'THE BEST OF . . .'
collections are intended to present the
representative stories of the masters of
science fiction in chronological order, their
aim being to provide science fiction readers
with a selection of short stories that
demonstrate the authors' literary
development and at the same time providing
new readers with a sound introduction to
their work.

The collections were compiled with the help
and advice of the authors concerned,
together with the invaluable assistance of
numerous fans, without whose good work,
time and patience they would not have been
published.

In particular the advice of Roger Peyton,
Gerald Bishop, Peter Weston and Leslie
Flood is appreciated.

ANGUS WELLS, *Editor*, 1974

The Best of
A. E. van Vogt

SPHERE BOOKS LIMITED
30/32 Gray's Inn Road, London WC1X 8JL

First published in Great Britain by Sphere Books Ltd 1974
Copyright © A. E. van Vogt 1974
Anthology copyright © Sphere Books Ltd 1974
Introduction copyright © A. E. van Vogt 1974
Bibliography copyright © Audvark House 1974

TRADE
MARK

Set in Monotype Times Roman

Printed in Great Britain by
Hazell Watson & Viney Ltd
Aylesbury, Bucks

ISBN 0 7221 8774 2

CONTENTS

ACKNOWLEDGMENTS

Vault of the Beast copyright © 1940 Street & Smith Publications; renewed 1967 by A. E. van Vogt

The Weapon Shop copyright © 1942 Street & Smith Publications

The Storm copyright © 1943 Street & Smith Publications; renewed 1970 by A. E. van Vogt

Juggernaut copyright © 1944 Street & Smith Publications

Hand of the Gods copyright © 1946 Street & Smith Publications

The Cataaaaa copyright © 1947 Fantasy Publishing Co.

The Monster copyright © 1948 Street & Smith Publications

Dear Pen Pal copyright © 1949 Arkham House

The Green Forest copyright © 1949 Street & Smith Publications

War of Nerves copyright © 1950 Clark Publishing Co.

The Expendables copyright © 1963 Galaxy Publishing Co.

Silkies in Space copyright © 1966 Galaxy Publishing Co.

The Proxy Intelligence copyright © 1968 Galaxy Publishing Co.

INTRODUCTION

'BEST' is what is called in General Semantics a defining word. What this means is that the word of itself implies a state, or level, of superiority in something.

But that, if you will think about it, is merely a value judgment of a person, a committee, or a group. That is, it is an intellectual, or emotional, consideration. As such, it can never be an operational term.

So we are not surprised when, each year in the U.S.A. these days, half a dozen publishers issue best-of-the-year science fiction. Worse, with a couple of well-advertised exceptions, none of the stories in one 'Best' is the same as those of any of the others.

Authors have lived with such contradictions with equanimity since the early days of sf.

Not too long ago, one of the best-of-that-year editors asked an sf writer if he had a story that had not already been anthologized too often. Said author presently sent along a story which he had selected because, until then, it had only been printed in a collection of his own stories. The editor accepted it as one of the best of the year without reading any of the other stories written by that author.

Now, it happened that the story which was submitted under these restricting requirements was the best short story ever written by that author. That year it won the Hugo award of the World Science Fiction Convention. None of the other 'Best' editors had had the foresight to include it in their anthologies.

I have a lesser example from my own experience. Years ago, the editor of a magazine asked me to select one of my stories for what was called an author's choice of his own best story. The editor, however, required that I limit my selection to a story printed in his magazine. The problem was he had only published three of my stories.

Like most sf authors I handled this situation with the total aplomb of someone who realizes that failure to make such a choice simply means your story is not included. P.S. I got the check.

Still – I should report – no one likes to be cynical.

Truth is, I have always had my own favorites among my stories, and occasionally re-read these.

Before I tell you my own choice, let me list for you those stories of mine which have repeatedly won the accolade of my particular readership.

Short stories: (early titles) 'Far Centaurus', 'Enchanted Village', 'The Monster'. This last has sometimes been titled 'Resurrection', (more recent title) 'Itself'.

Novelettes: (early titles) 'Black Destroyer', 'Cooperate – Or Else', 'The Weapon Shop', (recent titles) 'The Proxy Intelligence', 'The Silkie' – novelette version – and 'The Reflected Men'.

Novels: (early) *Slan*, *The Voyage of the Space Beagle* and *The World of Null-A*, (recent) *Quest for the Future* and *The Darkness on Diamondia*.

Now, why are those not my choices also? Well, I like far-out science fiction.

Does far-out – you may wonder – mean unscientific? Does it mean that I have a fantasy orientation as distinct from scientific extrapolation. Does it mean that I like it when an author creates bizarre but impossible situations.

No – to all three questions.

Take 'The Storm' – which I include in my list. Surely, at first look, some of the ideas in it are as far-fetched as you could ask for. A 'storm' in space. A planet revolving around the most fantastic sun in the known universe: S-Doradus.

I'll concentrate on that last item. When I got the idea, I wrote John W. Campbell, editor of *Astounding*, and asked him if it was possible to obtain any valid concept of such a planet. What would the sky look like? The plant life? etc. He wrote an astronomer friend. Among the three of us we evolved the planet as described in the story. So far as I know it's the only description in existence. And it's accurate.

There *is* an error in the original magazine version – and I have decided to let it stand in this present volume. Just to show you how difficult these matters are, let me describe the mistake. The astronomy texts I had available did not clearly identify which of the Magellanic Clouds contain S-Doradus. This particular point did not cross my mind during the correspondence. Suddenly, it was too late. I had to guess. Now, in those days I gave a lot of attention to the sounds of words. It was my belief that certain letters all by themselves conveyed a feeling. And so, when I wanted this feeling, or that, I would look for words with those sounds in them, and substitute them for words that might, otherwise, appear to be more suitable.

My critics presently took me apart on my use of the English language, particularly ridiculing such passages. So I abandoned the technique. However, before I was demolished, I decided that the word Lesser had a better feeling for my purposes that Greater. So, on this basis, I placed the great and glorious S-Doradus in the Lesser Magellanic Cloud.

A few years later, while I was looking up something else in another text, there was the truth. Meaning, it was in the Greater Magellanic Cloud.

Those things happen to sf authors, alas.

Another example: I read an entire text book on the production and manufacture of steel and its by-products. I used the terminology in a little short story, titled, 'Juggernaut'. To my dismay, a reader wrote in with a puzzled appraisal, stating that I seemed to know something about the subject; but that, as a steel man himself, he had to report that he had never heard any of the terms.

It developed that I had read a book about British steel production.

A third story needing comment is 'The Ghost'. It appeared originally in *Unknown Worlds*, a fantasy magazine. Well, it's science fiction. The idea in it derives from the time theories of a British philosopher, named Dunne. He called his time concept *serial time*.

When I was age eighteen – and a would-be writer – I loved the lush style of A. Merritt, the cosmic stories of E. E. Smith, and the western yarns of Max Brand. By the time I got around to eighteen a second time (age thirty-six, for you people who can't add) I was myself a science fiction writer, and had in fact written most of the stories which were subsequently regarded as my 'Best'. I spent my third eighteen years making a study of human behavior. During this time, I wrote a non-fiction book, *The Hypnotism Handbook* for a psychologist. In 1962, *The Violent Man*, my Red China novel (not science fiction) was published by Farrar, Straus and Giroux. Another study begun in the fifties recently culminated in a second non-fiction title, *The Money Personality*. A third study – on women – will have an sf novel based on it (*The Secret Galactics*) to be published by Prentice-Hall, Inc. in March 1974.

In 1964 I again started to write science fiction. The first of my new stories was 'The Expendables'.

I am bemused by the possibility that what I wrote with a hammer and a chisel (so to speak) in my younger days, adhering rigidly to an 800-word-scene-method writing, is actually better than what I can now do when I am so much more knowledgeable. For example, today I feel that I understand human behavior, money, women, men (though not children), exercise, dreams, and writing technique as never before. Then, I just let character happen according to the needs of the story. Now, I know at all times what I'm doing, and why. It feels better. And I really think it's going to turn out better.

Here, without further preliminary discussion, is my list of my favorites: shorter stories: (early) 'The Monater', 'War of Nerves', (later) 'The Ultra Man'; novelettes: (early) 'Vault of the Beast', 'The Storm', 'Hand of the Gods', (later) 'Silkies in Space', 'The Proxy Intelligence'; novels: (early) *The World of Null-A*, (later) *The Silkie*, *The Battle of Forever*.

Those are my very top choices. Following close behind these are: 'Dear Pen Pal', 'The Cataaaaa', and 'Juggernaut' (short); 'Expendables', 'The Ghost', 'The Weapon Shop', 'Secret Unattainable', and 'The Green Forest' (novelettes); and the novels, *The Weapon Shops of Isher*, *The Wizard of Linn* and *Future Glitter*.

I want to make a brief comment about a couple of those choices. 'Proxy Intelligence' is a sequel to an early novella, 'Asylum', which at one time I considered one of my best stories. I still do; but I prefer 'Proxy'. (At some future time there will be another sequel, titled 'I.Q. 10,000' – at the moment I don't quite feel up to doing that.)

It is very likely that, of my Linn stories, 'Hand of the Gods' is the most perfectly organized. These first Linn stories were to some extent unconsciously modeled on Robert Graves's *I, Claudius* – so I had pointed out to me later. But I had done such a vast amount of reading in that particular Roman period that I really thought it was Roman history. However, the Linn family tree was modeled on the Medici line of Florence. So Clane is a combination of Claudius and Lorenzo. Transferred to 12,000 A.D., the whole thing acquired a life of its own, and even won a grudging accolade from my principal U.S. critic Damon Knight.

The stories printed in this present volume, and the novels I have named, qualify for my personal accolade because they are farther out than the stories not included in my list.

I recommend them to all my far-out reader types.

A. E. van Vogt,
Hollywood, Calif., 1973

VAULT OF THE BEAST

THE CREATURE crept. It whimpered from fear and pain, a thin, slobbering sound horrible to hear. Shapeless, formless thing yet changing shape and form with every jerky movement.

It crept along the corridor of the space freighter, fighting the terrible urge of its elements to take the shape of its surroundings. A gray blob of disintegrating stuff, it crept, it cascaded, it rolled, flowed, dissolved, every movement an agony of struggle against the abnormal need to become a stable shape.

Any shape! The hard, chilled-blue metal wall of the Earth-bound freighter, the thick, rubbery floor. The floor was easy to fight. It wasn't like the metal that pulled and pulled. It would be easy to become metal for all eternity.

But something prevented. An implanted purpose. A purpose that drummed from electron to electron, vibrated from atom to atom with an unvarying intensity that was like a special pain: *Find the greatest mathematical mind in the Solar System, and bring it to the vault of the Martian ultimate metal. The Great One must be freed! The prime number time lock must be opened!*

That was the purpose that hummed with unrelenting agony through its elements. That was the thought that had been seared into its fundamental consciousness by the great and evil minds that had created it.

There was movement at the far end of the corridor. A door opened. Footsteps sounded. A man whistling to himself. With a metallic hiss, almost a sigh, the creature dissolved, looking momentarily like diluted mercury. Then it turned brown like the floor. It became the floor, a slightly thicker stretch of dark-brown rubber spread out for yards.

It was ecstasy just to lie there, to be flat and to have shape, and to be so nearly dead that there was no pain. Death was so sweet, so utterly desirable. And life such an unbearable torment of agony, such a throbbing, piercing nightmare of anguished convulsion. If only the life that was approaching would pass swiftly. If the life stopped, it would pull it into shape. Life could do that. Life was stronger than metal, stronger than anything. The approaching life meant torture, struggle, pain.

The creature tensed its now flat, grotesque body – the body that could develop muscles of steel – and waited in terror for the death struggle.

Spacecraftsman Parelli whistled happily as he strode along the gleaming corridor that led from the engine room. He had just received a wireless from the hospital. His wife was doing well, and it was a boy. Eight pounds, the radiogram had said. He suppressed a desire to whoop and dance. A boy. Life sure was good.

Pain came to the thing on the floor. Primeval pain that sucked through its elements like acid burning, burning. The brown floor shuddered in every atom as Parelli strode over it. The aching urge to pull toward him, to take his shape. The thing fought its horrible desire, fought with anguish and shivering dread, more consciously now that it could think with Parelli's brain. A ripple of floor rolled after the man.

Fighting didn't help. The ripple grew into a blob that momentarily seemed to become a human head. Gray, hellish nightmare of demoniac shape. The creature hissed metallically in terror, then collapsed palpitating, slobbering with fear and pain and hate as Parelli strode on rapidly – too rapidly for its creeping pace.

The thin, horrible sound died; the thing dissolved into brown floor, and lay quiescent yet quivering in every atom from its unquenchable, uncontrollable urge to live – live in spite of pain, in spite of abysmal terror and primordial

13

longing for stable shape. To live and fulfill the purpose of its lusting and malignant creators.

Thirty feet up the corridor, Parelli stopped. He jerked his mind from its thoughts of child and wife. He spun on his heels, and stared uncertainly along the passageway from the engine room.

'Now, what the devil was that?' he pondered aloud.

A sound – a queer, faint yet unmistakably horrid sound was echoing and re-echoing through his consciousness. A shiver ran the length of his spine. That sound – that devilish sound.

He stood there, a tall, magnificently muscled man, stripped to the waist, sweating from the heat generated by the rockets that were decelerating the craft after its meteoric flight from Mars. Shuddering, he clenched his fists, and walked slowly back the way he had come.

The creature throbbed with the pull of him, a gnawing, writhing, tormenting struggle that pierced into the deeps of every restless, agitated cell, stabbing agonizingly along the alien nervous system; and then became terrifyingly aware of the inevitable, the irresistible need to take the shape of the life.

Parelli stopped uncertainly. The floor moved under him, a visible wave that reared brown and horrible before his incredulous eyes and grew into a bulbous, slobbering, hissing mass. A venomous demon head reared on twisted, half-human shoulders. Gnarled hands on apelike, mal-formed arms clawed at his face with insensate rage – and changed even as they tore at him.

'Good God!' Parelli bellowed.

The hands, the arms that clutched him grew more normal, more human, brown, muscular. The face assumed familiar lines, sprouted a nose, eyes, a red gash of mouth. The body was suddenly his own, trousers and all, sweat and all.

' – God!' his image echoed; and pawed at him with letching fingers and an impossible strength.

Gasping, Parelli fought free, then launched one crushing blow straight into the distorted face. A drooling scream of agony came from the thing. It turned and ran, dissolving as it ran, fighting dissolution, uttering strange half-human cries.

And, struggling against horror, Parelli chased it, his knees weak and trembling from sheer funk and incredulity. His arm reached out, and plucked at the disintegrating trousers. A piece came away in his hand, a cold, slimy, writhing lump like wet clay.

The feel of it was too much. His gorge rising in disgust, he faltered in his stride. He heard the pilot shouting ahead:

'What's the matter?'

Parelli saw the open door of the storeroom. With a gasp, he dived in, came out a moment later, wild-eyed, an ato-gun in his fingers. He saw the pilot, standing with staring, horrified brown eyes, white face and rigid body, facing one of the great windows.

'There it is!' the man cried.

A gray blob was dissolving into the edge of the glass, becoming glass. Parelli rushed forward, ato-gun poised. A ripple went through the glass, darkening it; and then, briefly, he caught a glimpse of a blob emerging on the other side of the glass into the cold of space.

The officer stood gaping beside him; the two of them watched the gray, shapeless mass creep out of sight along the side of the rushing freight liner.

Parelli sprang to life. 'I got a piece of it!' he grasped. 'Flung it down on the floor of the storeroom.'

It was Lieutenant Morton who found it. A tiny section of floor reared up, and then grew amazingly large as it tried to expand into human shape. Parelli with distorted, crazy eyes scooped it up in a shovel. It hissed; it nearly became a part of the metal shovel, but couldn't because Parelli was so close. Changing, fighting for shape, it slobbered and hissed as Parelli staggered with it behind his superior officer. He

15

was laughing hysterically. 'I touched it,' he kept saying, 'I touched it.'

A large blister of metal on the outside of the space freighter stirred into sluggish life, as the ship tore into the Earth's atmosphere. The metal walls of the freighter grew red, then white-hot, but the creature, unaffected, continued its slow transformation into gray mass. Vague thought came to the thing, realization that it was time to act.

Suddenly, it was floating free of the ship, falling slowly, heavily, as if somehow the gravitation of Earth had no serious effect upon it. A minute distortion in its electrons started it falling faster, as in some alien way it suddenly became more allergic to gravity.

The Earth was green below; and in the dim distance a gorgeous and tremendous city of spires and massive buildings glittered in the sinking Sun. The thing slowed, and drifted like a falling leaf in a breeze toward the still-distant Earth. It landed in an arroyo beside a bridge at the outskirts of the city.

A man walked over the bridge with quick, nervous steps. He would have been amazed, if he had looked back, to see a replica of himself climb from the ditch to the road, and start walking briskly after him.

Find the – greatest mathematician!

It was an hour later; and the pain of that throbbing thought was a dull, continuous ache in the creature's brain, as it walked along the crowded street. There were other pains, too. The pain of fighting the pull of the pushing, hurrying mass of humanity that swarmed by with unseeing eyes. But it was easier to think, easier to hold form now that it had the brain and body of a man.

Find – mathematician!

'Why?' asked the man's brain of the thing; and the whole body shook with startled shock at such heretical questioning. The brown eyes darted in fright from side to side, as if

16

expecting instant and terrible doom. The face dissolved a little in that brief moment of mental chaos, became successively the man with the hooked nose who swung by, the tanned face of the tall woman who was looking into the shop window, the —

With a second gasp, the creature pulled its mind back from fear, and fought to readjust its face to that of the smooth-shaven young man who sauntered idly in from a side street. The young man glanced at him, looked away, then glanced back again startled. The creature echoed the thought in the man's brain: 'Who the devil is that? Where have I seen that fellow before?'

Half a dozen women in a group approached. The creature shrank aside as they passed, its face twisted with the agony of the urge to become woman. Its brown suit turned just the faintest shade of blue, the color of the nearest dress, as it momentarily lost control of its outer atoms. Its mind hummed with the chatter of clothes and 'My dear, didn't she look dreadful in that awful hat?'

There was a solid cluster of giant buildings ahead. The thing shook its human head consciously. So many buildings meant metal; and the forces that held metal together would pull and pull at its human shape. The creature comprehended the reason for this with the understanding of the slight man in a dark suit who wandered by dully. The slight man was a clerk; the thing caught his thought. He was thinking enviously of his boss who was Jim Brender, of the financial firm of J. P. Brender & Co.

The overtones of that thought struck along the vibrating elements of the creature. It turned abruptly and followed Lawrence Pearson, bookkeeper. If people ever paid attention to other people on the street, they would have been amazed after a moment to see two Lawrence Pearsons proceeding down the street, one some fifty feet behind the other. The second Lawrence Pearson had learned from the mind of the first that Jim Brender was a Harvard graduate in mathematics, finance and political economy, the latest of a long line of financial geniuses, thirty years old, and the head of the tremendously wealthy J. P. Brender & Co. Jim Brender had just married the most beautiful girl in the world; and this was the reason for Lawrence Pearson's discontent with life.

'Here I'm thirty, too,' his thoughts echoed in the creature's mind, 'and I've got nothing. He's got everything – everything – while all I've got to look forward to is the same old boardinghouse till the end of time.'

It was getting dark as the two crossed the river. The creature quickened its pace, striding forward with aggressive alertness that Lawrence Pearson in the flesh could never have managed. Some glimmering of its terrible purpose communicated itself in that last instant to the victim. The slight man turned; and let out a faint squawk as those steel-muscled fingers jerked at his throat, a single, fearful snap.

The creature's brain went black with dizziness as the brain of Lawrence Pearson crashed into the night of death. Gasping, whimpering, fighting dissolution, it finally gained control of itself. With one sweeping movement, it caught the dead body and flung it over the cement railing. There was a splash below, then a sound of gurgling water.

The thing that was now Lawrence Pearson walked on hurriedly, then more slowly till it came to a large, rambling brick house. It looked anxiously at the number, suddenly uncertain if it had remembered rightly. Hesitantly, it opened the door.

A streamer of yellow light splashed out, and laughter vibrated in the thing's sensitive ears. There was the same hum of many thoughts and many brains, as there had been in the street. The creature fought against the inflow of thought that threatened to crowd out the mind of Lawrence Pearson. A little dazed by the struggle, it found itself in a large, bright hall, which looked through a door into a room where a dozen people were sitting around a dining table.

'Oh, it's you, Mr Pearson,' said the landlady from the head of the table. She was a sharp-nosed, thin-mouthed woman at whom the creature stared with brief intentness. From her mind, a thought had come. She had a son who was a mathematics teacher in a high school. The creature shrugged. In one penetrating glance, the truth throbbed along the intricate atomic structure of its body. This woman's son was as much an intellectual lightweight as his mother.

'You're just in time,' she said incuriously. 'Sarah, bring Mr Pearson's plate.'

'Thank you, but I'm not feeling hungry,' the creature replied; and its human brain vibrated to the first silent, ironic laughter that it had ever known. 'I think I'll just lie down.'

All night long it lay on the bed of Lawrence Pearson, bright-eyed, alert, becoming more and more aware of itself. It thought:

'I'm a machine, without a brain of my own. I use the brains of other people, but somehow my creators made it possible for me to be more than just an echo. I use people's brains to carry out my purpose.'

It pondered about those creators, and felt a surge of panic sweeping along its alien system, darkening its human mind. There was a vague physiological memory of pain unutterable, and of tearing chemical action that was frightening.

The creature rose at dawn, and walked the streets till half past nine. At that hour, it approached the imposing marble entrance of J. P. Brender & Co. Inside, it sank down in the comfortable chair initialed L. P.; and began painstakingly to work at the books Lawrence Pearson had put away the night before.

At ten o'clock, a tall young man in a dark suit entered the arched hallway and walked briskly through the row after row of offices. He smiled with easy confidence to every side.

The thing did not need the chorus of 'Good morning, Mr Brender' to know that its prey had arrived.

Terrible in its slow-won self-confidence, it rose with a lithe, graceful movement that would have been impossible to the real Lawrence Pearson, and walked briskly to the washroom. A moment later, the very image of Jim Brender emerged from the door and walked with easy confidence to the door of the private office which Jim Brender had entered a few minutes before.

The thing knocked and walked in and simultaneously became aware of three things: The first was that it had found the mind after which it had been sent. The second was that its image mind was incapable of imitating the finer subtleties of the razor-sharp brain of the young man who was staring up from dark-gray eyes that were a little startled. And the third was the large metal bas-relief that hung on the wall.

With a shock that almost brought chaos, it felt the overpowering tug of that metal. And in one flash it knew that this was ultimate metal, product of the fine craft of the ancient Martians, whose metal cities, loaded with treasures of furniture, art and machinery were slowly being dug up by enterprising human beings from the sands under which they had been buried for thirty or fifty million years.

The ultimate metal! The metal that no heat would even warm, that no diamond or other cutting device, could scratch, never duplicated by human beings, as mysterious as the ieis force which the Martians made from apparent nothingness.

All these thoughts crowded the creature's brain, as it explored the memory cells of Jim Brender. With an effort that was a special pain, the thing wrenched its mind from the metal, and fastened its eyes on Jim Brender. It caught the full flood of the wonder in his mind, as he stood up.

'Good lord,' said Jim Brender, 'who are you?'

'My name's Jim Brender,' said the thing, conscious of

grim amusement, conscious, too, that it was progress for it to be able to feel such an emotion.

The real Jim Brender had recovered himself. 'Sit down, sit down,' he said heartily. 'This is the most amazing coincidence I've ever seen.'

He went over to the mirror that made one panel of the left wall. He stared, first at himself, then at the creature. 'Amazing,' he said. 'Absolutely amazing.'

'Mr Brender,' said the creature, 'I saw your picture in the paper, and I thought our astounding resemblance would make you listen, where otherwise you might pay no attention. I have recently returned from Mars, and I am here to persuade you to come back to Mars with me.'

'That,' said Jim Brender, 'is impossible.'

'Wait,' the creature said, 'until I have told you why. Have you ever heard of the Tower of the Beast?'

'The Tower of the Beast!' Jim Brender repeated slowly. He went around his desk and pushed a button.

A voice from an ornamental box said: 'Yes, Mr Brender?'

'Dave, get me all the data on the Tower of the Beast and the legendary city of Li in which it is supposed to exist.'

'Don't need to look it up,' came the crisp reply. 'Most Martian histories refer to it as the beast that fell from the sky when Mars was young – some terrible warning connected with it – the beast was unconscious when found – said to be the result of its falling out of sub-space. Martians read its mind; and were so horrified by its subconscious intentions they tried to kill it, but couldn't. So they built a huge vault, about fifteen hundred feet in diameter and a mile high – and the beast, apparently of these dimensions, was locked in. Several attempts have been made to find the city of Li, but without success. Generally believed to be a myth. That's all, Jim.'

'Thank you!' Jim Brender clicked off the connection, and turned to his visitor. 'Well?'

21

'It is not a myth. I know where the Tower of the Beast is; and I also know that the beast is still alive.'

'Now, see here,' said Brender good-humoredly, 'I'm intrigued by your resemblance to me; and as a matter of fact I'd like Pamela – my wife – to see you. How about coming over to dinner? But don't, for Heaven's sake, expect me to believe such a story. The beast, if there is such a thing, fell from the sky when Mars was young. There are some authorities who maintain that the Martian race died out a hundred million years ago, though twenty-five million is the conservative estimate. The only things remaining of their civilization are their constructions of ultimate metal. Fortunately, toward the end they built almost everything from that indestructible metal.'

'Let me tell you about the Tower of the Beast,' said the thing quietly. 'It is a tower of gigantic size, but only a hundred feet or so projected above the sand when I saw it. The whole top is a door, and that door is geared to a time lock, which in turn has been integrated along a line of ieis to the ultimate prime number.'

Jim Brender stared; and the thing caught his startled thought, the first uncertainty, and the beginning of belief.

'Ultimate prime number!' Brender ejaculated. 'What do you mean?' he caught himself. 'I know of course that a prime number is a number divisible only by itself and by one.'

He snatched at a book from the little wall library beside his desk, and rippled through it. 'The largest known prime is – ah, here it is – is 230584300921393951. Some others, according to this authority, are 77843839397, 182521213001, and 78875943472201.'

He frowned. 'That makes the whole thing ridiculous. The ultimate prime would be an indefinite number.' He smiled at the thing. 'If there is a beast, and it is locked up in a vault of ultimate metal, the door of which is geared to a time lock, integrated along a line of ieis to the ultimate prime number –

then the beast is caught. Nothing in the world can free it.'

'To the contrary,' said the creature. 'I have been assured by the beast that it is within the scope of human mathematics to solve the problem, but that what is required is a born mathematical mind, equipped with all the mathematical training that Earth science can afford. You are that man.'

'You expect me to release this evil creature – even if I could perform this miracle of mathematics.'

'Evil nothing!' snapped the thing. 'That ridiculous fear of the unknown which made the Martians imprison it has resulted in a very grave wrong. The beast is a scientist from another space, accidentally caught in one of his experiments. I say "his" when of course I do not know whether this race has a sexual differentiation.'

'You actually talked with the beast?'

'It communicated with me by mental telepathy.'

'It has been proven that thoughts cannot penetrate ultimate metal.'

'What do humans know about telepathy? They cannot even communicate with each other except under special conditions.' The creature spoke contemptuously.

'That's right. And if your story is true, then this is a matter for the Council.'

'This is a matter for two men, you and I. Have you forgotten that the vault of the beast is the central tower of the great city of Li – billions of dollars' worth of treasure in furniture, art and machinery? The beast demands release from its prison before it will permit anyone to mine that treasure. You can release it. We can share the treasure.'

'Let me ask you a question,' said Jim Brender. 'What is your real name?'

'P-Pierce Lawrence!' the creature stammered. For the moment, it could think of no greater variation of the name of its first victim than reversing the two words, with a slight change on 'Pearson'. Its thoughts darkened with confusion as the voice of Brender pounded:

'On what ship did you come from Mars?'

'O-on *F4961*,' the thing stammered chaotically, fury adding to the confused state of its mind. It fought for control, felt itself slipping, suddenly felt the pull of the ultimate metal that made up the bas-relief on the wall, and knew by that tug that it was dangerously near dissolution.

'That would be a freighter,' said Jim Brender. He pressed a button. 'Carltons, find out if the *F4961* had a passenger or person aboard, named Pierce Lawrence. How long will it take?'

'About a minute, sir.'

'You see,' said Jim Brender, leaning back, 'this is mere formality. If you were on that ship, then I shall be compelled to give serious attention to your statements. You can understand, of course, that I could not possibly go into a thing like this blindly. I —'

The buzzer rang. 'Yes?' said Jim Brender.

'Only the crew of two was on the *F4961* when it landed yesterday. No such person as Pierce Lawrence was aboard.'

'Thank you.' Jim Brender stood up. He said coldly, 'Good-by, Mr Lawrence. I cannot imagine what you hoped to gain by this ridiculous story. However, it has been most intriguing, and the problem you presented was very ingenious indeed —'

The buzzer was ringing. 'What is it?'

'Mr Gorson to see you, sir.'

'Very well, send him right in.'

The thing had greater control of its brain now, and it saw in Brender's mind that Gorson was a financial magnate, whose business ranked with the Brender firm. It saw other things, too; things that made it walk out of the private office, out of the building, and wait patiently until Mr Gorson emerged from the imposing entrance. A few minutes later, there were two Mr Gorsons walking down the street.

Mr Gorson was a vigorous man in his early fifties. He had

lived a clean, active life; and the hard memories of many climates and several planets were stored away in his brain. The thing caught the alertness of this man on its sensitive elements, and followed him warily, respectfully, not quite decided whether it would act.

It thought: 'I've come a long way from the primitive life that couldn't hold its shape. My creators, in designing me, gave to me powers of learning, developing. It is easier to fight dissolution, easier to be human. In handling this man, I must remember that my strength is invincible when properly used.'

With minute care, it explored in the mind of its intended victim the exact route of his walk to his office. There was the entrance to a large building clearly etched on his mind. Then a long, marble corridor, into an automatic elevator up to the eighth floor, along a short corridor with two doors. One door led to the private entrance of the man's private office. The other to a storeroom used by the janitor. Gorson had looked into the place on various occasions; and there was in his mind, among other things, the memory of a a large chest —

The thing waited in the storeroom till the unsuspecting Gorson was past the door. The door creaked. Gorson turned, his eyes widening. He didn't have a chance. A fist of solid steel smashed his face to a pulp, knocking the bones back into his brain.

This time, the creature did not make the mistake of keeping its mind tuned to that of its victim. It caught him viciously as he fell, forcing its steel fist back to a semblance of human flesh. With furious speed, it stuffed the bulky and athletic form into the large chest, and clamped the lid down tight.

Alertly, it emerged from the storeroom, entered the private office of Mr Gorson, and sat down before the gleaming desk of oak. The man who responded to the pressing of a button saw John Gorson sitting there, and heard John Gorson say:

'Crispins, I want you to start selling these stocks through the secret channels right away. Sell until I tell you to stop, even if you think it's crazy. I have information of something big on.'

Crispins glanced down the row after row of stock names; and his eyes grew wider and wider. 'Good lord, man!' he gasped finally, with that familiarity which is the right of a trusted adviser, 'these are all the gild-edged stocks. Your whole fortune can't swing a deal like this.'

'I told you I'm not in this alone.'

'But it's against the law to break the market,' the man protested.

'Crispins, you heard what I said. I'm leaving the office. Don't try to get in touch with me. I'll call you.'

The thing that was John Gorson stood up, paying no attention to the bewildered thoughts that flowed from Crispins. It went out of the door by which it had entered. As it emerged from the building, it was thinking: 'All I've got to do is kill half a dozen financial giants, start their stocks selling, and then —'

By one o'clock it was over. The exchange didn't close till three, but at one o'clock, the news was flashed on the New York tickers. In London, where it was getting dark, the papers brought out an extra. In Hankow and Shanghai, a dazzling new day was breaking as the newsboys ran along the streets in the shadows of skyscrapers, and shouted that J. P. Brender & Co. had assigned; and that there was to be an investigation —

'We are facing,' said the chairman of the investigation committee, in his opening address the following morning, 'one of the most astounding coincidents in all history. An ancient and respected firm, with world-wide affiliations and branches, with investments in more than a thousand companies of every description, is struck bankrupt by an unexpected crash in every stock in which the firm was interested. It will require months to take evidence on the responsibility for the short-selling which brought about this disaster. In the meantime, I see no reason, regrettable as the action must be to all the old friends of the late J. P. Brender, and of his son, why the demands of the creditors should not be met, and the properties liquidated through auction sales and such other methods as may be deemed proper and legal —'

'Really, I don't blame her,' said the first woman, as they wandered through the spacious rooms of the Brenders' Chinese palace. 'I have no doubt she does love Jim Brender, but no one could seriously expect her to remain married to him *now*. She's a woman of the world, and it's utterly impossible to expect her to live with a man who's going to be a mere pilot or space hand or something on a Martian spaceship —'

Commander Hughes of Interplanetary Spaceways entered the office of his employer truculently. He was a small man, but extremely wiry; and the thing that was Louis Dyer gazed at him tensely, conscious of the force and power of this man.

Hughes began: 'You have my report on this Brender case?'

The thing twirled the mustache of Louis Dyer nervously; then picked up a small folder, and read out loud:

'Dangerous for psychological reasons . . . to employ Brender . . . So many blows in succession. Loss of wealth, position and wife . . . No normal man could remain normal under . . . circumstances. Take him into office . . . befriend him . . . give him a sinecure, or position where his undoubted great ability . . . but not on a spaceship, where the utmost hardiness, both mental, moral, spiritual and physical is required —'

Hughes interrupted: 'Those are exactly the points which I am stressing. I knew you would see what I meant, Louis.'

'Of course, I see,' said the creature, smiling in grim amusement, for it was feeling very superior these days. 'Your thoughts, your ideas, your code and your methods are stamped irrevocably on your brain and' – it added hastily – 'you have never left me in doubt as to where you stand. However, in this case, I must insist. Jim Brender will not take an ordinary position offered by his friends. And it is ridiculous to ask him to subordinate himself to men to whom he is in every way superior. He has commanded his own space yacht; he knows more about the mathematical end of the work than our whole staff put together; and that is no reflection on our staff. He knows the hardships connected with space flying, and believes that it is exactly what he needs. I, therefore, command you, for the first time in our long association, Peter, to put him on space freighter *F4961* in the place of Spacecraftsman Parelli who collapsed into a nervous breakdown after that curious affair with the creature from space, as Lieutenant Morton described it — By the way, did you find the . . . er . . . sample of that creature yet?'

'No, sir, it vanished the day you came in to look at it. We've searched the place high and low – queerest stuff you ever saw. Goes through glass as easy as light; you'd think it was some form of light-stuff – scares me, too. A pure sympodial development – actually more adaptable to environment than anything hitherto discovered; and that's putting it mildly. I tell you, sir — But see here, you can't steer me off the Brender case like that.'

'Peter, I don't understand your attitude. This is the first time I've interfered with your end of the work and —'

'I'll resign,' groaned that sorely beset man.

The thing stifled a smile. 'Peter, you've built up the staff of Spaceways. It's your child, your creation; you can't give it up, you know you can't —'

The words hissed softly into alarm; for into Hughes' brain had flashed the first real intention of resigning. Just hearing of his accomplishments and the story of his beloved job brought such a rush of memories, such a realization of how tremendous an outrage was this threatened interference. In one mental leap, the creature saw what this man's resignation would mean: The discontent of the men; the swift perception of the situation by Jim Brender; and his refusal to accept the job. There was only one way out – that Brender would get to the ship without finding out what had happened. Once on it, he must carry through with one trip to Mars; and that was all that was needed.

The thing pondered the possibility of imitating Hughes' body; then agonizingly realized that it was hopeless. Both Louis Dyer and Hughes must be around until the last minute.

'But, Peter, listen!' the creature began chaotically. Then it said, 'Damn!' for it was very human in its mentality; and the realization that Hughes took its words as a sign of weakness was maddening. Uncertainty descended like a black cloud over its brain.

'I'll tell Brender when he arrives in five minutes how I feel about all this!' Hughes snapped; and the creature knew that the worst had happened. 'If you forbid me to tell him, then I resign. I — Good God, man, your face!'

Confusion and horror came to the creature simultaneously. It knew abruptly that its face had dissolved before the threatened ruin of its plans. It fought for control, leaped to its feet, seeing the incredible danger. The large office just beyond the frosted glass door – Hughes' first outcry would bring help —

With a half sob, it sought to force its arm into an imitation of a metal fist, but there was no metal in the room to pull it into shape. There was only the solid maple desk. With a harsh cry, the creature leaped completely over the desk, and sought to bury a pointed shaft of stick into Hughes' throat.

Hughes cursed in amazement, and caught at the stick with furious strength. There was sudden commotion in the outer office, raised voices, running feet —

29

It was quite accidental the way it happened. The surface cars swayed to a stop, drawing up side by side as the red light blinked on ahead. Jim Brender glanced at the next car.

A girl and a man sat in the rear of the long, shiny streamlined affair, and the girl was desperately striving to crouch down out of his sight, striving with equal desperation not to be too obvious in her intention. Realizing that she was seen, she smiled brilliantly, and leaned out of the window.

'Hello, Jim, how's everything?'

'Hello, Pamela!' Jim Brender's fingers tightened on the steering wheel till the knuckles showed white, as he tried to keep his voice steady. He couldn't help adding: 'When does the divorce become final?'

'I get my papers tomorrow,' she said, 'but I suppose you won't get yours till you return from your first trip. Leaving today, aren't you?'

'In about fifteen minutes.' He hesitated. 'When is the wedding?'

The rather plump, white-faced man who had not participated in the conversation so far, leaned forward.

'Next week,' he said. He put his fingers possessively over Pamela's hand. 'I wanted it tomorrow but Pamela wouldn't – er, good-by.'

His last words were hastily spoken, as the traffic lights switched, and the cars rolled on, separating at the first corner.

The rest of the drive to the spaceport was a blur. He hadn't expected the wedding to take place so soon. Hadn't, when he came right down to it, expected it to take place at all. Like a fool, he had hoped blindly —

Not that it was Pamela's fault. Her training, her very life made this the only possible course of action for her. But – *one week!* The spaceship would be one fourth of the long trip to Mars —

He parked his car. As he paused beside the runway that led to the open door of *F4961* – a huge globe of shining

30

metal, three hundred feet in diameter – he saw a man running toward him. Then he recognized Hughes.

The thing that was Hughes approached, fighting for calmness. The whole world was a flame of cross-pulling forces. It shrank from the thoughts of the people milling about in the office it had just left. Everything had gone wrong. It had never intended to do what it now had to do. It had intended to spend most of the trip to Mars as a blister of metal on the outer shield of the ship. With an effort, it controlled its funk, its terror, its brain.

'We're leaving right away,' it said.

Brender looked amazed. 'But that means I'll have to figure out a new orbit under the most difficult —'

'Exactly,' the creature interrupted. 'I've been hearing a lot about your marvelous mathematical ability. It's time the words were proved by deeds.'

Jim Brender shrugged. 'I have no objection. But how is it that you're coming along?'

'I always go with a new man.'

It sounded reasonable. Brender climbed the runway, closely followed by Hughes. The powerful pull of the metal was the first real pain the creature had known for days. For a long month, it would now have to fight the metal, fight to retain the shape of Hughes – and carry on a thousand duties at the same time.

That first stabbing pain tore along its elements, and smashed the confidence that days of being human had built up. And then, as it followed Brender through the door, it heard a shout behind it. It looked back hastily. People were streaming out of several doors, running toward the ship.

Brender was several yards along the corridor. With a hiss that was almost a sob, the creature leaped inside, and pulled the lever that clicked the great door shut.

There was an emergency lever that controlled the anti-gravity plates. With one jerk, the creature pulled the heavy lever hard over. There was a sensation of lightness and a sense of falling.

Through the great plate window, the creature caught a flashing glimpse of the field below, swarming with people. White faces turning upward, arms waving. Then the scene grew remote, as a thunder of rockets vibrated through the ship.

'I hope,' said Brender, as Hughes entered the control room, 'you wanted me to start the rockets.'

'Yes,' the thing replied, and felt brief panic at the chaos in its brain, the tendency of its tongue to blur. 'I'm leaving the mathematical end entirely in your hands.'

It didn't dare stay so near the heavy metal engines, even with Brender's body there to help it keep its human shape. Hurriedly, it started up the corridor. The best place would be the insulated bedroom —

Abruptly, it stopped in its head-long walk, teetered for an instant on tiptoes. From the control room it had just left, a thought was trickling – a thought from Brender's brain. The creature almost dissolved in terror as it realized that Brender was sitting at the radio, answering an insistent call from Earth —

It burst into the control room, and braked to a halt, its eyes widening with humanlike dismay. Brender whirled from before the radio with a single twisting step. In his fingers, he held a revolver. In his mind, the creature read a dawning comprehension of the whole truth. Brender cried:

'You're the . . . thing that came to my office, and talked about prime numbers and the vault of the beast.'

He took a step to one side to cover an open doorway that led down another corridor. The movement brought the telescreen into the vision of the creature. In the screen was the image of the real Hughes. Simultaneously, Hughes saw the thing.

'Brender,' he bellowed, 'it's the monster that Morton and Parelli saw on their trip from Mars. It doesn't react to heat

32

or any chemicals, but we never tried bullets. Shoot, you fool!'

It was too much, there was too much metal, too much confusion. With a whimpering cry, the creature dissolved. The pull of the metal twisted it horribly into thick half metal; the struggle to be human left it a malignant structure of bulbous head, with one eye half gone, and two snakelike arms attached to the half metal of the body.

Instinctively, it fought closer to Brender, letting the pull of his body make it more human. The half metal became fleshlike stuff that sought to return to its human shape.

'Listen, Brender!' Hughes' voice came urgently. 'The fuel vats in the engine room are made of ultimate metal. One of them is empty. We caught a part of this thing once before, and it couldn't get out of the small jar of ultimate metal. If you could drive it into the vat while it's lost control of itself, as it seems to do very easily — '

'I'll see what lead can do!' Brender rapped in a brittle voice.

Bang! The half-human creature screamed from its half-formed slit of mouth, and retreated, its legs dissolving into gray dough.

'It hurts, doesn't it?' Brender ground out. 'Get over into the engine room, you damned thing, into the vat!'

'Go on, go on!' Hughes was screaming from the telescreen.

Brender fired again. The creature made a horrible slobbering sound, and retreated once more. But it was bigger again, more human; and in one caricature hand a caricature of Brender's revolver was growing.

It raised the unfinished, unformed gun. There was an explosion, and a shriek from the thing. The revolver fell, a shapeless, tattered blob, to the floor. The little gray mass of it scrambled frantically toward the parent body, and attached itself like some monstrous canker to the right foot.

And then, for the first time, the mighty and evil brains that had created the thing, sought to dominate their robot. Furious, yet conscious that the game must be carefully played, the Controller forced the terrified and utterly beaten thing to its will. Scream after agonized scream rent the air, as the change was forced upon the unstable elements. In an instant, the thing stood in the shape of Brender, but instead of a revolver, there grew from one browned, powerful hand a pencil of shining metal. Mirror bright, it glittered in every facet like some incredible gem.

The metal glowed ever so faintly, an unearthly radiance. And where the radio had been, and the screen with Hughes' face on it, there was a gaping hole. Desperately, Brender pumped bullets into the body before him, but though the shape trembled, it stared at him now, unaffected. The shining weapon swung toward him.

'When you are quite finished,' it said, 'perhaps we can talk.'

It spoke so mildly that Brender, tensing to meet death, lowered his gun in amazement. The thing went on:

'Do not be alarmed. This which you hear and see is a robot, designed by us to cope with your space and number world. Several of us are working here under the most difficult conditions to maintain this connection, so I must be brief.

'We exist in a time world immeasurably more slow than your own. By a system of synchronization, we have geared a number of these spaces in such fashion that, though one of our days is millions of your years, we can communicate. Our purpose is to free our colleague, Kalorn, from the Martian vault. Kalorn was caught accidentally in a time warp of his own making and precipitated onto the planet you know as Mars. The Martians, needlessly fearing his great size, constructed a most diabolical prison, and we need your knowledge of the mathematics peculiar to your space and number world – and to it alone – in order to free him.'

The calm voice continued, earnest but not offensively so, insistent but friendly. He regretted that their robot had killed human beings. In greater detail, he explained that every space was constructed on a different numbers system, some all negative, some all positive, some a mixture of the two, the whole an infinite variety, and every mathematic interwoven into the very fabric of the space it ruled.

Ieis force was not really mysterious. It was simply a flow from one space to another, the result of a difference in potential. This flow, however, was one of the universal forces, which only one other force could affect, the one he had used a few minutes before. Ultimate metal was *actually* ultimate.

In their space they had a similar metal, built up from negative atoms. He could see from Brender's mind that the Martians had known nothing about minus numbers, so that they must have built it up from ordinary atoms. It could be done that way, too, though not so easily. He finished:

'The problem narrows down to this: Your mathematic must tell us how, with our universal force, we can short-circuit the ultimate prime number – that is, factor it – so that the door will open any time. You may ask how a prime can be factored when it is divisible only by itself and by one. That problem is, for your system, solvable only by your mathematics. Will you do it?'

Brender realized with a start that he was still holding his revolver. He tossed it aside. His nerves were calm as he said:

'Everything you have said sounds reasonable and honest. If you were desirous of making trouble, it would be the simplest thing in the world to send as many of your kind as you wished. Of course, the whole affair must be placed before the Council —'

'Then it is hopeless – the Council could not possibly accede —'

'And you expect me to do what you do not believe the

highest governmental authority in the System would do?' Brender exclaimed.

'It is inherent in the nature of a democracy that it cannot gamble with the lives of its citizens. We have such a government here; and its members have already informed us that, in a similar condition, they would not consider releasing an unknown beast upon their people. Individuals, however, can gamble where governments must not. You have agreed that our argument is logical. What system do men follow if not that of logic?'

The Controller, through its robot, watched Brender's thoughts alertly. It saw doubt and uncertainty, opposed by a very human desire to help, based upon the logical conviction that it was safe. Probing his mind, it saw swiftly that it was unwise, in dealing with men, to trust too much to logic. It pressed on:

'To an individual we can offer – everything. In a minute, with your permission, we shall transfer this ship to Mars; not in thirty days, but in thirty seconds: The knowledge of how this is done will remain with you. Arrived at Mars, you will find yourself the only living person who knows the whereabouts of the ancient city of Li, of which the vault of the beast is the central tower. In this city will be found literally billions of dollars' worth of treasure made of ultimate metal; and according to the laws of Earth, fifty per cent will be yours. Your fortune re-established, you will be able to return to Earth this very day, and reclaim your former wife, and your position. Poor silly child, she loves you still, but the iron conventions and training of her youth leave her no alternative. If she were older, she would have the character to defy those conventions. You must save her from herself. Will you do it?'

Brender was as white as a sheet, his hands clenching and unclenching. Malevolently, the thing watched the flaming thought sweeping through his brain – the memory of a pudgy white hand closing over Pamela's fingers, watched the reaction of Brender to its words, those words that expressed exactly what he had always thought. Brender looked up with tortured eyes.

'Yes,' he said, 'I'll do what I can.'

A bleak range of mountains fell away into a valley of reddish gray sand. The thin winds of Mars blew a mist of sand against the building.

Such a building! At a distance, it had looked merely big. A bare hundred feet projected above the desert, a hundred feet of length and *fifteen hundred feet of diameter*. Literally thousands of feet must extend beneath the restless ocean of sand to make the perfect balance of form, the graceful flow, the fairylike beauty, which the long-dead Martians demanded of all their constructions, however massive. Brender felt suddenly small and insignificant as the rockets of his spacesuit pounded him along a few feet above the sand toward that incredible building.

At close range the ugliness of sheer size was miraculously lost in the wealth of the decorative. Columns and pilasters assembled in groups and clusters, broke up the façades, gathered and dispersed again restlessly. The flat surfaces of wall and roof melted into a wealth of ornaments and imitation stucco work, vanished and broke into a play of light and shade.

The creature floated beside Brender; and its Controller said: 'I see that you have been giving considerable thought to the problem, but this robot seems incapable of following abstract thoughts, so I have no means of knowing the course of your speculations. I see however that you seem to be satisfied.'

'I think I've got the answer,' said Brender, 'but first I wish to see the time lock. Let's climb.'

They rose into the sky, dipping over the lip of the building. Brender saw a vast flat expanse; and in the center → He caught his breath!

The meager light from the distant sun of Mars shone down on a structure located at what seemed the exact center of the great door. The structure was about fifty feet high, and seemed nothing less than a series of quadrants coming together at the center, which was a metal arrow pointing straight up.

The arrow head was not solid metal. Rather it was as if the metal had divided in two parts, then curved together again. But not quite together. About a foot separated the two sections of metal. But that foot was bridged by a vague, thin, green flame of ieis force.

'The time lock!' Brender nodded. 'I thought it would be something like that, though I expected it would be bigger, more substantial.'

'Do not be deceived by its fragile appearance,' answered the thing. 'Theoretically, the strength of ultimate metal is infinite; and the ieis force can only be affected by the universal I have mentioned. Exactly what the effect will be, it is impossible to say as it involves the temporary derangement of the whole number system upon which that particular area of space is built. But now tell us what to do.'

'Very well.' Brender eased himself onto a bank of sand, and cut off his antigravity plates. He lay on his back, and stared thoughtfully into the blue-black sky. For the time being all doubts, worries and fears were gone from him, forced out by sheer will power. He began to explain:

'The Martian mathematic, like that of Euclid and Pythagoras, was based on endless magnitude. Minus numbers were beyond their philosophy. On Earth, however, beginning with Descartes, an analytical mathematic was evolved. Magnitude and perceivable dimensions were replaced by that of variable relation-values between positions in space.

'For the Martians, there was only one number between 1 and 3. Actually, the totality of such numbers is an infinite aggregate. And with the introduction of the idea of the square root of minus one – or *i* – and the complex numbers, mathematics definitely ceased to be a simple thing of magnitude, perceivable in pictures. Only the intellectual step from the infinitely small quantity to the lower limit of every possible finite magnitude brought out the conception of a variable number which oscillated beneath any assignable number that was not zero.

'The prime number, being a conception of pure magnitude, had no reality in *real* mathematics, but in this case was rigidly bound up with the reality of the ieis force. The Martians knew ieis as a pale-green flow about a foot in length and developing say a thousand horsepower. (It was actually 12.171 inches and 1021.23 horsepower, but that was unimportant.) The power produced never varied, the length never varied, from year end to year end, for tens of thousands of years. The Martians took the length as their basis of measurement, and called it one "el"; they took the power as their basis of power and called it one "rb". And because of the absolute invariability of the flow they knew it was eternal.

'They knew furthermore that nothing could be eternal without being prime; their whole mathematic was based on numbers which could be factored, that is, disintegrated, destroyed, rendered less than they had been; and numbers which could not be factored, disintegrated or divided into smaller groups.

'Any number which could be factored was incapable of being infinite. Contrariwise, the infinite number must be prime.

'Therefore, they built a lock and integrated it along a line of ieis, to operate when the ieis ceased to flow – which would be at the end of Time, provided it was not interfered with. To prevent interference, they buried the motivating mechanism of the flow in ultimate metal, which could not be destroyed or corroded in any way, According to their mathematic, that settled it.'

'But you have the answer,' said the voice of the thing eagerly.

'Simply this: The Martians set a value on the flow of one "rb". If you interfere with that flow to no matter what small degree, you no longer have an "rb". You have something less. The flow, which is a universal, becomes automatically less than a universal, less than infinite. The prime number ceases to be prime. Let us suppose that you interfere with it to the extent of *infinity minus one*. You will then have a number divisible by two. As a matter of fact, the number, like most large numbers, will immediately break into thousands of pieces, i.e., it will be divisible by tens of thousands of smaller numbers. If the present time falls anywhere near one of those breaks, the door would open then. In other words, the door will open immediately if you can so interfere with the flow that one of the factors occurs in immediate time.'

'That is very clear,' said the Controller with satisfaction and the image of Brender was smiling triumphantly. 'We shall now use this robot to manufacture a universal; and Kalorn shall be free very shortly.' He laughed aloud. 'The poor robot is protesting violently at the thought of being destroyed, but after all it is only a machine, and not a very good one at that. Besides, it is interfering with my proper reception of your thoughts. Listen to it scream, as I twist it into shape.'

The cold-blooded words chilled Brender, pulled him from the heights of his abstract thought. Because of the prolonged intensity of his thinking, he saw with sharp clarity something that had escaped him before.

'Just a minute,' he said. 'How is it that the robot, introduced from your world, is living at the same time rate as I am, whereas Kalorn continues to live at your time rate?'

'A very good question.' The face of the robot was twisted

40

into a triumphant sneer, as the Controller continued. 'Because, my dear Brender, you have been duped. It is true that Kalorn is living in our time rate, but that was due to a shortcoming in our machine. The machine which Kalorn built, while large enough to transport him, was not large enough in its adaptive mechanism to adapt him to each new space as he entered it. With the result that he was transported but not adapted. It was possible of course for us, his helpers, to transport such a small thing as the robot, though we have no more idea of the machine's construction than you have.

'In short, we can use what there is of the machine, but the secret of its construction is locked in the insides of our own particular ultimate metal, and in the brain of Kalorn. Its invention by Kalorn was one of those accidents which, by the law of averages, will not be repeated in millions of our years. Now that you have provided us with the method of bringing Kalorn back, we shall be able to build innumerable interspace machines. Our purpose is to control all spaces, all worlds – particularly those which are inhabited. We intend to be absolute rulers of the entire Universe.'

The ironic voice ended; and Brender lay in his prone position the prey of horror. The horror was twofold, partly due to the Controller's monstrous plan, and partly due to the thought that was pulsing in his brain. He groaned, as he realized that warning thought must be ticking away on the automatic receiving brain of the robot. 'Wait,' his thought was saying, 'that adds a new factor. Time —'

There was a scream from the creature as it was forcibly dissolved. The scream choked to a sob, then silence. An intricate machine of shining metal lay there on that great gray-brown expanse of sand and ultimate metal.

The metal glowed; and then the machine was floating in the air. It rose to the top of the arrow, and settled over the green flame of ieis.

41

Brender jerked on his antigravity screen, and leaped to his feet. The violent action carried him some hundred feet into the air. His rockets sputtered into staccato fire, and he clamped his teeth against the pain of acceleration.

Below him, the great door began to turn, to unscrew, faster and faster, till it was like a flywheel. Sand flew in all directions in a miniature storm.

At top acceleration, Brender darted to one side.

Just in time. First, the robot machine was flung off that tremendous wheel by sheer centrifugal power. Then the door came off, and, spinning now at an incredible rate, hurtled straight into the air, and vanished into space.

A puff of black dust came floating up out of the blackness of the vault. Supressing his horror, yet perspiring from awful relief, he rocketed to where the robot had fallen into the sand.

Instead of glistening metal, a time-dulled piece of junk lay there. The dull metal flowed sluggishly and assumed a quasi-human shape. The flesh remained gray and in little rolls as if it were ready to fall apart from old age. The thing tried to stand up on wrinkled, horrible legs, but finally lay still. Its lips moved, mumbled:

'I caught your warning thought, but I didn't let them know. Now, Kalorn is dead. They realized the truth as it was happening. End of Time came —'

It faltered into silence; and Brender went on: 'Yes, end of Time came when the flow became momentarily less than eternal – came at the factor point which occurred a few minutes ago.'

'I was . . . only partly . . . within its . . . influence, Kalorn all the way . . . . Even if they're lucky . . . will be years before . . . they invent another machine . . . and one of their years is billions . . . of yours . . . . I didn't tell them . . . . I caught your thought . . . and kept it . . . from them —'

'But why did you do it? Why?'

'Because they were hurting me. They were going to destroy

me. Because . . . I liked . . . being human. I was . . . some-body!'

The flesh dissolved. It flowed slowly into a pool of lavalike gray. The lava crinkled, split into dry, brittle pieces. Brender touched one of the pieces. It crumbled into a fine powder of gray dust. He gazed out across that grim, deserted valley of sand, and said aloud, pityingly:

'Poor Frankenstein.'

He turned toward the distant spaceship, toward the swift trip to Earth. As he climbed out of the ship a few minutes later, one of the first persons he saw was Pamela.

She flew into his arms. 'Oh, Jim, Jim,' she sobbed. 'What a fool I've been. When I heard what had happened, and realized you were in danger, I — Oh Jim!'

Later, he would tell her about their new fortune.

THE WEAPON SHOP

The village at night made a curiously timeless picture. Fara walked contentedly beside his wife along the street. The air was like wine; and he was thinking dimly of the artist who had come up from Imperial City, and made what the telestats called – he remembered the phrase vividly – 'a symbolic painting reminiscent of a scene in the electrical age of seven thousand years ago'.

Fara believed that utterly. The street before him with its weedless, automatically tended gardens, its shops set well back among the flowers, its perpetual hard, grassy sidewalks, and its street lamps that glowed from every pore of their structure – this was a restful paradise where time had stood still.

And it was like being a part of life that the great artist's picture of this quiet, peaceful scene before him was now in the collection of the empress herself. She had praised it, and naturally the thrice-blest artist had immediately and humbly begged her to accept it.

What a joy it must be to be able to offer personal homage to the glorious, the divine, the serenely gracious and lovely Innelda Isher, one thousand one hundred eightieth of her line.

As they walked, Fara half turned to his wife. In the dim light of the nearest street lamp, her kindly, still youthful face was almost lost in shadow. He murmured softly, instinctively muting his voice to harmonize with the pastel shades of night:

'She said – our empress said – that our little village of Glay seemed to her to have in it all the wholesomeness, the gentleness, that constitutes the finest qualities of her people. Wasn't that a wonderful thought, Creel? She must be a marvelously understanding woman. I —'

44

He stopped. They had come to a side street, and there was something about a hundred and fifty feet along it that —

'Look!' Fara said hoarsely.

He pointed with rigid arm and finger at a sign that glowed in the night, a sign that read:

FINE WEAPONS
THE RIGHT TO BUY WEAPONS IS THE RIGHT
TO BE FREE

Fara had a strange, empty feeling as he stared at the blazing sign. He saw that other villagers were gathering. He said finally, huskily:

'I've heard of these shops. They're places of infamy, against which the government of the empress will act one of these days. They're built in hidden factories, and then transported whole to towns like ours and set up in gross defiance of property rights. That one wasn't there an hour ago.'

Fara's face hardened. His voice had a harsh edge in it, as he said:

'Creel, go home.'

Fara was surprised when Creel did not move off at once. All their married life, she had had a pleasing habit of obedience that had made cohabitation a wonderful thing. He saw that she was looking at him wide-eyed, and that it was a timid alarm that held her there. She said:

'Fara, what do you intend to do? You're not thinking of —'

'Go home!' Her fear brought out all the grim determination in his nature. 'We're not going to let such a monstrous thing desecrate our village. Think of it' – his voice shivered before the appalling thought – 'this fine, old-fashioned community, which we had resolved always to keep exactly as the empress has it in her picture gallery, debauched now, ruined by this . . . this thing — But we won't have it; that's all there is to it.'

Creel's voice came softly out of the half-darkness of the street corner, the timidity gone from it: 'Don't do anything rash, Fara. Remember it is not the first new building to come into Glay – since the picture was painted.'

Fara was silent. This was a quality of his wife of which he did not approve, this reminding him unnecessarily of unpleasant facts. He knew exactly what she meant. The gigantic, multitentacled corporation, Automatic Atomic Motor Repair Shops, Inc., had come in under the laws of the State with their flashy building, against the wishes of the village council – and had already taken half of Fara's repair business.

'That's different!' Fara growled finally. 'In the first place people will discover in good time that these new automatic repairers do a poor job. In the second place its fair competition. But this weapon shop is a defiance of all the decencies that make life under the House of Isher such a joy. Look at the hypocritical sign: "The right to buy weapons —" Aaaaahh!'

He broke off with: 'Go home, Creel. We'll see to it that they sell no weapons in this town.'

He watched the slender woman-shape move off into the shadows. She was halfway across the street when a thought occurred to Fara. He called:

'And if you see that son of ours hanging around some street corner, take him home. He's got to learn to stop staying out so late at night.'

The shadowed figure of his wife did not turn; and after watching her for a moment moving along against the dim background of softly glowing street lights, Fara twisted on his heel, and walked swiftly toward the shop. The crowd was growing larger every minute, and the night pulsed with excited voices.

Beyond doubt, here was the biggest thing that had ever happened to the village of Glay.

The sign of the weapon shop was, he saw, a normal-illusion affair. No matter what his angle of view, he was always looking straight at it. When he paused finally in front of the great display window, the words had pressed back against the store front, and were staring unwinkingly down at him.

Fara sniffed once more at the meaning of the slogan, then forgot the simple thing. There was another sign in the window, which read:

THE FINEST ENERGY WEAPONS IN THE KNOWN UNIVERSE

A spark of interest struck fire inside Fara. He gazed at that brilliant display of guns, fascinated in spite of himself. The weapons were of every size, ranging from tiny little finger pistols to express rifles. They were made of every one of the light, hard, ornamental substances: glittering glassein, the colorful but opaque Ordine plastic viridescent magnesitic beryllium. And others.

It was the very deadly extent of the destructive display that brought a chill to Fara. So many weapons for the little village of Glay, where not more than two people to his knowledge had guns, and those only for hunting. Why, the thing was absurd, fantastically mischievous, utterly threatening.

Somewhere behind Fara, a man said: 'It's right on Lan Harris' lot. Good joke on that old scoundrel. Will he raise a row!'

There was a faint titter from several men, that made an odd patch of sound on the warm, fresh air. And Fara saw that the man had spoken the truth. The weapon shop had a forty-foot frontage. And it occupied the very center of the green, gardenlike lot of tight-fisted, old Harris.

Fara frowned. The clever devils, the weapon-shop people, selecting the property of the most disliked man in town, coolly taking it over and giving everybody an agreeable titillation. But the very cunning of it made it vital that the trick shouldn't succeed.

He was still scowling anxiously when he saw the plump figure of Mel Dale, the mayor. Fara edged toward him hurriedly, touched his hat respectfully, and said:

'Where's Jor?'

'Here.' The village constable elbowed his way through a little bundle of men. 'Any plans?' he said.

'There's only one plan,' said Fara boldly. 'Go in and arrest them.'

To Fara's amazement, the two men looked at each other, then at the ground. It was the big constable who answered shortly:

'Door's locked. And nobody answers our pounding. I was just going to suggest we let the matter ride until morning.'

'Nonsense!' His very astonishment made Fara impatient. 'Get an ax and we'll break the door down. Delay will only encourage such riffraff to resist. We don't want their kind in our village for so much as a single night. Isn't that so?'

There was a hasty nod of agreement from everybody in his immediate vicinity. Too hasty. Fara looked around puzzled at eyes that lowered before his level gaze. He thought: 'They are all scared. And unwilling.' Before he could speak, Constable Jor said:

'I guess you haven't heard about those doors or these shops. From all account, you can't break into them.'

It struck Fara with a sudden pang that it was he who would have to act here. He said, 'I'll get my atomic cutting machine from my shop. That'll fix them. Have I your permission to do that, Mr Mayor?'

In the glow of the weapon-shop window, the plump man was sweating visibly. He pulled out a handkerchief, and wiped his forehead. He said:

'Maybe I'd better call the commander of the Imperial garrison at Ferd, and ask them.'

'No!' Fara recognized evasion when he saw it. He felt himself steel; the conviction came that all the strength in this village was in him. 'We must act ourselves. Other communities have let these people get in because they took no decisive action. We've got to resist to the limit. Beginning now. This minute. Well?'

The mayor's 'All right!' was scarcely more than a sigh of sound. But it was all Fara needed.

He called out his intention to the crowd; and then, as he pushed his way out of the mob, he saw his son standing with some other young men staring at the window display.

Fara called: 'Cayle, come and help me with the machine.'

Cayle did not even turn; and Fara hurried on, seething. That wretched boy! One of these days he, Fara, would have to take firm action there. Or he'd have a no-good on his hands.

The energy was soundless – and smooth. There was no sputter, no fireworks. It glowed with a soft, pure white light, almost caressing the metal panels of the door – but not even beginning to sear them.

Minute after minute, the dogged Fara refused to believe the incredible failure, and played the boundlessly potent energy on that resisting wall. When he finally shut off his machine, he was perspiring freely.

'I don't understand it,' he gasped. 'Why – no metal is supposed to stand up against a steady flood of atomic force. Even the hard metal plates used inside the blast chamber of a motor take the explosions in what is called infinite series, so that each one has unlimited rest. That's the theory, but actually steady running crystallizes the whole plate after a few months.'

'It's as Jor told you,' said the mayor. 'These weapon shops are – big. They spread right through the empire, *and they don't recognize the empress.*'

Fara shifted his feet on the hard grass, disturbed. He didn't like this kind of talk. It sounded – sacrilegious. And besides it was nonsense. It must be. Before he could speak, a man said somewhere behind him:

'I've heard it said that that door will open only to those who cannot harm the people inside.'

The words shocked Fara out of his daze. With a start, and for the first time, he saw that his failure had had a bad psychological effect. He said sharply:

'That's ridiculous! If there were doors like that, we'd all have them. We —'

The thought that stopped his words was the sudden realization that he had not seen anybody try to open the door; and with all this reluctance around him it was quite possible that —

He stepped forward, grasped at the doorknob, and pulled. The door opened with an unnatural weightlessness that gave him the fleeting impression that the knob had come loose into his hand. With a gasp, Fara jerked the door wide open.

'Jor!' he yelled. 'Get in!'

The constable made a distorted movement – distorted by what must have been a will to caution, followed by the instant realization that he could not hold back before so many. He leaped awkwardly toward the open door – and it closed in his face.

Fara stared stupidly at his hand, which was still clenched. And then, slowly, a hideous thrill coursed along his nerves. The knob had – withdrawn. It had twisted, become viscous, and slipped amorphously from his straining fingers. Even the memory of that brief sensation gave him a feeling of unnormal things.

He grew aware that the crowd was watching with a silent intentness. Fara reached again for the knob, not quite so eagerly this time; and it was only a sudden realization of his reluctance that made him angry when the handle neither turned nor yielded in any way.

50

Determination returned in full force, and with it came a thought. He motioned to the constable. 'Go back, Jor, while I pull.'

The man retreated, but it did no good. And tugging did not help. The door would not open. Somewhere in the crowd, a man said darkly:

'It decided to let you in, then it changed its mind.'

'What foolishness are you talking!' Fara spoke violently. '*It* changed its mind. Are you crazy? A door has no sense.'

But a surge of fear put a half-quaver into his voice. It was the sudden alarm that made him bold beyond all his normal caution. With a jerk of his body, Fara faced the shop.

The building loomed there under the night sky, in itself bright as day, huge in width and length, and alien, menacing, no longer easily conquerable. The dim queasy wonder came as to what the soldiers of the empress would do if they were invited to act. And suddenly – a bare, flashing glimpse of grim possibility – the feeling grew that even they would be able to do nothing.

Abruptly, Fara was conscious of horror that such an idea could enter his mind. He shut his brain tight, said wildly:

'The door opened for me once. It will open again.'

It did. Quite simply it did. Gently, without resistance, *with* that same sensation of weightlessness, the strange, sensitive door followed the tug of his fingers. Beyond the threshold was dimness, a wide, darkened alcove. He heard the voice of Mel Dale behind him, the mayor saying:

'Fara, don't be a fool. What will you do inside?'

Fara was vaguely amazed to realize that he had stepped across the threshold. He turned, startled, and stared at the blur of faces. 'Why – ' he began blankly; then he brightened; he said, 'Why, I'll buy a gun, of course.'

The brilliance of his reply, the cunning implicit in it, dazzled Fara for half a minute longer. The mood yielded slowly, as he found himself in the dimly lighted interior of the weapon shop.

It was preternaturally quiet inside. Not a sound penetrated from the night from which he had come; and the startled thought came that the people of the shop might actually be unaware that there was a crowd outside.

Fara walked gingerly on a rugged floor that muffled his footsteps utterly. After a moment, his eyes accustomed themselves to the soft lighting, which came like a reflection from the walls and ceilings. In a vague way, he had expected ultranormalness; and the ordinariness of the atomic lighting acted like a tonic to his tensed nerves.

He shook himself angrily. Why should there be anything really superior? He was getting as bad as those credulous idiots out in the street.

He glanced around with gathering confidence. The place looked quite common. It was a shop, almost scantily furnished. There were showcases on the walls and on the floor, glitteringly lovely things, but nothing unusual, and not many of them – a few dozens. There was in addition a double, ornate door leading to a back room —

Fara tried to keep one eye on that door, as he examined several showcases, each with three or four weapons either mounted or arranged in boxes or holsters.

Abruptly, the weapons began to excite him. He forgot to watch the door, as the wild thought struck that he ought to grab one of those guns from a case, and then the moment someone came, force him outside where Jor would perform the arrest and —

Behind him, a man said quietly: 'You wish to buy a gun?'

Fara turned with a jump. Brief rage flooded him at the way his plan had been wrecked by the arrival of the clerk.

The anger died as he saw that the intruder was a fine-looking, silver-haired man, older than himself. That was immeasurably disconcerting. Fara had an immense and almost automatic respect for age, and for a long second he could only stand there gaping. He said at last, lamely:

'Yes, yes, a gun.'

'For what purpose?' said the man in his quiet voice.

Fara could only look at him blankly. It was too fast. He wanted to get mad. He wanted to tell these people what he thought of them. But the age of this representative locked his tongue, tangled his emotions. He managed speech only by an effort of will:

'For hunting.' The plausible word stiffened his mind. 'Yes, definitely for hunting. There is a lake to the north of here,' he went on more fulsomely, glibly, 'and —'

He stopped, scowling, startled at the extent of his dishonesty. He was not prepared to go so deeply into prevarication. He said curtly:

'For hunting.'

Fara was himself again. Abruptly, he hated the man for having put him so completely at a disadvantage. With smoldering eyes he watched the old fellow click open a showcase, and take out a green-shining rifle.

As the man faced him, weapon in hand, Fara was thinking grimly, 'Pretty clever, having an old man as a front.' It was the same kind of cunning that had made them choose the property of Miser Harris. Icily furious, taut with his purpose, Fara reached for the gun; but the man held it out of his reach, saying:

'Before I can even let you test this, I am compelled by the by-laws of the weapon shops to inform you under what circumstances you may purchase a gun.'

So they had private regulations. What a system of psychological tricks to impress gullible fools. Well, let the old scoundrel talk. As soon as he, Fara, got hold of the rifle, he'd put an end to hypocrisy.

'We weapon makers,' the clerk was saying mildly, 'have evolved guns that can, in their particular ranges, destroy any machine or object made of what is called matter. Thus whoever possesses one of our weapons is the equal and more of any soldier of the empress. I say more because each gun is the center of a field of force which acts as a perfect screen against immaterial destructive forces. That screen offers no resistance to clubs or spears or bullets, or other material substances, but it would require a small atomic cannon to penetrate the superb barrier it creates around its owner.

'You will readily comprehend,' the man went on, 'that such a potent weapon could not be allowed to fall, unmodified, into irresponsible hands. Accordingly, no gun purchased from us may be used for aggression or murder. In the case of the hunting rifle, only such specified game birds and animals as we may from time to time list in our display windows may be shot. Finally, no weapon can be resold without our approval. Is that clear?'

Fara nodded dumbly. For the moment, speech was impossible to him. The incredible, fantastically stupid words were still going round and around in his head. He wondered if he ought to laugh out loud, or curse the man for daring to insult his intelligence so tremendously.

So the gun mustn't be used for murder or robbery. So only certain birds and animals could be shot. And as for reselling it, suppose – suppose he bought this thing, took a trip of a thousand miles, and offered it to some wealthy stranger for two credits – who would ever know?

Or suppose he held up the stranger. Or shot him. How would the weapon shop ever find out? The thing was so ridiculous that —

He grew aware that the gun was being held out to him stock first. He took it eagerly, and had to fight the impulse to turn the muzzle directly on the old man. Mustn't rush this, he thought tautly. He said:

'How does it work?'

'You simply aim it, and pull the trugger. Perhaps you would like to try it on a target we have.'

Fara swung the gun up. 'Yes,' he said triumphantly, 'and you're it. Now, just get over there to the front door, and then outside.'

He raised his voice: 'And if anybody's thinking of coming through the back door, I've got that covered, too.'

He motioned jerkily at the clerk. 'Quick now, move! I'll shoot! I swear I will.'

The man was cool, unflustered. 'I have no doubt you would. When we decided to attune the door so that you could enter despite your hostility, we assumed the capacity for homicide. However, this is our party. You had better adjust yourself accordingly, and look behind you —'

There was silence. Finger on trigger, Fara stood moveless. Dim thoughts came of all the *half-things* he had heard in his days about the weapon shops: that they had secret supporters in every district, that they had a private and ruthless hidden government, and that once you got into their clutches, the only way out was death and —

But what finally came clear was a mind picture of himself, Fara Clark, family man, faithful subject of the empress, standing here in this dimly lighted store, deliberately fighting an organization so vast and menacing that — He must have been mad.

Only – here he was. He forced courage into his sagging muscles. He said:

'You can't fool me with pretending there's someone behind me. Now, get to that door. And *fast!*'

The firm eyes of the old man were looking past him. The man said quietly: 'Well, Rad, have you all the data?'

'Enough for a primary,' said a young man's baritone voice behind Fara. 'Type A-7 conservative. Good average intelligence, but a Monaric development peculiar to small towns. One-sided outlook fostered by the Imperial schools present in exaggerated form. Extremely honest. Reason would be useless. Emotional approach would require extended treatment. I see no reason why we should bother. Let him live his life as it suits him.'

'If you think,' Fara said shakily, 'that that trick is going

55

to make me turn, you're crazy. That's the left wall of the building. I know there's no one there.'

'I'm all in favor, Rad,' said the old man, 'of letting him live his life. But he was the prime mover of the crowd outside. I think he should be discouraged.'

'We'll advertise his presence,' said Rad. 'He'll spend the rest of his life denying the charge.'

Fara's confidence in the gun had faded so far that, as he listened in puzzled uneasiness to the incomprehensible conversation, he forgot it completely. He parted his lips, but before he could speak, the old man cut in, persistently:

'I think a little emotion might have a long-run effect. Show him the palace.'

Palace! The startling word tore Fara out of his brief paralysis. 'See here,' he began, 'I can see now that you lied to me. This gun isn't loaded at all. It's —'

His voice failed him. Every muscle in his body went rigid. He stared like a madman. *There was no gun in his hands.*

'Why, you – ' he began wildly. And stopped again. His mind heaved with imbalance. With a terrible effort he fought off the spinning sensation, thought finally, tremblingly: Somebody must have sneaked the gun from him. That meant – there was someone behind him. The voice was no mechanical thing. Somehow, they had —

He started to turn – and couldn't. What in the name of — He struggled, pushing with his muscles. And couldn't move, couldn't budge, couldn't even —

The room was growing curiously dark. He had difficulty seeing the old man and — He would have shrieked then if he could. Because the weapon shop was gone. He was —

He was standing in the sky above an immense city.

In the sky, and nothing beneath him, nothing around him but air, and blue summer heaven, and the city a mile, two miles below.

Nothing, nothing — He would have shrieked, but his breath seemed solidly embedded in his lungs. Sanity came

56

back as the remote awareness impinged upon his terrified mind that he was actually standing on a hard floor, and that the city must be a picture somehow focused directly into his eyes.

For the first time, with a start, Fara recognized the metropolis below. It was the city of dreams, Imperial City, capital of the glorious Empress Isher — From his great height, he could see the gardens, the gorgeous grounds of the silver palace, the official Imperial residence itself —

The last tendrils of his fear were fading now before a gathering fascination and wonder; they vanished utterly as he recognized with a ghastly thrill of uncertain expectancy that the palace was drawing nearer at great speed.

'Show him the palace,' they had said. Did that mean, could it mean —

That spray of tense thoughts splattered into nonexistence, as the glittering roof flashed straight at his face. He gulped, as the solid metal of it passed through him, and then other walls and ceilings.

His first sense of imminent and mind-shaking desecration came as the picture paused in a great room where a score of men sat around a table at the head of which sat – a young woman.

The inexorable, sacrilegious, limitlessly powered cameras that were taking the picture swung across the table, and caught the woman full face.

It was a handsome face, but there was passion and fury twisting it now, and a very blaze of fire in her eyes, as she leaned forward, and said in a voice at once familiar – how often Fara had heard its calm, measured tones on the telestats – and distorted. Utterly distorted by anger and an insolent certainty of command. That caricature of a beloved voice slashed across the silence as clearly as if he, Fara, was there in that room:

'I want that skunk killed, do you understand? I don't

care how you do it, but I want to hear by tomorrow night that he's dead.'

The picture snapped off and instantly – it was as swift as that – Fara was back in the weapon shop. He stood for a moment, swaying, fighting to accustom his eyes to the dimness; and then —

His first emotion was contempt at the simpleness of the trickery – a motion picture. What kind of a fool did they think he was, to swallow something as transparently unreal as that? He'd —

Abruptly, the appalling lechery of the scheme, the indescribable wickedness of what was being attempted here brought red rage.

'Why, you scum!' he flared. 'So you've got somebody to act the part of the empress, trying to pretend that — Why, you —'

'That will do,' said the voice of Rad; and Fara shook as a big young man walked into his line of vision. The alarmed thought came that people who would besmirch so vilely the character of her imperial majesty would not hesitate to do physical damage to Fara Clark. The young man went on in a steely tone:

'We do not pretend that what you saw was taking place this instant in the palace. That would be too much of a coincidence. But it was taken two weeks ago; the woman *is* the empress. The man whose death she ordered is one of her many former lovers. He was found murdered two weeks ago; his name, if you care to look it up in the news files, is Banton McCreddie. However, let that pass. We're finished with you now and —'

'But I'm not finished,' Fara said in a thick voice. 'I've never heard or seen so much infamy in all my life. If you think this town is through with you, you're crazy. We'll have a guard on this place day and night, and nobody will get in or out. We'll —'

'That will do.' It was the silver-haired man; and Fara

stopped out of respect for age, before he thought. The old man went on: 'The examination has been most interesting. As an honest man, you may call on us if you are ever in trouble. That is all. Leave through the side door.'

It *was* all. Impalpable forces grabbed him, and he was shoved at a door that appeared miraculously in the wall, where seconds before the palace had been.

He found himself standing dazedly in a flower bed, and there was a swarm of men to his left. He recognized his fellow townsmen and that he was – outside.

The incredible nightmare was over.

'Where's the gun?' said Creel, as he entered the house half an hour later.

'The gun?' Fara stared at his wife.

'It said over the radio a few minutes ago that you were the first customer of the new weapon shop. I thought it was queer, but —'

He was eerily conscious of her voice going on for several words longer, but it was the purest jumble. The shock was so great that he had the horrible sensation of being on the edge of an abyss.

So that was what the young man had meant: 'Advertise! We'll advertise his presence and —'

Fara thought: His reputation! Not that his was a great name, but he had long believed with a quiet pride that Fara Clark's motor repair shop was widely known in the community and countryside.

First, his private humiliation inside the shop. And now this – lying – to people who didn't know why he had gone into the store. Diabolical.

His paralysis ended, as a frantic determination to rectify the base charge drove him to the telestat. After a moment, the plump, sleepy face of Mayor Mel Dale appeared on the plate. Fara's voice made a barrage of sound, but his hopes dashed, as the man said:

'I'm sorry, Fara. I don't see how you can have free time on the telestat. You'll have to pay for it. They did.'

'They did!' Fara wondered vaguely if he sounded as empty as he felt.

'And they've just paid Lan Harris for his lot. The old man asked top price, and got it. He just phoned me to transfer the title.'

'Oh!' The world was shattering. 'You mean nobody's going to do anything. What about the Imperial garrison at Ferd?'

Dimly, Fara was aware of the mayor mumbling something about the empress' soldiers refusing to interfere in civilian matters.

'Civilian matters!' Fara exploded. 'You mean these people are just going to be allowed to come here whether we want them or not, illegally forcing the sale of lots by first taking possession of them?'

A sudden thought struck him breathless. 'Look, you haven't changed your mind about having Jor keep guard in front of the shop?'

With a start, he saw that the lump face in the telestat plate had grown impatient. 'Now, see here, Fara,' came the pompous words, 'let the constituted authorities handle this matter.'

'But you're going to keep Jor there,' Fara said doggedly.

The mayor looked annoyed, said finally peevishly: 'I promised, didn't I? So he'll be there. And now – do you want to buy time on the telestat? It's fifteen credits for one minute. Mind you, as a friend, I think you're wasting your money. No one has ever caught up with a false statement.'

Fara said grimly: 'Put two on, one in the morning, one in the evening.'

'All right. We'll deny it completely. Good night.'

The telestat went blank; and Fara sat there. A new thought hardened his face. 'That boy of ours – there's going to be a showdown. He either works in my shop, or he gets no more allowance.'

Creel said: 'You've handled him wrong. He's twenty-three, and you treat him like a child. Remember, at twenty-three, you were a married man.'

'That was different,' said Fara. 'I had a sense of responsibility. Do you know what he did tonight?'

He didn't quite catch her answer. For the moment, he thought she said: 'No; in what way did you humiliate him first?'

Fara felt too impatient to verify the impossible words. He rushed on: 'He refused in front of the whole village to give me help. He's a bad one, all bad.'

'Yes,' said Creel in a bitter tone, 'he is all bad. I'm sure you don't realize how bad. He's as cold as steel, but without steel's strength or integrity. He took a long time, but he hates even me now, because I stood up for your side so long, knowing you were wrong.'

'What's that?' said Fara, startled; then gruffly: 'Come, come, my dear, we're both upset. Let's go to bed.'

He slept poorly.

There were days then when the conviction that this was a personal fight between himself and the weapon shop lay heavily on Fara. Grimly, though it was out of his way, he made a point of walking past the weapon shop, always pausing to speak to Constable Jor and —

On the fourth day, the policeman wasn't there.

Fara waited patiently at first, then angrily; then he walked hastily to his shop, and called Jor's house. No, Jor wasn't home. He was guarding the weapon store.

Fara hesitated. His own shop was piled with work, and he had a guilty sense of having neglected his customers for the first time in his life. It would be simple to call up the mayor and report Jor's dereliction. And yet —

He didn't want to get the man into trouble —

Out in the street, he saw that a large crowd was gathering

in front of the weapon shop. Fara hurried. A man he knew greeted him excitedly:

'Jor's been murdered, Fara!'

'Murdered!' Fara stood stock-still, and at first he was not clearly conscious of the grisly thought that was in his mind: Satisfaction! A flaming satisfaction. Now, he thought, even the soldiers would have to act. They —

With a gasp, he realized the ghastly tenor of his thoughts. He shivered, but finally pushed the sense of shame out of his mind. He said slowly:

'Where's the body?'

'Inside.'

'You mean, those . . . scum —' In spite of himself, he hesitated over the epithet; even now, it was difficult to think of the fine-faced, silver-haired old man in such terms. Abruptly, his mind hardened; he flared: 'You mean those scum actually killed him, then pulled his body inside?'

'Nobody saw the killing,' said a second man beside Fara, 'but he's gone, hasn't been seen for three hours. The mayor got the weapon shop on the telestat, but they claim they don't know anything. They've done away with him, that's what, and now they're pretending innocence. Well, they won't get out of it as easily as that. Mayor's gone to phone the soldiers at Ferd to bring up some big guns and —'

Something of the intense excitement that was in the crowd surged through Fara, the feeling of big things brewing. It was the most delicious sensation that had ever tingled along his nerves, and it was all mixed with a strange pride that he had been so right about this, that he at least had never doubted that here was evil.

He did not recognize the emotion as the full-flowering joy that comes to a member of a mob. But his voice shook, as he said:

'Guns? Yes, that will be the answer, and the soldiers will have to come, of course.'

Fara nodded to himself in the immensity of his certainty

that the Imperial soldiers would now have no excuse for not acting. He started to say something dark about what the empress would do if she found out that a man had lost his life because the soldiers had shirked their duty, but the words were drowned in a shout:

'Here comes the mayor! Hey, Mr Mayor, when are the atomic cannons due?'

There was more of the same general meaning, as the mayor's sleek, all-purpose car landed lightly. Some of the questions must have reached his honor, for he stood up in the open two-seater, and held up his hand for silence.

To Fara's astonishment, the plump-faced man looked at him with accusing eyes. The thing seemed so impossible that, quite instinctively, Fara looked behind him. But he was almost alone; everybody else had crowded forward.

Fara shook his head, puzzled by that glare; and then, astoundingly, Mayor Dale pointed a finger at him, and said in a voice that trembled:

'There's the man who's responsible for the trouble that's come upon us. Stand forward, Fara Clark, and show yourself. You've cost this town seven hundred credits that we could ill afford to spend.'

Fara couldn't have moved or spoken to save his life. He just stood there in a maze of dumb bewilderment. Before he could even think, the mayor went on, and there was quivering self-pity in his tone:

'We've all known that it wasn't wise to interfere with these weapon shops. So long as the Imperial government leaves them alone, what right have we to set up guards, or act against them? That's what I've thought from the beginning, but this man . . . this . . . this Fara Clark kept after all of us, forcing us to move against our wills, and so now we've got a seven-hundred-credit bill to meet and —'

He broke off with: 'I might as well make it brief. When I called the garrison, the commander just laughed and said

63

that Jor would turn up. And I had barely disconnected when there was a money call from Jor. He's on Mars.'

He waited for the shouts of amazement to die down. 'It'll take three weeks for him to come back by ship, and we've got to pay for it, and Fara Clark is responsible. He —'

The shock was over. Fara stood cold, his mind hard. He said finally, scathingly: 'So you're giving up, and trying to blame me all in one breath. I say you're all fools.'

As he turned away, he heard Mayor Dale saying something about the situation not being completely lost, as he had learned that the weapon shop had been set up in Glay because the village was equidistant from four cities, and that it was the city business the shop was after. This would mean tourists, and accessory trade for the village stores and —

Fara heard no more. Head high, he walked back toward his shop. There were one or two catcalls from the mob, but he ignored them.

He had no sense of approaching disaster, simply a gathering fury against the weapon shop, which had brought him to this miserable status among his neighbors.

The worst of it, as the days passed, was the realization that the people of the weapon shop had no personal interest in him. They were remote, superior, undefeatable. That unconquerableness was a dim, suppressed awareness inside Fara.

When he thought of it, he felt a vague fear at the way they had transferred Jor to Mars in a period of less than three hours, when all the world knew that the trip by fastest spaceship required nearly three weeks.

Fara did not go to the express station to see Jor arrive home. He had heard that the council had decided to charge Jor with half of the expense of the trip, on the threat of losing his job if he made a fuss.

On the second night after Jor's return, Fara slipped down to the constable's house, and handed the officer one hundred seventy-five credits. It wasn't that he was responsible, he told Jor, but —

The man was only too eager to grant the disclaimer, provided the money went with it. Fara returned home with a clearer conscience.

It was on the third day after that that the door of his shop banged open and a man came in. Fara frowned as he saw who it was: Castler, a village hanger-on. The man was grinning:

'Thought you might be interested, Fara. Somebody came out of the weapon shop today.'

Fara strained deliberately at the connecting bolt of a hard plate of the atomic motor he was fixing. He waited with a gathering annoyance that the man did not volunteer further information. Asking questions would be a form of recognition of the worthless fellow. A developing curiosity made him say finally, grudgingly:

'I suppose the constable promptly picked him up.'

He supposed nothing of the kind, but it was an opening.

'It wasn't a man. It was a girl.'

Fara knitted his brows. He didn't like the idea of making trouble for women. But – the cunning devils! Using a girl, just as they had used an old man as a clerk. It was a trick that deserved to fail, the girl probably a tough one who needed rough treatment. Fara said harshly:

'Well, what's happened?'

'She's still out, bold as you please. Pretty thing, too.'

The bolt off, Fara took the hard plate over to the polisher, and began patiently the long, careful task of smoothing away the crystals that heat had seared on the once shining metal. The soft throb of the polisher made the background to his next words:

'Has anything been done?'

'Nope. The constable's been told, but he says he doesn't fancy being away from his family for another three weeks, and paying the cost into the bargain.'

Fara contemplated that darkly for a minute, as the polisher throbbed on. His voice shook with suppressed fury, when he said finally:

'So they're letting them get away with it. It's all been as clever as hell. Can't they see that they mustn't give an inch before these . . . these transgressors. It's like giving countenance to sin.'

From the corner of his eye, he noticed that there was a curious grin on the face of the other. It struck Fara suddenly that the man was enjoying his anger. And there was something else in that grin; something – a secret knowledge.

Fara pulled the engine plate away from the polisher. He faced the ne'er-do-well, scathed at him:

'Naturally, that sin part wouldn't worry you much.'

'Oh,' said the man nonchalantly, 'the hard knocks of life make people tolerant. For instance, after you know the girl better, you yourself will probably come to realize that there's good in all of us.'

It was not so much the words, as the curious I've-got-secret-information tone that made Fara snap:

'What do you mean – if I get to know the girl better! I won't even speak to the brazen creature.'

'One can't always choose,' the other said with enormous casualness. 'Suppose he brings her home.'

'Suppose who brings who home?' Fara spoke irritably. 'Castler, you —'

He stopped; a dead weight of dismay plumped into his stomach; his whole being sagged. 'You mean — ' he said.

'I mean,' replied Castler with a triumphant leer, 'that the boys aren't letting a beauty like her be lonesome. And, naturally, your son was the first to speak to her.'

He finished: 'They're walkin' together now on Second Avenue, comin' this way, so — '

'Get out of here!' Fara roared. 'And stay away from me with your gloating. Get out!'

The man hadn't expected such an ignominious ending.

66

He flushed scarlet, then went out, slamming the door.

Fara stood for a moment, every muscle stiff; then, with an abrupt, jerky movement, he shut off his power, and went out into the street.

The time to put a stop to that kind of thing was – now!

He had no clear plan, just that violent determination to put an immediate end to an impossible situation. And it was all mixed up with his anger against Cayle. How could he have had such a worthless son, he who paid his debts and worked hard, and tried to be decent and to live up to the highest standards of the empress?

A brief, dark thought came to Fara that maybe there was some bad blood on Creel's side. Not from her mother, of course – Fara added the mental thought hastily. *There* was a fine, hard-working woman, who hung on to her money, and who would leave Creel a tidy sum one of these days.

But Creel's father had disappeared when Creel was only a child, and there had been some vague scandal about him having taken up with a telestat actress.

And now Cayle with this weapon-shop girl. A girl who had let herself be picked up —

He saw them, as he turned the corner onto Second Avenue. They were walking a hundred feet distant, and heading away from Fara. The girl was tall and slender, almost as big as Cayle, and, as Fara came up, she was saying:

'You have the wrong idea about us. A person like you can't get a job in our organization. You belong in the Imperial Service, where they can use young men of good education, good appearance and no scruples. I —'

Fara grasped only dimly that Cayle must have been trying to get a job with these people. It was not clear; and his own mind was too intent on his purpose for it to mean anything at the moment. He said harshly:

'Cayle!'

The couple turned, Cayle with the measured unhurriedness of a young man who has gone a long way on the road to steellike nerves; the girl was quicker, but withal dignified.

Fara had a vague, terrified feeling that his anger was too great, self-destroying, but the very violence of his emotions ended that thought even as it came. He said thickly:

'Cayle, get home – at once.'

Fara was aware of the girl looking at him curiously from strange, gray-green eyes. No shame, he thought, and his rage mounted several degrees, driving away the alarm that came at the sight of the flush that crept into Cayle's cheeks.

The flush faded into a pale, tight-lipped anger; Cayle half-turned to the girl, said:

'This is the childish old fool I've got to put up with. Fortunately, we seldom see each other; we don't even eat together. What do you think of him?'

The girl smiled impersonally: 'Oh, we know Fara Clark; he's the backbone of the empress in Glay.'

'Yes,' the boy sneered. 'You ought to hear him. He thinks we're living in heaven; and the empress is the divine power. The worst part of it is that there's no chance of his ever getting that stuffy look wiped off his face.'

They walked off; and Fara stood there. The very extent of what had happened had drained anger from him as if it had never been. There was the realization that he had made a mistake so great that —

He couldn't grasp it. For long, long now, since Cayle had refused to work in his shop, he had felt this building up to a climax. Suddenly, his own uncontrollable ferocity stood revealed as a partial product of that – deeper – problem.

Only, now that the smash was here, he didn't want to face it —

All through the day in his shop, he kept pushing it out of his mind, kept thinking:

Would this go on now, as before, Cayle and he living in the same house, not even looking at each other when they

68

met, going to bed at different times, getting up, Fara at 6:30, Cayle at noon? Would *that* go on through all the days and years to come?

When he arrived home, Creel was waiting for him. She said:

'Fara, he wants you to loan him five hundred credits, so that he can go to Imperial City.'

Fara nodded wordlessly. He brought the money back to the house the next morning, and gave it to Creel, who took it into the bedroom.

She came out a minute later. 'He says to tell you good-by.'

When Fara came home that evening, Cayle was gone. He wondered whether he ought to feel relieved or – what?

The days passed. Fara worked. He had nothing else to do, and the gray thought was often in his mind that now he would be doing it till the day he died. Except —

Fool that he was – he told himself a thousand times how big a fool – he kept hoping that Cayle would walk into the shop and say:

'Father, I've learned my lesson. If you can ever forgive me, teach me the business, and then you retire to a well-earned rest.'

It was exactly a month to a day after Cayle's departure that the telestat clicked on just after Fara had finished lunch. 'Money call,' it sighed, 'money call.'

Fara and Creel looked at each other. 'Eh,' said Fara finally, 'money call for us.'

He could see from the gray look in Creel's face the thought that was in her mind. He said under his breath: 'Damn that boy!'

But he felt relieved. Amazingly, relieved! Cayle was beginning to appreciate the value of parents and —

He switched on the viewer. 'Come and collect,' he said.

The face that came on the screen was heavy-jowled, beetle-browed – and strange. The man said:

'This is Clerk Pearton of the Fifth Bank of Ferd. We have received a sight draft on you for ten thousand credits. With carrying charges and government tax, the sum required will be twelve thousand one hundred credits. Will you pay it now or will you come in this afternoon and pay it?'

'B-but . . . b-but – ' said Fara. 'W-who —'

He stopped, conscious of the stupidity of the question, dimly conscious of the heavy-faced man saying something about the money having been paid out to one Cayle Clark, that morning, in Imperial City. At last, Fara found his voice:

'But the bank had no right,' he expostulated, 'to pay out the money without my authority. I —'

The voice cut him off coldly: 'Are we then to inform our central that the money was obtained under false pretenses? Naturally, an order will be issued immediately for the arrest of your son.'

'Wait . . . wait —' Fara spoke blindly. He was aware of Creel beside him, shaking her head at him. She was as white as a sheet, and her voice was a sick, stricken thing, as she said:

'Fara, let him go. He's through with us. We must be as hard – let him go.'

The words rang senselessly in Fara's ears. They didn't fit into any normal pattern. He was saying:

'I . . . I haven't got — How about my paying . . . installments? I —'

'If you wish a loan,' said Clerk Pearton, 'naturally we will be happy to go into the matter. I might say that when the draft arrived, we checked up on your status, and we are prepared to loan you eleven thousand credits on indefinite call with your shop as security. I have the form here, and if you are agreeable, we will switch this call through the registered circuit, and you can sign at once.'

'Fara, no.'

The clerk went on: 'The other eleven hundred credits will have to be paid in cash. Is that agreeable?'

'Yes, yes, of course, I've got twenty-five hund —' He stopped his chattering tongue with a gulp; then: 'Yes, that's satisfactory.'

The deal completed, Fara whirled on his wife. Out of the depths of his hurt and bewilderment, he raged:

'What do you mean, standing there and talking about not paying it? You said several times that I was responsible for him being what he is. Besides, we don't know why he needed the money. He —'

Creel said in a low, dead tone: 'In one hour, he's stripped us of our life work. He did it deliberately, thinking of us as two old fools, who wouldn't know any better than to pay it.'

Before he could speak, she went on: 'Oh, I know I blamed you, but in the final issue, I knew it was he. He was always cold and calculating, but I was weak, and I was sure that if you handled him in a different . . . and besides I didn't want to see his faults for a long time. He —'

'All I see,' Fara interrupted doggedly, 'is that I have saved our name from disgrace.'

His high sense of duty rightly done lasted until mid-afternoon, when the bailiff from Ferd came to take over the shop.

'But what —' Fara began.

The bailiff said: 'The Automatic Atomic Repair Shops, Limited, took over your loan from the bank, and are fore-closing. Have you anything to say?'

'It's unfair,' said Fara. 'I'll take it to court. I'll —'

He was thinking dazedly: 'If the empress ever learned of this, she'd . . . she'd —'

The courthouse was a big, gray building; and Fara felt emptier and colder every second, as he walked along the gray corridors. In Glay, his decision not to give himself into the hands of a bloodsucker of a lawyer had seemed a wise act. Here, in these enormous halls and palatial rooms, it seemed the sheerest folly.

He managed, nevertheless, to give an articulate account of the criminal act of the bank in first giving Cayle the money, then turning over the note to his chief competitor, apparently within minutes of his signing it. He finished with:

'I'm sure, sir, the empress would not approve of such goings-on against honest citizens. I —'

'How dare you,' said the cold-voiced creature on the bench, 'use the name of her holy majesty in support of your own gross self-interest?'

Fara shivered. The sense of being intimately a member of the empress' great human family yielded to a sudden chill and a vast mind-picture of the ten million icy courts like this, and the myriad malevolent and heartless men – *like this* – who stood between the empress and her loyal subject, Fara.

He thought passionately: If the empress knew what was happening here, how unjustly he was being treated, she would —

Or would she?

He pushed the crowding, terrible doubt out of his mind – came out of his hard reverie with a start, to hear the Cadi saying:

'Plaintiff's appeal dismissed, with costs assessed at seven hundred credits, to be divided between the court and the defense solicitor in the ratio of five to two. See to it that the appellant does not leave till the costs are paid. Next case —'

Fara went alone the next day to see Creel's mother. He called first at 'Farmer's Restaurant' at the outskirts of the village. The place was, he noted with satisfaction in the thought of the steady stream of money flowing in, half full, though it was only midmorning. But madame wasn't there. Try the feed store.

He found her in the back of the feed store, overseeing the weighing out of grain into cloth measures. The hard-faced old woman heard his story without a word. She said finally, curtly:

'Nothing doing, Fara. I'm one who has to make loans often from the bank to swing deals. If I tried to set you up in business, I'd find the Automatic Atomic Repair people getting after me. Besides, I'd be a fool to turn money over to a man who lets a bad son squeeze a fortune out of him. Such a man has no sense about worldly things.

'And I won't give you a job because I don't hire relatives in my business.' She finished: 'Tell Creel to come and live at my house. I won't support a man, though. That's all.'

He watched her disconsolately for a while, as she went on calmly superintending the clerks who were manipulating the old, no longer accurate measuring machines. Twice her voice echoed through the dust-filled interior, each time with a sharp: 'That's overweight, a gram at least. Watch your machine.'

Though her back was turned, Fara knew by her posture that she was still aware of his presence. She turned at last with an abrupt movement, and said:

'Why don't you go to the weapon shop? You haven't anything to lose, and you can't go on like this.'

Fara went out, then, a little blindly. At first the suggestion that he buy a gun and commit suicide had no real personal application. But he felt immeasurably hurt that his mother-in-law should have made it.

Kill himself? Why, it was ridiculous. He was still only a young man, going on fifty. Given the proper chance, with his skilled hands, he could wrest a good living even in a world where automatic machines were encroaching everywhere. There was always room for a man who did a good job. His whole life had been based on that credo.

Kill himself —

He went home to find Creel packing. 'It's the common-sense thing to do,' she said. 'We'll rent the house and move into rooms.'

He told her about her mother's offer to take her in, watching her face as he spoke. Creel shrugged.

'I told her "No" yesterday,' she said thoughtfully. 'I wonder why she mentioned it to you.'

Fara walked swiftly over to the great front window overlooking the garden, with its flowers, its pool, its rockery. He tried to think of Creel away from this garden of hers, this home of two thirds a lifetime, Creel living in rooms – and knew what her mother had meant. There was one more hope –

He waited till Creel went upstairs, then called Mel Dale on the telestat. The mayor's plump face took on an uneasy expression as he saw who it was.

But he listened pontifically, said finally: 'Sorry, the council does not loan money; and I might as well tell you, Fara – I have nothing to do with this, mind you – but you can't get a license for a shop any more.'

'W-what?'

'I'm sorry!' The mayor lowered his voice. 'Listen, Fara, take my advice and go to the weapon shop. These places have their uses.'

There was a click, and Fara sat staring at the blank face of the viewing screen.

So it was to be – death!

He waited until the street was empty of human beings, then slipped across the boulevard, past a design of flower gardens, and so to the door of the shop. The brief fear came that the door wouldn't open, but it did, effortlessly.

As he emerged from the dimness of the alcove into the shop proper, he saw the silver-haired old man sitting in a corner chair, reading under a softly bright light. The old man looked up, put aside his book, then rose to his feet.

'It's Mr Clark,' he said quietly. 'What can we do for you?'

A faint flush crept into Fara's cheeks. In a dim fashion, he had hoped that he would not suffer the humiliation of

74

being recognized; but now that his fear was realized, he stood his ground stubbornly. The important thing about killing himself was that there be no body for Creel to bury at great expense. Neither knife nor poison would satisfy that basic requirement.

'I want a gun,' said Fara, 'that can be adjusted to disintegrate a body six feet in diameter in a single shot. Have you that kind?'

Without a word, the old man turned to a showcase, and brought forth a sturdy gem of a revolver that glinted with all the soft colors of the inimitable Ordine plastic. The man said in a precise voice:

'Notice the flanges on this barrel are little more than bulges. This makes the model ideal for carrying in a shoulder holster under the coat; it can be drawn very swiftly because, when properly attuned, it will leap toward the reaching hand of its owner. At the moment it is attuned to me. Watch while I replace it in its holster and —'

The speed of the draw was absolutely amazing. The old man's fingers moved; and the gun, four feet away, was in them. There was no blur of movement. It was like the door the night that it had slipped from Fara's grasp, and slammed noiselessly in Constable Jor's face. *Instantaneous!*

Fara, who had parted his lips as the old man was explaining, to protest the utter needlessness of illustrating any quality of the weapon except what he had asked for, closed them again. He stared in a brief, dazed fascination; and something of the wonder that was here held his mind and his body.

He had seen and handled the guns of soldiers, and they were simply ordinary metal or plastic things that one used clumsily like any other material substance, not like this at all, not possessed of a dazzling life of their own, leaping with an intimate eagerness to assist with all their superb power the will of their master. They —

With a start, Fara remembered his purpose. He smiled wryly, and said:

'All this is very interesting. But what about the beam that can fan out?'

The old man said calmly: 'At pencil thickness, this beam will pierce any body except certain alloys of lead up to four hundred yards. With proper adjustment of the firing nozzle, you can disintegrate a six-foot object at fifty yards or less. This screw is the adjustor.'

He indicated a tiny device in the muzzle itself. 'Turn it to the left to spread the beam, to the right to close it.'

Fara said. 'I'll take the gun. How much is it?'

He saw that the old man was looking at him thoughtfully; the oldster said finally, slowly: 'I have previously explained our regulations to you, Mr Clark. You recall them, of course?'

'Eh!' said Fara, and stopped, wide-eyed. It wasn't that he didn't remember them. It was simply —

'You mean,' he gasped, 'those things actually apply. They're not —'

With a terrible effort, he caught his spinning brain and blurring voice. Tense and cold, he said:

'All I want is a gun that will shoot in self-defense, but which I can turn on myself if I have to or – want to.'

'Oh, suicide!' said the old man. He looked as if a great understanding had suddenly dawned on him. 'My dear sir, we have no objection to you killing yourself at any time. That is your personal privilege in a world where privileges grow scanter every year. As for the price of this revolver, it's four credits.'

'Four cre . . . only four credits!' said Fara.

He stood, absolutely astounded, his whole mind snatched from its dark purpose. Why, the plastic alone was – and the whole gun with its fine, intricate workmanship – twenty-five credits would have been dirt cheap.

He felt a brief thrall of utter interest; the mystery of the weapon shops suddenly loomed as vast and important as his own black destiny. But the old man was speaking again:

'And now, if you will remove your coat, we can put on the holster —'

Quite automatically, Fara complied. It was vaguely startling to realize that, in a few seconds, he would be walking out of here, equipped for self-murder, and that there was now not a single obstacle to his death.

Curiously, he was disappointed. He couldn't explain it, but somehow there had been in the back of his mind a hope that these shops might, just might – what?

What indeed? Fara sighed wearily – and grew aware again of the old man's voice, saying:

'Perhaps you would prefer to step out of our side door. It is less conspicuous than the front.'

There was no resistance in Fara. He was dimly conscious of the man's fingers on his arm, half guiding him; and then the old man pressed one of several buttons on the wall – so that's how it was done – and there was the door.

He could see flowers beyond the opening; without a word he walked toward them. He was outside almost before he realized it.

Fara stood for a moment in the neat little pathway, striving to grasp the finality of his situation. But nothing would come except a curious awareness of many men around him; for a long second, his brain was like a log drifting along a stream at night.

Through that darkness grew a consciousness of something wrong; the wrongness was there in the back of his mind, as he turned leftward to go to the front of the weapon store.

Vagueness transformed to a shocked, startled sound. For – he was not in Glay, and the weapon shop *wasn't* where it had been. In its place —

A dozen men brushed past Fara to join a long line of men farther along. But Fara was immune to their presence, their strangeness. His whole mind, his whole vision, his very being was concentrating on the section of machine that stood where the weapon shop had been.

A machine, oh, a machine —

His brain lifted up, up in his effort to grasp the tremendousness of the dull-metaled immensity of what was spread here under a summer sun beneath a sky as blue as a remote southern sea.

The machine towered into the heavens, five great tiers of metal, each a hundred feet high; and the superbly streamlined five hundred feet ended in a peak of light, a gorgeous spire that tilted straight up a sheer two hundred feet farther, and matched the very sun for brightness.

And it *was* a machine, not a building, because the whole lower tier was alive with shimmering lights, mostly green, but sprinkled colorfully with red and occasionally a blue and yellow. Twice, as Fara watched, green lights directly in front of him flashed unscintillatingly into red.

The second tier was alive with white and red lights, although there were only a fraction as many lights as on the lowest tier. The third section had on its dull-metal surface only blue and yellow lights; they twinkled softly here and there over the vast area.

The fouth tier was a series of signs, that brought the beginning of comprehension. The whole sign was:

WHITE	—	BIRTHS
RED	—	DEATHS
GREEN	—	LIVING
BLUE	—	IMMIGRATION TO EARTH
YELLOW	—	EMIGRATION

The fifth tier was also all sign, finally explaining:

POPULATIONS

SOLAR SYSTEM	19,174,463,747
EARTH	11,193,247,361
MARS	1,097,298,604
VENUS	5,141,053,811
MOONS	1,742,863,971

The numbers changed, even as he looked at them, leaping up and down, shifting below and above what they had first been. People were dying, being born, moving to Mars, to Venus, to the moons of Jupiter, to Earth's moon, and others coming back again, landing minute by minute in the thousands of spaceports. Life went on in its gigantic fashion – and here was the stupendous record. Here was —

'Better get in line,' said a friendly voice beside Fara. 'It takes quite a while to put through an individual case, I understand.'

Fara stared at the man. He had the distinct impression of having had senseless words flung at him. 'In line?' he started – and stopped himself with a jerk that hurt his throat.

He was moving forward, blindly, ahead of the younger man, thinking a curious jumble about that this must have been how Constable Jor was transported to Mars – when another of the man's words penetrated.

'Case?' said Fara violently. 'Individual case!'

The man, a heavy-faced, blue-eyed young chap of around thirty-five, looked at him curiously: 'You must know why you're here,' he said. 'Surely, you wouldn't have been sent through here unless you had a problem of some kind that the weapon shop courts will solve for you; there's no other reason for coming to Information Center.'

Fara walked on because he was in the line now, a fast moving line that curved him inexorably around the machine; and seemed to be heading him toward a door that led into the interior of the great metal structure.

So it was a building as well as a machine.

A problem, he was thinking, why, of course, he had a problem, a hopeless, insoluble, completely tangled problem, so deeply rooted in the basic structure of Imperial civilization that the whole world would have to be overturned to make it right.

With a start, he saw that he was at the entrance. And the

awed thought came: In seconds he would be committed irrevocably to – what?

Inside was a long, shining corridor, with scores of completely transparent hallways leading off the main corridor. Behind Fara, the young man's voice said:

'There's one, practically empty. Let's go.'

Fara walked ahead; and suddenly he was trembling. He had already noticed that at the end of each side hallway were some dozen young women sitting at desks, interviewing men and . . . and, good heavens, was it possible that all this meant —

He grew aware that he had stopped in front of one of the girls.

She was older than she had looked from a distance, over thirty, but good-looking, alert. She smiled pleasantly, but impersonally, and said:

'Your name, please?'

He gave it before he thought and added a mumble about being from the village of Glay. The woman said:

'Thank you. It will take a few minutes to get your file. Won't you sit down?'

He hadn't noticed the chair. He sank into it; and his heart was beating so wildly that he felt choked. The strange thing was that there was scarcely a thought in his head, nor a real hope; only an intense, almost mind-wrecking excitement.

With a jerk, he realized that the girl was speaking again, but only snatches of her voice came through that screen of tension in his mind:

' – Information Center is . . . in effect . . . a bureau of statistics. Every person born . . . registered here . . . their education, change of address . . . occupation . . . and the highlights of their life. The whole is maintained by . . . combination of . . . Imperial Chamber of Statistics and . . . through medium of agents . . . in every community —'

It seemed to Fara that he was missing vital information, and that if he could only force his attention and hear more —

80

He strained, but it was no use; his nerves were jumping madly and —

Before he could speak, there was a click, and a thin, dark plate slid onto the woman's desk. She took it up, and examined it. After a moment, she said something into a mouthpiece, and in a short time two more plates precipitated out of the empty air onto her desk. She studied them impassively, looked up finally.

'You will be interested to know,' she said, 'that your son, Cayle, bribed himself into a commission in the Imperial army with five thousand credits.'

'Eh?' said Fara. He half rose from his chair, but before he could say anything, the young woman was speaking again, firmly:

'I must inform you that the weapon shops take no action against individuals. Your son can have his job, the money he stole; we are not concerned with moral correction. That must come naturally from the individual, and from the people as a whole – and now if you will give me a brief account of your problem for the record and the court.'

Sweating, Fara sank back into his seat; his mind was heaving; most desperately, he wanted more information about Cayle. He began:

'But . . . but what . . . how —' He caught himself; and in a low voice described what had happened. When he finished, the girl said:

'You will proceed now to the Name Room; watch for your name, and when it appears go straight to Room 474. Remember, 474 – and now, the line is waiting, if you please —'

She smiled politely, and Fara was moving off almost before he realized it. He half turned to ask another question, but an old man was sinking into his chair. Fara hurried on, along a great corridor, conscious of curious blasts of sound coming from ahead.

Eagerly, he opened the door; and the sound crashed at

81

him with all the impact of a sledge-hammer blow.

It was such a colossal, incredible sound that he stopped short, just inside the door, shrinking back. He stood then trying to blink sense into a visual confusion that rivaled in magnitude that incredible tornado of noise.

Men, men, men everywhere; men by the thousands in a long, broad auditorium, packed into rows of seats, pacing with an abandon of restlessness up and down aisles, and all of them staring with a frantic interest at a long board marked off into squares, each square lettered from the alphabet, from A, B, C and so on to Z. The tremendous board with its lists of names ran the full length of the immense room.

The Name Room, Fara was thinking shakily, as he sank into a seat – and his name would come up in the C's, and then —

It was like sitting in at a no-limit poker game, watching the jewel-precious cards turn up. It was like playing the exchange with all the world at stake during a stock crash. It was nerve-racking, dazzling, exhausting, fascinating, terrible, mind-destroying, stupendous. It was —

It was like nothing else on the face of the earth.

New names kept flashing on to the twenty-six squares; and men would shout like insane beings and some fainted, and the uproar was absolutely shattering; the pandemonium raged on, one continuous, unbelievable sound.

And every few minutes a great sign would flash along the board, telling everyone:

'WATCH YOUR OWN INITIALS.'

Fara watched, trembling in every limb. Each second it seemed to him that he couldn't stand it an instant longer. He wanted to scream at the room to be silent; he wanted to jump up to pace the floor, but others who did that were yelled at hysterically, threatened wildly, hated with a mad, murderous ferocity.

Abruptly, the blind savagery of it scared Fara. He thought

82

unsteadily: 'I'm not going to make a fool of myself. I —'

'Clark, Fara — ' winked the board. 'Clark, Fara —'

With a shout that nearly tore off the top of his head, Fara leaped to his feet. 'That's me!' he shrieked. 'Me!'

No one turned; no one paid the slightest attention. Shamed, he slunk across the room where an endless line of men kept crowding into a corridor beyond.

The silence in the long corridor was almost as shattering as the mind-destroying noise it replaced. It was hard to concentrate on the idea of a number – 474.

It was completely impossible to imagine what could lie beyond – 474.

The room was small. It was furnished with a small, business-type table and two chairs. On the table were seven neat piles of folders, each pile a different color. The piles were arranged in a row in front of a large, milky-white globe, that began to glow with a soft light. Out of its depths, a man's baritone voice said:

'Fara Clark?'

'Yes,' said Fara.

'Before the verdict is rendered in your case,' the voice went on quietly, 'I want you to take a folder from the blue pile. The list will show the Fifth Interplanetary Bank in its proper relation to yourself and the world, and it will be explained to you in due course.'

The list, Fara saw, was simply that, a list of the names of companies. The names ran from A to Z, and there were about five hundred of them. The folder carried no explanation; and Fara slipped it automatically into his side pocket, as the voice came again from the shining globe:

'It has been established,' the words came precisely, 'that the Fifth Interplanetary Bank perpetrated upon you a gross swindle, and that it is further guilty of practicing scavengery, deception, blackmail and was accessory in a criminal conspiracy.

'The bank made contact with your son, Cayle, through

what is quite properly known as a scavenger, that is an employee who exists by finding young men and women who are morally capable of drawing drafts on their parents or other victims. The scavenger obtains for this service a commission of eight percent, which is always paid by the person making the loan, in this case your son.

'The bank practiced deception in that its authorized agents deceived you in the most culpable fashion by pretending that it had already paid out the ten thousand credits to your son, whereas the money was not paid over until your signature had been obtained.

'The blackmail guilt arises out of the threat to have your son arrested for falsely obtaining a loan, a threat made at a time when no money had exchanged hands. The conspiracy consists of the action whereby your note was promptly turned over to your competitor.

'The bank is accordingly triple-fined, thirty-six thousand three hundred credits. It is not in our interest, Fara Clark, for you to know how this money is obtained. Suffice to know that the bank pays it, and that of the fine the weapon shops allocate to their own treasury a total of one half. The other half —'

There was a *plop*; a neatly packaged pile of bills fell onto the table. 'For you,' said the voice; and Fara, with trembling fingers, slipped the package into his coat pocket. It required the purest mental and physical effort for him to concentrate on the next words that came:

'You must not assume that your troubles are over. The re-establishment of your motor repair shop in Glay will require force and courage. Be discreet, brave and determined, and you cannot fail. Do not hesitate to use the gun you have purchased in defense of your rights. The plan will be explained to you. And now, proceed through the door facing you —'

Fara braced himself with an effort, opened the door and walked through.

It was a dim, familiar room that he stepped into, and there was a silver-haired, fine-faced man who rose from a reading chair, and came forward in the dimness, smiling gravely.

The stupendous, fantastic, exhilarating adventure was over; and he was back in the weapon shop of Glay.

He couldn't get over the wonder of it – this great and fascinating organization established here in the very heart of a ruthless civilization, a civilization that had in a few brief weeks stripped him of everything he possessed.

With a deliberate will, he stopped that glowing flow of thought. A dark frown wrinkled his solidly built face; he said:

'The . . . judge —' Fara hesitated over the name, frowned again, annoyed at himself, then went on: 'The judge said that, to re-establish myself I would have to —'

'Before we go into that,' said the old man quietly, 'I want you to examine the blue folder you brought with you.'

'Folder?' Fara echoed blankly. It took a long moment to remember that he had picked up a folder from the table in Room 474.

He studied the list of company names with a gathering puzzlement, noting that the name Automatic Atomic Motor Repair Shops was well down among the A's, and the Fifth Interplanetary Bank only one of several great banks included. Fara looked up finally:

'I don't understand,' he said; 'are these the companies you have had to act against?'

The silver-haired man smiled grimly, shook his head. 'That is not what I mean. These firms constitute only a fraction of the eight hundred thousand companies that are constantly in our books.'

He smiled again, humorlessly: 'These companies all know that, because of us, their profits on paper bear no relation to their assets. What they don't know is how great the difference really is; and, as we want a general improvement in business morals, not merely more skillful scheming to outwit us, we prefer them to remain in ignorance.'

He paused, and this time he gave Fara a searching glance, said at last: 'The unique feature of the companies on this particular list is that they are every one wholly owned by Empress Isher.'

He finished swiftly: 'In view of your past opinions on that subject, I do not expect you to believe me.'

Fara stood as still as death, for – he did believe with unquestioning conviction, completely, finally. The amazing, the unforgivable thing was that all his life he had watched the march of ruined men into the oblivion of poverty and disgrace – and blamed *them*.

Fara groaned. 'I've been like a madman,' he said. 'Everything the empress and her officials did was right. No friendship, no personal relationship could survive with me that did not include belief in things as they were. I suppose if I started to talk against the empress I would receive equally short shrift.'

'Under no circumstances,' said the old man grimly, 'must you say anything against her majesty. The weapon shops will not countenance any such words, and will give no further aid to anyone who is so indiscreet. The reason is that, for the moment, we have reached an uneasy state of peace with the Imperial government. We wish to keep it that way; beyond that I will not enlarge on our policy.

'I am permitted to say that the last great attempt to destroy the weapon shops was made seven years ago, when the glorious Innelda Isher was twenty-five years old. That was a secret attempt, based on a new invention; and failed by purest accident because of our sacrifice of a man from seven thousand years in the past. That may sound mysterious to you, but I will not explain.

'The worst period was reached some forty years ago when every person who was discovered receiving aid from us was murdered in some fashion. You may be surprised to know that your father-in-law was among those assassinated at that time.'

'Creel's father!' Fara gasped. 'But —'

He stopped. His brain was reeling; there was such a rush of blood to his head that for an instant he could hardly see.

'But,' he managed at last, 'it was reported that he ran away with another woman.'

'They always spread a vicious story of some kind,' the old man said; and Fara was silent, stunned.

The other went on: 'We finally put a stop to their murders by killing the three men from the top down, *excluding* the royal family, who gave the order for the particular execution involved. But we do not again want that kind of bloody murder.

'Nor are we interested in any criticism of our toleration of so much that is evil. It is important to understand that *we do not interfere in the main stream of human existence*. We right wrongs; we act as a barrier between the people and their more ruthless exploiters. Generally speaking, we help only honest men; that is not to say that we do not give assistance to the less scrupulous, but only to the extent of selling them guns – which is a very great aid indeed, and which is one of the reasons why the government is relying almost exclusively for its power on an economic chicanery.

'In the four thousand years since the brilliant genius, Walter S. DeLany invented the vibration process that made the weapon shops possible, and laid down the first principles of weapon shop political philosophy, we have watched the tide of government swing backward and forward between democracy under a limited monarchy to complete tyranny. And we have discovered one thing:

'*People always have the kind of government they want.* When they want change, they must change it. As always we shall remain an incorruptible core – and I mean that literally; we have a psychological machine that never lies about a man's character – I repeat, an incorruptible core of human idealism, devoted to relieving the ills that arise inevitably under any form of government.

'But now – your problem. It is very simple, really. You must fight, as all men have fought since the beginning of time for what they valued, for their just rights. As you know the Automatic Repair people removed all your machinery and tools within an hour of foreclosing on your shop. This material was taken to Ferd, and then shipped to a great warehouse on the coast.

'We recovered it, and with our special means of transportation have now replaced the machines in your shop. You will accordingly go there and —'

Fara listened with a gathering grimness to the instructions, nodded finally, his jaw clamped tight.

'You can count on me,' he said curtly. 'I've been a stubborn man in my time; and though I've changed sides, I haven't changed *that*.'

Going outside was like returning from life to – death; from hope to – reality.

Fara walked along the quiet streets of Glay at darkest night. For the first time it struck him that the weapon shop Information Center must be halfway around the world, for it had been day, brilliant day.

The picture vanished as if it had never existed, and he grew aware again, preternaturally aware of the village of Glay asleep all around him. Silent, peaceful – yet ugly, he thought, ugly with the ugliness of evil enthroned.

He thought: The right to buy weapons – and his heart swelled into his throat; the tears came to his eyes.

He wiped his vision clear with the back of his hand, thought of Creel's long dead father, and strode on, without shame. Tears were good for an angry man.

The shop was the same, but the hard, metal padlock yielded before the tiny, blazing, supernal power of the revolver. One flick of fire; the metal dissolved – and he was inside.

It was dark, too dark to see, but Fara did not turn on the lights immediately. He fumbled across to the window control, turned the windows to darkness vibration, and then clicked on the lights.

He gulped with awful relief. For the machines, his precious tools that he had seen carted away within hours after the bailiff's arrival, were here again, ready for use.

Shaky from the pressure of his emotion, Fara called Creel on the telestat. It took a little while for her to appear; and she was in her dressing robe. When she saw who it was she turned a dead white.

'Fara, oh, Fara, I thought —'

He cut her off grimly: 'Creel, I've been to the weapon shop. I want you to do this: go straight to your mother. I'm here at my shop. I'm going to stay here day and night until it's settled that I *stay* . . . . I shall go home later for some food and clothing, but I want you to be gone by then. Is that clear?'

Color was coming back into her lean, handsome face. She said: 'Don't you bother coming home, Fara. I'll do everything necessary. I'll pack all that's needed into the carplane including a folding bed. We'll sleep in the back room at the shop.'

Morning came palely, but it was ten o'clock before a shadow darkened the open door; and Constable Jor came in. He looked shamefaced.

'I've got an order here for your arrest,' he said.

'Tell those who sent you,' Fara replied deliberately, 'that I resisted arrest – with a gun.'

The deed followed the words with such rapidity that Jor blinked. He stood like that for a moment, a big, sleepy-looking man, staring at that gleaming, magical revolver; then:

'I have a summons here ordering you to appear at the great court of Ferd this afternoon. Will you accept it?'

'Certainly.'

'Then you will be there?'

'I'll send my lawyer,' said Fara. 'Just drop the summons on the floor there. Tell them I took it.'

The weapon shop man had said: 'Do not ridicule by word any legal measure of the Imperial authorities. Simply disobey them.'

Jor went out, and seemed relieved. It took an hour before Mayor Mel Dale came pompously through the door.

'See here, Fara Clark,' he bellowed from the doorway. 'You can't get away with this. This is defiance of the law.'

Fara was silent as his honor waddled farther into the building. It was puzzling, almost amazing, that Mayor Dale would risk his plump, treasured body. Puzzlement ended as the mayor said in a low voice:

'Good work, Fara; I knew you had it in you. There's dozens of us in Glay behind you, so stick it out. I had to yell at you just now, because there's a crowd outside. Yell back at me, will you? Let's have a real name calling. But, first, a word of warning: the manager of the Automatic Repair shop is on his way here with his bodyguards, two of them —'

Shakily, Fara watched the mayor go out. The crisis was at hand. He braced himself, thought: 'Let them come, let them —'

It was easier than he had thought – for the men who entered the shop turned pale when they saw the holstered revolver. There was a violence of blustering, nevertheless, that narrowed finally down to:

'Look here,' the man said, 'we've got your note for twelve thousand one hundred credits. You're not going to deny you owe that money.'

'I'll buy it back,' said Fara in a stony voice, 'for exactly half, not a cent more.

The strong-jawed young man looked at him for a long time. 'We'll take it,' he said finally, curtly.

Fara said: 'I've got the agreement here —'

His first customer was old man Miser Lan Harris. Fara stared at the long-faced oldster with a vast surmise, and his first, amazed comprehension came of how the weapon shop must have settled on Harris' lot – by arrangement.

It was an hour after Harris had gone that Creel's mother stamped into the shop. She closed the door.

'Well,' she said, 'you did it, eh? Good work. I'm sorry if I seemed rough with you when you came to my place, but we weapon-shop supporters can't afford to take risks for those who are not on our side.

'But never mind that. I've come to take Creel home. The important thing is to return everything to normal as quickly as possible.'

It was over; incredibly it was over. Twice, as he walked home that night, Fara stopped in midstride, and wondered if it had not all been a dream. The air was like wine. The little world of Glay spread before him, green and gracious, a peaceful paradise where time had stood still.

THE STORM

OVER the miles and the years, the gases drifted. Waste matter from ten thousand suns, a diffuse miasm of spent explosions, of dead hell fires and the furies of a hundred million raging sunspots – formless, purposeless.

But it was the beginning.

Into the great dark the gases crept. Calcium was in them, and sodium, and hydrogen; and the speed of the drift varied up to twenty miles a second.

There was a timeless period while gravitation performed its function. The inchoate mass became masses. Great blobs of gas took a semblance of shape in widely separate areas, and moved on and on and on.

They came finally to where a thousand flaring seetee suns had long before doggedly 'crossed the street' of the main stream of terrene suns. Had crossed, and left *their* excrement of gases.

The first clash quickened the vast worlds of gas. The electron haze of terrene plunged like spurred hordes and sped danger into the equally violently reacting positron haze of contraterrene. Instantly, the lighter orbital positrons and electrons went up in a blaze of hard radiation.

The storm was on.

The stripped seetee nuclei carried now terrific and unbalanced negative charges and repelled electrons, but tended to attract terrene atom nuclei. In their turn the stripped terrene nuclei attracted contraterrene.

Violent beyond all conception were the resulting cancellations of charges.

The two opposing masses heaved and spun in a cataclysm of partial adjustment. They had been heading in different directions. More and more they became one tangled, seething whirlpool.

The new course, uncertain at first, steadied and became a line drive through the midnight heavens. On a front of nine light years, at a solid fraction of the velocity of light, the storm roared toward its destiny.

Suns were engulfed for half a hundred years – and left behind with only a hammering of cosmic rays to show that they had been the centers of otherwise invisible, impalpable atomic devastation.

In its four hundred and ninetieth Sidereal year, the storm intersected the orbit of a Nova at the flash moment.

It began to move!

On the three-dimensional map at weather headquarters on the planet Kaider III, the storm was colored orange. Which meant it was the biggest of the four hundred odd storms raging in the Fifty Suns region of the Lesser Magellanic Cloud.

It showed as an uneven splotch fronting at Latitude 473, Longitude 228, Center 190 parsecs, but that was a special Fifty. Suns degree system which had no relation to the magnetic center of the Magellanic Cloud as a whole.

The report about the Nova had not yet been registered on the map. When that happened the storm color would be changed to an angry red.

They had stopped looking at the map. Maltby stood with the councilors at the great window staring up at the Earth ship.

The machine was scarcely more than a dark sliver in the distant sky. But the sight of it seemed to hold a deadly fascination for the older men.

Maltby felt cool, determined, but also sardonic. It was sardonic. It was funny, these – these people of the Fifty Suns in this hour of their danger calling upon *him*.

He unfocused his eyes from the ship, fixed his steely,

laconic gaze on the plump, perspiring chairman of the Kaider III government – and, tensing his mind, forced the man to look at him. The councilor, unaware of the compulsion, conscious only that he had turned, said:

'You understand your instructions, Captain Maltby?'

Maltby nodded. 'I do.'

The curt words must have evoked a vivid picture. The fat face rippled like palsied jelly and broke out in a new trickle of sweat.

'The worst part of it all,' the man groaned, 'is that the people of the ship found us by the wildest accident. They had run into one of our meteorite stations and captured its attendant. The attendant sent a general warning and then forced them to kill him before they could discover which of the fifty million suns of the Lesser Magellanic Cloud was us.

'Unfortunately, they did discover that he and the rest of us were all descendants of the robots who had escaped the massacre of the robots in the main galaxy fifteen thousand years ago.

'But they were baffled, and without a clue. They started home, stopping off at planets on the way on a chance basis. The seventh stop was us. Captain Maltby —'

The man looked almost beside himself. He shook. His face was as colorless as a white shroud. He went on hoarsely:

'Captain Maltby, you must not fail. They have asked for a meteorologist to guide them to Cassidor VII, where the central government is located. They mustn't reach there. You must drive them into the great storm at 473.

'We have commissioned you to do this for us because you have the two minds of the Mixed Men. We regret that we have not always fully appreciated your services in the past. But you must admit that, after the wars of the Mixed Men, it was natural that we should be careful about —'

Maltby cut off the lame apology. 'Forget it,' he said. 'The Mixed Men are robots, too, and therefore as deeply involved, as I see it, as the Dellians and non-Dellians. Just what the Hidden Ones of my kind think, I don't know, nor do I care. I assure you I shall do my best to destroy this ship.'

'Be careful!' the chairman urged anxiously. 'This ship could destroy us, our planet, our sun in a single minute. We never dreamed that Earth could have gotten so far ahead of us and produced such a devastatingly powerful machine. After all, the non-Dellian robots and, of course, the Mixed Men among us are capable of research work; the former have been laboring feverishly for thousands of years.

'But, finally, remember that you are not being asked to commit suicide. The battleship is absolutely invincible. Just how it will survive a real storm we were not told when we were shown around. But it will. What happens, however, is that everyone aboard becomes unconscious.

'As a Mixed Man you will be the first to revive. Our combined fleets will be waiting to board the ship the moment you open the doors. Is that clear?'

It had been clear the first time it was explained, but these non-Dellians had a habit of repeating themselves, as if thoughts kept growing vague in their minds. As Maltby closed the door of the great room behind him, one of the councilors said to his neighbor:

'Has he been told that the storm has gone Nova?'

The fat man overheard. He shook his head. His eyes gleamed as he said quietly: 'No. After all, he is one of the Mixed Men. We can't trust him too far no matter what his record.'

All morning the reports had come in. Some showed progress, some didn't. But her basic good humor was untouched by the failures.

The great reality was that her luck had held. She had found a planet of the robots. Only one planet so far, but —

Grand Captain Laurr smiled grimly. It wouldn't be long

now. Being a supreme commander was a terrible business. But she had not shrunk from making the deadly threat: provide all required information, or the entire planet of Kaider III would be destroyed.

The information was coming in: Population of Kaider III two billion, one hundred million, two-fifths Dellian, three-fifths non-Dellian robots.

Dellians physically and mentally the higher type, but completely lacking in creative ability. Non-Dellians dominated in the research laboratories.

The forty-nine other suns whose planets were inhabited were called, in alphabetical order: Assora, Atmion, Bresp, Buraco, Cassidor, Corrab — They were located at (1) Assora: Latitude 931, Longitude 27, Center 201 parsecs; (2) Atmion —

It went on and on. Just before noon she noted with steely amusement that there was still nothing coming through from the meteorology room, nothing at all about storms.

She made the proper connection and flung her words: 'What's the matter, Lieutenant Cannons? Your assistants have been making prints and duplicates of various Kaider maps. Aren't you getting anything?'

The old meteorologist shook his head. 'You will recall, noble lady, that when we captured that robot in space, he had time to send out a warning. Immediately on every Fifty Suns planet, all maps were despoiled, civilian meteorologists were placed aboard spaceships, that were stripped of receiving radios, with orders to go to a planet on a chance basis, and stay there for ten years.

'To my mind, all this was done before it was clearly grasped that their navy hadn't a chance against us. Now they are going to provide us with a naval meteorologist, but we shall have to depend on our lie detectors as to whether or not he is telling us the truth.'

'I see.' The woman smiled. 'Have no fear. They don't dare oppose us openly. No doubt there is a plan being built up against us, but it cannot prevail now that we can take action to enforce our unalterable will. Whoever they send must tell us the truth. Let me know when he comes.'

Lunch came, but she ate at her desk, watching the flashing pictures on the astro, listening to the murmur of voices, storing the facts, the general picture, into her brain.

'There's no doubt, Captain Turgess,' she commented once, savagely, 'that we're being lied to on a vast scale. But let it be so. We can use psychological tests to verify all the vital details.

'For the time being it is important that you relieve the fears of everyone you find it necessary to question. We must convince these people that Earth will accept them on an equal basis without bias or prejudice of any kind because of their robot orig —'

She bit her lip. 'That's an ugly word, the worst kind of propaganda. We must eliminate it from our thoughts.'

'I'm afraid,' the officer shrugged, 'not from our thoughts.'

She stared at him, narrow-eyed, then cut him off angrily. A moment later she was talking into the general transmitter: 'The word robot must not be used – by any of our personnel – under pain of fine —'

Switching off, she put a busy signal on her spare receiver, and called Psychology House. Lieutenant Neslor's face appeared on the plate.

'I heard your order just now, noble lady,' the woman psychologist said. 'I'm afraid, however, that we're dealing with the deepest instincts of the human animal – hatred or fear of the stranger, the alien.

'Excellency, we come from a long line of ancestors who, in their time, have felt superior to others because of some slight variation in the pigmentation of the skin. It is even recorded that the color of the eyes has influenced the egoistic in historical decisions. We have sailed into very deep waters, and it will be the crowning achievement of our life if we sail out in a satisfactory fashion.'

There was an eager lilt in the psychologist's voice; and the grand captain experienced a responsive thrill of joy. If there was one thing she appreciated, it was the positive outlook, the kind of people who faced all obstacles short of the recognizably impossible with a youthful zest, a will to win. She was still smiling as she broke the connection.

The high thrill sagged. She sat cold with her problem. It was a problem. Hers. All aristocratic officers had *carte blanche* powers, and were expected to solve difficulties involving anything up to whole groups of planetary systems.

After a minute she dialed the meteorology room again.

'Lieutenant Cannons, when the meteorology officer of the Fifty Suns navy arrives, please employ the following tactics —'

Maltby waved dismissal to the driver of his car. The machine pulled away from the curb and Maltby stood frowning at the flaming energy barrier that barred farther progress along the street. Finally, he took another look at the Earth ship.

It was directly above him now that he had come so many miles across the city toward it. It was tremendously high up, a long, black torpedo shape almost lost in the mist of distance.

But high as it was it was still visibly bigger than anything ever seen by the Fifty Suns, an incredible creature of metal from a world so far away that, almost, it had sunk to the status of myth.

Here was the reality. There would be tests, he thought, penetrating tests before they'd accept any orbit he planned. It wasn't that he doubted the ability of his double mind to overcome anything like that, but —

Well to remember that the frightful gap of years which separated the science of Earth from that of the Fifty Suns had already shown unpleasant surprises. Maltby shook himself grimly and gave his full attention to the street ahead.

A fan-shaped pink fire spread skyward from two machines that stood in the center of the street. The flame was a very pale pink and completely transparent. It looked electronic, deadly.

Beyond it were men in glittering uniforms. A steady trickle of them moved in and out of buildings. About three blocks down the avenue a second curtain of pink fire flared up.

There seemed to be no attempt to guard the sides. The men he could see looked at ease, confident. There was murmured conversation, low laughter and – they weren't all men.

As Maltby walked forward, two fine-looking young women in uniform came down the steps of the nearest of the requisitioned buildings. One of the guards of the flame said something to them. There was a twin tinkle of silvery laughter. Still laughing, they strode off down the street.

It was suddenly exciting. There was an air about these people of far places, of tremendous and wonderful lands beyond the farthest horizons of the staid Fifty Suns.

He felt cold, then hot, then he glanced up at the fantastically big ship; and the chill came back. One ship, he thought, but so big, so mighty that thirty billion people didn't dare send their own fleets against it. They —

He grew aware that one of the brilliantly arrayed guards was staring at him. The man spoke into a wrist radio, and after a moment a second man broke off his conversation with a third soldier and came over. He stared through the flame barrier at Maltby.

'Is there anything you desire? Or are you just looking?'

He spoke English, curiously accented – but English! His manner was mild, almost gentle, cultured. The whole effect had a naturalness, an unalienness that was pleasing. After all, Maltby thought, he had never had the fear of these people that the others had. His very plan to defeat the ship was based upon his own fundamental belief that the robots

99

were indestructible in the sense that no one could ever wipe them out completely.

Quietly, Maltby explained his presence.

'Oh, yes,' the man nodded, 'we've been expecting you. I'm to take you at once to the meteorological room of the ship. Just a moment —'

The flame barrier went down and Maltby was led into one of the buildings. There was a long corridor, and the transmitter that projected him into the ship must have been focused somewhere along it.

Because abruptly he was in a very large room. Maps floated in half a dozen antigravity pits. The walls shed light from millions of tiny point sources. And everywhere were tables with curved lines of very dim but sharply etched light on their surfaces.

Maltby's guide was nowhere to be seen. Coming toward him, however, was a tall, fine-looking old man. The oldster offered his hand.

'My name is Lieutenant Cannons, senior ship meteorologist. If you will sit down here we can plan an orbit and the ship can start moving within the hour. The grand captain is very anxious that we get started.'

Maltby nodded casually. But he was stiff, alert. He stood quite still, feeling around with that acute second mind of his, his Dellian mind, for energy pressures that would show secret attempts to watch or control his mind.

But there was nothing like that.

He smiled finally, grimly. It was going to be as simple as this, was it? Like hell it was.

As he sat down, Maltby felt suddenly cozy and alive. The pure exhilaration of existence burned through him like a flame. He recognized the singing excitement for the battle thrill it was and felt a grim joy that for the first time in fifteen years he could do something about it.

During his long service in the Fifty Suns navy, he had

faced hostility and suspicion because he was a Mixed Man. And always he had felt helpless, unable to do anything about it. Now, here was a far more basic hostility, however veiled, and a suspicion that must be like a burning fire.

And this time he could fight. He could look this skillfully voluble, friendly old man squarely in the eye and —

Friendly?

'It makes me smile sometimes,' the old man was saying, 'when I think of the unscientific aspects of the orbit we have to plan now. For instance, what is the time lag on storm reports out here?'

Maltby could not suppress a smile. So Lieutenant Cannons wanted to know things, did he? To give the man credit, it wasn't really a lame opening. The truth was, the only way to ask a question was – well – to ask it. Maltby said:

'Oh, three, four months. Nothing unusual. Each space meteorologist takes about that length of time to check the bounds of the particular storm in his area, and then he reports, and we adjust our maps.

'Fortunately' – he pushed his second mind to the fore as he coolly spoke the great basic lie – 'there are no major storms between the Kaidor and Cassidor suns.'

He went on, sliding over the untruth like an eel breasting wet rock:

'However, several suns prevent a straight line movement. So if you would show me some of your orbits for twenty-five hundred light years, I'll make a selection of the best ones.'

He wasn't, he realized instantly, going to slip over his main point as easily as that.

'No intervening storms?' the old man said. He pursed his lips. The fine lines in his long face seemed to deepen. He looked genuinely nonplused; and there was no doubt at all that he hadn't expected such a straightforward statement. 'Hm-m-m, no storms. That does make it simple, doesn't it?'

101

He broke off. 'You know, the important thing about two' – he hesitated over the word, then went on – 'two people, who have been brought up in different cultures, under different scientific standards, is that they make sure they are discussing a subject from a common viewpoint.

'Space is so big. Even this comparatively small system of stars, the Lesser Magellanic Cloud, is so vast that it defies our reason. We on the battleship *Star Cluster* have spent ten years surveying it, and now we are able to say glibly that it comprises two hundred sixty billion cubic light years, and contains fifty millions of suns.

'We located the magnetic center of the Cloud, fixed our zero line from center to the great brightest star, S—Doradus; and now, I suppose, there are people who would be fools enough to think we've got the system stowed away in our brainpans.'

Maltby was silent because he himself was just such a fool. This was warning. He was being told in no uncertain terms that they were in a position to check any orbit he gave them with respect to all intervening suns.

It meant much more. It showed that Earth was on the verge of extending her tremendous sway to the Lesser Magellanic Cloud. Destroying this ship now would provide the Fifty Suns with precious years during which they would have to decide what they intended to do.

But that would be all. Other ships would come; the inexorable pressure of the stupendous populations of the main galaxy would burst out even farther into space. Always under careful control, shepherded by mighty hosts of invincible battleships, the great transports would sweep into the Cloud, and every planet everywhere, robot or non-robot, would acknowledge Earth suzerainty.

Imperial Earth recognized no separate nations of any description anywhere. The robots, Dellian, non-Dellian and Mixed, would need every extra day, every hour; and it was lucky for them all that he was not basing his hope of destroying this ship on an orbit that would end inside a sun.

Their survey had magnetically placed all the suns for them. But they couldn't know about the storms. Not in ten years or in a hundred was it possible for one ship to locate possible storms in an area that involved twenty-five hundred light years of length.

Unless their psychologists could uncover the special qualities of his double brain, he had them. He grew aware that Lieutenant Cannons was manipulating the controls of the orbit table.

The lines of light on the surface flickered and shifted. Then settled like the balls in a game of chance. Maltby selected six that ran deep into the great storm. Ten minutes after that he felt the faint jar as the ship began to move. He stood up, frowning. Odd that they should act without *some* verification of his —

'This way,' said the old man.

Maltby thought sharply: This couldn't be all. Any minute now they'd start on him and —

His thought ended.

He was in space. Far, far below was the receding planet of Kaider III. To one side gleamed the vast dark hull of the battleship; and on every other side, and up, and down, were stars and the distances of dark space.

In spite of all his will, the shock was inexpressibly violent.

His active mind jerked. He staggered physically; and he would have fallen like a blindfolded creature except that, in the movement of trying to keep on his feet, he recognized that he *was* still on his feet.

His whole being steadied. Instinctively, he – tilted – his second mind awake, and pushed it forward. Put its more mechanical and precise qualities, its Dellian strength, between his other self and whatever the human beings might be doing against him.

Somewhere in the mist of darkness and blazing stars, a woman's clear and resonant voice said:

'Well, Lieutenant Neslor, did the surprise yield any psychological fruits?'

The reply came from a second, an older-sounding woman's voice:

'After three seconds, noble lady, his resistance leaped to I.Q. 900. Which means they've sent us a Dellian. Your excellency, I thought you specifically asked that their representative be not a Dellian.'

Maltby said swiftly into the night around him: 'You're quite mistaken. I am not a Dellian. And I assure you that I will lower my resistance to zero if you desire. I reacted instinctively to surprise, naturally enough.'

There was a click. The illusion of space and stars snapped out of existence. Maltby saw what he had begun to suspect, that he was, had been all the time, in the meteorology room.

Nearby stood the old man, a thin smile on his lined face. On a raised dais, partly hidden behind a long instrument board, sat a handsome young woman. It was the old man who spoke. He said in a stately voice:

'You are in the presence of Grand Captain, the Right Honorable Gloria Cecily, the Lady Laurr of Noble Laurr. Conduct yourself accordingly.'

Maltby bowed but he said nothing. The grand captain frowned at him, impressed by his appearance. Tall magnificent-looking body – strong, supremely intelligent face. In a single flash she noted all the characteristics common to the first-class human being and robot.

These people might be more dangerous than she had thought. She said with unnatural sharpness for her:

'As you know, we have to question you. We would prefer that you do not take offense. You have told us that Cassidor VII, the chief planet of the Fifty Suns, is twenty-five hundred light years from here. Normally, we would spend more than sixty years *feeling* our way across such an immense gap of uncharted, star-filled space. But you have given us a choice of orbits.

'We must make sure those orbits are honest, offered without guile or harmful purpose. To that end we have to ask you to open your mind and answer our questions under the strictest psychological surveillance.'

'I have orders,' said Maltby, 'to cooperate with you in every way.'

He had wondered how he would feel, now that the hour of decision was upon him. But there was nothing unnormal. His body was a little stiffer, but his minds —

He withdrew his *self* into the background and left his Dellian mind to confront all the questions that came. His Dellian mind that he had deliberately kept apart from his thoughts. That curious mind, which had no will of its own, but which, by remote control, reacted with the full power of an I.Q. of 191.

Sometimes, he marveled himself at that second mind of his. It had no creative ability, but its memory was machine-like, and its resistance to outside pressure was, as the woman psychologist had so swiftly analyzed, over nine hundred. To be exact, the equivalent of I.Q. 917.

'What is your name?'

That was the way it began: His name, distinction — He answered everything quietly, positively, without hesitation. When he had finished, when he had sworn to the truth of every word about the storms, there was a long moment of dead silence. And then a middle-aged woman stepped out of the nearby wall.

She came over and motioned him into a chair. When he was seated she tilted his head and began to examine it. She did it gently; her fingers were caressing as a lover's. But when she looked up she said sharply:

'You're not a Dellian or a non-Dellian. And the molecular structure of your brain and body is the most curious I've ever seen. All the molecules are twins. I saw a similar arrangement once in an artificial electronic structure where an attempt was being made to balance an unstable electronic structure. The parallel isn't exact, but – mm-m-m, I must try to remember what the end result was of that experiment.'

She broke off: 'What is your explanation? What are you?'

Maltby sighed. He had determined to tell only the one main lie. Not that it mattered so far as his double brain was concerned. But untruths effected slight variations in blood pressure, created neural spasms and disturbed muscular integration. He couldn't take the risk of even one more than was absolutely necessary.

'I'm a Mixed Man,' he explained. He described briefly how the cross between the Dellian and non-Dellian, so long impossible, had finally been brought about a hundred years before. The use of cold and pressure —

'Just a moment,' said the psychologist.

She disappeared. When she stepped again out of the wall transmitter, she was thoughtful.

'He seems to be telling the truth,' she confessed, almost reluctantly.

'What is this?' snapped the grand captain. 'Ever since we ran into that first citizen of the Fifty Suns, the psychology department has qualified every statement it issues. I thought psychology was the only perfect science. Either he is telling the truth or he isn't.'

The older woman looked unhappy. She stared very hard at Maltby, seemed baffled by his cool gaze, and finally faced her superior, said:

'It's that double molecule structure of his brain. Except for that, I see no reason why you shouldn't order full acceleration.'

The grand captain smiled. 'I shall have Captain Maltby to dinner tonight. I'm sure he will co-operate then with any further studies you may be prepared to make at that time. Meanwhile I think —'

She spoke into a communicator: 'Central engines, step up to half light year a minute on the following orbit —'

Maltby listened, estimating with his Dellian mind. Half a light year a minute; it would take a while to attain that speed, but – in eight hours they'd strike the storm.

In eight hours he'd be having dinner with the grand captain.

Eight hours!

The full flood of a contraterrene Nova impinging upon terrene gases already infuriated by seetee gone insane – that was the new, greater storm.

The exploding, giant sun added weight to the diffuse, maddened thing. And it added something far more deadly.

Speed! From peak to peak of velocity the tumult of ultrafire leaped. The swifter crags of the storm danced and burned with an absolutely hellish fury.

The sequence of action was rapid almost beyond the bearance of matter. First raced the light of the Nova, blazing its warning at more than a hundred and eighty-six thousand miles a second to all who knew that it flashed from the edge of an interstellar storm.

But the advance glare of warning was nullified by the colossal speed of the storm. For weeks and months it drove through the vast night at a velocity that was only a bare measure short of that of light itself.

The dinner dishes had been cleared away. Maltby was thinking: In half an hour – *half an hour!*

He was wondering shakily just what did happen to a battleship suddenly confronted by thousands of gravities of deceleration. Aloud he was saying:

'My day? I spent it in the library. Mainly, I was interested in the recent history of Earth's interstellar colonization. I'm curious as to what is done with groups like the Mixed Men. I mentioned to you that, after the war in which they were defeated largely because there was so few of them, the Mixed Men hid themselves from the Fifty Suns. I was one of the captured children who —'

There was an interruption, a cry from the wall communicator: '*Noble lady, I've solved it!*'

A moment fled before Maltby recognized the strained voice of the woman psychologist. He had almost forgotten that she was supposed to be studying him. Her next words chilled him:

'Two minds! I thought of it a little while ago and rigged up a twin watching device. Ask him, *ask* him the question about the storms. Meanwhile stop the ship. At once!'

Maltby's dark gaze clashed hard with the steely, narrowed eyes of the grand captain. Without hesitation he concentrated his two minds on her, forced her to say:

'Don't be silly, lieutenant. One person can't have two brains. Explain yourself further.'

His hope was delay. They had ten minutes in which they could save themselves. He must waste every second of that time, resist all their efforts, try to control the situation. If only his special three-dimensional hypnotism worked through communicators —

It didn't. Lines of light leaped at him from the wall and crisscrossed his body, held him in his chair like so many unbreakable cables. Even as he was bound hand and foot by palpable energy, a second complex of forces built up before his face, barred his thought pressure from the grand captain, and finally coned over his head like a dunce cap.

He was caught as neatly as if a dozen men had swarmed with their strength and weight over his body. Maltby relaxed and laughed.

'Too late,' he taunted. 'It'll take at least an hour for this ship to reduce to a safe speed; and at this velocity you can't turn aside in time to avoid the greatest storm in this part of the Universe.'

That wasn't strictly true. There was still time and room

108

to sheer off before the advancing storm in any of the fronting directions. The impossibility was to turn toward the storm's tail or its great, bulging sides.

His thought was interrupted by the first cry from the young woman; a piercing cry: 'Central engines! Reduce speed! Emergency!'

There was a jar that shook the walls and a pressure that tore at his muscles. Maltby adjusted and then stared across the table at the grand captain. She was smiling, a frozen mask of a smile; and she said from between clenched teeth:

'Lieutenant Neslor, use any means physical or otherwise, but make him talk. There must be something.'

'His second mind is the key,' the psychologist's voice came. 'It's not Dellian. It has only normal resistance. I shall subject it to the greatest concentration of conditioning ever focused on a human brain, using the two basics: sex and logic. I shall have to use you, noble lady, as the object of his affections.'

'Hurry!' said the young woman. Her voice was like a metal bar.

Maltby sat in a mist, mental and physical. Deep in his mind was awareness that he was an entity, and that irresistible machines were striving to mold his thought.

He resisted. The resistance was as strong as his life, as intense as all the billions and quadrillions of impulses that had shaped his being, could make it.

But the outside thought, the pressure, grew stronger. How silly of him to resist Earth – when this lovely woman of Earth loved him, loved him, loved him. Glorious was that civilization of Earth and the main galaxy. Three hundred million billion people. The very first contact would rejuvenate the Fifty Suns. How lovely she is; I must save her. She means everything to me.

As from a great distance, he began to hear his own voice, explaining what must be done, just how the ship must be turned, in what direction, how much time there was. He tried to stop himself, but inexorably his voice went on, mouthing the words that spelled defeat for the Fifty Suns.

The mist began to fade. The terrible pressure eased from his straining mind. The damning stream of words ceased to pour from his lips. He sat up shakily, conscious that the energy cords and the energy cap had been withdrawn from his body. He heard the grand captain say into a communicator:

'By making a point 0100 turn we shall miss the storm by seven light weeks. I admit it is an appallingly sharp curve, but I feel that we should have at least that much leeway.'

She turned and stared at Maltby: 'Prepare yourself. At half a light year a minute even a hundredth of a degree turn makes some people black out.'

'Not me,' said Maltby, and tensed his Dellian muscles.

She fainted three times during the next four minutes as he sat there watching her. But each time she came to within seconds.

'We human beings,' she said wanly, finally, 'are a poor lot. But at least we know how to endure.'

The terrible minutes dragged. And dragged. Maltby began to feel the strain of that infinitesimal turn. He thought at last: Space! How could these people ever hope to survive a direct hit on a storm?

Abruptly, it was over; a man's voice said quietly: 'We have followed the prescribed course, noble lady, and are now out of dang —'

He broke off with a shout: 'Captain, the light of a Nova sun has just flashed from the direction of the storm. We —'

In those minutes before disaster struck, the battleship *Star Cluster*, glowed like an immense and brilliant jewel. The warning glare from the Nova set off an incredible roar of emergency clamor through all of her hundred and twenty decks.

From end to end her lights flicked on. They burned row by row straight across her four thousand feet of length with the hard tinkle of cut gems. In the reflection of that light, the black mountain that was her hull looked like the fabulous planet of Cassidor, her destination, as seen at night from a far darkness, sown with diamond shining cities.

Silent as a ghost, grand and wonderful beyond all imagination, glorious in her power, the great ship slid through the blackness along the special river of time and space which was her plotted course.

Even as she rode into the storm there was nothing visible. The space ahead looked as clear as any vacuum. So tenuous were the gases that made up the storm that the ship would not even have been aware of them if it had been travelling at atomic speeds.

Violent the disintegration of matter in that storm might be, and the sole source of cosmic rays the hardest energy in the known universe. But the immense, the cataclysmic danger to the *Star Cluster* was a direct result of her own terrible velocity.

If she had had time to slow, the storm would have meant nothing.

Striking that mass of gas at half a light year a minute was like running into an unending solid wall. The great ship shuddered in every plate as the deceleration tore at her gigantic strength.

In seconds she had run the gamut of all the recoil systems her designers had planned for her as a unit.

She began to break up.

And still everything was according to the original purpose of the superb engineering firm that had built her. The limit of unit strain reached, she dissolved into her nine thousand separate sections.

Streamlined needles of metal were those sections, four hundred feet long, forty feet wide; sliverlike shapes that

111

sinuated cunningly through the gases, letting the pressure of them slide off their smooth hides.

But it wasn't enough. Metal groaned from the torture of deceleration. In the deceleration chambers, men and women lay at the bare edge of consciousness, enduring agony that seemed on the verge of being beyond endurance.

Hundreds of the sections careered into each other in spite of automatic screens, and instantaneously fused into white-hot coffins.

And still, in spite of the hideously maintained velocity, that mass of gases was not bridged; light years of thickness had still to be covered.

For those sections that remained, once more all the limits of human strength were reached. The final action was chemical, directly on the human bodies that remained of the original thirty thousand. Those bodies for whose sole benefit all the marvelous safety devices had been conceived and constructed, the poor, fragile, human beings who through all the ages had persisted in dying under normal conditions from a pressure of something less than fifteen gravities.

The prompt reaction of the automatics in rolling back every floor, and plunging every person into the deceleration chambers of each section – that saving reaction was abruptly augmented as the deceleration chamber was flooded by a special type of gas.

Wet was that gas, and clinging. It settled thickly on the clothes of the humans, soaked through to the skin and *through* the skin, into every part of the body.

Sleep came gently, and with it a wonderful relaxation. The blood grew immune to shock; muscles that, in a minute before, had been drawn with anguish – loosened; the brain impregnated with life-giving chemicals that relieved it of all shortages remained untroubled even by dreams.

Everybody grew enormously flexible to gravitation pressures – a hundred – a hundred and fifty gravities of deceleration; and still the life force clung.

112

The great heart of the Universe beat on. The storm roared along its inescapable artery, creating the radiance of life, purging the dark of its poisons – and at last the tiny ships in their separate courses burst its great bounds.

They began to come together, to seek each other, as if among them there was an irresistible passion that demanded intimacy of union.

Automatically, they slid into their old positions; the battleship *Star Cluster* began again to take form – but there were gaps. Segments destroyed, and segments lost.

On the third day Acting Grand Captain Rutgers called the surviving captains to the forward bridge, where he was temporarily making his headquarters. After the conference a communique was issued to the crew:

At 008 hours this morning a message was received from Grand Captain, the Right Honorable Gloria Cecily, the Lady Laurr of Noble Laurr, I.C., C.M., G.K.R. She has been forced down on the planet of a yellow-white sun. Her ship crashed on landing, and is unrepairable. As all communication with her has been by nondirectional sub-space radio, and as it will be utterly impossible to locate such an ordinary type sun among so many millions of other suns, the Captains in Session regret to report that our noble lady's name must now be added to that longest of all lists of naval casualties: the list of those who have been lost forever on active duty.

The admiralty lights will burn blue until further notice.

Her back was to him as he approached. Maltby hesitated, then tensed his mind, and held her there beside the section of ship that had been the main bridge of the *Star Cluster*.

The long metal shape lay half buried in the marshy ground of the great valley, its lower end jutting down into the shimmering deep yellowish black waters of a sluggish river.

Maltby paused a few feet from the tall, slim woman, and,

113

still holding her unaware of him, examined once again the environment that was to be their life.

The fine spray of dark rain that had dogged his exploration walk was retreating over the yellow rim of valley to the 'west'.

As he watched, a small yellow sun burst out from behind a curtain of dark, ocherous clouds and glared at him brilliantly. Below it an expanse of jungle glinted strangely brown and yellow.

Everywhere was that dark-brown and intense, almost liquid yellow.

Maltby sighed – and turned his attention to the woman, willed her not to see him as he walked around in front of her.

He had given a great deal of thought to the Right Honorable Gloria Cecily during his walk. Basically, of course, the problem of a man and a woman who were destined to live the rest of their lives together, alone, on a remote planet, was very simple. Particularly in view of the fact that one of the two had been conditioned to be in love with the other.

Maltby smiled grimly. He could appreciate the artificial origin of that love. But that didn't dispose of the profound fact of it.

The conditioning machine had struck to his very core. Unfortunately, it had not touched her at all; and two days of being alone with her had brought out one reality:

The Lady Laurr of Noble Laurr was not even remotely thinking of yielding herself to the normal requirements of the situation.

It was time that she was made aware, not because an early solution was necessary or even desirable, but because she had to realize that the problem existed.

He stepped forward and took her in his arms.

She was a tall, graceful woman; she fitted into his embrace as if she belonged there; and, because his control of her made her return the kiss, its warmth had an effect beyond his intention.

He had intended to free her mind in the middle of the kiss. He didn't.

When he finally released her, it was only a physical release. Her mind was still completely under his domination.

There was a metal chair that had been set just outside one of the doors. Maltby walked over, sank into it and stared up at the grand captain.

He felt shaken. The flame of desire that had leaped through him was a telling tribute to the conditioning he had undergone. But it was entirely beyond his previous analysis of the intensity of his own feelings.

He had thought he was in full control of himself, and he wasn't. Somehow, the sardonicism, the half detachment, the objectivity, which he had fancied was the keynote of his own reaction to this situation, didn't apply at all.

The conditioning machine had been thorough.

He loved this woman with such a violence that the mere touch of her was enough to disconnect his will from operations immediately following.

His heart grew quieter; he studied her with a semblance of detachment.

She was lovely in a handsome fashion; though almost all robot women of the Dellian race were better-looking. Her lips, while medium full, were somehow a trifle cruel; and there was a quality in her eyes that accentuated that cruelty.

There were built-up emotions in this woman that would not surrender easily to the idea of being marooned for life on an unknown planet.

It was something he would have to think over. Until then —

Maltby sighed. And released her from the three-dimensional hypnotic spell that his two minds had imposed on her.

He had taken the precaution of turning her away from him. He watched her curiously as she stood, back to him, for a

115

moment, very still. Then she walked over to a little knob of trees above the springy, soggy marsh land.

She climbed up it and gazed in the direction from which he had come a few minutes before. Evidently looking for him.

She turned finally, shaded her face against the yellow brightness of the sinking sun, came down from the hillock and saw him.

She stopped; her eyes narrowed. She walked over slowly. She said with an odd edge in her voice:

'You came very quietly. You must have circled and walked in from the west.'

'No,' said Maltby deliberately, 'I stayed in the east.'

She seemed to consider that. She was silent, her lean face creased into a frown. She pressed her lips together, finally; there was a bruise there that must have hurt, for she winced, then she said:

'What did you discover? Did you find any —'

She stopped. Consciousness of the bruise on her lip must have penetrated at that moment. Her hand jerked up, her fingers touched the tender spot. Her eyes came alive with the violence of her comprehension. Before she could speak, Maltby said:

'Yes, you're quite right.'

She stood looking at him. Her stormy gaze quietened. She said finally, in a stony voice:

'If you try that again I shall feel justified in shooting you.'

Maltby shook his head. He said, unsmiling:

'And spend the rest of your life here alone? You'd go mad.'

He saw instantly that her basic anger was too great for that kind of logic. He went on swiftly:

'Besides, you'd have to shoot me in the back. I have no doubt you could do that in the line of duty. But not for personal reasons.'

Her compressed lips – separated. To his amazement

116

there were suddenly tears in her eyes. Anger tears, obviously. But tears!

She stepped forward with a quick movement and slapped his face.

'You robot!' she sobbed.

Maltby stared at her ruefully; then he laughed. Finally he said, a trace of mockery in his tone:

'If I remember rightly, the lady who just spoke is the same one who delivered a ringing radio address to all the planets of the Fifty Suns swearing that in fifteen thousand years Earth people had forgotten all their prejudices against robots.

'Is it possible,' he finished, 'that the problem on *closer* investigation is proving more difficult?'

There was no answer. The Honorable Gloria Cecily brushed past him and disappeared into the interior of the ship.

She came out again a few minutes later.

Her expression was more serene; Maltby noted that she had removed all trace of the tears. She looked at him steadily, said:

'What did you discover when you were out? I've been delaying my call to the ship till you returned.'

Maltby said: 'I thought they asked you to call at 010 hours.'

The woman shrugged; and there was an arrogant note in her voice as she replied:

'They'll take my calls when I make them. Did you find any sign of intelligent life?'

Maltby allowed himself brief pity for a human being who had as many shocks still to absorb as had Grand Captain Laurr.

One of the books he had read while aboard the battleship about colonists of remote planets had dealt very specifically with castaways.

He shook himself and began his description. 'Mostly marsh land in the valley and there's jungle, very old. Even some of the trees are immense, though sections show no growth rings – some interesting beasts and a four-legged, two-armed thing that watched me from a distance. It carried a spear but it was too far away for me to use my hypnotism on it. There must be a village somewhere, perhaps on the valley rim. My idea is that during the next months I'll cut the ship into small sections and transport it to drier ground.

'I would say that we have the following information to offer the ship's scientists: We're on a planet of a G-type sun. The sun must be larger than the average yellow-white type and have a larger surface temperature.

'It must be larger and hotter because, though it's far away, it is hot enough to keep the northern hemisphere of this planet in a semitropical condition.

'The sun was quite a bit north at midday, but now it's swinging back to the south. I'd say offhand the planet must be tilted at about forty degrees, which means there's a cold winter coming up, though that doesn't fit with the age and type of the vegetation.'

The Lady Laurr was frowning. 'It doesn't seem very helpful,' she said. 'But, of course, I'm only an executive.'

'And I'm only a meteorologist.'

'Exactly. Come in. Perhaps my astrophysicist can make something of it.'

'*Your* astrophysicist!' said Maltby. But he didn't say it aloud.

He followed her into the segment of ship and closed the door.

Maltby examined the interior of the main bridge with a wry smile as the young woman seated herself before the astroplate.

The very imposing glitter of the instrument board that occupied one entire wall was ironical now. All the machines it had controlled were far away in space. Once it had dominated the entire Lesser Magellanic Cloud; now his own hand gun was a more potent instrument.

He grew aware that Lady Laurr was looking up at him. 'I don't understand it,' she said. 'They don't answer.'

'Perhaps' – Maltby could not keep the faint sardonicism out of his tone – 'perhaps they may really have had a good reason for wanting you to call at 010 hours.'

The woman made a faint, exasperated movement with her facial muscles but she did not answer. Maltby went on coolly:

'After all, it doesn't matter. They're only going through routine motions, the idea being to leave no loophole of rescue unlooked through. I can't even imagine the kind of miracle it would take for anybody to find us.'

The woman seemed not to have heard. She said, frowning:

'How is it that we've never heard a single Fifty Suns broadcast? I intended to ask about that before. Not once during our ten years in the Lesser Cloud did we catch so much as a whisper of radio energy.'

Maltby shrugged. 'All radios operate on an extremely complicated variable wave length – changes every twentieth of a second. Your instruments would register a tick once every ten minutes, and —'

He was cut off by a voice from the astroplate. A man's face was there – Acting Grand Captain Rutgers.

'Oh, there you are, captain,' the woman said. 'What kept you?'

'We're in the process of landing our forces on Cassidor VII,' was the reply. 'As you know, regulations require that the grand captain —'

'Oh, yes. Are you free now?'

'No. I've taken a moment to see that everything is right with you, and then I'll switch you over to Captain Planston.'

'How is the landing proceeding?'

'Perfectly. We have made contact with the government.

They seem resigned. But now I must leave. Good-by, my lady.'

His face flickered and was gone. The plate went blank. It was about as curt a greeting as anybody had ever received. But Maltby, sunk in his own gloom, scarcely noticed.

So it was all over. The desperate scheming of the Fifty Suns leaders, his own attempt to destroy the great battleship, proved futile against an invincible foe.

For a moment he felt very close to the defeat, with all its implications. Consciousness came finally that the fight no longer mattered in his life. But the knowledge failed to shake his dark mood.

He saw that the Right Honorable Gloria Cecily had an expression of mixed elation and annoyance on her fine strong face; and there was no doubt that she didn't *feel* – disconnected – from the mighty events out there in space. Nor had she missed the implications of the abruptness of the interview.

The astroplate grew bright and a face appeared on it – one that Maltby hadn't seen before. It was of a heavy-jowled, oldish man with a ponderous voice that said:

'Privilege your ladyship – hope we can find something that will enable us to make a rescue. Never give up hope, I say, until the last nail's driven in your coffin.'

He chuckled; and the woman said: 'Captain Maltby will give you all the information he had, then no doubt you can give him some advice, Captain Planston. Neither he nor I, unfortunately, are astrophysicists.'

'Can't be experts on every subject,' Captain Planston puffed. 'Er, Captain Maltby, what do you know?'

Maltby gave his information briefly, then waited while the other gave instructions. There wasn't much:

'Find out length of seasons. Interested in that yellow effect of the sunlight and the deep brown. Take the following photographs, using orthosensitive film – use three dyes, a red sensitive, a blue and a yellow. Take a spectrum reading – what I want to check on is that maybe you've got a strong

120

blue sun there, with the ultraviolet barred by a heavy atmosphere, and all the heat and light coming in on the yellow band.

'I'm not offering much hope, mind you – the Lesser Cloud is packed with blue suns – five hundred thousand of them brighter than Sirius.

'Finally, get that season information from the natives. Make a point of it. Good-by!'

The native was wary. He persisted in retreating elusively into the jungle; and his four legs gave him a speed advantage of which he seemed to be aware. For he kept coming back, tantalizingly.

The woman watched with amusement, then exasperation.

'Perhaps,' she suggested, 'if we separated, and I drove him toward you?'

She saw the frown on the man's face as Maltby nodded reluctantly. His voice was strong, tense.

'He's leading us into an ambush. Turn on the sensitives in your helmet and carry your gun. Don't be too hasty about firing, but don't hesitate in a crisis. A spear can make an ugly wound; and we haven't got the best facilities for handling anything like that.'

His orders brought a momentary irritation. He seemed not to be aware that she was as conscious as he of the requirements of the situation.

The Right Honorable Gloria sighed. If they had to stay on this planet there would have to be some major psychological adjustments, and not – she thought grimly – only by herself.

'*Now!*' said Maltby beside her, swiftly. 'Notice the way the ravine splits in two. I came this far yesterday and they join about two hundred yards farther on. He's gone up the left fork. I'll take the right. You stop here, let him come back to see what's happened, then drive him on.'

He was gone, like a shadow, along a dark path that wound under thick foliage.

121

Silence settled.

She waited. After a minute she felt herself alone in a yellow and black world that had been lifeless since time began.

She thought: This was what Maltby had meant yesterday when he had said she wouldn't dare shoot him – and remain alone. It hadn't penetrated then.

It did now. Alone, on a nameless planet of a mediocre sun, one woman waking up every morning on a moldering ship that rested its unliving metal shape on a dark, muggy, yellow marsh land.

She stood somber. There was no doubt that the problem of robot and human being would have to be solved here as well as out there.

A sound pulled her out of her gloom. As she watched, abruptly more alert, a catlike head peered cautiously from a line of bushes a hundred yards away across the clearing.

It was an interesting head; its ferocity not the least of its fascinating qualities. The yellowish body was invisible now in the underbrush, but she had caught enough glimpses of it earlier to recognize that it was the CC type, of the almost universal Centaur family. Its body was evenly balanced between its hind and forelegs.

It watched her, and its great glistening black eyes were round with puzzlement. Its head twisted from side to side, obviously searching for Maltby.

She waved her gun and walked forward. Instantly the creature disappeared. She could hear it with her sensitives, running into distance. Abruptly, it slowed; then there was no sound at all.

'He's got it,' she thought.

She felt impressed. These two-brained Mixed Men, she thought, were bold and capable. It would really be too bad if antirobot prejudice prevented them from being absorbed into the galactic civilization of Imperial Earth.

She watched him a few minutes later, using the block

system of communication with the creature. Maltby looked up, saw her. He shook his head as if puzzled.

'He says its always been warm like this, and that he's been alive for thirteen hundred moons. And that a moon is forty suns – forty days. He wants us to come up a little farther along this valley, but that's too transparent for comfort. Our move is to make a cautious, friendly gesture, and —'

He stopped short. Before she could even realize anything was wrong, her mind was caught, her muscles galvanized. She was thrown sideways and downward so fast that the blow of striking the ground was pure agony.

She lay there stunned, and out of the corner of her eye she saw the spear plunge through the air where she had been.

She twisted, rolled over – her own free will now – and jerked her gun in the direction from which the spear had come. There was a second centaur there, racing away along a bare slope. Her finger pressed on the control; and then —

'Don't!' It was Maltby, his voice low. 'It was a scout the others sent ahead to see what was happening. He's done his work. It's all over.'

She lowered her gun and saw with annoyance that her hand was shaking, her whole body trembling. She parted her lips to say: 'Thanks for saving my life!' Then she closed them again. Because the words would have quavered. And because —

Saved her life! Her mind poised on the edge of blankness with the shock of the thought. Incredibly – she had never before been in personal danger from an individual creature.

There had been the time when her battleship had run into the outer fringes of a sun; and there was the cataclysm of the storm, just past.

But those had been impersonal menaces to be met with technical virtuosities and the hard training of the service.

This was different.

All the way back to the segment of ship she tried to fathom what the difference meant.

It seemed to her finally that she had it.

'Spectrum featureless.' Maltby gave his findings over the astro. 'No dark lines at all; two of the yellow bands so immensely intense that they hurt my eyes. As you suggested, apparently what we have here is a blue sun whose strong violet radiation is cut off by the atmosphere.

'However,' he finished, 'the uniqueness of that effect is confined to our planet here, a derivation of the thick atmosphere. Any questions?'

'No-o!' The astrophysicist looked thoughtful. 'And I can give you no further instructions. I'll have to examine this material. Will you ask Lady Laurr to come in? Like to speak to her privately, if you please.'

'Of course.'

When she had come, Maltby went outside and watched the moon come up. Darkness – he had noticed it the previous night – brought a vague, overall violet haze. Explained now!

An eighty-degree temperature on a planet that, the angular diameter of the sun being what it was, would have been minus one hundred eighty degrees, if the sun's apparent color had been real.

A blue sun, one of five hundred thousand — Interesting but — Maltby smiled savagely – Captain Planston's 'No further instructions!' had a finality about it that —

He shivered involuntarily. And after a moment tried to picture himself sitting, like this, a year hence, staring up at an unchanged moon. Ten years, twenty —

He grew aware that the woman had come to the doorway and was gazing at him where he sat on the chair.

Maltby looked up. The stream of white light from inside the ship caught the queer expression on her face, gave her a strange, bleached look after the yellowness that had seemed a part of her complexion all day.

'We shall receive no more astro-radio calls,' she said and, turning, went inside.

Maltby nodded to himself, almost idly. It was hard and

brutal, this abrupt cutting off of communication. But the regulations governing such situations were precise.

The marooned ones must realize with utter clarity, without false hopes and without the curious illusions produced by radio communication, that they were cut off forever. Forever on their own.

Well, so be it. A fact was a fact, to be faced with resolution. There had been a chapter on castaways in one of the books he had read on the battleship. It had stated that nine hundred million human beings had, during recorded history, been marooned on then undiscovered planets. Most of these planets had eventually been found; and on no less than ten thousand of them great populations had sprung from the original nucleus of castaways.

The law prescribed that a castaway could not withhold himself or herself from participating in such population increases – regardless of previous rank. Castaways must forget considerations of sensitivity and individualism, and think of themselves as instruments of race expansion.

There were penalties; naturally inapplicable if no rescue was effected, but ruthlessly applied whenever recalcitrants were found.

Conceivably the courts might determine that a human being and a robot constituted a special case.

Half an hour must have passed while he sat there. He stood up finally, conscious of hunger. He had forgotten all about supper.

He felt a qualm of self-annoyance. Damn it, this was not the night to appear to be putting pressure on her. Sooner or later she would have to be convinced that she ought to do her share of the cooking.

But not tonight.

He hurried inside, toward the compact kitchen that was part of every segment of ship. In the corridor, he paused.

A blaze of light streamed from the kitchen door. Somebody was whistling softly and tunelessly but cheerfully; and there was an odor of cooking vegetables, and hot *lak* meat.

They almost bumped in the doorway. 'I was just going to call you,' she said.

The supper was a meal of silences, quickly over. They put the dishes into the automatic and went and sat in the great lounge; Maltby saw finally that the woman was studying him with amused eyes.

'Is there any possibility,' she said abruptly, 'that a Mixed Man and a human woman can have children?'

'Frankly,' Maltby confessed, 'I doubt it.'

He launched into a detailed description of the cold and pressure process that had molded the protoplasm to make the original Mixed Men. When he finished he saw that her eyes were still regarding him with a faint amusement. She said in an odd tone:

'A very curious thing happened to me today, after that native threw his spear. I realized' – she seemed for a moment to have difficulty in speaking – 'I realized that I had, so far as I personally was concerned, solved the robot problem.

'Naturally,' she finished quietly, 'I would not have withheld myself in any event. But it is pleasant to know that I like you without' – she smiled – 'qualifications'.

Blue sun that looked yellow. Maltby sat in the chair the following morning puzzling over it. He half expected a visit from the natives, and so he was determined to stay near the ship that day.

He kept his eyes aware of the clearing edges, the valley rims, the jungle trails, but —

There was a law, he remembered, that governed the shifting of light to other wave bands, to yellow for instance. Rather complicated, but in view of the fact that all the instruments of the main bridge were controls of instruments, not the machines themselves, he'd have to depend on mathematics if he ever hoped to visualize the kind of sun that was out there.

Most of the heat probably came through the ultraviolet range. But that was uncheckable. So leave it alone and stick to the yellow.

He went into the ship. Gloria was nowhere in sight, but her bedroom door was closed. Maltby found a notebook, returned to his chair and began to figure.

An hour later he stared at the answer: One million three hundred thousand million miles. About a fifth of a light year.

He laughed curtly. That was that. He'd have to get better data than he had or —

Or would he?

His mind poised. In a single flash of understanding, the stupendous truth burst upon him.

With a cry he leaped to his feet, whirled to race through the door as a long, black shadow slid across him.

The shadow was so vast, instantly darkening the whole valley, that, involuntarily, Maltby halted and looked up.

The battleship *Star Cluster* hung low over the yellow-brown jungle planet, already disgorging a lifeboat that glinted a yellowish silver as it circled out into the sunlight, and started down.

Maltby had only a moment with the woman before the lifeboat landed. 'To think,' he said, 'that I just now figured out the truth.'

She was, he saw, not looking at him. Her gaze seemed far away. He went on:

'As for the rest, the best method, I imagine, is to put me in the conditioning chamber, and —'

Still without looking at him, she cut him off:

'Don't be ridiculous. You must not imagine that I feel embarrassed because you have kissed me. I shall receive you later in my quarters.'

A bath, new clothes – at last Maltby stepped through the transmitter into the astrophysics department. His own first realization of the tremendous truth, while generally accurate, had lacked detailed facts.

'Ah, Maltby!' The chief of the department came forward, shook hands. 'Some sun you picked there – we suspected from your first description of the yellowness and the black. But naturally we couldn't rouse your hopes — Forbidden, you know.

'The axial tilt, the apparent length of a summer in which jungle trees of great size showed no growth rings – very suggestive. The featureless spectrum with its complete lack of dark lines – almost conclusive. Final proof was that the orthosensitive film was overexposed, while the blue and red sensitives were badly underexposed.

'This star-type is so immensely hot that practically all of its energy radiation is far in the ultravisible. A secondary radiation – a sort of fluorescence in the star's own atmosphere – produces the visible yellow when a minute fraction of the appalling ultraviolet radiation is transformed into longer wave lengths by helium atoms. A fluorescent lamp, in a fashion – but on a scale that is more than ordinarily cosmic in its violence. The total radiation reaching the planet was naturally tremendous; the surface radiation, after passing through miles of absorbing ozone, water vapor, carbondioxide and other gases, was very different.

'No wonder the native said it had always been hot. The summer lasts four thousand years. The normal radiation of that special appalling star type – the aeon-in-aeon-out radiation rate – is about equal to a full-fledged Nova at its catastrophic maximum of violence. It has a period of a few hours, and is equivalent to approximately a hundred million ordinary suns. Nova O, we call that brightest of all stars; and there's only one in the Lesser Magellanic Cloud, the great and glorious S-Doradus.

'When I asked you to call Grand Captain Laurr, and I told her that out of thirty million suns she had picked —'

It was at that point that Maltby cut him off. 'Just a minute,' he said, 'did you say you told Lady Laurr *last night!*'

'Was it night down there?' Captain Planston said, interested. 'Well, well — By the way, I almost forgot – this marrying and giving in marriage is not so important to me now that I am an old man. But congratulations.'

The conversation was too swift for Maltby. His minds were still examining the first statement. That she had known all the time. He came up, groping, before the new words.

'Congratulations?' he echoed.

'Definitely time she had a husband,' boomed the captain. 'She's been a career woman, you know. Besides, it'll have a revivifying effect on the other robots . . . pardon me. Assure you, the name means nothing to me.

'Anyway, Lady Laurr herself made the announcement a few minutes ago, so come down and see me again.'

He turned away with a wave of a thick hand.

Maltby headed for the nearest transmitter. She would probably be expecting him by now.

She would not be disappointed.

JUGGERNAUT

THE MAN – his name was Pete Creighton, though that doesn't matter – saw the movement out of the corner of his eye, as he sat reading his evening paper.

A hand reached out of the nothingness of thin air about two feet above the rug. It seemed to grope, then drew back into nothingness. Almost instantly it reappeared, this time holding a small, dully glinting metal bar. The fingers let go of the bar, and drew out of sight, even as the metal thing started to fall towards the floor.

THUD! The sound was vibrant. It shook the room.

Creighton sat jerkily up in his chair, and lowered his paper. Then he remembered what he had seen. Automatically, his mind rejected the memory. But the fantastic idea of it brought him mentally further into the room.

He found himself staring at an ingot of iron about a foot long and two inches square. That was all. It lay there on the rug, defying his reason.

'Cripes!' said Creighton.

His wife, a sad-faced woman, came out of the kitchen. She stared at him gloomily: 'What's the matter now?' she intoned.

'That iron bar!' Her husband, half-choked, pointed. 'Who threw that in here?'

'Bar?' The woman looked at the ingot in surprise. Her face cleared. 'Johnny must have brought it in from the outside.'

She paused, frowned again; then added: 'Why all the fuss about a piece of scrap iron?'

'It fell,' Creighton babbled. 'I saw it out of the corner of my eye. A hand dropped it right out of the —'

He stopped. Realization came out of what he was saying.

He swallowed hard. His eyes widened. He bent sideways in his chair, and grabbed convulsively for the metal bar.

It came up in his strong fingers. It was quite heavy. Its weight and its drab appearance dimmed his desire to examine it thoroughly. It was a solid ingot of iron, nothing more, nor less. His wife's tired voice came again:

'Johnny must have stood it up on one end, and it fell over.'

'Huh-uh!' said her husband.

He found himself anxious to accept the explanation. The curious sense of alien things faded before the normalness of it. He must have been daydreaming. He must have been crazy.

He put the bar down on the floor. 'Give it to the next scrap drive!' he said gruffly.

Hour after hour, the Vulcan Steel & Iron Works roared and yammered at the undefended skies. The din was an unceasing dirge, lustily and horrendously sounding the doom of the Axis. It was a world of bedlam; and not even an accident could stop that over-all bellowing of metal being smashed and tormented into new shapes.

The accident added a minor clamor to the dominating theme of stupendous sound. There was a screech from a cold roller machine, than a thumping and a sound of metal tearing.

One of the men operating the machine emitted some fanciful verbal sounds, and frantically manipulated the controls. The thumping and the tearing ceased. An assistant foreman came over.

'What's wrong, Bill?'

'That bar!' muttered Bill. 'I was just starting to round it, and it bent one of the rollers.'

'*That* bar!' echoed the assistant foreman incredulously.

He stared at the little thing. It was a big bar to be going through a roller. But compared to the sizable steel extrusions and moldings turned out by the Vulcan works, it was tiny.

It was six feet long, and it had originally been two inches

square. About half of its length had been rolled once. At the point where the strength of the rollers had been bested, the metal of the bar looked exactly the same as that which had gone before. Except that it had refused to round.

The assistant foreman spluttered, and then fell back on a technicality. 'I thought it was understood,' he said, 'that in the Vulcan plants nothing over an inch and a half is rounded by rollers.'

'I have had dozens of 'em,' said Bill. He added doggedly: 'When they come, I do 'em.'

There was nothing to do but accept the reality. Other firms, the assistant foreman knew, made a common practise of rolling two-inchers. He said:

'O.K., take your helper and report to Mr Johnson. I'll have a new roller put in here. The bent one and that bar go to the scrap heap.'

He could not refrain from adding: 'Hereafter send two-inch bars to the hammers.'

The bar obediently went through the furnace again. A dozen things could have happened to it. It could have formed part of a large molding. It could have, along with other metal, endured an attempt to hammer it into sheer steel.

It would have been discovered then, its basic shape and hardness exposed.

But the wheels of chance spun – and up went a mechanical hammer, and down onto the long, narrow, extruded shape of which the original ingot was a part.

The hammer was set for one and one quarter inches, and it clanged with a curiously solid sound. It was a sound not unfamiliar to the attendant, but one which oughtn't to be coming from the pummeling of white-hot metal.

It was his helper, however, who saw the dents in the base of the hammer. He uttered a cry, and pulled out the clutch. The older man jerked the bar clear, and stared at the havoc it had wrought.

'Yumpin' yimminy!' he said. 'Hey, Mr Yenkins, come over here, and look at this.'

Jenkins was a big, chubby man who had contributed fourteen ideas for labor-saving devices before and since he was made foreman. The significance of what he saw now was not lost on him.

'Ernie's sick today,' he said. 'Take over his drill for a couple of hours, you two, while I look into this.'

He phoned the engineering department; and after ten minutes Boothby came down, and examined the hammer.

He was a lean-built, precise young man of thirty-five. On duty he wore horned-rimmed glasses, behind which gleamed a pair of bright-blue eyes. He was a craftsman, a regular hound for precision work.

He measured the dents. They were a solid two inches wide; and the hammer and its base shared the depth equally.

In both, the two-inch wide, one-foot long gouge was exactly three eighths of an inch deep, a total for the two of three quarters of an inch.

'Hm-m-m,' said Boothby, 'what have we got here . . . a super-super hard alloy, accidentally achieved?'

'My mind jumped that way,' said Mr Jenkins modestly. 'My name is Jenkins, Wilfred Jenkins.'

Boothby grinned inwardly. He recognized that he was being told very quietly to whom the credit belonged for any possible discovery. He couldn't help his reaction. He said:

'Who was on this machine?'

Jenkins' heavy face looked unhappy. He hesitated.

'Some Swede,' he said reluctantly. 'I forget his name.'

'Find it out,' said Boothby. 'His prompt action in calling you is very important. Now, let's see if we can trace this bar back to its source.'

He saw that Jenkins was happy again. 'I've already done that,' the foreman said. 'It came out of a pot, all the metal of which was derived from shop scrap. Beyond that, of course, it's untraceable.'

Boothby found himself appreciating Jenkins a little more. It always made him feel good to see a man on his mental toes.

He had formed a habit of giving praise when it was deserved. He gave it now, briefly, then finished:

'Find out if any other department has recently run up against a very hard metal. No, wait, I'll do that. You have this bar sent right up to the metallurgical lab.'

'Sent up hot?' asked Jenkins.

'Now!' said Boothby, 'whatever its condition. I'll ring up Nadderly . . . er, Mr Nadderly, and tell him to expect it.'

He was about to add: 'And see that your men don't make a mistake, and ship the wrong one.'

He didn't add it. There was a look on Jenkins' face, an unmistakable look. It was the look of a man who strongly suspected that he was about to win his fifteenth bonus in two and a half years.

There would be no mistake.

A steel bar 2 in × 2 in × 12 in – tossed out of hyper-space into the living room of one, Pete Creighton, who didn't matter —

None of the individuals mattered. They were but pawns reacting according to a pattern, from which they could vary only if some impossible change took place in their characters. Impossible because they would have had to become either more or less than human.

When a machine in a factory breaks down, its operator naturally has to call attention to the fact. All the rest followed automatically out of the very nature of things. An alert foreman, an alert engineer, a skillful metallurgist; these were normal Americans, normal Englishmen, normal – Germans!

No, the individuals mattered not. There was only the steel ingot, forming now a part of a long, narrow bar.

On the thirtieth day, Boothby addressed the monthly

meeting of the Vulcan's board of directors. He was first on the agenda, so he had had to hustle. But he was in a high good humor as he began:

'As you all know, obtaining information from a metallurgist' – he paused and grinned inoffensively at Nadderly, whom he had invited down – 'is like obtaining blood from a turnip. Mr Nadderly embodies in his character and his science all the caution of a Scotchman who realizes that it's time he set up the drinks for everybody, but who is waiting for some of the gang to depart.

'I might as well warn you, gentlemen, that he is fully aware that any statement he has made on this metal might be used against him. One of his objections is that thirty days is a very brief period in the life of an alloy. There is an aluminium alloy, for instance, that requires forty days to age harden.

'Mr Nadderly wishes that stressed because the original hard alloy, which seems to have been a bar of about two inches square by a foot long, has in fifteen days *imparted* its hardness to the rest of the bar, of which it is a part.

'Gentlemen' – he looked earnestly over the faces – 'the hardness of this metal cannot be stated or estimated. It is not just so many times harder than chromium or molybdenum steel. It is hard beyond all calculation.

'Once hardened, it cannot be machined, not even by tools made of itself. It won't grind. Diamonds do not even scratch it. Cannon shells neither dent it nor scratch it. Chemicals have no effect. No heat we have been able to inflict on it has any softening effect.

'Two pieces welded together – other metal attaches to it readily – impart the hardness to the welding. Apparently, any metal once hardened by contact with the hard metal, will impart the hardness to any metal with which it in turn comes into contact.

'The process is cumulative and endless, though, as I have said, it seems to require fifteen days. It is during this fortnight that the metal can be worked.

'Mr Nadderley thinks that the hardness derives from atomic, not molecular processes, and that the impulse of hardness is imparted much as radium will affect metals with which it is placed in contact. It seems to be harmless, unlike radium, but —'

Boothby paused. He ran his gaze along the line of intent faces, down one side of the board table and up the other.

'The problem is this: Can we after only thirty days, long before we can be sure we know all its reactions, throw this metal into the balance against the Axis?'

Boothby sat down. No one seemed to have expected such an abrupt ending, and it was nearly a minute before the chairman of the board cleared his throat and said:

'I have a telegram here from the Del-Air Corporation, which puzzled me when I received it last night, but which seems more understandable in the light of what Mr Boothby has told us. The telegram is from the president of Del-Air. I will read it, if you please.'

He read:

' "We have received from the United States Air Command, European Theater, an enthusiastic account of some new engines which we dispatched overseas some thirteen days ago by air. Though repeatedly struck by cannon shells, the cylinder blocks of these engines sustained no damage, and continued in operation. These cylinders were bored from steel blocks sent from your plant twenty days ago. Please continue to send us this marvelous steel, which you have developed, and congratulations." '

The chairman looked up. 'Well?' he said.

'But it's not probable,' Boothby protested. 'None of the alloy has been sent out. It's up in the metallurgical lab right now.'

He stopped, his eyes widening. 'Gentlemen,' he breathed, 'is it possible that any metal, which has been in contact with the super-hard steel for however brief a period, goes through the process of age-hardening? I am thinking of the fact that the original ingot has twice at least been through an arc furnace, and that it has touched various other machines.'

He stopped again, went on shakily: 'If that is so, then our problem answers itself. We *have* been sending out super-steel.'

He finished quietly, but jubilantly: 'We can, therefore, only accept the miracle, and try to see to it that no super-tanks or super-machines fall into the hands of our enemies.'

After thirty days, the metal impulse was flowing like a streak. In thirty more days it had crossed the continent and the oceans myriad times.

What happens when every tool in a factory is turning out two hundred and ten thousand different parts, every tool is sharing with its product the gentle impulse of an atomically generated force? And when a thousand, ten thousand factories are affected.

That's what happened.

Limitless were the potentialities of that spread, yet there was a degree of confinement. The area between the battle forces in Europe was like an uncrossable moat.

The Germans retreated too steadily. It was the Allies who salvaged abandoned Nazi trucks and tanks, not the other way around. Bombing of cities had stopped. There were no cities.

The gigantic air fleets roared over the German lines, and shed their bombs like clouds of locusts. By the time anything was touched by the atomic flow, the battle line had advanced a mile or more; and the Allies had the affected area.

Besides, far more than ninety per cent of the bombs were from storerooms in that mighty munitions dump which was England. For years the millions of tons of *matériel* had been piling up underground. It was brought up only when needed, and almost immediately and irretrievably exploded.

The few affected bombs didn't shatter. But no one, no German had time to dig them out of the ground.

Day after day after day, the impulse in the metal crept along the battle front, but couldn't cross over.

During those first two months, the Vulcan office staff was busy. There were vital things to do. Every customer had to be advised that the metal must be 'worked' within a certain set time. Before that paper job was completed, the first complaints had started to come in.

Boothby only grinned when he read them. 'Metal too hard, breaking our tools —' That was the gist.

'They'll learn,' he told the third board meeting he attended. 'I think we should concentrate our attention on the praises of the army and navy. After all, we are now as never before, working hand-and-glove with the government. Some of these battle-front reports are almost too good to be true. I like particularly the frequent use of the word "irresistible".'

It was two days after that that his mind, settling slowly to normalcy from the excitement of the previous ten weeks, gave birth to a thought. It was not a complete thought, not final. It was a doubt that brought a tiny bead of perspiration out on his brow, and it prompted him to sit down, a very shaken young man, and draw a diagrammatic tree.

The tree began with a line that pointed at the word 'Vulcan'. It branched out to 'Factories', then to other factories. It branched again, and again and again, and again and again and again.

It raced along railway tracks. It bridged the seas in ships and planes. It moved along fences and into mines. It ceased to have a beginning and an end. There was no end.

There was no color in Boothby's face now. His eyes behind their owlish spectacles had a glazed look. Like an old man, he swayed up finally from his chair, and, hatless, wandered out into the afternoon. He found his way home like a sick dog, and headed straight for his workroom.

138

He wrote letters to Nadderly, to the chairman of the board of Vulcan, and to the chief army and navy agent attached to the enormous steel and iron works. He staggered to the nearest mailbox with the letters, then returned to his workroom, and headed straight for the drawer where he kept his revolver.

The bullet splashed his brain out over the floor.

Ogden Tait, chairman of the board, had just finished reading the letter from Boothby when the urgent call came for him to come to the smelter.

The letter and the call arriving so close upon one another confused him concerning the contents of the letter. Something about —

Startled, he hurried down to answer the urgent call. An array of plant engineers were there, waiting for him. They had cleared all workmen away from one of the electric arc furnaces. An executive engineer explained the disaster.

Fumbling Boothby's letter, alternately stunned and dismayed, the chairman listened to the chilling account.

'But it's impossible,' he gasped finally. 'How could the ore arrive here super-hard? It came straight by lake boat from the ore piles at Iron Mountain.'

None of the engineers was looking at him. And in the gathering silence, the first glimmer of understanding of what was here began to come to Ogden Tait. He remembered some of the phrases from Boothby's letter: '. . . two million tons of steel and iron sent out in two and one half months . . . spread everywhere . . . no limit —'

His brain began to sway on its base, as the landslide of possibilities unreeled before it. New tracking, Boothby had mentioned, for the interior of the mines. Or new ore cars, or new —

Not only new. Newness didn't matter. Contact was enough; simple, momentary contact. The letter had gone on to say that —

In a blank dismay, he brought it up in his shaking fingers.

When he had re-read it, he looked up dully.

'Just what,' he said vaguely, 'in as few words as possible, will this mean?'

The executive engineer said in a level voice:

'It means that in a few weeks not a steel or iron plant in the United States will be in operation. This is Juggernaut with a capital Hell.'

It is the people who are not acquainted with all the facts who are extremists. In this group will be found the defeatists of 1940 and the super optimists of 1943. Careless of logistics, indifferent to realities partially concealed for military reasons, they blunt their reasons and madden their minds with positivities.

In this group were Boothby and the engineers of the Vulcan Steel & Iron Works; and, until he arrived in Washington, the day after sending a dozen terrified telegrams, in this group also was Ogden Tait, chairman of the Vulcan board.

His first amazement came when the members of the war-planning board greeted him cheerfully.

'The important thing,' said the Great Man, who was chairman of *that* board, 'is that there be no morale slump. I suggest that all the iron ore and metal that is still workable be turned into peace-time machinery, particularly machinery for farm use, which must be heavy as well as strong. There will always be a certain amount of unaffected ore and scrap; and, since any machinery, once completed, will endure forever, it should not take long to supply all the more essential needs of the nation.'

'But – but – but – ' stammered Ogden Tait. 'The w-war!'

He saw, bewildered, that the men were smiling easily. A member glanced at the Great Man.

'May I tell him?'

He was given permission. He turned to Ogden Tait.

'We have generously,' he said, 'decided to share our

secret and wonderful metal with the Axis. Even now our planes are hovering over German and Japanese mines, ore piles, factories, dropping chunks of super-hard steel.'

Ogden Tait waited. For the first time in his long, comfortable life, he had the feeling that he was not being very bright. It was a radical thought.

The member was continuing: 'In a few months, what remains of the Axis steel industry, after our past bombings, will suspend operations.'

He paused, smiling.

'But,' Ogden Tait pointed out, 'they'll have had three months production while we —'

'Let them have their three months,' the member said calmly. 'Let them have six months, a year. What do you think we've been doing these last few years? You bet we have. We've been building up supplies. Mountains, oceans, continents of supplies. We've got enough on hand to fight two years of continuous battle.

'The Germans, on the other hand, cannot get along for a single month without fresh munitions.

'The war is accordingly won.'

The Great Man interjected at that point: 'Whatever prank of fate wished this Juggernaut upon us has also solved the peace forever. If you will think about it for a moment, you will realize that, without steel, there can be no war —'

Whatever prank of fate! . . . A hand reaching out of nothingness into Pete Creighton's living room . . . deliberately dropping an ingot of steel.

HAND OF THE GODS

AT TWENTY, Clane wrote his first book. It was a cautiously worded, thin volume about old legends. And what was important about it was not that it attempted to dispel supersitions about the banished golden era which the atom gods had destroyed, but that for weeks it required him to go every day into the palace library, where, with the help of three secretary-slaves – two men and a woman – he did the necessary research work.

It was in the library that the Lady Lydia, his stepgrandmother, saw him one day.

She had almost forgotten that he existed. But she saw him now for the first time under conditions that were favorable to his appearance. He was modestly attired in the fatigue gown of a temple scientist, a costume which was effective for covering up his physical deformations. There were folds of cloth to conceal his mutated arms so skillfully that his normal human hands came out into the open as if they were the natural extensions of a healthy body. The cloak was drawn up into a narrow, not unattractive band around his neck, which served to hide the subtly mutated shoulders and the unhuman chest formation. Above the collar, Lord Clane's head reared with all the pride of a young lordling.

It was a head to make any woman look twice, delicately beautiful, with a remarkably clear skin. Lydia, who had never seen her husband's grandson, except at a distance – Clane had made sure of that – felt a constricting fear in her heart.

'By Uranium!' she thought. 'Another great man. As if I didn't have enough trouble trying to get Tews back from exile.'

It hardly seemed likely that death would be necessary for a mutation. But if she ever hoped to have Tews inherit the empire, then all the more direct heirs would have to be taken care of in some way. Standing there, she added this new relative to her list of the more dangerous kin of the ailing Lord Leader.

She saw that Clane was looking at her. His face had changed, stiffened, lost some of its good looks, and that brought a memory of things she had heard about him. That he was easily upset emotionally. The prospect interested her. She walked towards him, a thin smile on her long, handsome countenance.

Twice, as she stood tall before him, he tried to get up. And failed each time. All the color was gone from his cheeks, his face even more strained looking than it had been, ashen and unnatural, twisted, changed, the last shape of beauty gone from it. His lips worked with the effort at speech, but only a routed burst of unintelligible sounds issued forth.

Lydia grew aware that the young slave woman-secretary was almost as agitated as her master. The creature looked beseechingly at Lydia, finally gasped:

'May I speak, your excellency?'

That shocked. Slaves didn't speak except when spoken to. It was not just a rule or a regulation dependent upon the whim of the particular owner; it was the law of the land, and anybody could report breach as a misdemeanor, and collect half the fine which was subsequently levied from the slave's master. What dazed Lady Lydia was that *she* should have been the victim of such a degrading experience. She was so stunned that the young woman had time to gasp:

'You must forgive him. He is subject to fits of nervous paralysis, when he can neither move nor speak. The sight of his illustrious grandmother coming upon him by surprise —'

That was as far as she got. Lydia found her voice. She snapped:

143

'It is too bad that all slaves are not similarly afflicted. How dare you speak to me?'

She stopped, catching herself sharply. It was not often that she lost her temper, and she had no intention of letting the situation get out of hand. The slave girl was sagging away as if she had been struck with a violence beyond her power to resist. Lydia watched the process of disintegration curiously. There was only one possible explanation for a slave speaking up so boldly for her master. She must be one of his favorite mistresses. And the odd thing, in this case, was that the slave herself seemed to approve of the relationship, or she wouldn't have been so anxious for him.

It would appear, thought Lydia, *that this mutation relative of mine can make himself attractive in spite of his deformities, and that it isn't only a case of a slave girl compelled by her circumstances.*

It seemed to her that the moment had potentialities. 'What,' she said, 'is your name?'

'Selk.' The young woman spoke huskily.

'Oh, a Martian.'

The Martian war, some years before, had produced some hundreds of thousands of husky, good-looking boy and girl Martians for the slave schools to train.

Lydia's plan grew clear. She would have the girl assassinated, and so put the first desperate fear into the mutation. That should hold him until she had succeeded in bringing Tews back from exile to supreme power. After all, he was too important. It would be impossible for a despised mutation ever to become Lord Leader.

He had to be put out of the way in the long run, because the Linn party would otherwise try to make use of him against Tews and herself.

She paused for a last look down at Clane. He was sitting as rigid as a board, his eyes glazed, his face still colorless and unnatural. She made no effort to conceal her contempt

144

as, with a flounce of her skirt, she turned and walked away, followed by her ladies and personal slaves.

Slaves were sometimes trained to be assassins. The advantage of using them was that they could not be witnesses in court either for or against the accused. But Lydia had long discovered that, if anything went wrong, if a crisis arose as a result of the murder attempt, a slave assassin did not have the same determination to win over obstacles. Slaves took to their heels at the slightest provocation, and returned with fantastic accounts of the odds that had defeated them.

She used former knights and sons of knights, whose families had been degraded from their rank because they were penniless. Such men had a desperate will to acquire money, and when they failed she could usually count on a plausible reason.

She had a horror of not knowing the facts. For more than thirty of her fifty-five years her mind had been a non-saturable sponge for details and ever more details.

It was accordingly of more than ordinary interest to her when the two knights she had hired to murder her step-grandson's slave girl, Selk, reported that they had been unable to find the girl.

'There is no such person now attached to Lord Clane's city household.'

Her informant, a slim youth named Meerl, spoke with that mixture of boldness and respect which the more devil-may-care assassins affected when talking to high personages.

'Lady,' he went on with a bow and a smile, 'I think you have been outwitted.'

'I'll do the thinking,' said Lydia with asperity. 'You're a sword or a knife with a strong arm to wield. Nothing more.'

'And a good brain to direct it,' said Meerl.

Lydia scarcely heard. Her retort had been almost automatic. Because – could it be? Was it possible that Clane had realized what she would do?

What startled her was the decisiveness of it, the prompt action that had been taken on the basis of what would only have been a suspicion. The world was full of people who never did anything about their suspicions. The group that did was always in a special class. If Clane had consciously frustrated her, then he was even more dangerous than she had thought. She'd have to plan her next move with care.

She grew aware that the two men were still standing before her. She glared at them.

'Well, what you waiting for? You know there is no money if you fail.'

'Gracious lady,' said Meerl, 'we did not fail. You failed.'

Lydia hesitated, impressed by the fairness of the thrust. She had a certain grudging respect for this particular assassin.

'Fifty per cent,' she said.

She tossed forward a pouch of money. It was skillfully caught. The men bowed quickly, stiffly, with a flash of white teeth and a clank of steel. They whirled and disappeared through thick portieres that concealed the door by which they had entered.

Lydia sat alone with her thoughts, but not for long. A knock came on another door, and one of her ladies in waiting entered, holding a sealed letter in her hand.

'This arrived, madam, while you were engaged.'

Lydia's eyebrows went up a little when she saw that the letter was from Clane. She read it, tight-lipped:

To My Most Gracious Grandmother:

I offer my sincere apologies for the insult and distress which I caused your ladyship yesterday in the library. I can only plead that my nervous afflictions are well known in the family, and that, when I am assailed, it is beyond my power to control myself.

146

I also offer apologies for the action of my slave girl in speaking to you. It was my first intention to turn her over to you for punishment. But then it struck me that you were so tremendously busy at all times, and besides she scarcely merited your attention. Accordingly, I have had her sold in the country to a dealer in labor, and she will no doubt learn to regret her insolence.

With renewed humble apologies, I remain,

Your obedient grandson,

Clane

Reluctantly, the Lady Linn was compelled to admire the letter. Now she would never know whether she had been outwitted or victorious.

I suppose, she thought acridly, *I could at great expense discover if he merely sent her to his country estate, there to wait until I have forgotten what she looks like. Or could I even do that?*

She paused to consider the difficulties. She would have to send as an investigator someone who had seen the girl. Who? She looked up.

'Dalat.'

The woman who had brought the letter curtsied.

'Yes?'

'What did that slave girl in the library yesterday look like?'

Dalat was disconcerted. 'W-why, I don't think I noticed, your ladyship. A blonde, I think.'

'A blonde!' Explosively. 'Why, you numbskull. That girl had the most fancy head of golden hair that I've seen in several years – and you didn't notice.'

Dalat was herself again. 'I am not accustomed to remembering slaves,' she said.

'Get out of here,' said Lydia. But she said it in a flat tone, without emotion.

Here was defeat.

She shrugged finally. After all, it was only an idea she had

147

had. Her problem was to get Tews back to Linn. Lord Clane, the only mutation ever born into the family of the Lord Leader, could wait.

Nevertheless, the failure rankled.

The Lord Leader had over a period of years become an ailing old man, who could not make up his mind. At seventy-one, he was almost blind in his left eye, and only his voice remained strong. He had a thunderous baritone that still struck terror into the hearts of criminals when he sat on the chair of high judgment, a duty which, because of its sedentary nature, he cultivated more and more as the swift months of his declining years passed by.

He was greatly surprised one day to see Clane turn up in the palace court as a defense counsel for a knight. He stopped the presentation of the case to ask some questions.

'Have you experience in the lower courts?'

'Yes, Leader.'

'Hm-m-m, why was I not told?'

The mutation had suddenly a strained look on his face, as if the pressure of being the center of attention was proving too much for him. The Lord Leader recalled the young man's affliction, and said hastily:

'Proceed with the case. I shall talk to you later.'

The case was an unimportant one involving equity rights. It had obviously been taken by Clane because of its simple, just aspects. For a first case in the highest court it had been well selected. The old man was pleased, and gave the favorable verdict with satisfaction.

As usual, however, he had over-estimated his strength. And so, he was finally forced to retire quickly, with but a word to Clane:

'I shall come to call on you one of these days. I have been wanting to see your home.'

That night he made the mistake of sitting on the balcony too long without a blanket. He caught a cold, and spent the whole of the month that followed in bed. It was there, helpless on his back, acutely aware of his weak body, fully, clearly conscious at last that he had at most a few years to live, that the Lord Leader realized finally the necessity of selecting an heir. In spite of his personal dislike for Tews, he found himself listening, at first grudgingly, then more amenably, to his wife.

'Remember,' she said, again and again, 'your dream of bequeathing to the world a unified empire. Surely, you cannot become sentimental about it at the last minute. Lords Jerrin and Draid are still too young. Jerrin, of course, is the most brilliant young man of his generation. He is obviously a future Lord Leader, and should be named so in your will. But not yet. You cannot hand over the solar system to a youngster of twenty-four.'

The Lord Leader stirred uneasily. He noticed that there was not a word in her argument about the reason for Tews' exile. And that she was too clever ever to allow into her voice the faintest suggestion that, behind her logic, was the emotional fact that Tews was her son.

'There are of course,' Lydia went on, 'the boy's uncles on their mother's side, both amiable administrators but lacking in will. And then there are your daughters and sons-in-law, and their children, and your nieces and nephews.'

'Forget them.' The Lord Leader, gaunt and intent on the pillow, moved a hand weakly in dismissal of the suggestion. He was not interested in the second-raters. 'You have forgotten,' he said finally, 'Clane.'

'A mutation!' said Lydia, surprised. 'Are you serious?'

The lord of Linn was silent. He knew better, of course. Mutations were despised, hated, and, paradoxically, feared. No normal person would ever accept their domination. The suggestion was actually meaningless. But he knew why he had made it. Delay. He realized he was being pushed inexorably to choosing as his heir Lydia's plumpish son by her first husband.

'If you considered your own blood only,' urged Lydia, 'it would be just another case of imperial succession so common among our tributary monarchies and among the barbarians of Aiszh and Venus and Mars. Politically it would be meaningless. If, however, you strike across party lines, your action will speak for your supreme patriotism. In no other way could you so finally and unanswerably convince the world that you have only its interest at heart.'

The old scoundrel, dimmed though his spirit and intellect were by illness and age, was not quite so simple as that. He knew what they were saying under the pillars, that Lydia was molding him like a piece of putty to her plans.

Not that such opinions disturbed him very much. The tireless propaganda of his enemies and of mischief makers and gossips had dinned into his ears for nearly fifty years, and he had become immune to the chatter.

In the end the decisive factor was only partly Lydia's arguments, only partly his own desperate realization that he had little choice. The unexpected factor was a visit to his bedside by the younger of his two daughters by his first marriage. She asked that he grant her a divorce from her present husband, and permit her to marry the exiled Tews.

'I have always,' she said, 'been in love with Tews, and only Tews, and I am willing to join him in exile.'

The prospect was so dazzling that, for once, the old man was completely fooled. It did not even occur to him that Lydia had spent two days convincing the cautious Gudrun that here was her only chance of becoming first lady of Linn.

'Otherwise,' Lydia had pointed out, 'you'll be just another relative, dependent upon the whim of the reigning Lady Leader.'

The Linn of Linn suspected absolutely nothing of that behind-the-scenes connivance. His daughter married to Lord Tews. The possibilities warmed his chilling blood. She was too old, of course, to have any more children, but she

150

would serve Tews as Lydia had him, a perfect foil, a perfect representative of his own political group. *His* daughter!

I must, he thought, *go and see what Clane thinks. Meanwhile I can send for Tews on a tentative basis.*

He didn't say that out loud. No one in the family except himself realized the enormous extent of the knowledge that the long-dead temple scientist Joquin had bequeathed to Clane. The Lord Leader preferred to keep the information in his own mind. He knew Lydia's propensity for hiring assassins, and it wouldn't do to subject Clane to more than ordinary danger from that source.

He regarded the mutation as an unsuspected stabilizing force during the chaos that might follow his death. He wrote the letter inviting Tews to return to Linn, and, a week later, finally out of bed, had himself carried to Clane's residence in the west suburbs. He remained overnight, and, returning the next day, began to discharge a score of key men whom Lydia had slipped into administrative positions on occasions when he was too weary to know what the urgent business was for which he was signing papers.

Lydia said nothing, but she noted the sequence of events. A visit to Clane, then action against her men. She pondered that for some days, and then, the day before Tews was due, she paid her first visit to the modest looking home of Lord Clane Linn, taking care that she was not expected. She had heard vague accounts of the estate.

The reality surpassed anything she had ever imagined or heard.

For seven years, Tews had lived on Awai in the Great Sea. He had a small property on the largest island of the group, and, after his disgrace, his mother had suggested that he retire there rather than to one of his more sumptuous mainland estates. A shrewd, careful man, he recognized the value of the advice. His role, if he hoped to remain alive, must be sackcloth and ashes.

151

At first it was purposeful cunning. In Linn, Lydia wracked her brains for explanations and finally came out with the statement that her son had wearied and sickened of politics, and retired to a life of meditation beyond the poisoned waters. For a long time, so plausible and convincing was her sighing, tired way of describing his feelings – as if she, too, longed for the surcease of rest from the duties of her position – that the story was actually believed. Patrons, governors and ambassadors, flying out in spaceships from Linn to the continents across the ocean, paused as a matter of course to pay their respects to the son of Lydia.

Gradually, they began to catch on that he was out of favor. Desperately, terribly dangerously out of favor. The stiff-faced silence of the Lord Leader when Tews was mentioned was reported finally among administrators and oliticians everywhere. People were tremendously astute, once they realized. It was recalled that Tews had hastily departed from Linn at the time when the news of the death of General Lord Creg, son of the Lord Leader, was first brought from Mars. At the time his departure had scarcely been remarked. Now it was remembered and conclusions drawn. Great ships, carrying high government officials, ceased to stop, so that the officials could float down for lunch with Lord Tews. But that was the least important aspect. The deadly danger was that some zealous and ambitious individual knight might seek to gain the favor of Linn of Linn by murdering his stepson.

Lydia herself nipped several such plots in the bud. But each conspiracy was such a visible strain on her nervous system that the Lord Leader unfroze sufficiently to bestow on Tews a secondary military position on Awai. It was actually an insulting offer, but the panic-stricken Lydia persuaded Tews to accept it as a means of preserving his life until she could do more for him. The position, and the power that went with it, arrived just in time.

He had formed a habit of attending lectures at the University of Awai. One day, a term having expired, and a new one scheduled to begin, he made the customary application for renewal. The professor in charge took the opportunity during the first lecture of the first semester of the new term – the first lecture was free and open to the public – to inform him before the entire audience that, since the lists were full, his application was being rejected, and would have to be put over until the following year, when, of course, it would be considered again 'on its merits'.

It was the act of a neurotic fool. But Tews would have let it pass for the time being if the audience, recognizing a fallen giant, had not started catcalling and threatening. The uproar grew with the minutes, and, experienced leader of men that he was, Tews realized that a mob mood was building up, which must be smashed if he hoped to continue living in safety on the island. He climbed to his feet, and, since most of the audience was standing on seats and benches he managed to reach the outside before the yelling individuals who saw him were able to attract the attention of the yelling crowd that didn't.

Tews went straight to the outdoor restaurant where his new guard was waiting. It was a rowdy crew, but recently arrived from Linn, and with enough basic discipline to follow him back into the lecture room. There was a pause in the confusion when the glinting line of spears wedged towards the platform. In a minute, before an abruptly subdued audience, the startled professor was being stripped and tied to a chair. The twenty-five lashes that he received then ended for good the outburst of hatred against Tews.

He returned to his villa that afternoon, and made no further effort to participate in the activities of the community. The isolation affected him profoundly. He became tremendously observant. He noticed in amazement for the first time that the islanders swam at night in the ocean. Swam! In water that had been poisoned since legendary times by the atom gods. Was it possible the water

153

was no longer deadly? He noted the point for possible future reference, and for the first time grew interested in the name the islanders had for the great ocean. Passfic. Continental people had moved inland to escape the fumes of the deadly seas, and they had forgotten the ancient names.

During the long months of aloneness that followed his retreat to his villa, Tews' mind dwelt many times critically upon his life in Linn. He began to see the madness of it, and the endless skulduggery. He read with more and more amazement the letters of his mother, outlining what she was doing. It was a tale of endless cunnings, conspiracies and murders, written in a simple code that was effective because it was based on words the extra-original meanings of which were known only to his mother and himself.

His amazement became disgust, and disgust grew into the first comprehension of the greatness of his stepfather, the Lord Leader.

But he's wrong, Tews thought intently. *The way to a unified empire is not through a continuation of absolute power for one man. The old republic never had a chance, since the factions came up from the days of the two-king system. But now, after decades of virtual nonparty patriotism under my honorable stepfather, it should be possible to restore the republic with the very good possibility that this time it will work. That must be my task if I can ever return to Linn.*

The messenger from the Lord Leader inviting his return arrived on the same ship as another letter from his mother. Hers sounded as if it had been written in breathless haste, but it contained an explanation of how his recall had been accomplished. The price shocked Tews.

What, he thought, *marry Gudrun!*

It took an hour for his nerves to calm sufficiently for him even to consider the proposition. His plan, it seemed to him finally, was too important to be allowed to fail because of his distaste for a woman whose interest in men ran not so much to quality as quantity. And it wasn't as if he was bound to another woman. His wife, seven years before, on discovering that his departure from Linn might be permanent, hastily persuaded her father to declare them divorced.

Yes, he was free to marry.

Lydia, on the way to the home of her stepgrandson, pondered her situation. She was not satisfied. A dozen of her schemes were coming to a head; and here she was going to see Lord Clane, a completely unknown factor. Thinking about it from that viewpoint, she felt astonished. What possible danger, she asked herself again and again, could a mutation be to her?

Even as those thoughts infuriated the surface of her mind, deep inside she knew better. There was something here. *Something*. The old man would never bother with a nonentity. He was either quiet with the quietness of weariness, or utterly impatient. Young people particularly enraged him easily, and if Clane was an exception, then there was a reason.

From a distance, Clane's residence looked small. There was brush in the foreground, and a solid wall of trees across the entire eight-hundred-foot front of the estate. The house peaked a few feet above a mantle of pines and evergreens. As her chair drew nearer it, Lydia decided it was a three-storey building, which was certainly minuscule beside the palaces of the other Linns. Her bearers puffed up a hill, trotted past a pleasant arbor of trees, and came after a little to a low, massive fence that had not been visible from below. Lydia, always alert for military obstacles, had her chair put down. She climbed out, conscious that a cool, sweet breeze was blowing where, a moment before, had been only the dead heat of a stifling summer day. The air was rich with the perfume of trees and green things.

She walked slowly along the fence, noting that it was skillfully hidden from the street below by an unbroken hedge, although it showed through at this close range. She recognized the material as similar to that of which the temples of the scientists was constructed, only there was no visible lead lining. She estimated the height of the fence at three feet, and its thickness about three and a half. It was fat and squat and defensively useless.

When I was young, she thought, *I could have jumped over it myself.*

She returned to the chair, annoyed because she couldn't fathom its purpose, and yet couldn't quite believe it had no purpose. It was even more disconcerting to discover a hundred feet farther along the walk that the gate was not a closure but an opening in the wall, and that there was no guard in sight. In a minute more, the bearers had carried her inside, through a tunnel of interwoven shrubs shadowed by towering trees, and then to an open lawn. That was where the real surprise began.

'Stop!' said the Lady Leader Lydia.

An enormous combination meadow and garden spread from the edge of the trees. She had an eye for size, and, without consciously thinking about it, she guessed that fifteen acres were visible from her vantage point. A gracious stream meandered diagonally across the meadow. Along its banks scores of guest homes had been built, low, sleek, be-windowed structures, each with its overhanging shade trees. The house, a square-built affair, towered to her right. At the far end of the grounds were five spaceships neatly laid out side by side. And everywhere were people. Men and women singly and in groups, sitting in chairs, walking, working, reading, writing, drawing and painting. Thoughtfully, Lydia walked over to a painter, who sat with his easel and palette a scant dozen yards from her. He was painting the scene before him, and he paid no attention to her. She was not accustomed to being ignored. She said sharply:

'What is all this?' She waved one arm to take in the activities of the estate. 'What is going on here?'

156

The young man shrugged. He dabbed thoughtfully at the scene he was painting, then, still without looking up, said:

'Here, madam, you have the center of Linn. Here the thought and opinion of the empire is created and cast into molds for public consumption. Ideas born here, once they are spread among the masses, become the mores of the nation and the solar system. To be invited here is an unequaled honor, for it means that your work as a scholar or artist has received the ultimate recognition that power and money can give. Madam, whoever you are, I welcome you to the intellectual center of the world. You would not be here if you had not some unsurpassed achievement to your credit. However, I beg of you, please do not tell me what it is until this evening when I shall be happy to lend you both my ears. And now, old and successful woman, good day to you.'

Lydia withdrew thoughtfully. Her impulse, to have the young man stripped and lashed, yielded before a sudden desire to remain incognito as long as possible while she explored this unsuspected outdoor salon.

It was a universe of strangers. Not once did she see a face she recognized. These people, whatever their achievements, were not the publicized great men of the empire. She saw no patrons and only one man with the insignia of a knight on his coat. And when she approached him, she recognized from the alien religious symbol connected with the other markings, that his knighthood was of provincial origin.

He was standing beside a fountain near a cluster of guest homes. The fountain spewed forth a skillfully blended mixture of water and smoke. It made a pretty show, the smoke rising up in thin, steamlike clouds. As she paused beside the fountain there was a cessation of the cooling breeze, and she felt a wave of heat that reminded her of steaming hot lower town. Lydia concentrated on the man and on her desire for information.

'I'm new here,' she said engagingly. 'Has this center been long in existence?'

'About three years, madam. After all, our young prince is only twenty-four!'

'Prince?' asked Lydia.

The knight, a rugged-faced individual of forty, was apologetic.

'I beg your pardon. It is an old word of my province, signifying a leader of high birth. I discovered on my various journeys into the pits, where the atom gods live, and where once cities existed, that the name was of legendary origin. This is according to old books I found in remnants of buildings.'

Lydia said, shocked: 'You went down into one of the reputed homes of the gods, where the eternal fires burn?'

The knight chuckled. 'Some of them are less eternal than others, I discovered.'

'But weren't you afraid of being physically damaged?'

'Madam,' shrugged the other, 'I am nearly fifty years old. Why should I worry if my blood is slightly damaged by the aura of the gods.'

Lydia hesitated, interested. But she had let herself be drawn from her purpose. 'Prince,' she repeated now, grimly. Applied to Clane, the title had a ring she didn't like. Prince Clane. It was rather stunning to discover that there were men who thought of him as a leader. What had happened to the old prejudices against mutations? She was about to speak again when, for the first time, she actually looked at the fountain.

She pulled back with a gasp. The water was bubbling. A mist of steam arose from it. Her gaze shot up to the spout, and now she saw that it was not smoke and water spewing up from it. It was boiling, steaming water. Water that roiled and rushed and roared. More hot water than she had ever seen from an artificial source. Memory came of the blackened pots in which slaves heated her daily hot water needs.

And she felt a spurt of pure jealousy at the extravagant luxury of a fountain of boiling water on one's grounds.

'But how does he do it?' she gasped. 'Has he tapped an underground hot spring?'

'No madam, the water comes from the stream over there.' The knight pointed. 'It is brought here in tiled pipes, and then runs off into the various guest homes.'

'Is there some arrangement of hot coals?'

'Nothing, madam.' The knight was beginning to enjoy himself visibly. 'There is an opening under the fountain, and you can look in if you wish.'

Lydia wished. She was fascinated. She realized that she had let herself be distracted, but for the moment that was of secondary importance. She watched with bright eyes as the knight opened the little door in the cement, and then she stooped beside him to peer in. It took several seconds to become accustomed to the dim light inside, but finally she was able to make out the massive base of the spout, and then the six-inch pipe that ran into it. Lydia straightened slowly. The man shut the door matter-of-factly. As he turned, she asked:

'But how does it work?'

The knight shrugged. 'Some say that the water gods of Mars have been friendly to him ever since they helped his late father to win the war against the Martians. You will recall that the canal waters boiled in a frightful fury, thus confusing the Martians as they were attacked. And then, again, others say that it is the atom gods helping their favorite mutation.'

'Oh!' said Lydia. This was the kind of talk she could understand. She had never in her life worried about what the gods might think of her actions. And she was not going to start now. She straightened and glared imperiously at the man.

'Don't be such a fool,' she said. 'A man who has dared to penetrate the homes of the gods should have more sense than to repeat old wives' tales like that.'

The man gaped. She turned away before he could speak, and marched off to her chair. 'To the house!' she commanded her slaves.

They had her at the front entrance of the residence before it struck her that she had not learned the tremendous and precious secret of the boiling fountain.

She caught Clane by surprise. She entered the house in her flamboyant manner, and by the time a slave saw her, and ran to his master's laboratory to bring the news of her coming, it was too late. She loomed in the doorway, as Clane turned from a corpse he was dissecting. To her immense disappointment he did not freeze up in one of his emotional spasms. She had expected it, and her plan was to look over the laboratory quietly and without interference.

But Clane came towards her. 'Honorable grandmother,' he said. And knelt to kiss her hand. He came up with an easy grace. 'I hope,' he said with an apparent eagerness, 'that you will have the time and inclination to see my home and my work. Both have interesting features.'

His whole manner was so human, so engaging, that she was disconcerted anew, not an easy emotion for her to experience. She shook off the weakness impatiently. Her first words affirmed her purpose in visiting him:

'Yes,' she said, 'I shall be happy to see your home. I have been intending for some years to visit you, but I have been so busy.' She sighed. 'The duties of statecraft can be very onerous.'

The beautiful face looked properly sympathetic. A delicate hand pointed at the dead body, which those slim fingers had been working over. The soft voice informed that the purpose of the dissection was to discover the position pattern of the organs and muscles and bones.

'I have cut open dead mutations,' Clane said, 'and compared them with normal bodies.'

Lydia could not quite follow the purpose. After all, each

mutation was different, depending upon the way the god forces had affected them. She said as much. The glowing blue eyes of the mutation looked at her speculatively.

'It is commonly known,' he said, 'that mutations seldom live beyond the age of thirty. Naturally,' he went on, with a faint smile, 'since I am now within six years of that milestone, the possibility weighs upon me. Joquin, that astute old scientist, who unfortunately is now dead, believed that the deaths resulted from inner tensions, due to the manner in which mutations were treated by their fellows. He felt that if those tensions could be removed, as they have been to some extent in me, a normal span of life would follow as also would normal intelligence. I'd better correct that. He believed that a mutation, given a chance, would be able to realize his normal *potentialities*, which might be either super- or sub-normal compared to human beings.'

Clane smiled. 'So far,' he said, 'I have noticed nothing out of the ordinary in myself.'

Lydia thought of the boiling fountain, and felt a chill. *That old fool, Joquin,* she thought in a cold fury. *Why didn't I pay more attention to what he was doing? He's created an alien mind in our midst within striking distance of the top of the power group of the empire.*

The sense of immense disaster possibilities grew. *Death,* she thought, *within hours after the old man is gone. No risks can be taken with this creature.*

Suddenly, she was interested in nothing but the accessibility of the various rooms of the house to assassins. Clane seemed to realize her mood, for after a brief tour of the laboratory, of which she remembered little, he began the journey from room to room. Now, her eyes and attention sharpened. She peered into doors, examined window arrangements, and did not fail to note with satisfaction the universal carpeting of the floors. Meerl would be able to attack without warning sounds.

'And your bedroom?' she asked finally.

161

'We're coming to it,' said Clane. 'It's downstairs, adjoining the laboratory. There's something else in the lab that I want to show you. I wasn't sure at first that I would, but now' – his smile was angelic – 'I will.'

The corridor that led from the living room to the bedroom was almost wide enough to be an ante-room. The walls were hung with drapes from floor to ceiling, which was odd. Lydia, who had no inhibitions, lifted one drape, and peered under it. The wall was vaguely warm, like an ember, and it was built of temple stone. She looked at Clane questioningly.

'I have some god metals in the house. Naturally, I am taking no chances. There's another corridor leading from the laboratory to the bedroom.'

What interested Lydia was that neither door of the bedroom had either a lock or a bolt on it. She thought about that tensely, as she followed Clane through the ante-room that led to the laboratory. He wouldn't, it seemed to her, leave himself so unprotected forever.

The assassins must strike before he grew alarmed, the sooner the better. Regretfully, she decided it would have to wait until Tews was confirmed as heir to the throne. She grew aware that Clane had paused beside a dark box.

'Gelo Greeant,' he said, 'brought this to me from one of his journeys into the realms of the gods. I'm going to step inside, and you go around to the right there, and look into the dark glass. You will be amazed.'

Lydia obeyed, puzzled. For a moment, after Clane had disappeared inside, the glass remained dark. Then it began to glow faintly. She retreated a step before that alien shining-ness, then, remembering who she was, stood her ground. And then she screamed.

A skeleton glowed through the glass. And the shadow of a beating heart, the shadow of expanding and contracting lungs. As she watched, petrified now, the skeleton arm moved, and seemed to come towards her, but drew back again. To her paralyzed brain came at last comprehension.

She was looking at the inside of a living human being. At Clane. Abruptly, that interested her. *Clane*. Like lightning, her eyes examined his bone structure. She noticed the cluster of ribs around his heart and lungs, the special thickness of his collar bones. Her gaze flashed down towards his kidneys, but this time she was too slow. The light faded, and went out. Clane emerged from the box.

'Well,' he asked, pleased, 'what do you think of my little gift from the gods?'

The phraseology startled Lydia. All the way home, she thought of it. Gift from the gods! In a sense it was. The atom gods had sent their mutation a method for seeing himself, for studying his own body. What could *their* purpose be?

She had a conviction that, if the gods really existed, and if, as seemed evident, they were helping Clane, then the Deities of the Atom were again – as they had in legendary times – interfering with human affairs.

The sinking sensation that came had only one hopeful rhythm. And that was like a drumbeat inside her: Kill! And soon. *Soon!*

But the days passed. And the demands of political stability absorbed all her intention. Nevertheless, in the midst of a score of new troubles, she did not forget Clane.

The return of Tews was a triumph for his mother's diplomacy and a great moment for himself. His ship came down in the square of the pillars, and there, before an immense cheering throng, he was welcomed by the Lord Leader and the entire patronate. The parade that followed was led by a unit of five thousand glitteringly arrayed horse-mounted troops, followed by ten thousand foot soldiers, one thousand engineers and scores of mechanical engines for throwing weights and rocks at defensive barriers. Then came the Lord Leader, Lydia and Tews, and the three hundred patrons and six hundred knights of the empire. The rear of the parade was brought up by another cavalry unit of five thousand men.

From the rostrum that jutted out from the palace, the Lord Leader, his lion's voice undimmed by age, welcomed his stepson. All the lies that had ever been told about the reason for Tews' exile were coolly and grandly confirmed now. He had gone away to meditate. He had wearied of the cunnings and artifices of government. He had returned only after repeated pleadings on the part of his mother and of the Lord Leader.

'As you know,' concluded the Lord Leader, 'seven years ago, I was bereft of my natural heir in the moment of the greatest military triumph the empire has ever experienced, the conquest of the Martians. Today, as I stand before you, no longer young, no longer able to bear the full weight of either military or political command, it is an immeasurable relief to me to be able to tell the people with confidence and conviction: Here in this modest and unassuming member of my family, the son of my dear wife, Lydia, I ask you to put your trust. To the soldiers I say, this is no weakling. Remember the Cimbri, conquered under his skillful generalship when he was but a youth of twenty-five. Particularly, I direct my words to the hard-pressed soldiers on Venus, where false leaders have misled the island provinces of the fierce Venusian tribes to an ill-fated rebellion. Ill-fated, I say, because as soon as possible Tews will be there with the largest army assembled by the empire since the war of the Martians. I am going to venture a prediction. I am going to predict that within two years the Venusian leaders will be hanging on long lines of posts of the type they are now using to murder prisoners. I predict that these hangings will be achieved by *Co-Lord Leader* General Tews, whom I now publicly appoint my heir and successor, and on whose behalf I now say, Take warning, all those who would have ill befall the empire. Here is the man who will confound you and your schemes.'

The dazzled Tews, who had been advised by his mother of the extent of the victory she had won for him, stepped forward to acknowledge the cheers and to say a few words. 'Not too much,' his mother had warned him. 'Be non-committal.' But Lord Tews had other plans. He had carefully thought out the pattern of his future actions, and he had one announcement to make, in addition to a ringing acceptance of the military leadership that had been offered him, and a promise that the Venusian leaders would indeed suffer the fate which the Linn of Linn had promised them. The announcement had to do with the title of Co-Lord Leader, which had been bestowed on him.

'I am sure,' he told the crowd, 'that you will agree with me that the title of Lord Leader belongs uniquely to the first and greatest man of Linn. I therefore request, and will hold it mandatory upon government leaders, that I be addressed as Lord Adviser. It shall be my pleasure to act as adviser to both the Lord Leader and to the patronate, and it is in this role that I wish to be known henceforth to the people of the mighty Linnan empire. Thank you for listening to me, and I now advise you that there will be games for three days in the bowls, and that free food will be served throughout the city during that time at my expense. Go and have a good time, and may the gods of the atoms bring you all good luck.'

During the first minute after he had finished, Lydia was appalled. Was Tews mad to have refused the title of Lord Leader? The joyful yelping of the mob soothed her a little, and then, slowly, as she followed Tews and the old man along the promenade that led from the rostrum to the palace gates, she began to realize the cleverness of the new title. Lord Adviser. Why, it would be a veritable shield against the charges of those who were always striving to rouse the people against the absolute government of the

Linns. It was clear that the long exile had sharpened rather than dulled the mind of her son.

The Lord Leader, too, as the days passed, and the new character of Tews came to the fore, was having regrets. Certain restrictions, which he had imposed upon his stepson during his residence on Awai, seemed unduly severe and ill-advised in retrospect. He should not, for instance, have permitted Tews' wife to divorce him, but should instead have insisted that she accompany him.

It seemed to him now that there was only one solution. He rushed the marriage between Tews and Gudrun, and then dispatched them to Venus on their honeymoon, taking the precaution of sending a quarter of a million men along, so that the future Lord Leader could combine his love-making with war-making.

Having solved his main troubles, the Lord Leader gave himself up to the chore of aging gracefully and of thinking out ways and means whereby his other heirs might be spared from the death which the thoughtful Lydia was undoubtedly planning for them.

The Lord Leader was dying. He lay in his bed of pillows sweating out his last hours. All the wiles of the palace physician – including an ice-cold bath, a favorite remedy of his, failed to rally the stricken great man. In a few hours, the patronate was informed, and state leaders were invited to officiate at the death bed. The Linn of Linn had some years before introduced a law to the effect that no ruler was ever to be allowed to die incommunicado. It was a thoughtful precaution against poisoning, which he had considered extremely astute at the time, but which now, as he watched the crowds surging outside the open doors of his bedroom, and listened to the subdued roar of voices, seemed somewhat less than dignified.

He motioned to Lydia. She came gliding over, and nodded at his request that the door be closed. Some of the people in the bedroom looked at each other, as she shooed them away, but the mild voice of the Lord Leader urged them, and so they trooped out. It took about ten minutes to clear the room. The Lord Leader lay, then, looking sadly up at his wife. He had an unpleasant duty to perform, and the unfortunate atmosphere of imminent death made the affair not less but more sordid. He began without preliminary:

'In recent years I have frequently hinted to you about fears I have had about the health of my relatives. Your reactions have left me no recourse but to doubt that you now have left in your heart any of the tender feelings which are supposed to be the common possession of womankind.'

'What's this?' said Lydia. She had her first flash of insight as to what was coming. She said grimly, 'My dear husband, have you gone out of your head?'

The Lord Leader went on calmly: 'For once, Lydia, I am not going to speak in diplomatic language. Do not go through with your plans to have my relatives assassinated as soon as I am dead.'

The language was too strong for the woman. The color deserted her cheeks, and she was suddenly as pale as lead. 'I,' she breathed, 'kill your kin!'

The once steel-gray, now watery eyes stared at her with remorseless purpose. 'I have put Jerrin and Draid beyond your reach. They are in command of powerful armies, and my will leaves explicit instructions about their future. Some of the men, who are administrators, are likewise protected to some extent. The women are not so fortunate. My own two daughters are safe, I think. The elder is childless and without ambition, and Gudrun is now the wife of Tews. But I want a promise from you that you will not attempt to harm her, and that you will similarly refrain from taking any action against her three children, by her first marriage. I want your promise to include the children of my two cousins, my brother and sister, and all their descendants, and finally I want a promise from you about the Lady Tania, her two daughters, and her son, Lord Clane.'

'Clane!' said Lydia. Her mind had started working as he talked. It leaped past the immense insult she was being offered, past all the names, to that one individual. She spoke the name again, more loudly: '*Clane!*'

Her eyes were distorted pools. She glared at her husband with a bitter intensity. 'And what,' she said, 'makes you think, who suspect me capable of such crimes, that I would keep such a promise to a dead man?'

The old man was suddenly less bleak. 'Because, Lydia,' he said quietly, 'you are more than just a mother protecting her young. You are the Lady Leader whose political sagacity and general intelligence made possible the virtually united empire, which Tews will now inherit. You are at heart an honest woman, and if you made me a promise I think you would keep it.'

She knew he was merely hoping now. And her calmness came back. She watched him with bright eyes, conscious of how weak was the power of a dying man, no matter how desperately he strove to fasten his desires and wishes upon his descendants.

'Very well, my old darling,' she soothed him, 'I will make you the promise you wish. I guarantee not to murder any of these people you have mentioned.'

The Lord Leader gazed at her in despair. He had, he realized, not remotely touched her. This woman's basic integrity – and he knew it was there – could no longer be reached through her emotions. He abandoned that line immediately.

'Lydia,' he said, 'don't anger Clane by trying to kill him.'

'Anger him!' said Lydia. She spoke sharply, because the phrase was so unexpected. She gazed at her husband with a startled wonder, as if she couldn't be quite sure that she had heard him correctly. She repeated the words slowly, listening to them as if she somehow might catch their secret meaning: 'Anger him?'

'You must realize,' said the Lord Leader, 'that you have from fifteen to twenty years of life to endure after my death, provided you hoard your physical energies. If you spend those years trying to run the world through Tews, you will quickly and quite properly be discarded by him. That is something which is not yet clear to you, and so I advise you to reorientate yourself. You must seek your power through other men. Jerrin will not need you, and Draid needs only Jerrin. Tews can and will dispense with you. That leaves Clane, of the great men. He can use you. Through him, therefore, you will be able to retain a measure of your power.'

Her gaze was on his mouth every moment that he talked. She listened as his voice grew weaker, and finally trailed into nothingness. In the silence that fell between them, Lydia sat comprehending at last, so it seemed to her. This was Clane talking through his dying grandfather. This was Clane's cunning appeal to the fears she might have for her own future. The Clane who had frustrated her designs on the slave girl, Selk, was now desperately striving to anticipate her designs on him.

Deep inside her, as she sat there watching the old man die, she laughed. Three months before, recognizing the signals of internal disintegration in her husband, she had insisted that Tews be recalled from Venus, and Jerrin appointed in his place. Her skill in timing was now bearing fruit, and it was working out even better than she had hoped. It would be at least a week before Tews' spaceship would arrive at Linn. During that week the widow Lydia would be all-powerful.

It was possible that she would have to abandon her plans against some of the other members of the family. But they at least were human. It was Clane, the alien, the creature, the nonhuman, who must be destroyed at any cost.

She had one week in which she could, if necessary, use three whole legions and a hundred spaceships to smash him and the gods that had made him.

169

The long, tense conversation had dimmed the spark of life in the Lord Leader. Ten minutes before sunset, the great throngs outside saw the gates open, and Lydia leaning on the arms of two old patrons came dragging out, followed by a crowd of noblemen. In a moment it was general knowledge that the Linn of Linn was dead.

Darkness settled over a city that for fifty years had known no other ruler.

Lydia wakened lazily on the morrow of the death of the Lord Leader. She stretched and yawned deliciously, reveling in the cool, clean sheets. Then she opened her eyes, and stared at the ceiling. Bright sunlight was pouring through open windows, and Dalat hovered at the end of the bed.

'You asked to be wakened early, honorable lady,' she said.

There was a note of respect in her voice that Lydia had never noticed before. Her mind poised, pondering the imponderable difference. And then she got it. The Linn was dead. For one week, she was not the legal but the *de facto* head of the city and state. None would dare to oppose the mother of the new Leader – uh, the Lord Adviser Tews. Glowing, Lydia sat up in the bed.

'Has there been any word yet from Meerl?'

'None, gracious lady.'

She frowned over that. Her assassin had formed a relationship with her, which she had first accepted reluctantly, then, recognizing its value, with smiling grace. He had access to her bedroom at all hours of the day or night. And it was rather surprising that he to whom she had intrusted such an important errand, should not have reported long since.

Dalat was speaking again. 'I think, madam, you should inform him, however, that it is unwise for him to have parcels delivered here addressed to himself in your care.'

Lydia was climbing out of bed. She looked up, astounded and angry.

'Why, the insolent fool, has he done that? Let me see the parcel.'

She tore off the wrapping, furiously. And found herself staring down at a vase filled with ashes. A note was tied around the lip of the vase. Puzzled, she turned it over and read:

Dear Madam:

Your assassin was too moist. The atom gods, once roused, become frantic in the presence of moisture.

Signed, Uranium

For the council of gods.

CRASH! The sound of the vase smashing on the floor shocked her out of a blur of numbness. Wide-eyed, she stared down at the little pile of ashes amid the broken pieces of pottery. With tense fingers she reached down, and picked up the note. This time, not the meaning of the note, but the signature, snatched at her attention: *Uranium.*

It was like a dash of cold water. With bleak eyes, she gazed at the ashes of what had been Meerl, her most trustworthy assassin. She realized consciously that she felt this death more keenly than that of her husband. The old man had hung on too long. So long as life continued in his bones, he had the power to make changes. When he had finally breathed his last, she had breathed easily for the first time in years, as if a weight had lifted from her soul.

But now – a new weight began to settle in its place, and her breath came in quick gasps. She kicked viciously at the ashes, as if she would shove the meaning of them out of her life. How could Meerl have failed? Meerl, the cautious, the skillful, Meerl the bold and brave and daring!

'Dalat!'

'Yes, Lady?'

With narrowed eyes and pursed lips, Lydia considered the action she was contemplating. But not for long.

'Call Colonel Maljan. Tell him to come at once.'

She had one week to kill a man. It was time to come out into the open.

Lydia had herself carried to the foot of the hill that led up to the estate of Lord Clane. She wore a heavy veil and used as carriers slaves who had never appeared with her in public, and an old, unmarked chair of one of her ladies in waiting. Her eyes, that peered out of this excellent disguise, were bright with excitement.

The morning was unnaturally hot. Blasts of warm air came sweeping down the hill from the direction of Clane's house. And, after a little, she saw that the soldiers one hundred yards up the hill, had stopped. The pause grew long and puzzling, and she was just about to climb out of the chair, when she saw Maljan coming towards her. The dark-eyed, hawk-nosed officer was sweating visibly.

'Madam,' he said, 'we cannot get near that fence up there. It seems to be on fire.'

'I can see no flame.' Curtly.

'It isn't that kind of a fire.'

Lydia was amazed to see that the man was trembling with fright. 'There's something unnatural up there,' he said. 'I don't like it.'

She came out of her chair then, the chill of defeat settling upon her. 'Are you an idiot?' she snarled. 'If you can't get past the fence, drop men from spaceships into the grounds.'

'I've already sent for them,' he said, 'but —'

'BUT!' said Lydia, and it was a curse. 'I'll go up and have a look at that fence myself.'

She went up, and stopped short where the soldiers were gasping on the ground. The heat had already blasted at her, but at that point it took her breath away. She felt as if her lungs would sear inside her. In a minute her throat was ash dry.

She stooped behind a bush. But it was no good. She saw that the leaves had seared and darkened. And then she was retreating behind a little knoblike depression in the hill. She crouched behind it, too appalled to think. She grew aware of Maljan working up towards her. He arrived, gasping, and it was several seconds before he could speak. Then he pointed up.

'The ships!' he said.

She watched them creep in low over the trees. They listed a little as they crossed the fence, then sank out of sight behind the trees that hid the meadow of Clane's estate. Five ships in all came into sight and disappeared over the rim of the estate. Lydia was keenly aware that their arrival relieved the soldiers sprawling helplessly all around her.

'Tell the men to get down the hill,' she commanded hoarsely, and made the hastiest retreat of all.

The street below was still almost deserted. A few people had paused to watch in a puzzled fashion the activities of the soldiers, but they moved on when commanded to do so by guards who had been posted in the road.

It was something to know that the campaign was still a private affair.

She waited. No sound came from beyond the trees where the ships had gone. It was as if they had fallen over some precipice into an abyss of silence. Half an hour went by, and then, abruptly, a ship came into sight. Lydia caught her breath, then watched the machine float towards them over the trees, and settle in the road below. A man in uniform came out. Maljan waved at him, and ran over to meet him. The conversation that followed was very earnest. At last Maljan turned, and with evident reluctance came towards her. He said in a low tone:

'The house itself is offering an impregnable heat barrier. But they have talked to Lord Clane. He wants to speak to you.'

She took that with a tense thoughtfulness. The realization had already penetrated deep that this stalemate might go on for days.

If I could get near him, she decided, remorselessly, *by pretending to consider his proposals —*

It seemed to work perfectly. By the time the spaceship lifted her over the fence, the heat that exuded from the walls of the house had died away to a bearable temperature. And, incredibly, Clane agreed that she could bring a dozen soldiers into the house as guards.

As she entered the house, she had her first sense of eeriness. There was no one around, not a slave, not a movement of life. She headed in the direction of the bedroom, more slowly with each step. The first grudging admiration came. It seemed unbelievable that his preparations could have been so thorough as to include the evacuation of all his slaves. And yet it all fitted. Not once in her dealings with him had he made a mistake.

'Grandmother, I wouldn't come any closer.'

She stopped short. She saw that she had come to within a yard of the corridor that led to his bedroom. Clane was standing at the far end, and he seemed to be quite alone and undefended.

'Come any nearer,' he said, 'and death will strike you automatically.'

She could see nothing unusual. The corridor was much as she remembered it. The drapes had been taken down from the walls, revealing the temple stone underneath. And yet, standing there, she felt a faint warmth, unnatural and, suddenly, deadly. It was only with an effort that she threw off the feeling. She parted her lips to give the command, but Clane spoke first:

'Grandmother, do nothing rash. Consider, before you defy the powers of the atom. Has what happened today not yet penetrated to your intelligence? Surely, you can see that whom the gods love no mortal can harm.'

The woman was bleak with her purpose. 'You have misquoted the old saying,' she said drably. 'Whom the gods love die young.'

And yet, once more, she hesitated. The stunning thing was that he continued to stand there less than thirty feet away, unarmed, unprotected, a faint smile on his lips. How far he has come, she thought. His nervous affliction, conquered now. And what a marvelously beautiful face, so calm, so confident.

Confident! Could it be that there *were* gods?

Could it be?

'Grandmother, I warn you, make no move. If you must prove that the gods will strike on my behalf, send your soldiers. BUT DO NOT MOVE YOURSELF.'

She felt weak, her legs numb. The conviction that was pouring through her, the certainty that he was not bluffing brought a parallel realization that she could not back down. And yet she must.

She recognized that there was insanity in her terrible indecision. And knew, then, that she was not a person who was capable of conscious suicide. Therefore, quit, retreat, accept the reality of rout.

She parted her lips to give the order to retire when it happened.

What motive impelled the soldier to action was never clear. Perhaps he grew impatient. Perhaps he felt there would be promotion for him. Whatever the reason, he suddenly cried out, 'I'll get his gizzard for you!' And leaped forward.

He had not gone more than a half dozen feet past Lydia when he began to disintegrate. He crumpled like an empty sack. Where he had been, a mist of ashes floated lazily to the floor.

There was one burst of heat, then. It came in a gust of unearthly hot wind, barely touched Lydia, who had instinctively jerked aside, but struck the soldiers behind her. There was a hideous masculine squalling and whimpering, followed by a mad scramble. A door slammed, and she was alone. She straightened, conscious that the air from the corridor was still blowing hot. She remained cautiously where she was, and called:

'Clane!'

The answer came instantly. 'Yes, grandmother?'

175

For a moment, then, she hesitated, experiencing all the agony of a general about to surrender. At last, slowly:

'What do you want?'

'An end to attacks on me. Full political co-operation, but people must remain unaware of it as long as we can possibly manage it.'

'Oh!'

She began to breathe easier. She had had a fear that he would demand public recognition.

'And if I don't?' she said at last.

'Death!'

It was quietly spoken. The woman did not even think to doubt. She was being given a chance. But there was one thing more, one tremendous thing more.

'Clane, is your ultimate goal the Lord Leadership?'

'No!'

His answer was too prompt. She felt a thrill of disbelief, a sick conviction that he was lying. But she was glad after a moment that he had denied. In a sense it bound him. Her thoughts soared to all the possibilities of the situation, then came down again to the sober necessity of this instant.

'Very well,' she said, and it was little more than a sigh, 'I accept.'

Back at the palace, she sent an assassin to perform an essential operation against the one outsider who knew the Lady Lydia had suffered a major defeat. It was late afternoon when the double report came in: The exciting information that Tews had landed sooner than anticipated, and was even then on his way to the palace. And the satisfying words that Colonel Maljan lay dead in an alleyway with a knife in one of his kidneys.

It was only then that it struck her that she was now in the exact position that her dead husband had advised for her own safety and well-being.

Tears and the realization of her great loss came as late as that.

THE CATAAAAA

THE USUAL group was gathering in the bar. Cathy was already pretending she was far gone, Ted was busy putting on his stupid look. Myra giggled three times the way a musician tunes his instrument for the evening. Jones was talking to Gord, in his positive fashion. Gord said 'Glub!' every few seconds, just as if he was listening. And Morton tried to draw attention to himself by remaining aloof and intellectual looking far down in his chair.

No one noticed the slight, slim man sitting on a stool before the bar. The man kept glancing at the group; but just when he joined them, or who invited him, no one had any clear idea. Nor did it occur to anyone to tell him to go away.

The stranger said, 'You were talking about the basic characteristics of human nature —'

Myra giggled, 'Is that what we were talking about? I wondered.'

The laughter that followed did not deter the newcomer.

'It so happens that I have had an experience which illustrates the point. It began one day when I was glancing through the newspaper, and I ran across a circus advertisement . . .'

At the top of the ad (he went on) was a large question mark followed by some equally large exclamation marks. Then:

WHAT IS IT?
IT'S THE CAT
COME AND SEE THE CAT
THE CAT WILL STARTLE YOU
THE CAT WILL AMAZE YOU
SEE THE CAT AT THE FREAK SHOW

177

In smaller letters at the bottom of the ad was the information that the cat was being 'shown under the personal direction of Silkey Travis'.

Until that point I had been reading with a vague interest and curiosity. The name made me jump.

Good lord! I thought. *It's him. It's Silkey Travis on that card.*

I hurried to my desk, and took out a card that had come in the mail two days before. At the time it had made no sense to me at all. The words written on the back in a fine script seemed pure gibberish, and the photograph on the front, though familiar, unlocked no real memory. It was of a man with a haunted look on his face, sitting in a small cage. I now recognized it as being a likeness of Silkey Travis, not as I had known him fifteen or so years before, but plumper, older, as he would be now.

I returned to my chair, and sat musing about the past.

Even in those days, his name had fitted Silkey Travis. At high school he organized the bathing beauty contest, and gave the first prize to his cousin and the second prize to the girl who was the teacher's pet of the most teachers. The students' science exhibition, a collection of local lizards, snakes, insects and a few Indian artifacts, was an annual affair, which brought a turnout of admiring parents. Invariably, it was Silkey who organized it. Plays, holiday shows and other paraphernalia of school pastimes felt the weight of his guiding hand and circus spirit.

After graduating from high school, I went on to State college to major in biology, and I lost sight of Silkey for seven years. Then I saw an item in one of the papers to the effect that local boy Silkey Travis was doing well in the big town, having just purchased a 'piece' of a vaudeville show, and that he also owned a 'piece' in a beach concession in New Jersey.

Again, there was silence. And now, here he was, no doubt 'piece' owner of the circus freak show.

178

Having solved the mystery of the postcard, so it seemed to me, I felt amused and tolerant. I wondered if Silkey had sent the card to all his former school companions. I decided not to puzzle any more about the meaning of the words written on the back. The scheme behind them was all too obvious.

Sitting there, I had absolutely no intention of going to the circus. I went to bed at my usual hour, and woke up with a start some hours later to realize that I was not alone. The sensations that came to me as I lay there have been described by Johnson in his book on morbid fears.

I lived in a quiet neighborhood, and the silence was intense. Presently, I could hear the labored pounding of my heart. Poisons surged into my stomach; gas formed and leaked up to my mouth bringing a bitter taste. I had to fight to keep my breath steady.

And still I could see nothing. The dark fears ran their courses, and the first thought came that I must have had a nightmare. I began to feel ashamed of myself. I mumbled:

'Who's there?'

No answer.

I climbed out of bed, and turned on the light. The room was empty. But still I wasn't satisfied. I went out into the hall; then I examined the clothes closet and bathroom. Finally, dissatisfied, I tested the window fastening – and it was there I received my shock. Painted on the outer side of the pane of one of the windows were the letters:

The cat requests that you come to the circus.

I went back to bed so furious that I thought of having Silkey arrested. When I woke up in the morning the sign was gone from the window.

By the time breakfast was over, my temper of the night had cooled. I was even able to feel a pitying amusement at the desperate desire of Silkey to let his old acquaintances know what a big shot he was. Before starting off to my morning classes at State, I looked under my bedroom window. I found what looked like footprints, but they were not human, so I decided that Silkey must have taken care to leave no tracks of his own.

At class, just before noon, one of the students asked me whether there was any good explanation in biological science for freaks. I gave the usual explanation of variabilities, nutritional deficiencies, diseases, frustration of brain development affecting the shape of the body, and so on. I finished dryly that for further information I would direct him to my old friend, Silkey Travis, director of freaks at the Pagley-Matterson circus.

The offhand remark caused a sensation. I was informed that a freak at the circus had prompted the original question. 'A strange, cat-like creature,' the student said in a hushed voice, 'that examines you with the same interest that you examine it.'

The bell rang at that moment, and I was spared the necessity of making a comment. I remember thinking, however, that people hadn't changed much. They were still primarily interested in eccentricity whereas, as a scientist, the processes of normalcy seemed to me far more fascinating.

I still had no intention of going to the circus. But on the way home that afternoon I put my hand in my breast pocket, and drew out the postcard with the photograph of Silkey on the front. I turned it over absently, and read again the message that was on it:

The interspatial problem of delivering mail involves enormous energy problems, which affect time differentials. Accordingly, it is possible that this card will arrive before I know who you are. As a precaution I am sending another one to the circus with your name and address on it, and the two cards will go out together.

Do not worry too much about the method of delivery. I simply put an instrument into a mailbox. This precipitates the cards into the box on Earth, and they will then be picked up and delivered in the usual fashion. The precipitator then dissolves.

The photograph speaks for itself.

It didn't. Which is what began to irritate me again. I jammed the card back into my pocket, half-minded to phone up Silkey and ask him what the silly thing meant, if anything. I refrained, of course. It wasn't important enough.

When I got out of bed the next morning, the words *The cat wants to talk to you!* were scrawled on the outside of the same window pane. They must have been there for a long time. Because, even as I stared at them, they began to fade. By the time I finished breakfast they were gone.

I was disturbed now rather than angry. Such persistence on Silkey's part indicated neurotic overtones in his character. It was possible that I ought to go to his show, and so give him the petty victory that would lay to rest his ghost, which had now haunted me two nights running. However, it was not till after lunch that a thought occurred to me that suddenly clinched my intention. I remembered Virginia.

For two years I had been professor of biology at State. It was an early ambition which, now that I had realized it, left me at a loose end for the first time in my life. Accordingly, for the first time in my rather drab existence the mating urge was upon me. Virginia was the girl, and, unfortunately, she regarded me as a cross between a fossil and a precision brain. I felt sure that the idea of marrying me had not yet occurred to her.

For some time it had seemed to me that if I could only convince her, without loss of dignity, that I was a romantic fellow she might be fooled into saying yes. What better method than to pretend that I still got excited over circuses, and as a grand climax to the evening I would take her in to see Silkey Travis, and hope that my acquaintance with such a character would thrill her exotic soul.

181

The first hurdle was bridged when I called her up, and she agreed to go to the circus with me. I put the best possible face on for the preliminaries, riding the ferris wheel and such juvenilia. But the moment of the evening for me came when I suggested that we go and see the freaks being shown by my old friend, Silkey Travis.

It really went over. Virginia stopped and looked at me almost accusingly.

'Philip,' she said, 'you're not trying to pretend that you know a person called Silkey?' She drew a deep breath. 'That I have to see.'

Silkey came through beautifully. He was not in when we entered, but the ticket taker called into some rear compartment. And a minute later Silkey came charging into the main freak tent. He was plump with the plumpness of a well-fed shark. His eyes were narrowed as if he had spent the past fifteen years calculating the best methods of using other people for his own advantage. He had none of the haunted look of the photograph, but there were ghosts in his face. Ghosts of greed and easy vices, ghosts of sharp dealing and ruthlessness. He was all that I had hoped for, and, best of all, he was pathetically glad to see me. His joy had the special quality of the lonely nomad who is at last looking longingly at the settled side of life. We both overdid the greeting a little, but we were about equally pleased at each other's enthusiasm. The hellos and introductions over, Silkey grew condescending.

'Brick was in a while ago. Said you were teaching at State. Congrats. Always knew you had it in you.'

I passed over that as quickly as possible. 'How about showing us around, Silkey, and telling us about yourself?'

We had already seen the fat woman and the human skeleton, but Silkey took us back and told us *his* life history with them. How he had found them, and helped them to their present fame. He was a little verbose, so on occasion I had to hurry him along. But finally we came to a small tent

182

within the tent, over the closed canvas entrance of which was painted simply, THE CAT. I had noticed it before, and the chatter of the barker who stood in front of it had already roused my curiosity:

'The cat . . . come in and see the cat. Folks, this is no ordinary event, but the thrill of a lifetime. Never before has such an animal as this been seen in a circus. A biological phenomenon that has amazed scientists all over the country. . . . Folks, this is special. Tickets are twenty-five cents, but if you're not satisfied you can get your money back. That's right. That's what I said. You can get your money back merely by stepping up and asking for it. . . .'

And so on. However, his ballyhoo was not the most enticing angle. What began to titillate my nerves was the reaction of the people who went inside. They were allowed to enter in groups, and there must have been a guide inside, because his barely audible voice would mumble on for some minutes, and then it would rise to a hearable level, as he said, 'And now, folks, I will draw aside the curtain and show you – the cat!'

The curtain must have been pulled with a single jerk, on a carefully timed basis. For the word *cat* was scarcely out of his mouth, when the audience reaction would sound:

'Aaaaaa!'

Distinct, unmistakable exhalation of the breaths of a dozen startled people. There would follow an uncomfortable silence. Then, slowly, the people would emerge and hurry to the outer exit. Not one, that I was aware of, asked for his money back.

There was a little embarrassment at the gate. Silkey started to mumble something about only owning part of the show, so he couldn't give passes. But I ended that by quickly purchasing the necessary tickets, and we went inside with the next group.

The animal that sat in an armchair on the dais was about

five feet long and quite slender. It had a cat's head and vestiges of fur. It looked like an exaggerated version of the walkie-talkie animals in comic books.

At that point resemblance to normalcy ended.

It was alien. It was not a cat at all. I recognized that instantly. The structure was all wrong. It took me a moment to identify the radical variations.

The head! High foreheaded it was, and not low and receding. The face was smooth and almost hairless. It had character and strength, and intelligence. The body was well balanced on long, straight legs. The arms were smooth, ending in short but unmistakable fingers, surmounted by thin, sharp claws.

But it was the eyes that were really different. They looked normal enough, slightly slanted, properly lidded, about the same size as the eyes of human beings. *But they danced.* They shifted twice, even three times as swiftly as human eyes. Their balanced movement at such a high speed indicated vision that could read photographically reduced print across a room. What sharp, what incredibly sharp images that brain must see.

All this I saw within the space of a few seconds. Then the creature moved.

It stood up, not hurriedly, but casually, easily, and yawned and stretched. Finally, it took a step forward. Brief panic ensued among the women in the audience, that ended as the guide said quietly:

'It's all right, folks. He frequently comes down and looks us over. He's harmless.'

The crowd stood its ground, as the cat came down the steps from the dais and approached me. The animal paused in front of me, and peered at me curiously. Then it reached gingerly forward, opened my coat, and examined the inside breast pocket.

It came up holding the postcard with the picture of Silkey on it. I had brought it along, intending to ask Silkey about it.

For a long moment the cat examined the card, and then it held it out to Silkey. Silkey looked at me.

'Okay?' he said.

I nodded. I had a feeling that I was witnessing a drama the motivations of which I did not understand. I realized that I was watching Silkey intently.

He looked at the picture on the card, and then started to hand it to me. Then he stopped. Jerkily, he pulled the card back, and stared at the photograph.

'For cripes sake,' he gasped. 'It's a picture of me.'

There was no doubt about his surprise. It was so genuine that it startled me. I said, 'Didn't you send that to me? Didn't you write what's on the back there?'

Silkey did not answer immediately. He turned the card over and glared down at the writing. He began to shake his head.

'Doesn't make sense,' he muttered. 'Hmm, it was mailed in Marstown. That's where we were three days last week.'

He handed it back to me. 'Never saw it before in my life. Funny.'

His denial was convincing. I held the card in my hand, and looked questioningly at the cat. But it had already lost interest. As we stood there, watching, it turned and climbed back up to the dais, and slumped into a chair. It yawned. It closed its eyes.

And that's all that happened. We all left the tent, and Virginia and I said goodbye to Silkey. Later, on our way home, the episode seemed even more meaningless than when it had happened.

I don't know how long I had been asleep before I wakened. I turned over intending to go right back to sleep. And then I saw that my bedside light was burning. I sat up with a start.

The cat was sitting in a chair beside the bed, not more than three feet away.

There was silence. I couldn't have spoken at the beginning.

185

Slowly, I sat up. Memory came of what the guide at the show had said, '. . . Harmless!' But I didn't believe that anymore.

Three times now this beast had come here, twice to leave messages. I let my mind run over those messages, and I quailed. '. . . The cat wants to talk to you!' Was it possible that this thing could talk?

The very inactivity of the animal finally gave me courage. I licked my lips and said, 'Can you talk?'

The cat stirred. It raised an arm in the unhurried fashion of somebody who does not want to cause alarm. It pointed at the night table beside my bed. I followed the pointing finger and saw that an instrument was standing under the lamp. The instrument spoke at me:

'I cannot emit human sounds with my own body, but as you can hear this is an excellent intermediary.'

I have to confess that I jumped, that my mind scurried into a deep corner of my head – and only slowly came out again as the silence continued, and no attempt was made to harm me. I don't know why I should have assumed that its ability to speak through a mechanical device was a threat to me. But I had.

I suppose it was really a mental shrinking, my mind unwilling to accept the reality that was here. Before I could think clearly, the instrument on the table said:

'The problem of conveying thoughts through an electronic device depends on rhythmic utilization of brain energies.'

The statement stirred me. I had read considerably on that subject, beginning with Professor Hans Berger's report on brain rhythms in 1929. The cat's statements didn't quite fit.

'Isn't the energy potential too small?' I asked. 'And besides, you have your eyes open. The rhythms are always interfered with when the eyes are open, and in fact such a large part of the cortex yields to the visual centers that no rhythm whatever is detectable at such times.'

It didn't strike me then, but I think now that I actually

distracted the animal from its purpose. 'What measurements have been taken?' it asked. Even through the mind radio, it sounded interested.

'Photoelectric cells,' I said, 'have measured as much (or as little, which is really more accurate) as fifty microvolts of energy, mostly in the active regions of the brain. Do you know what a microvolt is?'

The creature nodded. It said after a moment, 'I won't tell you what energy my brain develops. It would probably frighten you, but it isn't all intelligence. I am a student on a tour of the galaxy, what might be called a post-graduate tour. Now, we have certain rules —' It stopped. 'You opened your mouth. Did you wish to say something?'

I felt dumb, overwhelmed. Then, weakly, 'You said galaxy.'

'That is correct.'

'B-but wouldn't that take years?' My brain was reaching out, striving to grasp, to understand.

'My tour will last about a thousand of your years,' said the cat.

'You're immortal?'

'Oh, no.'

'But —'

There I stopped. I couldn't go on. I sat there, blank-brained, while the creature went on:

'The rules of the fraternity of students require that we tell one person about ourselves before we leave the planet. And that we take with us a symbolical souvenir of the civilization of the beings on it. I'm curious to know what you would suggest as a souvenir of Earth. It can be anything, so long as it tells at a glance the dominating character of the race.'

The question calmed me. My brain stopped its alternation of mad whirling followed by blankness. I began to feel distinctly better. I shifted myself into a more comfortable position and stroked my jaw thoughtfully. I sincerely hoped

187

that I was giving the impression that I was an intelligent person whose opinion would be worthwhile.

A sense of incredible complications began to seize on me. I had realized it before, but now, with an actual decision to make, it seemed to me that human beings were really immensely intricate creatures. How could anybody pick one facet of their nature and say, 'This is man!' Or 'This represents man!' I said slowly:

'A work of art, science, or any useful article – you include those?'

'Anything.'

My interest was now at its peak. My whole being accepted the wonderfulness of what had happened. It seemed tremendously important that the great race that could travel the breadth and length of the galaxy should have some true representation of man's civilization. It amazed me, when I finally thought of the answer, that it had taken me so long. But the moment it occurred to me, I knew I had it.

'Man,' I said, 'is primarily a religious animal. From times too remote to have a written record, he has needed a faith in something. Once, he believed almost entirely in animate gods like rivers, storms, plants, then his gods became invisible; now they are once more becoming animate. An economic system, science – whatever it will be, the dominating article of it will be that he worships it without regard to reason, in other words in a purely religious fashion.'

I finished with a quiet satisfaction. 'All you need is an image of a man in a durable metal, his head tilted back, his arms raised to the sky, a rapt expression on his face, and written on the base of the inscription, "I believe".'

I saw that the creature was staring at me. 'Very interesting,' it said at last. 'I think you are very close to it, but you haven't quite got the answer.'

It stood up. 'But now I want you to come with me.'

'Eh?'

'Dress, please.'

It was unemotionally said. The fear that had been held deep inside me for minutes came back like a fire that had reached a new cycle of energy.

I drove my car. The cat sat beside me. The night was cool and refreshing, but dark. A fraction of a moon peered out occasionally from scurrying clouds, and there were glimpses of star-filtered dark blue sky. The realizaton that, from somewhere up there, this creature had come down to our Earth dimmed my tenderness. I ventured:

'Your people – have they progressed much farther than we to the innermost meaning of truth?'

It sounded drab and precise, a pedagogical rather than a vitally alive question. I added quickly:

'I hope you won't mind answering a few questions.'

Again it sounded inadequate. It seemed to me in an abrupt agony of despair that I was muffing the opportunity of the centuries. Silently, I cursed my professional training that made my every word sound as dry as dust.

'That card,' I said. 'You sent that?'

'Yes.' The machine on the cat's lap spoke quietly but clearly.

'How did you know my address and my name?'

'I didn't.'

Before I could say anything, the cat went on, 'You will understand all that before the night's over.'

'Oh!' The words held me for a second. I could feel the tightness crawling into my stomach. I had been trying not to think of what was going to happen before this night was over. '. . . Questions?' I croaked. 'Will you answer them?'

I parted my lips to start a machine-gun patter of queries. And then I closed them again. *What did I want to know?* The vast implications of that reply throttled my voice. Why, oh, why, are human beings so emotional at the great moments of their lives? I couldn't think, for what seemed an endless time. And when I finally spoke again, my first question was trite and not at all what I intended. I said, 'You came in a spaceship?'

The cat looked at me thoughtfully. 'No,' it replied slowly. 'I use the energy in my brain.'

'Eh! You came through space in your own body?'

'In a sense. One of these years human beings will make the initial discoveries about the rhythmic use of energy. It will be a dazzling moment for science.'

'We have,' I said, 'already made certain discoveries about our nervous systems and rhythm.'

'The end of that road,' was the answer, 'is control of the powers of nature. I will say no more about that.'

I was silent, but only briefly. The questions were bubbling now. 'Is it possible,' I asked, 'to develop an atomic-powered spaceship?'

'Not in the way you think,' said the cat. 'An atomic explosion cannot be confined except when it is drawn out in a series of timed frustrations. And that is an engineering problem, and has very little to do with creative physics.'

'Life,' I mumbled, 'where did life come from?'

'Electronic accidents occurring in a suitable environment.'

I had to stop there. I couldn't help it. 'Electronic accidents. What do you mean?'

'The difference between an inorganic and an organic atom is the arrangement of the internal structure. The hydro-carbon compounds being the most easily affected under certain conditions are the most common form of life. But now that you have atomic energy you will discover that life can be created from any element or compound of elements. Be careful. The hydrocarbon is a weak life structure that could be easily overwhelmed in its present state of development.'

I felt a chill. I could just picture the research that would be going on in government laboratories.

'You mean,' I gulped, 'there are life forms that would be dangerous the moment they are created?'

190

'Dangerous to man,' said the cat. It pointed suddenly. 'Turn up that street, and then through a side entrance into the circus grounds.'

I had been wondering tensely where we were going. Strangely, it was a shock to realize the truth.

A few minutes later we entered the dark, silent tent of the freaks. And I knew that the final drama of the cat on Earth was about to be enacted.

A tiny light flickered in the shadows. It came nearer, and I saw that there was a man walking underneath it. It was too dark to recognize him, but the light grew stronger, and I saw that it had no source. And suddenly I recognized Silkey Travis.

He was sound asleep.

He came forward, and stood in front of the cat. He looked unnatural, forlorn, like a woman caught without her makeup on. One long, trembling look I took at him, and then I stammered: 'What are you going to do?'

The machine the cat carried did not reply immediately. The cat turned and stared at me thoughtfully; then it touched Silkey's face, gently, with one finger. Silkey's eyes opened, but he made no other reaction. I realized that one part of his consciousness had been made aware of what was happening. I whispered: 'Can he hear?'

The cat nodded.

'Can he think?'

The cat shook its head; and then it said:

'In your analysis of the basic nature of human beings, you selected a symptom only. Man is religious because of a certain characteristic. I'll give you a clue. When an alien arrives on an inhabited planet, there is usually only one way that he can pass among the intelligent beings on that planet without being recognized for what he is. When you find that method, you have attained understanding of the fundamental character of the race.'

It was hard for me to think. In the dim emptiness of the

freak tent, the great silence of the circus grounds all around, what was happening seemed unnatural. I was not afraid of the cat. But there was a fear inside me, as strong as terror, as dark as night. I looked at the unmoving Silkey with all the lines of his years flabby on his face. And then I stared at the light that hovered above him. And finally I looked at the cat, and I said:

'Curiosity. You mean, man's curiosity. His interest in strange objects makes him accept them as natural when he sees them.'

The cat said, 'It seems incredible that you, an intelligent man, have never realized the one character of all human beings.' It turned briskly, straightening. 'But now, enough of this conversation. I have fulfilled the basic requirements of my domicile here. I have lived for a period without being suspected, and I have told one inhabitant that I have been here. It remains for me to send home a significant artifact of your civilization – and then I can be on my way . . . elsewhere.'

I ventured, shakily, 'Surely, the artifact isn't Silkey.'

'We seldom,' said the cat, 'choose actual inhabitants of a planet, but when we do we give them a compensation designed to balance what we take away. In his case, virtual immortality.'

I felt desperate, suddenly. Seconds only remained; and it wasn't that I had any emotion for Silkey. He stood there like a clod, and even though later he would remember, it didn't matter. It seemed to me that the cat had discovered some innate secret of human nature which I, as a biologist, must know.

'For God's sake,' I said, 'you haven't explained anything yet. What is this basic human characteristic? And what about the postcard you sent me? And —'

'You have all the clues.' The creature started to turn away. 'Your inability to comprehend is no concern of mine. We have a code, we students, that is all.'

192

'But what,' I asked desperately, 'shall I tell the world? Have you no message for human kind, something —'

The cat was looking at me again. 'If you can possibly restrain yourself,' it said, 'don't tell anyone anything.'

This time, when it moved away, it did not look back. I saw, with a start, that the mist of light above Silkey's head was expanding, growing. Brighter, vaster, it grew. It began to pulse with a gentle but unbroken rhythm. Inside its coalescing fire the cat and Silkey were dim forms, like shadows in a fire.

Abruptly, the shadows faded; and then the mist of light began to dim. Slowly, it sagged to the ground, and lay for minutes blurring into the darkness.

Of Silkey and the creature there was no sign.

The group sitting around the table in the bar was briefly silent. Finally, Gord said, 'Glub!' and Jones said in a positive fashion, 'You solved the problem of the postcard, of course?'

The slim, professorish man nodded. 'I think so. The reference in the card to time differentials is the clue. The card was sent *after* Silkey was put on exhibition in the school museum of the cat people, but because of time variations in transmission it arrived *before* I knew Silkey would be in town.'

Morton came up out of the depths of his chair. 'And what about this basic human characteristic, of which religion is merely an outward expression?'

The stranger made a gesture. 'Silkey, exhibiting freaks, was really exhibiting himself. Religion is self-dramatization before a god. Self-love, narcissism – in our own little way we show ourselves off . . . and so a strange being could come into our midst unsuspected.'

Cathy hiccoughed, and said, 'The love interest is what I like. Did you marry Virginia? You are the professor of biology at State, aren't you?'

193

The other shook his head. 'I was,' he said. 'I should have followed the cat's advice. But I felt it was important to tell other people what had happened. I was dismissed after three months, and I won't tell you what I'm doing now. But I must go on. The world must know about the weakness that makes us so vulnerable. Virginia? She married a pilot with one of the big air firms. She fell for his line of self-dramatization.'

He stood up. 'Well, I guess I'll be on my way. I've got a lot of bars to visit tonight.'

When he had gone, Ted paused momentarily in his evening's task of looking stupid. 'There,' he said, 'is a guy who really has a line. Just imagine. He's going to tell that story about five times tonight. What a set-up for a fellow who wants to be the center of attention.'

Myra giggled. Jones began to talk to Gord in his know-it-all fashion. Gord said, 'Glub!' every few seconds, just as if he was listening. Cathy put her head on the table and snored drunkenly. And Morton sagged lower and lower into his chair.

THE MONSTER

'No SIGN of war damage!' The bodiless voice touched his ears momentarily. Enash turned it out.

On the ground he collapsed his bubble. He found himself in a walled inclosure overgrown with weeds. Several skeletons lay in the tall grass beside the rakish building. They were of long, two-legged, two-armed beings with the skulls in each case mounted at the end of a thin spine. The skeletons, all of adults, seemed in excellent preservation, but when he bent down and touched one, a whole section of it crumbled into a fine powder. As he straightened, he saw that Yoal was floating down nearby. Enash waited until the historian had stepped out of his bubble, then he said:

'Do you think we ought to use our method of reviving the long dead?'

Yoal was thoughtful. 'I have been asking questions of the various people who have landed, and there is something wrong here. This planet has no surviving life, not even insect life. We'll have to find out what happened before we risk any colonization.'

Enash said nothing. A soft wind was blowing. It rustled through a clump of trees nearby. He motioned toward the trees. Yoal nodded and said, 'Yes, the plant life has not been harmed, but plants after all are not affected in the same way as the active life forms.'

There was an interruption. A voice spoke from Yoal's receiver: 'A museum has been found at approximately the center of the city. A red light has been fixed on the roof.'

Enash said, 'I'll go with you, Yoal. There might be skeletons of animals and of the intelligent being in various stages of his evolution. You didn't answer my question. Are you going to revive these beings?'

Yoal said slowly, 'I intend to discuss the matter with the council, but I think there is no doubt. We must know the cause of this disaster.' He waved one sucker vaguely to take in half the compass. He added as an afterthought, 'We shall proceed cautiously, of course, beginning with an obviously early development. The absence of the skeletons of children indicates that the race had developed personal immortality.'

The council came to look at the exhibits. It was, Enash knew, a formal preliminary only. The decision was made. There would be revivals. It was more than that. They were curious. Space was vast, the journeys through it long and lonely, landing always a stimulating experience, with its prospect of new life forms to be seen and studied.

The museum looked ordinary. High-domed ceilings, vast rooms. Plastic models of strange beasts, many artifacts – too many to see and comprehend in so short a time. The life span of a race was imprisoned here in a progressive array of relics. Enash looked with the others, and was glad when they came to the line of skeletons and preserved bodies. He seated himself behind the energy screen, and watched the biological experts take a preserved body out of a stone sarcophagus. It was wrapped in windings of cloth, many of them. The experts did not bother to unravel the rotted material. Their forceps reached through, pinched a piece of skull – that was the accepted procedure. Any part of the skeleton could be used, but the most perfect revivals, the most complete reconstructions resulted when a certain section of the skull was used.

Hamar, the chief biologist, explained the choice of body. 'The chemicals used to preserve this mummy show a sketchy knowledge of chemistry. The carvings on the sarcophagus indicate a crude and unmechanical culture. In such a civilization there would not be much development of the potentialities of the nervous system. Our speech experts have been analyzing the recorded voice mechanism which is a part of each exhibit, and though many languages are in-

196

volved – evidence that the ancient language spoken at the time the body was alive has been reproduced – they found no difficulty in translating the meanings. They have now adapted our universal speech machine, so that anyone who wishes to need only speak into his communicator, and so will have his words translated into the language of the revived person. The reverse, naturally, is also true. Ah, I see we are ready for the first body.'

Enash watched intently with the others as the lid was clamped down on the plastic reconstructor, and the growth processes were started. He could feel himself becoming tense. For there was nothing haphazard about what was happening. In a few minutes a full-grown ancient inhabitant of this planet would sit up and stare at them. The science involved was simple and always fully effective.

. . . Out of the shadows of smallness, life grows. The level of beginning and ending, of life and – not life; in that dim region matter oscillates easily between old and new habits. The habit of organic, or the habit of inorganic. Electrons do not have life and un-life values. Atoms know nothing of inanimateness. But when atoms form into molecules, there is a step in the process, one tiny step, that is of life – if life begins at all. One step, and then darkness. Or aliveness.

A stone or a living cell. A grain of gold or a blade of grass, the sands of the sea or the equally numerous animalcules inhabiting the endless fishy waters – the difference is there in the twilight zone of matter. Each living cell has in it the whole form. The crab grows a new leg when the old one is torn from its flesh. Both ends of the planarian worm elongate, and soon there are two worms, two identities, two digestive systems each as greedy as the original, each a whole, unwounded, unharmed by its experience. Each cell can be the whole. Each cell remembers in a detail so intricate that no totality of words could ever describe the completeness achieved.

But – paradox – memory is not organic. An ordinary wax

record remembers sounds. A wire recorder easily gives up a duplicate of the voice that spoke into it years before. Memory is a physiological impression, a mark on matter, a change in the shape of a molecule, so that when a reaction is desired the *shape* emits the same rhythm of response.

Out of the mummy's skull had come the multi-quadrillion memory shapes from which a response was now being evoked. As ever, the memory held true.

A man blinked, and opened his eyes.

'It is true, then,' he said aloud, and the words were translated into the Ganae tongue as he spoke them. 'Death is merely an opening into another life – but where are my attendants?' At the end, his voice took on a complaining tone.

He sat up, and climbed out of the case, which had automatically opened as he came to life. He saw his captors. He froze, but only for a moment. He had a pride and a very special arrogant courage, which served him now. Reluctantly, he sank to his knees and made obeisance, but doubt must have been strong in him. 'Am I in the presence of the gods of Egypt?' He climbed to his feet. 'What nonsense is this? I do not bow to nameless demons.'

Captain Gorsid said, 'Kill him!'

The two-legged monster dissolved, writhing, in the beam of a ray gun.

The second revived man stood up, pale, and trembled with fear. 'My God, I swear I won't touch the stuff again. Talk about pink elephants —'

Yoal was curious. 'To what *stuff* do you refer, revived one?'

'The old hooch, the poison in the hip pocket flask, the juice they gave me at that speak . . . my lordie!'

Captain Gorsid looked questioningly at Yoal. 'Need we linger?'

Yoal hesitated. 'I am curious.' He addressed the man. 'If I were to tell you that we were visitors from another star, what would be your reaction?'

198

The man stared at him. He was obviously puzzled, but the fear was stronger. 'Now, look,' he said, 'I was driving along, minding my own business. I admit I'd had a shot or two too many, but it's the liquor they serve these days. I swear I didn't see the other car – and if this is some new idea of punishing people who drink and drive, well, you've won. I won't touch another drop as long as I live, so help me.'

Yoal said, 'He drives a "car" and thinks nothing of it. Yet we saw no cars. They didn't even bother to preserve them in the museums.'

Enash noticed that everyone waited for everyone else to comment. He stirred as he realized the circle of silence would be complete unless he spoke. He said, 'Ask him to describe the car. How does it work?'

'Now, you're talking,' said the man. 'Bring on your line of chalk, and I'll walk it, and ask any questions you please. I may be so tight that I can't see straight, but I can always drive. How does it work? You just put her in gear, and step on the gas.'

'Gas,' said engineering officer Veed. 'The internal combustion engine. That places him.'

Captain Gorsid motioned to the guard with the ray gun.

The third man sat up, and looked at them thoughtfully. 'From the stars?' he said finally. 'Have you a system, or was it blind chance?'

The Ganae councilors in that domed room stirred uneasily in their curved chairs. Enash caught Yoal's eye on him. The shock in the historian's eyes alarmed the meteorologist. He thought: 'The two-legged one's adjustment to a new situation, his grasp of realities, was unnormally rapid. No Ganae could have equalled the swiftness of the reaction.'

Hamar, the chief biologist, said, 'Speed of thought is not necessarily a sign of superiority. The slow, careful thinker has his place in the hierarchy of intellect.'

But Enash found himself thinking it was not the speed;

199

it was the accuracy of the response. He tried to imagine himself being revived from the dead, and understanding instantly the meaning of the presence of aliens from the stars. He couldn't have done it.

He forgot his thought, for the man was out of the case. As Enash watched with the others, he walked briskly over to the window and looked out. One glance, and then he turned back.

'Is it all like this?' he asked.

Once again, the speed of his understanding caused a sensation. It was Yoal who finally replied.

'Yes. Desolation. Death. Ruin. Have you any idea as to what happened?'

The man came back and stood in front of the energy screen that guarded the Ganae. 'May I look over the museum? I have to estimate what age I am in. We had certain possibilities of destruction when I was last alive, but which one was realized depends on the time elapsed.'

The councilors looked at Captain Gorsid, who hesitated; then, 'Watch him,' he said to the guard with the ray gun. He faced the man. 'We understand your aspirations fully. You would like to seize control of this situation and insure your own safety. Let me reassure you. Make no false moves, and all will be well.'

Whether or not the man believed the lie, he gave no sign. Nor did he show by a glance or a movement that he had seen the scarred floor where the ray gun had burned his two predecessors into nothingness. He walked curiously to the nearest doorway, studied the other guard who waited there for him, and then, gingerly, stepped through. The first guard followed him, then came the mobile energy screen, and finally, trailing one another, the councilors.

Enash was the third to pass through the doorway. The room contained skeletons and plastic models of animals. The room beyond that was what, for want of a better term, Enash called a culture room. It contained the artifacts from

200

a single period of civilization. It looked very advanced. He had examined some of the machines when they first passed through it, and had thought: Atomic energy. He was not alone in his recognition. From behind him, Captain Gorsid said to the man:

'You are forbidden to touch anything. A false move will be the signal for the guards to fire.'

The man stood at ease in the center of the room. In spite of a curious anxiety, Enash had to admire his calmness. He must have known what his fate would be, but he stood there thoughtfully, and said finally, deliberately, 'I do not need to go any farther. Perhaps you will be able to judge better than I of the time that has elapsed since I was born and these machines were built. I see over there an instrument which, according to the sign above it, counts atoms when they explode. As soon as the proper number have exploded it shuts off the power automatically, and for just the right length of time to prevent a chain explosion. In my time we had a thousand crude devices for limiting the size of an atomic reaction, but it required two thousand years to develop those devices from the early beginnings of atomic energy. Can you make a comparison?'

The councilors glanced at Veed. The engineering officer hesitated. At last, reluctantly, he said, 'Nine thousand years ago we had a thousand methods of limiting atomic explosions.' He paused, then even more slowly, 'I have never heard of an instrument that counts out atoms for such a purpose.'

'And yet,' murmured Shuri, the astronomer, breathlessly, 'the race was destroyed.'

There was silence. It ended as Gorsid said to the nearest guard, 'Kill the monster!'

But it was the guard who went down, bursting into flame. Not just one guard, but the guards! Simultaneously down, burning with a blue flame. The flame licked at the screen, recoiled, and licked more furiously, recoiled and burned brighter. Through a haze of fire, Enash saw that the man had retreated to the far door, and that the machine that counted atoms was glowing with a blue intensity.

Captain Gorsid shouted into his communicator, 'Guard all exits with ray guns. Spaceships stand by to kill alien with heavy guns.'

Somebody said, 'Mental control. Some kind of mental control. What have we run into?'

They were retreating. The blue flame was at the ceiling, struggling to break through the screen. Enash had a last glimpse of the machine. It must still be counting atoms, for it was a hellish blue. Enash raced with the others to the room where the man had been resurrected. There, another energy screen crashed to their rescue. Safe now, they retreated into their separate bubbles and whisked through outer doors and up to the ship. As the great ship soared, an atomic bomb hurtled down from it. The mushroom of flame blotted out the museum and the city below.

'But we still don't know why the race died,' Yoal whispered into Enash's ear, after the thunder had died from the heavens behind them.

The pale yellow sun crept over the horizon on the third morning after the bomb was dropped, the eighth day since the landing. Enash floated with the others down on a new city. He had come to argue against any further revival.

'As a meteorologist,' he said, 'I pronounce this planet safe for Ganae colonization. I cannot see the need for taking any risks. This race has discovered the secrets of its nervous system, and we cannot afford —'

He was interrupted. Hamar, the biologist, said dryly, 'If they knew so much why didn't they migrate to other star systems and save themselves?'

'I will concede,' said Enash, 'that very possibly they had not discovered our system of locating stars with planetary families.' He looked earnestly around the circle of his friends. 'We have agreed that was a unique accidental discovery. We were lucky, not clever.'

He saw by the expressions on their faces that they were mentally refuting his arguments. He felt a helpless sense of imminent catastrophe. For he could see that picture of a great race facing death. It must have come swiftly, but not so swiftly that they didn't know about it. There were too many skeletons in the open, lying in the gardens of magnificent homes, as if each man and his wife had come out to wait for the doom of his kind. He tried to picture it for the council, that last day long, long ago, when a race had calmly met its ending. But his visualization failed somehow, for the others shifted impatiently in the seats that had been set up behind the series of energy screens, and Captain Gorsid said, 'Exactly what aroused this intense emotional reaction in you, Enash?'

The question gave Enash pause. He hadn't thought of it as emotional. He hadn't realized the nature of his obsession, so subtly had it stolen upon him. Abruptly now, he realized.

'It was the third one,' he said, slowly. 'I saw him through the haze of energy fire, and he was standing there in the distant doorway watching us curiously, just before we turned to run. His bravery, his calm, the skilful way he had duped us – it all added up.'

'Added up to his death!' said Hamar. And everybody laughed.

'Come now, Enash,' said Vice-captain Mayad good-humoredly, 'you're not going to pretend that this race is braver than our own, or that, with all the precautions we have now taken, we need fear one man?'

Enash was silent, feeling foolish. The discovery that he had had an emotional obsession abashed him. He did not want to appear unreasonable. He made a final protest. 'I merely wish to point out,' he said doggedly, 'that this desire to discover what happened to a dead race does not seem absolutely essential to me.'

Captain Gorsid waved at the biologist. 'Proceed,' he said, 'with the revival.'

To Enash, he said, 'Do we dare return to Gana, and recommend mass migrations – and then admit that we did not actually complete our investigations here? It's impossible, my friend.'

It was the old argument, but reluctantly now Enash admitted there was something to be said for that point of view. He forgot that, for the fourth man was stirring.

The man sat up. And vanished.

There was a blank, startled, horrified silence. Then Captain Gorsid said harshly, 'He can't get out of there. We know that. He's in there somewhere.'

All around Enash, the Ganae were out of their chairs, peering into the energy shell. The guards stood with ray guns held limply in their suckers. Out of the corner of his eye, he saw one of the protective screen technicians beckon to Veed, who went over. He came back grim. He said, 'I'm told the needles jumped ten points when he first disappeared. That's on the nucleonic level.'

'By ancient Ganae!' Shuri whispered. 'We've run into what we've always feared.'

Gorsid was shouting into the communicator. 'Destroy all the locators on the ship. Destroy them, do you hear!'

He turned with glaring eyes. 'Shuri,' he bellowed, 'they don't seem to understand. Tell those subordinates of yours to act. All locators and reconstructors must be destroyed.'

'Hurry, hurry!' said Shuri weakly.

When that was done they breathed more easily. There were grim smiles and a tensed satisfaction. 'At least,' said Vice-captain Mayad, 'he cannot now ever discover Gana. Our great system of locating suns with planets remains our secret. There can be no retaliation for —' He stopped, said slowly, 'What am I talking about? We haven't done anything. We're not responsible for the disaster that has befallen the inhabitants of this planet.'

But Enash knew what he had meant. The guilt feelings came to the surface at such moments as this – the ghosts of all the races destroyed by the Ganae, the remorseless will that had been in them, when they first landed, to annihilate whatever was here. The dark abyss of voiceless hate and terror that lay behind them; the days on end when they had mercilessly poured poisonous radiation down upon the unsuspecting inhabitants of peaceful planets – all that had been in Mayad's words.

'I still refuse to believe he has escaped.' That was Captain Gorsid. 'He's in there. He's waiting for us to take down our screens, so he can escape. Well, we won't do it.'

There was silence again as they stared expectantly into the emptiness of the energy shell. The reconstructor rested on its metal supports, a glittering affair. But there was nothing else. Not a flicker of unnatural light or shade. The yellow rays of the sun bathed the open spaces with a brilliance that left no room for concealment.

'Guards,' said Gorsid, 'destroy the reconstructor. I thought he might come back to examine it, but we can't take a chance on that.'

It burned with a white fury. And Enash, who had hoped somehow that the deadly energy would force the two-legged thing into the open, felt his hopes sag within him.

'But where can he have gone?' Yoal whispered.

Enash turned to discuss the matter. In the act of swinging around, he saw that the monster was standing under a tree a score of feet to one side, watching them. He must have arrived at *that* moment, for there was a collective gasp from the councilors. Everybody drew back. One of the screen technicians, using great presence of mind, jerked up an energy screen between the Ganae and the monster. The creature came forward slowly. He was slim of build, he held his head well back. His eyes shone as from an inner fire.

He stopped as he came to the screen, reached out and touched it with his fingers. It flared, blurred with changing colors. The colors grew brighter, and extended in an intricate pattern all the way from his head to the ground. The blur cleared. The pattern faded into invisibility. The man was through the screen.

He laughed, a soft curious sound; then sobered. 'When I first awakened,' he said, 'I was curious about the situation. The question was, what should I do with you?'

The words had a fateful ring to Enash on the still morning air of that planet of the dead. A voice broke the silence, a voice so strained and unnatural that a moment passed before he recognized it as belonging to Captain Gorsid.

'*Kill him!*'

When the blasters ceased their effort, the unkillable thing remained standing. He walked slowly forward until he was only a half a dozen feet from the nearest Ganae. Enash had a position well to the rear. The man said slowly:

'Two courses suggest themselves, one based on gratitude for reviving me, the other based on reality. I know you for what you are. Yes, *know* you – and that is unfortunate. It is hard to feel merciful. To begin with,' he went on, 'let us suppose you surrender the secret of the locator. Naturally, now that a system exists, we shall never again be caught as we were.'

Enash had been intent, his mind so alive with the potentialities of the disaster that was here that it seemed impossible that he could think of anything else. And yet, a part of his attention was stirred now. 'What did happen?' he asked.

The man changed color. The emotions of that far day thickened his voice. 'A nucleonic storm. It swept in from outer space. It brushed this edge of our galaxy. It was about ninety light-years in diameter, beyond the farthest limit of our power. There was no escape from it. We had dispensed with spaceships, and had no time to construct any. Castor, the only star with planets ever discovered by us, was also in the path of the storm.' He stopped. 'The secret?' he said.

Around Enash, the councilors were breathing easier. The fear of race destruction that had come to them was lifting.

Enash saw with pride that the first shock was over, and they were not even afraid for themselves.

'Ah,' said Yoal softly, 'you don't know the secret. In spite of all your great development, we alone can conquer the galaxy.' He looked at the others, smiling confidently. 'Gentlemen,' he said, 'our pride in a great Ganae achievement is justified. I suggest we return to our ship. We have no further business on this planet.'

There was a confused moment while their bubbles formed, when Enash wondered if the two-legged one would try to stop their departure. But when he looked back, he saw that the man was walking in a leisurely fashion along a street.

That was the memory Enash carried with him, as the ship began to move. That and the fact that the three atomic bombs they dropped, one after the other, failed to explode.

'We will not,' said Captain Gorsid, 'give up a planet as easily as that. I propose another interview with the creature.'

They were floating down again into the city, Enash and Yoal and Veed and the commander. Captain Gorsid's voice tuned in once more:

'. . . As I visualize it' – through the mist Enash could see the transparent glint of the other three bubbles around him – 'we jumped to conclusions about this creature, not justified by the evidence. For instance, when he awakened, he vanished. Why? Because he was afraid, of course. He wanted to size up the situation. *He* didn't believe he was omnipotent.'

It was sound logic. Enash found himself taking heart from it. Suddenly, he was astonished that he had become panicky so easily. He began to see the danger in a new light. Only one man alive on a new planet. If they were determined enough, colonists could be moved in as if he did not exist. It had been done before, he recalled. On several planets, small groups of the original populations had survived the destroying radiation, and taken refuge in remote areas. In almost every case, the new colonists gradually hunted them down. In two instances, however, that Enash remembered, native races were still holding small sections of their planets. In each case, it had been found impractical to destroy them because it would have endangered the Ganae on the planet. So the survivors were tolerated. One man would not take up very much room.

When they found him, he was busily sweeping out the lower floor of a small bungalow. He put the broom aside and stepped onto the terrace outside. He had put on sandals, and he wore a loose-fitting robe made of very shiny material. He eyed them indolently but he said nothing.

It was Captain Gorsid who made the proposition. Enash had to admire the story he told into the language machine. The commander was very frank. That approach had been decided on. He pointed out that the Ganae could not be expected to revive the dead of this planet. Such altruism would be unnatural considering that the ever-growing Ganae hordes had a continual need for new worlds. Each vast new population increment was a problem that could be solved by one method only. In this instance, the colonists would gladly respect the rights of the sole survivor of this world.

It was at that point that the man interrupted. 'But what is the purpose of this endless expansion?' He seemed genuinely curious. 'What will happen when you finally occupy every planet in this galaxy?'

Captain Gorsid's puzzled eyes met Yoal's, then flashed to Veed, then Enash. Enash shrugged his torso negatively, and felt pity for the creature. The man didn't understand, possibly never could understand. It was the old story of two different viewpoints, the virile and the decadent, the race that aspired to the stars and the race that declined the call of destiny.

'Why not,' urged the man, 'control the breeding chambers?'

'And have the government overthrown!' said Yoal.

He spoke tolerantly, and Enash saw that the others were smiling at the man's naïveté. He felt the intellectual gulf between them widening. The creature had no comprehension of the natural life forces that were at work. The man spoke again:

'Well, if you don't control them, we will control them for you.'

There was silence.

They began to stiffen. Enash felt it in himself, saw the signs of it in the others. His gaze flicked from face to face, then back to the creature in the doorway. Not for the first time, Enash had the thought that their enemy seemed helpless. 'Why,' he decided, 'I could put my suckers around him and crush him.'

He wondered if mental control of nucleonic, nuclear, and gravitonic energies included the ability to defend oneself from a macrocosmic attack. He had an idea it did. The exhibition of power two hours before might have had limitations, but if so, it was not apparent. Strength or weakness could make no difference. The threat of threats had been made: 'If you don't control – we will.'

The words echoed in Enash's brain, and, as the meaning penetrated deeper, his aloofness faded. He had always regarded himself as a spectator. Even when, earlier, he had argued against the revival, he had been aware of a detached part of himself watching the scene rather than being a part of it. He saw with a sharp clarity that that was why he had finally yielded to the conviction of the others. Going back beyond that to remoter days, he saw that he had never quite considered himself a participant in the seizure of the planets of other races. He was the one who looked on, and thought of reality, and speculated on a life that seemed to have no meaning. It was meaningless no longer. He was caught by a tide of irresistible emotion, and swept along. He felt himself sinking, merging with the Ganae mass being. All the strength and all the will of the race surged up in his veins.

He snarled, 'Creature, if you have any hopes of reviving your dead race, abandon them now.'

The man looked at him, but said nothing. Enash rushed on, 'If you could destroy us, you would have done so already. But the truth is that you operate within limitations. Our ship is so built that no conceivable chain reaction could be started in it. For every plate of potential unstable material in it there is a counteracting plate, which prevents the development of a critical pile. You might be able to set off explosions in our engines, but they, too, would be limited, and would merely start the process for which they are intended – confined in their proper space.'

He was aware of Yoal touching his arm. 'Careful,' warned the historian. 'Do not in your just anger give away vital information.'

Enash shook off the restraining sucker. 'Let us not be unrealistic,' he said harshly. 'This thing has divined most of our racial secrets, apparently merely by looking at our bodies. We would be acting childishly if we assumed that he has not already realized the possibilities of the situation.'

'*Enash!*' Captain Gorsid's voice was imperative.

As swiftly as it had come, Enash's rage subsided. He stepped back. 'Yes, commander.'

'I think I know what you intended to say,' said Captain Gorsid. 'I assure you I am in full accord, but I believe also that I, as the top Ganae official, should deliver the ultimatum.'

He turned. His horny body towered above the man. 'You have made the unforgivable threat. You have told us, in effect, that you will attempt to restrict the vaulting Ganae spirit.'

'Not the spirit,' said the man. He laughed softly. 'No, not the spirit.'

The commander ignored the interruption. 'Accordingly, we have no alternative. We are assuming that, given time to locate the materials and develop the tools, you might be able to build a reconstructor. In our opinion it will be at least two years before you can complete it, *even if you know how*. It is an immensely intricate machine, not easily assembled by the lone survivor of a race that gave up its machines millennia before disaster struck.

'You did not have time to build a spaceship. We won't give you time to build a reconstructor.

'Within a few minutes our ship will start dropping bombs. It is possible you will be able to prevent explosions in your vicinity. We will start, accordingly, on the other side of the planet. If you stop us there, then we will assume we need help. In six months of traveling at top acceleration, we can reach a point where the nearest Ganae planet would hear our messages. They will send a fleet so vast that all your powers of resistance will be overcome. By dropping a hundred or a thousand bombs every minute, we will succeed in devastating every city so that not a grain of dust will remain of the skeletons of your people.

'That is our plan. So it shall be. Now, do your worst to us who are at your mercy.'

The man shook his head. 'I shall do nothing – now!' he said. He paused, then thoughtfully, 'Your reasoning is fairly accurate. Fairly. Naturally, I am not all powerful, but it seems to me you have forgotten one little point. I won't tell you what it is. And now,' he said, 'good day to you. Get back to your ship, and be on your way. I have much to do.'

Enash had been standing quietly, aware of the fury building up in him again. Now, with a hiss, he sprang forward, suckers outstretched. They were almost touching the smooth flesh – when something snatched at him.

He was back on the ship.

He had no memory of movement, no sense of being dazed or harmed. He was aware of Veed and Yoal and Captain Gorsid standing near him as astonished as he himself. Enash remained very still, thinking of what the man had said: '. . . *Forgotten one little point*.' Forgotten? That meant they knew. What could it be? He was still pondering about it when Yoal said:

'We can be reasonably certain our bombs alone will not work.'

They didn't.

Forty light-years out from Earth, Enash was summoned to the council chambers. Yoal greeted him wanly, 'The monster is aboard.'

The thunder of that poured through Enash, and with it came a sudden comprehension. 'That was what he meant we had forgotten,' he said finally, aloud and wonderingly. 'That he can travel through space at will within a limit – what was the figure he once used – of ninety light-years.'

He sighed. He was not surprised that the Ganae, who had to use ships, would not have thought immediately of such a possibility. Slowly, he began to retreat from the reality. Now that the shock had come, he felt old and weary, a sense of his mind withdrawing again to its earlier state of aloofness. It required a few minutes to get the story. A physicist's assistant, on his way to the storeroom, had caught a glimpse of a man in a lower corridor. In such a heavily manned ship, the wonder was that the intruder had escaped earlier observation. Enash had a thought.

'But after all we are not going all the way to one of our planets. How does he expect to make use of us to locate it if we only use the video – ' he stopped. That was it, of course. Directional video beams would have to be used, and the man would travel in the right direction the instant contact was made.

Enash saw the decision in the eyes of his companions, the only possible decision under the circumstances. And yet, it seemed to him they were missing some vital point. He walked slowly to the great video plate at one end of the chamber. There was a picture on it, so sharp, so vivid, so majestic that the unaccustomed mind would have reeled

212

as from a stunning blow. Even to him, who knew the scene, there came a constriction, a sense of unthinkable vastness. It was a video view of a section of the milky way. Four hundred *million* stars as seen through telescopes that could pick up the light of a red dwarf at thirty thousand light-years.

The video plate was twenty-five yards in diameter – a scene that had no parallel elsewhere in the plenum. Other galaxies simply did not have that many stars.

Only one in two hundred thousand of those glowing suns had planets.

That was the colossal fact that compelled them now to an irrevocable act. Wearily, Enash looked around him.

'The monster has been very clever,' he said quietly. 'If we go ahead, he goes with us, obtains a reconstructor, and returns by his method to his planet. If we use the directional beam, he flashes along it, obtains a reconstructor, and again reaches his planet first. In either event, by the time our fleets arrived back here, he would have revived enough of his kind to thwart any attack we could mount.'

He shook his torso. The picture was accurate, he felt sure, but it still seemed incomplete. He said slowly, 'We have one advantage now. Whatever decision we make, there is no language machine to enable him to learn what it is. We can carry out our plans without his knowing what they will be. He knows that neither he nor we can blow up the ship. That leaves us one real alternative.'

It was Captain Gorsid who broke the silence that followed. 'Well, gentlemen, I see we know our minds. We will set the engines, blow up the controls, and take him with us.'

They looked at each other, race pride in their eyes. Enash touched suckers with each in turn.

An hour later, when the heat was already considerable, Enash had the thought that sent him staggering to the communicator, to call Shuri, the astronomer. 'Shuri,' he yelled, 'when the monster first awakened – remember Captain Gorsid had difficulty getting your subordinates to destroy the locators. We never thought to ask them what the delay was. Ask them . . . ask them —'

There was a pause, then Shuri's voice came weakly over the roar of the static, 'They . . . couldn't . . . get . . . into the . . . room. The door was locked.'

Enash sagged to the floor. They had missed more than one point, he realized. The man had awakened, realized the situation; and, when he vanished, he had gone to the ship, and there discovered the secret of the locator and possibly the secret of the reconstructor – if he didn't know it previously. By the time he reappeared, he already had from them what he wanted. All the rest must have been designed to lead them to this act of desperation.

In a few moments, now, *he* would be leaving the ship, secure in the knowledge that shortly no alien mind would know his planet existed. Knowing, too, that his race would live again, and this time never die.

Enash staggered to his feet, clawed at the roaring communicator, and shouted his new understanding into it. There was no answer. It clattered with the static of uncontrollable and inconceivable energy. The heat was peeling his armored hide as he struggled to the matter transmitter. It flashed at him with purple flame. Back to the communicator he ran shouting and screaming.

He was still whimpering into it a few minutes later when the mighty ship plunged into the heart of a blue-white sun.

DEAR PEN PAL

Planet Aurigae II

DEAR Pen Pal:

When I first received your letter from the interstellar correspondence club, my impulse was to ignore it. The mood of one who has spent the last seventy planetary periods – years I suppose you would call them – in an Aurigaen prison, does not make for a pleasant exchange of letters. However, life is very boring, and so I finally settled myself to the task of writing you.

Your description of Earth sounds exciting. I would like to live there for a while, and I have a suggestion in this connection, but I won't mention it till I have developed it further.

You will have noticed the material on which this letter is written. It is a highly sensitive metal, very thin, very flexible, and I have inclosed several sheets of it for your use. Tungsten dipped in any strong acid makes an excellent mark on it. It is important to me that you do write on it, as my fingers are too hot – literally – to hold your paper without damaging it.

I'll say no more just now. It is possible you will not care to correspond with a convicted criminal, and therefore I shall leave the next move up to you. Thank you for your letter. Though you did not know its destination, it brought a moment of cheer into my drab life.

Skander

Aurigae II

Dear Pen Pal:

Your prompt reply to my letter made me happy. I am sorry your doctor thought it excited you too much, and sorry, also, if I have described my predicament in such a way as to make you feel badly. I welcome your many questions, and I shall try to answer them all.

You say the international correspondence club has no record of having sent any letters to Aurigae. That, according to them, the temperature on the second planet of the Aurigae sun is more than 500 degrees Fahrenheit. And that life is not known to exist there. Your club is right about the temperature and the letters. We have what your people would call a hot climate, but then we are not a hydrocarbon form of life, and find 500 degrees very pleasant.

I must apologize for deceiving you about the way your first letter was sent to me. I didn't want to frighten you away by telling you too much at once. After all, I could not be expected to know that you would be enthusiastic to hear from me.

The truth is that I am a scientist, and, along with the other members of my race, I have known for some centuries that there were other inhabited systems in the galaxy. Since I am allowed to experiment in my spare hours, I amused myself in attempts at communication. I developed several simple systems for breaking in on galactic communication operations, but it was not until I developed a subspacewave control that I was able to draw your letter (along with several others, which I did not answer) into a cold chamber.

I use the cold chamber as both sending and receiving center, and since you were kind enough to use the material which I sent you, it was easy for me to locate your second letter among the mass of mail that accumulated at the nearest headquarters of the interstellar correspondence club.

How did I learn your language? After all, it is a simple one, particularly the written language seems easy. I had no difficulty with it. If you are still interested in writing me, I shall be happy to continue the correspondence.

Skander

Dear Pen Pal:

Your enthusiasm is refreshing. You say that I failed to answer your question about how I expected to visit Earth. I confess I deliberately ignored the question, as my experiment had not yet proceeded far enough. I want you to bear with me a short time longer, and then I will be able to give you the details. You are right in saying that it would be difficult for a being who lives at a temperature of 500 degrees Fahrenheit to mingle freely with the people of Earth. This was never my intention, so please relieve your mind. However, let us drop that subject for the time being.

I appreciate the delicate way in which you approach the subject of my imprisonment. But it is quite unnecessary. I performed forbidden experiments upon my body in a way that was deemed to be dangerous to the public welfare. For instance, among other things, I once lowered my surface temperature to 150 degrees Fahrenheit, and so shortened the radioactive cycle-time of my surroundings. This caused an unexpected break in the normal person to person energy flow in the city where I lived, and so charges were laid against me. I have thirty more years to serve. It would be pleasant to leave my body behind and tour the universe – but as I said I'll discuss that later.

I wouldn't say that we're a superior race. We have certain qualities which apparently your people do not have. We live longer, not because of any discoveries we've made about ourselves, but because our bodies are built of a more enduring element – I don't know your name for it, but the atomic weight is 52.9 ♯.* Our scientific discoveries are of the kind that would normally be made by a race with our kind of physical structure. The fact that we can work with temperatures of as high as – I don't know just how to put that – has been very helpful in the development of the subspace energies which are extremely hot, and require delicate adjustments. In the later stages these adjustments can be

*A radioactive isotope of chromium. – Author's note.

made by machinery, but in the development the work must be done by 'hand' – I put that word in quotes, because we have no hands in the same way that you have.

I am enclosing a photographic plate, properly cooled and chemicalized for your climate. I wonder if you would set it up and take a picture of yourself. All you have to do is arrange it properly on the basis of the laws of light – that is, light travels in straight lines, so stand in front of it – and when you are ready *think* 'Ready!' The picture will be automatically taken.

Would you do this for me? If you are interested, I will also send you a picture of myself, though I must warn you. My appearance will probably shock you.

Sincerely,
Skander

Planet Aurigae II

Dear Pen Pal:

Just a brief note in answer to your question. It is not necessary to put the plate into a camera. You describe this as a dark box. The plate will take the picture when you think, 'Ready!' I assure you it will be flooded with light.

Skander

Aurigae II

Dear Pen Pal:

You say that while you were waiting for the answer to my last letter you showed the photographic plate to one of the doctors at the hospital – I cannot picture what you mean by doctor or hospital, but let that pass – and he took the problem up with government authorities. Problem? I don't understand. I thought we were having a pleasant correspondence, private and personal.

I shall certainly appreciate your sending that picture of yourself.

Skander

Dear Pen Pal:

I assure you I am not annoyed at your action. It merely puzzled me, and I am sorry the plate has not been returned to you. Knowing what governments are, I can imagine that it will not be returned to you for some time, so I am taking the liberty of inclosing another plate.

I cannot imagine why you should have been warned against continuing this correspondence. What do they expect me to do? – eat you up at long distance? I'm sorry but I don't like hydrogen in my diet.

In any event, I would like your picture as a memento of our friendship, and I will send mine as soon as I have received yours. You may keep it or throw it away, or give it to your governmental authorities – but at least I will have the knowledge that I've given a fair exchange.

With all best wishes
Skander

Dear Pen Pal:

Your last letter was so slow in coming that I thought you had decided to break off the correspondence. I was sorry to notice that you failed to inclose the photograph, puzzled by your reference to having a relapse, and cheered by your statement that you would send it along as soon as you felt better – whatever that means. However, the important thing is that you did write, and I respect the philosophy of your club which asks its members not to write of pessimistic matters. We all have our own problems which we regard as overshadowing the problems of others. Here I am in prison, doomed to spend the next 30 years tucked away from the main stream of life. Even the thought is hard on my restless spirit, though I know I have a long life ahead of me after my release.

In spite of your friendly letter, I won't feel that you have completely re-established contact with me until you send the photograph.

Yours in expectation
Skander

Aurigae II

Dear Pen Pal:

The photograph arrived. As you suggest, your appearance startled me. From your description I thought I had mentally reconstructed your body. It just goes to show that words cannot really describe an object which has never been seen.

You'll notice that I've inclosed a photograph of myself, as I promised I would. Chunky, metallic looking chap, am I not, very different, I'll wager, than you expected? The various races with whom we have communicated become wary of us when they discover we are highly radioactive, and that literally we are a radioactive form of life, the only such (that we know of) in the universe. It's been very trying to be so isolated and, as you know, I have occasionally mentioned that I had hopes of escaping not only the deadly imprisonment to which I am being subjected but also the body which cannot escape.

Perhaps you'll be interested in hearing how far this idea has developed. The problem involved is one of exchange of personalities with someone else. Actually, it is not really an exchange in the accepted meaning of the word. It is necessary to get an impress of both individuals, of their mind and of their thoughts as well as their bodies. Since this phase is purely mechanical, it is simply a matter of taking complete photographs and of exchanging them. By complete I mean of course every vibration must be registered. The next step is to make sure the two photographs are exchanged, that is, that each party has somewhere near him a complete photograph of the other. (It is already too late, Pen Pal. I have set in motion the sub-space energy interflow between

220

the two plates, so you might as well read on.) As I have said it is not exactly an exchange of personalities. The original personality in each individual is suppressed, literally pushed back out of the consciousness, and the image personality from the 'photographic' plate replaces it.

You will take with you a complete memory of your life on Earth, and I will take along memory of my life on Aurigae. Simultaneously, the memory of the receiving body will be blurrily at our disposal. A part of us will always be pushing up, striving to regain consciousness, but always lacking the strength to succeed.

As soon as I grow tired of Earth, I will exchange bodies in the same way with a member of some other race. Thirty years hence, I will be happy to reclaim my body, and you can then have whatever body I last happened to occupy.

This should be a very happy arrangement for us both. You, with your short life expectancy, will have out-lived all your contemporaries and will have had an interesting experience. I admit I expect to have the better of the exchange – but now, enough of explanation. By the time you reach this part of the letter it will be me reading it, not you. But if any part of you is still aware, so long for now, Pen Pal. It's been nice having all those letters from you. I shall write you from time to time to let you know how things are going with my tour.

Skander

Aurigae II

Dear Pen Pal:

Thanks a lot for forcing the issue. For a long time I hesitated about letting you play such a trick on yourself. You see, the government scientists analyzed the nature of that first photographic plate you sent me, and so the final decision was really up to me. I decided that anyone as eager as you were to put one over should be allowed to succeed.

Now I know I didn't have to feel sorry for you. Your

plan to conquer Earth wouldn't have gotten anywhere, but the fact that you had the idea ends the need for sympathy.

By this time you will have realized for yourself that a man who has been paralyzed since birth, and is subject to heart attacks, cannot expect a long life span. I am happy to tell you that your once lonely pen pal is enjoying himself, and I am happy to sign myself with a name to which I expect to become accustomed.

> With best wishes
> Skander

THE GREEN FOREST

'HERE!' said Marenson.

He put the point of his pencil down in the center of a splotch of green. His eyes focused on the wiry man opposite him.

'Right here, Mr Clugy,' he said, 'is where the camp will be built.'

Clugy leaned forward and glanced at the spot. Then he looked up; and Marenson was aware of the spaceman's slate-grey eyes studying him. Clugy drew slowly back into his chair, and said in a monotone:

'Why that particular spot?'

'Oh,' said Marenson, 'I have a feeling we'll get more juice from there.'

'A *feeling!*' The words came explosively. Clugy swallowed hard, and said quietly: 'Mr Marenson, that's dangerous jungle country.' He stood up, and bent over the map of the Mira sun planet. 'Now, here,' he said briskly, 'in this mountain country it's bad enough, but the animal and plant life can be fought off, and the climate is bearable.'

Marenson shook his head, and put his pencil back to the green splotch. 'Here,' he said with finality.

Clugy went back to his chair and sat down. He was a lean man with the tan of many suns on his face. Marenson was aware of the spaceman's hard eyes studying him. The other seemed to be tensing himself for a violent verbal battle. Abruptly, he must have decided against a head-on clash with his superior.

'But why?' he said in a perplexed tone. 'After all, the problem is very simple. A big ship is being built, and we need the organic juice from the progeny of these Mira beasts.'

'Exactly,' said Marenson, 'so we locate our camp in the forest which is their main habitat.'

'Why not,' Clugy persisted, 'leave the job of selecting the camp site to the field men – the hunters?'

Marenson put his pencil down deliberately. He was accustomed to dealing with people who opposed his plans. He thought of himself as a calm man whose patience was exhausted.

There were times when he gave detailed reasons for his actions, and there were times when he didn't. This was one of the times when he didn't; under the rulings, actually, he couldn't. A glance at the wall clock showed that it was ten to four. Tomorrow at this hour he would be clearing his desk preliminary to leaving on a month's vacation with Janet. Between now and then he had a score of vital things to do. It was time to break off the interview. He said in a formal voice:

'I take full responsibility for my decision. And now, Mr Clugy —'

He stopped, conscious that he had said the wrong thing. It was not often that there were scenes in this sumptuous office with its hundred-story view of the capital of the galaxy. Usually the deep space men who came in here were properly impressed by Ancil Marenson and his resonant baritone voice. But he took one look now at Clugy's face, and realized he had handled the other in a wrong fashion.

Clugy hunched himself forward angrily. And it was the stupendousness of the emotional jump he made then that startled Marenson – from mildness, without any gradations, to unqualified anger.

'Easy talk,' he said now in a harsh, steely voice, 'from a man in the penguin division of the service.'

Marenson blinked. He parted his lips to speak, then closed them tight. He started to smile, but changed his mind. He had such a long space career behind him that he had never thought of himself as being in the armchair brigade. He cleared his throat.

'Mr Clugy,' he said mildly, 'I'm surprised that you introduce personalities into this purely governmental affair.'

Clugy's stare was unflinching. 'Mr Marenson,' he said with chilling politeness, 'a man who sends others into dangerous situations on a mere whim has already introduced the personal element. You're making a life-and-death decision involving several thousand brave men. What you don't seem to understand is that the Mira planet forest is a green hell. There's nothing else like it in the universe we know – unless the Yevd have something similar in their section of the galaxy. The year round it swarms with the progeny of the lymph beast. What puzzles me is why don't I get up and punch you one right in that handsome face of yours?'

It was the reference to the Yevd that gave Marenson the opening he'd been looking for. 'If you don't mind,' he said coldly, 'I'm going to have you tested for light illusion. I'm having endless trouble on all our supply lines from Yevd interference. There's something funny about a man who's fighting as hard as you are to prevent lymph juice from being delivered to the navy.'

Clugy smiled, showing his teeth. 'That's right,' he said. 'Attack is the best defense, isn't it? So now I'm a Yevd using my mastery of light and illusion to make you believe I'm a human being.'

He stood up. Before he could continue, Marenson said in a savage voice: 'It's a good thing that there are men like me in the background. Field people have a tendency to slack on the job, and take all the easy ways. My job is to deliver lymph juice to The Yards. Deliver it, understand. No excuses. No explaining that the hunters find it more convenient to commute from the mountains. I have to get the juice to the factories, or resign in favor of someone who can. Mr Clugy, I make a hundred thousand a year because I know what decisions to make.

Clugy said: 'We'll get the juice.'

'You haven't been.'

'We're just starting.' He leaned over the desk. His gray eyes were steely. 'My penguin friend,' he said softly, 'you've got yourself into a little neurotic corner, fancying the hard decision is always the right one. Well, I don't give a care about your job conditioning. I'm telling you this: When the order comes to me, it had better read, "Mountain camp", or you'll know the reason why.'

'Then I'll know the reason why.'

'Is that final?'

'That's final.'

Without a word, Clugy turned and headed for the door. It closed behind him with a crash.

Marenson hesitated, then called his wife. She came on the visiplate in her jaunty fashion, a slim, healthy young woman of thirty-five. She smiled when she saw who it was. Marenson explained what had happened, finished:

'So you see I've got to stay down here and figure out ways and means to prevent him from getting back at me. I'll be late, I expect.'

'All right. 'Bye.'

Marenson worked fast. In the early, friendly part of his conversation with Clugy he had mentioned his vacation. Now, he called Government Messenger Service, and sent the spaceship tickets for the trip to the Paradise Planet offices for validation. While he waited for the messenger to return, he checked on Clugy.

The man was registered with his son in a suite at the Spacemen's Club. Son? Marenson's eyes narrowed. If Clugy got rough, the boy might be the best method of striking back at him.

During the next hour, he discovered that Clugy had

important 'connections' in high government circles, that he had killed four men, *juris ultima thule* – beyond the law of the uttermost limit – and that he was known as a man who liked to do a job his own way.

The tickets were returned as he reached that point. He grinned down at the union stamp of 'validation' on them. If the spacemen's organization repudiated that, they would be open to a court suit for triple damages.

Round one, accordingly, was his.

His grin faded. It was a minor victory against a man who had killed four times.

'The important thing,' Marenson decided, 'is to stay out of trouble until Janet and I are aboard the Paradise liner tomorrow. That will give me a month.'

He realized he was perspiring. He shook his head sadly. 'I'm not the man I used to be.' He looked down at his long, strong body. 'I'm getting soft. I couldn't take a really bad beating up, even with hypnotic anaesthesia.' He felt better for the admission. 'Now, I'm getting down to realities.'

The phone rang, Marenson jumped, then answered it. The man whose face came on the video said: 'Mr Clugy is just leaving the Spacemen's Club. He was in his room for about fifteen minutes.'

'Do you know where he's going?'

'He is now entering a taxigyro. There goes his destination up on the meter. Just a moment, I can hardly see it . . . Y—A . . . I got it. The Yards.'

Marenson nodded gloomily. Clugy returning to The Yards could, of course, mean many things. They were long and had many points of interest.

'Shall we beat him up, sir?'

Marenson hesitated. Ten years ago he would have said yes. Beat your opponent to the punch. That was the first principle of war between two spacemen. But he wasn't a spaceman any more. He couldn't define it, but it had something to do with prestige. If he was hurt, it was news. In that sense Clugy had an advantage over him. Because if he was caught doing anything against the man, the powerful spacemen's union would ruin him. Whereas if Clugy took action against him, his union would probably defend him on the grounds that he was acting for the best interests of his men.

Marenson's hesitation ended. 'Follow him,' he ordered, 'and report to me.'

He recognized the action of a half measure. But, then, a man couldn't risk his career on the basis of one incident. He closed his desk, and headed for home.

He found Janet still packing. She listened to his account of what he had done, a faraway expression in her eyes, and finally said: 'You surely don't expect to win that way.'

There was a tone in her voice that stung. Marenson defended himself, finishing: 'So you see, I just can't take the risks I used to take.'

'It's not a matter of risks,' she said. 'It's a matter of thoroughness.' She frowned. 'My father used to say that no man today could afford to let down his standards.'

Marenson was silent. Her father had been a fleet admiral in his day, and she regarded him as a final authority in most matters. On this occasion he was half inclined to agree with her, and yet there was another factor.

'The important thing,' he said, 'is that we get away tomorrow evening on the Paradise liner. If I do anything directly against Clugy, I might have an injunction slapped on me, or a union official may order me to appear before an investigating committee – the whole setup is dangerous.'

'Is that really the best way to get lymph juice – the way you ordered it?'

Marenson nodded vigorously. 'Yes, it is. The records go back just over three hundred years. There have been five major periods of big ship building during that time. And on each occasion the men who actually had to do the hunting have kicked up a row. Every method was tried, and the

228

statistics show the method of living in the forest to be a full seventy-five per cent more effective than any other system.'

'Did you tell that to Clugy?'

'No.' Marenson shook his head grimly.

'Why not?'

'Two generations ago, a union lawyer got a smart decision rendered against the government. The Supreme Court ruled that new techniques of hunting *could* nullify all past experience. No basically new methods of hunting had or have been developed, you understand. But, having made that statement, they then went on to draw their conclusion as if the new methods actually existed. They held that, since new techniques could nullify past experience, therefore to mention the past was to engage in unfair tactics. The government, they said, meaning the navy, was the stronger party in the dispute, and there was always danger accordingly that the interests of the men would be ignored. Therefore, the past cannot be considered. Therefore, mention of the past must be regarded as an unfair tactic. Such a tactic would automatically mean that the navy would lose the dispute.'

Marenson smiled. 'Clugy was probably waiting to pounce on me if I used that argument. Of course I may be doing him an injustice. He may not know about the ruling.'

'Are these lymph beasts really dangerous?'

He said solemnly: 'The progeny are in their own special fashion probably the deadliest creatures ever developed by Nature.'

'What are they like?'

Marenson told her. When he had finished, Janet frowned and said: 'But why are they so important? Why do we need them?'

Marenson grinned at her. 'If I told you that,' he said, 'the next time I was tested for loyalty I would not only automatically lose my job but at the very least I would be imprisoned for the rest of my life. I might be executed for treason. No, thank you, Mrs Marenson.'

There was silence for a while; and Marenson discovered that his words had chilled him just a little. He had an empty feeling in the pit of his stomach. It was so easy, working in an office, to concentrate on the details of a job, and forget the deadlier reasons for that job.

More than two hundred years before, the Yevd had come from the region of the dark obscuring matter in the center of the galaxy. Their ability to control light with the cells of their bodies was not suspected until one day a 'man' was blasted while rifling the safe of the Research Council. As the human image dissolved into a rectangular cubelike shape with numerous reticulated legs and arms, human beings had their first inkling of the fantastic danger that threatened.

The fleet was mobilized, armed helicars flew along every street, using radar to silhouette the true shapes of the Yevd. It was afterwards discovered that by a more difficult control of energy, the Yevd could guard themselves against radar. But apparently in their contempt of man's defense systems, they had not bothered to do so. On Earth and on other systems inhabited by men, altogether thirty-seven million of the enemy were killed.

Thereafter, human and Yevd ships fought each other on sight. The intensity of the war waxed and waned, but a few years before, the Yevd had occupied a planetary system near to the solar system. When they refused to leave, the United Governments started the construction of the biggest ship ever planned. Already, though it was only half finished, the great machine towered into the lower heavens.

The Yevd were a carbon-hydrogen-oxygen-fluorine life form, tough of skin and muscle, and almost immune to chemicals and bacteria that affected men. The great compelling problem for man had been to find an organism in his own part of the galaxy that would enable him to experiment for bacteriological warfare.

The progeny of the lymph beast was that organism. *And*

more! The lymph juice, when chemically separated, yielded a high percentage of heavy water.

It was believed that if the Yevd ever discovered how tremendously man was depending on the lymph beasts, they would launch a suicidal attack on the entire Mira system. There were other sources of heavy water, but no other fluorine-metabolism creature that could be used against the Yevd had yet been discovered.

The heavy water was the surface secret. It was hoped that *that* was what the Yevd would uncover if they ever began to study the problem.

Janet broke the silence with a sigh. 'Life has certainly become complicated.' She made no further comment. As soon as dinner was over, she retired to her bedroom to finish her packing. When Marenson glanced in later, her light was out and she was in bed. He closed the door softly.

At ten o'clock there was still no call from Detective Jerred. Marenson went to bed, and he must have slept, because he woke with a start to the sound of his visiphone buzzing. A glance at the night clock showed that it was a few minutes after midnight, and a glance at the plate, when he had turned it on, that it was the detective calling him at last.

'I'm back at the club,' said Jerred. 'Here's what's been happening.'

On his arrival at The Yards, Clugy had gone directly to union headquarters, and a union court sat immediately on his appeal for a reversal of the decision. His petition was refused within three hours, on the grounds that the problem involved was supervisory, and did not concern the union.

Apparently, Clugy accepted the decision. For he did not request a full dress trial, which would have required the presence of Marenson as a witness. Instead, he returned to his club where he and his son had dinner in their room. Clugy went to a show by himself, and returned about half an hour ago. He was scheduled to have breakfast at the club, and then at eleven board the freighter that would drop him off at Mira 92, a few days later.

Jerred ended: 'Looks as if he made the appeal to satisfy any protests the men might make, then let it go.'

Marenson could see how that might be. He had run up against opposition before, and for the most part it was a simple matter of legal procedure. This seemed now to be in the same category.

Clugy would have to act fast if he hoped to change the camp order before his ship departed for Mira.

Marenson said: 'Keep somebody watching him till he leaves.'

He slept well, and he must have relaxed his vigilance. As he headed for his gyro on the roof after breakfast, he was only vaguely aware of the two men who came toward him.

'Mr Marenson?' one asked.

Marenson looked up. They were well-dressed, young, strong looking. 'Why, yes,' he said, 'What —'

A gas gun exploded in his face.

Marenson woke up mad. He could feel that fury tensing his body as he came slowly up out of the darkness. And just as he was about to become fully conscious, he recognized the anger for what it was. The anger of fear.

He stayed where he was, eyes closed, body very still, forcing his breath into the slow, deep pattern of a sleeper. He was lying on something that felt like a canvas cot. It sagged in the middle, but it was reasonably comfortable.

A faint breeze blew against his cheek, and it brought a thick rancid odor to his nostrils. Jungle, he thought. Rotting vegetation intermingled with the tangy scent of innumerable growing things. The mustiness of the damp earth and something else – an acridness in the air itself, an alien atmosphere that registered on human nostrils with an almost sulphurous sharpness.

He was in a jungle on a planet that was not Earth.

232

He remembered the two young men who had come out of the stairway entrance as he walked toward his gyro. Marenson groaned inwardly. *Gassed, by heaven*, he thought. *Caught by a simple trick like that. But why? Was it personal – or Yved?*

Involuntarily, at that final possibility, Marenson cringed. The anger faded out of him completely, and only a cold fear remained. He lay then for a while simulating deep sleep. But slowly his spirit revived, and his mind began to work again. His thoughts became analytical. He remembered Clugy, but realized he couldn't be sure. As head of the procurement division for the Ship, he had in his time offended many bold and dangerous individuals.

That was one aspect, one possibility.

The other one was that the Yevd enemy of man was using him in one of their intricate games to slow down the construction of the Ship. If the Yevd were responsible, it would be complicated. The masters of light had devious minds, and took it for granted that any simple scheme would be quickly suspected.

Marenson began to breathe more easily. He was still alive, his hands were not tied; and the biggest question was: What would happen when he opened his eyes?

He opened them.

He was staring up through dense foliage at a reddish glowing sky. The sky looked hot, and that gave him a sudden awareness that he was perspiring furiously. And, oddly, now that he knew about it, the heat almost smothered him. He shrank from the flamelike intensity, then slowly climbed to his feet.

It was as if he had given a signal. From his right, beyond a line of bushes, he heard the sounds of a large camp suddenly coming to life.

For the first time, Marenson noticed that he was dressed in a light mesh unit that incased him from head to foot. The material was transparent, and even covered his boots. The clothing shocked him. For it was the kind of hunting outfit used on primitive planets that swarmed with hostile life of every description.

Which planet, and why? He began to think now with more conviction that his predicament was Clugy's doing, and that this was the famous Mira world where the lymph beast lived.

He started off in the direction of the sounds.

The line of brush that had barred his view was, he discovered, about twenty feet thick, and the moment he was through it, he saw that it was not on the outskirts of the camp, but near the center. And now he noticed that the reddish sky was something of an illusion. It was part of a barrier that had been electronically raised around the camp. An energy screen. The red effect was merely the screen's method of reacting to the light of the particular sun that was shining down upon it.

Marenson began to breathe easier. All around were men and machines – men by the hundreds. Even the most cunning group of Yevd wouldn't try to create so massive an illusion. And, besides, their great skill in the use of light was personal to each individual, and not a mass phenomenon.

A clearing was being created out of a tangle of growth. There was so much movement it was hard to know what any individual was doing. Marenson's eye for such things was ten years out of practice, but in a few moments he had oriented himself. The plastic huts were going up to his left. Those at the right were merely waiting their turn to be moved into place. Clugy's office would be in the permanent part of the encampment.

Grimly, Marenson started towards the hut village. Twice 'digger' machines harumphed past him, sowing their insect poison, and he had to step gingerly over the loose earth; in its early stages the poison was as unfriendly to human

234

beings as to anything else. The upturned soil glittered with long, black, shiny worms writhing feebly, with the famous red Mira bugs that shocked their victims with electric currents, and with other *things* that he did not recognize.

He reached the huts, walked on, and came presently to a sign which read:

PRODUCTION SUPERINTENDENT

Ira Clugy

A youth of fifteen or sixteen lolled in an easy-chair behind the counter inside. He looked up with the lazy, insolent eyes of a clerk whose boss is absent. Then he turned his back.

Marenson went through the gate, and reached for the scruff of the kid's neck. There must have been a preliminary warning, for the neck twisted away, and like a cat the boy was on his feet. He came around with a snarl on his face.

Baffled and furious, Marenson retreated into words. 'Where's Clugy?'

'I'll have you broken for this!' the boy snapped. 'My father —'

Marenson cut him off. 'Look, Mr Big Shot, I'm Marenson from Administration. I'm not the kind that's broken. I break. You'd better start talking, and fast. Is Clugy your father?'

The boy stood stiff, then nodded.

'Where is he?'

'Out in the jungle.'

'How long will he be gone?'

The boy hesitated. 'Probably be in for lunch – sir.'

'I see.' Marenson pondered the information. He was surprised that Clugy had chosen to absent himself, and so leave Ancil Marenson temporarily in full control of the camp. But from his own point of view that was all to the good. Even as he made his plans, his mind reached to another thought. He asked: 'When's the next ship due?'

'In twenty days.'

Marenson nodded. It seemed to him that he was beginning to understand. Clugy had known he was due to leave on his vacation, and so he had decided to inconvenience him. Instead of pleasure on Paradise Planet, he'd spend his vacation on primitive and dangerous Mira 92. Having no other method of countering his order, Clugy was repaying him with personal discomfort.

Marenson's lips tightened. Then he said: 'What's your name?'

'Peter.'

'Well, Peter,' said Marenson grimly, 'I've got some work for you to do. So let's get busy.'

For a while, then, it was a case of 'Where's that, Peter?' And, 'Peter, how about the stamp for this kind of document?' Altogether, in one hour he wrote out five orders. He assigned himself a Model A hut. He authorized himself to make visiradio calls to Earth. He assigned himself to Clugy's food unit. And he requisitioned two blasters, the use of a helicar and a pilot to operate it.

While Peter raced around delivering four of the orders to the proper departments, Marenson wrote out a news item for the editor of the camp newspaper. When that also was delivered, and Peter was back, Marenson felt better. What could be done on the scene was done. And since he'd have to remain for twenty days, the men in the camp might as well believe he was here on an inspection tour. The newspaper account would see to that.

Frowning, but partially satisfied, he started for the radio hut. His requisition was not questioned. He sat down and waited while the long and involved connection was put through.

Outside, men and machines were forcing a malignant stretch of jungle to be temporarily friendly to the hothouse needs of human flesh. Inside, surrounded by embanked instrument boards, Marenson pondered his next move. He had no evidence. His presence here against his will was not transparently the fault of Clugy. He had a lot of obscure back trails to investigate.

'Here's your connection,' said the radio man at last. 'Booth Three.'

'Thank you.'

Marenson talked first to his lawyer. 'I want a court order,' he said after he had described his situation, 'authorizing the camp magistrate to question Clugy by means of a lie detector, and authorizing complete amnesia afterwards. That's for my protection during the rest of the time I'll have to spend in the camp with him. Can do?'

'Can,' said the lawyer, 'by tomorrow.'

Next, Marenson connected with Jerred, head of his protective staff. The detective's face lighted as he saw who it was. 'Man,' he demanded, 'where have you been?'

His listened soberly to Marenson's account, then nodded. 'The outrage has one favorable aspect,' he said, 'it puts us into a better legal position. Perhaps now we can find out who the woman was that called Clugy's room at eleven o'clock the night before you were kidnapped. Apparently, his son answered, and must have communicated the message to him.

'Woman?' said Marenson.

Jerred shrugged. 'I don't know who it was. My agent didn't report to me till the following morning. He had no opportunity to listen in.'

Marenson nodded, and said: 'Try to see if there were any eyewitnesses to my kidnapping, then we'll get a court order and find out from Clugy and his son who the woman was.'

'You can count on us to do everything possible,' said the detective heartily.

'I expect results,' said Marenson, and broke the connection.

His next call was to his apartment. The visiplate did not brighten, and after the proper length of time, a recorder sighed at him:

'Mr and Mrs Marenson have gone to Paradise Planet until August 26th. Do you wish to leave a message?'

Marenson hung up, shaken, and went quietly out of the hut.

The fear that had come faded before his determination not to be alarmed. There must be a rational explanation for Janet's departure. He couldn't quite see how the Yevd could be involved.

He was annoyed that his mind had leaped instantly to that possibility.

A minute later, wearily, he unlocked the door of the hut. Inside, he removed his boots and sprawled on the bed. But he was too restless to relax. After less than five minutes, he got up with the intention of going to Clugy's office, and waiting there for the man to return. He had a lot of hard things to say to Ira Clugy.

Outside, he stopped short. Climbing up to his hut, he hadn't realized what a vantage point he had. The hill reared up a hundred feet above the jungle and the main part of the camp. It gave him an unsurpassed view of a green splendor, of the endless, shining forest. Clugy had chosen his camp site well. Lacking the higher mountains hundreds of miles to the south, he had nevertheless found in the hilly jungle country a sizeable semimountain that sloped gradually up until it was about eight hundred feet above the main jungle. The hill where Marenson stood was the final peak of the long, jungle-robed slope.

Marenson saw the glint of rivers, the sparkling color of strange trees; and, as he looked, something of his old feeling for this universe of planets beyond Earth stirred within him. He glanced up at the famous and wonderful Mira sun, and the thrill that came ended only when he thought of his

238

situation and his purpose. Grimly, he started down the hill.

Both Clugy and his son were in the office when Marenson entered it a few minutes later. The spaceman stood up. He seemed curious rather than friendly. 'Peter was telling me about you being here,' he said. 'So you thought you'd come and look the territory over personally, eh?'

Marenson ignored the comment. Coldly, he made his accusation. He finished, 'You may think you're going to get away with this trick, but I assure you that you aren't.'

Clugy gazed at him in astonishment. 'What's all this nonsense?' the spaceman demanded.

'Do you deny you had me kidnapped?'

'Why, certainly, I deny it.' Clugy was indignant. 'I wouldn't pull a fool stunt like that in these days of authorized lie detector tests. Besides, I don't work that way.'

He sounded so sincere that for a moment Marenson was taken aback. He recovered swiftly. 'If you're so positive,' he said, 'how about coming down right now to the camp magistrate's office, and taking an immediate test.'

Clugy frowned at him. He seemed puzzled. 'I'll do just that,' he said. He spoke quietly. 'And you'd better be prepared to take such a test yourself. There's something funny about this whole business.'

'Come along!' Marenson said.

Clugy paused at the door. 'Peter, keep an eye on the office till I get back.'

'Sure, Pop.'

The man's swift acceptance of the challenge was in itself convincing, Marenson thought as he walked along at Clugy's side. It seemed to prove that he actually had accepted the ruling of his union. His part in this affair must have ended the very night of their argument.

But then, who had seized on the situation? Who was trying to take advantage of the quarrel? Yevd? There was no indication of it. But then who?

239

The two tests required slightly less than an hour and a half. And Clugy was telling the truth. And Marenson was telling the truth. Convinced, the two men gazed at each other in baffled amazement. It was Marenson who broke the silence.

'What about the woman who called up your son the night before you left Earth?'

'What woman?'

Marenson groaned. 'You mean to tell me you don't know anything about that either?' He broke off with a frown. 'Just a minute,' he said, 'how come Peter didn't tell you?'

His mind leaped to a fantastic possibility. He said in a hushed voice: 'I think we'd better surround your hut.'

But the superintendent's office, when they finally closed in on it, was empty. Nor was Peter discoverable at any of his usual haunts.

'Obviously,' said Clugy, his face the color of lead, 'when he heard me agree to a lie detector test, he realized the game was up.'

'We've got to trace this whole thing back,' Marenson said slowly. 'Somewhere along the line a Yevd was substituted for your son. He came with you to Solar City, and took no chances on being caught by one of the several traps we have around The Yards to catch Yevd spies. I mean by that, he stayed in his room, and apparently communicated with other Yevd agents by visiradio. That woman who called the Yevd who was impersonating your son was probably another Yevd, and there's still another one of them impersonating me —'

He stopped. Because that other one was with Janet. Marenson started hastily for the radio hut. 'I've got to contact Earth,' he called over his shoulder to Clugy.

The radio hut was a shambles. On the floor, with his head blown off, was a man – Marenson couldn't be sure it was the operator. There was blood splattered on dozens of instruments, and the whole intricate machinery of an interstellar radio system had been burned by innumerable crisscrosses of energy from a powerful blaster.

Marenson did not linger in the radio hut. Back in Clugy's office, he paused only long enough to find out from that distracted man that the nearest radio station was in a settlement some nine hundred miles to the south.

'It's all right,' he said to Clugy's offer of a requisition for a helicar and pilot. 'I signed one myself this morning.'

A few minutes later he was in the air.

The speed of the machine gradually soothed Marenson. The tenseness went out of his muscles, and his mind began to work smoothly again. He stared out over the green world of the jungle, and thought: *The purpose of the Yevd is to slow down procurement of lymph juice. That's the important thing to remember*. They must have struck first at the source of the juice, and did an easy imitation of a boy. That was their usual tactic of interference at the production level. Then a new factor came into the situation. They discovered that Ancil Marenson, head of the procurement department, could be fitted into an enlarged version of their sabotage plan. Accordingly, two Yevd who looked like human beings gassed him and put him aboard the Mira freighter.

At the same time, a Yevd image of Marenson must have continued on to the office, and later that day the duplicate and Janet had probably departed together for Paradise Planet.

But why did they let me live? Marenson wondered. *Why not get me completely out of the way?*

There was only one reasonable explanation. They wanted to make further use of him. First of all, he must establish his presence, and his authority, and then – and not till then – he would be killed. And another Marenson image would order Clugy to transfer his camp to the distant mountain. In that fashion they would convince the willing Clugy that Marenson, having come to see for himself, had recognized the justice of Clugy's arguments.

Marenson felt himself change color – because that stage *had* arrived. All they needed from him was his signature on the order to Clugy. And even that could possibly be dispensed with, if they had managed to obtain some copy of his signature in the time available to them. But how would the attempt on him be made?

Uneasily, Marenson gazed out of the small helicar. He felt unprotected. He had been hasty in leaving the camp. In his anxiety to secure the safety of Janet he had exposed himself in a small ship which could be destroyed all too easily. *I'd better go back*, he decided.

He called to the pilot, 'Turn back!'

'Back?' said the man. He sounded surprised.

Marenson waved and pointed. The man seemed to hesitate, and then – he turned the machine upside down. With a crash, Marenson was flung to the ceiling of the craft. As he scrambled and fought for balance, the machine was spun once again. This time he had hold of a crossbar, and he came down more easily. He struggled to pull out a blaster.

The helicar was plummeting down towards the jungle now, and the pilot was jerking it violently to and fro. Marenson guessed his purpose and his identity, and felt ill. What a fool he had been to rush so blindly into this trap. The Yevd, knowing that he would try to send a radio message, must have killed the regular pilot – and simply waited for that simpleton Ancil Marenson to do what it expected him to do.

Marenson had a glimpse of trees terribly near. And realized the enemy's plan. A crash landing. The weak human being would be knocked unconscious, or killed. The Yevd, a carbon-hydrogen-oxygen-fluorine life form, would survive.

The next moment, there was a thump that shook his bones. During the seconds that followed, he seemed to be continuously conscious. He was even aware that the branches of strong trees had broken the fall of the ship, and so possibly saved his life. More vaguely, he knew when his blasters were taken from him. The only period of blur occurred when he was dropped to the ground from the helicar.

When his vision cleared again, he was in time to see another helicar come down in a nearby open space among the trees. The image of young Peter Clugy stepped out of it, and joined the image of the pilot. The two Yevd stood looking down at him.

Marenson braced himself. He was as good as dead, but the will to meet death standing up and fighting made him try to climb to his feet. He couldn't. His hands were tied to his legs.

He lay back weakly. He had no memory of having been tied. Which meant that he was wrong in believing that he had not been unconscious. It didn't matter, of course. With sick eyes he gazed up at his captors.

'What happened to the real Peter Clugy?' he asked finally.

The two Yevd merely continued to look at him, bleakly. Not that an answer was needed. Somewhere along the line of their moves to this point, Clugy's son had been murdered. It was possible that these two individuals did not even know the details of the killing.

Marenson changed the subject, and said with a boldness he did not feel: 'I see I made a slight personal error. Well, I'll make a bargain with you. You release me, and I'll see to it that you get safely off the planet.'

The two images wavered ever so slightly, an indication that the Yevd were talking to each other by means of light waves above the human vision level. Finally, one of them said:

'We're in no danger. We'll get off this planet in our own good time.'

Marenson laughed curtly. The laugh sounded unconvincing in his own ears, but the fact that they had answered him at all was encouraging. He said savagely: 'The whole game

243

is up. When I called Earth, the merest suspicion that Yevd were involved set in motion a far-flung defense organization. And, actually, my call was not necessary. The discovery that Yevd were involved was made in connection with my wife, Janet.'

It was a shot in the dark, but he was desperately anxious to find out if Janet were all right. Once more, there was the faint unsteadiness in the human images, that indicated conversation. Then the Yevd who was imitating Peter Clugy said:

'That's impossible. The person who accompanied your wife to Paradise Planet had instructions to destroy her if she showed the faintest sign of suspicion.'

Marenson shrugged. 'You'd better believe me,' he said.

He was tingling. His own analysis had been confirmed. Janet had gone off on her vacation with someone she thought was her husband. It was a characteristic of Yevd imitating human beings that they liked to be with a real woman or man who would be able to do things for them. There were so many things that a Yevd could do only with great difficulty, so many places where it was dangerous for an individual Yevd to go. Thus the image of Peter Clugy had taken the risk of living with the real Peter's father, and the image of Ancil Marenson had gone along with the real Janet.

The pilot Yevd said: 'We don't have to worry too much about any small group of human beings. Long-married couples are not demonstrative with each other. Days go by without kissing. In other words, the person imitating you is protected from discovery by contact for at least a week. Our plan will be accomplished by then.'

Marenson said: 'Don't be a couple of fools. I can see you're going to be stupid and make us all die. That's where this kind of stuff is so depressing. We three will die. And no one will care. It's not as if we'll be heroes, any of us.

You'll be burned, trying to escape, and I —' He broke off. 'What's your plan for me?'

'First,' said young Clugy's image, 'we want you to sign a paper.'

He paused; and Marenson sighed. His analysis of the situation had been so completely right – too late.

'And if I don't?' he asked. His voice trembled the faintest bit.

'Your signature,' was the reply, 'would merely make things easier for us. In doing what we have done, we had to act swiftly, and so none of our people capable of imitating a signature is available on this planet. That can be rectified in a few days, but fortunately for you, we want quicker action. Accordingly, we are in a position to offer you the choice of signing or not signing.'

'O.K.,' said Marenson ironically. 'My choice is – I don't sign.'

'If you sign,' the Yevd went on in an inexorable tone, 'we'll kill you mercifully.'

'And if I don't?'

'We leave you here.'

Marenson blinked. For an instant it seemed a meaningless threat. And then:

'Yes,' said Peter's image with satisfaction, 'leave you here for the lymph beast's progeny. I understand they like to burrow into the flesh of anybody they catch – a very weight-reducing experience.'

He laughed. It was a human laugh, a remarkable reproduction considering that it was done by light wave activation of a sound box it carried in its abdomen.

Marenson did not answer immediately. Until this instant, he had taken it for granted that the Yevd knew as much about the habits of those deadly dangerous creatures as did men. Apparently, their information was vague, accurate as far as it went, but —

'Of course,' said Peter Clugy's image, 'we won't really go away. We'll just go over to the ship and watch. And when you've had enough, we'll get your signature. Does that meet with your approval?'

Marenson had caught a movement out of the corner of one eye. It seemed a little more than a series of shadows very close to the ground, more like a quiver in the soil than anything substantial. But the perspiration broke out on his forehead. *Dark forest of Mira,* he thought, *alive with the young of the lymph beast* — He held himself very still, looking neither to the right nor to the left, neither at the Yevd nor at the shadow things.

'Well' – it was the Yevd image of the pilot – 'we'll stick around and have a look at some of these creatures we've been hearing so much about.'

They were moving away as the speaker reached that point. But Marenson did not turn, did not look. He heard a jerky movement, and then bright flashes lit up the dark corridor under the trees. But Marenson did not even roll his eyes. He lay still as death, silent as a log. A thing slithered across his chest, paused while he grew half-paralyzed with fright – and then moved on with a gliding movement.

The lights flashed more brilliantly now, and more erratically. And there were thumping sounds as if heavy bodies were frantically flinging themselves around. Marenson didn't have to look to realize that the enemy pair were in their death throes.

Two more Yevd were discovering the hard way that human beings were interested in the brainless lymph things because they *were* as dangerous to man's cunning opponent as to man himself.

For Marenson, the effort to remain quiet was a special agony, but he held himself there until the light was as spasmodic as a guttering candle, and as dim. When the glow had completely died, and when there had been silence for

246

more than a minute, Marenson permitted himself the exquisite luxury of turning his head slightly.

Only one of the Yevd was in his line of vision. It lay on the ground, a long, almost black, rectangular shape, with a whole series of reticulated arms and legs. Except for the appendages, it looked more like a contorted bar of metal than a thing of flesh. Here and there over its surface, the body glittered with a black, glassy sheen, evidence that some of the light-controlling cells were still alive.

In that one look, Marenson saw no less than seven discolored gashes in the part of the Yevd body that he could see – which meant that at least seven of the young lymph beasts had crawled inside. Being mindless, they would be quite unaware that they had killed anything or that there had been a struggle.

They lived to eat, and they attacked any object that moved. If it ceased moving before they reached it, they forgot about it instantly. Utterly indiscriminate, they attacked leaves drifting in the wind, the waving branch of a tree, even moving water. Millions of the tiny snake-like things died every month making insensate attacks on inanimate objects that had moved for one reason or another. Only a very small percentage survived the first two months of their existence, and changed into their final form.

In the development of the lymph beast, Nature had achieved one of her most fantastic balancing acts. The ultimate shape of the lymph beast was a hard-shelled beehivelike construction *that could not move*. It was difficult to go far into the Mira jungle without stumbling across one of these structures. They were everywhere, on the ground and in trees, on hillsides and in valleys – wherever the young monster happened to be at the moment of the change, there the 'adult' settled. The final stage was short but prolific. The 'hive' lived entirely on the food it had stored up as a youngster. Being bisexual, it spent its brief existence in a sustained ecstasy of procreation. The young, however,

247

were not discharged from the body. They incubated inside it, and when the shell died ate what was left of the parent. They also ate each other, but there were thousands of them, and the process of birth was so rapid that a fairly large proportion simply ate themselves to comparative safety outside.

On rare occasions, the outer shell failed to soften quickly enough for the progeny to escape their own savage appetites. At such times, the total 'born' was greatly reduced.

Marenson had no trouble. As soon as he had carefully examined his surroundings, he climbed to his feet – and stood silent and cautious while he made another prolonged investigation. In that fashion, step by step, he moved toward the helicar that stood in the little open space just beyond where the first machine had crashed.

He reached it and a few minutes later was back at the camp. Clugy warned, and the entire camp finally on the alert, he took another pilot-guide – this time after both he and the pilot were tested for humanness – and flew to the distant pleasure town. News awaited him there.

The Yevd gang was caught. Janet had become suspicious of the Marenson image, and had skillfully aided in its capture. That put the security police on the trail, and it was a simple matter of following the back track of the persons involved.

It took another hour before Marenson was able to contact Janet on Paradise Planet. He sighed with relief when her face came onto the visiplate. 'I was sure worried,' he said, 'when the Yevd here told me that my image was counting on the habits of old married couples. They evidently didn't realize why we were taking the trip.'

Janet was anxious. 'A police ship will be calling at Mira tomorrow,' she said, 'be sure to get on it, and come here as fast as you can.'

She finished, 'I want to spend at least part of my second honeymoon with my husband.'

WAR OF NERVES

THE voyage of the Space Beagle – *Man's first expedition to the great galaxy, M33 in Andromeda – had produced some grisly incidents. Not once, but three times, deadly attacks by aliens had been made against the 900-odd scientists under Director Morton, and the 149 military personnel commanded by Captain Leeth – all this entirely aside from the tensions that had developed among the men themselves. Hate, dislike, anxiety, ambition – of which Chief Chemist Kent's desire to be Director was but one example – permeated every activity aboard.*

Elliott Grosvenor, the only Nexialist on the ship, sometimes had the feeling that even one more danger would be too much for the physically weary and emotionally exhausted men, who were now on the long return journey to Earth.

The danger came.

Elliott Grosvenor had just said to Korita, the archeologist aboard the *Space Beagle:* 'Your brief outline of cyclic history is what I've been looking for. I did have some knowledge of it, of course. It wasn't taught at the Nexial Foundation, since it's a form of philosophy. But a curious man picks up odds and ends of information.'

They had paused at the 'glass' room on Grosvenor's floor. It wasn't glass, and it wasn't, by strict definition, a room. It was an alcove of an outer wall corridor, and the 'glass' was an enormous curving plate made from a crystallized form of one of the Resistance metals. It was so limpidly transparent as to give the illusion that nothing at all was there – beyond was the vacuum and darkness of space.

Korita half-turned away, then said, 'I know what you mean by odds and ends. For instance, I've learned just enough about Nexialism to envy you the mind trainings you received.'

At that moment, it happened – Grosvenor had noticed absently that the ship was almost through the small star cluster it had been traversing. Only a score of suns were still visible of the approximately five thousand stars that made up the system. The cluster was one of a hundred star groups accompanying Earth's galaxy through space.

Grosvenor parted his lips to say, 'I'd certainly like to talk to you again, Mr Korita.' — He didn't say it. A slightly blurred double image of a woman wearing a feathered hat was taking form in the glass directly in front of him. The image flickered and shimmered. Grosvenor felt an unnormal tensing of the muscles of his eyes. For a moment, his mind went blank. That was followed rapidly by sounds, flashes of light, a sharp sensation of pain – hypnotic hallucinations! The awareness was like an electric shock. The recognition saved him. He whirled, stumbled over the unconscious body of Korita, and then he was racing along the corridor.

As he ran, he had to look ahead in order to see his way. And yet, he had to keep blinking to break the pattern of the light flashes that came at his eyes from other images on the walls. At first, it seemed to him that the images were everywhere. Then, he noticed that the woman-like shapes – some oddly double, some single – occupied transparent or translucent wall sections. There were hundreds of such reflecting areas, but at least it was a limitation. At least he knew where he had to run fastest, and where he could slow down.

He saw more men. They lay at uneven intervals along his line of flight. Twice, he came upon conscious men. One stood in his path with unseeing eyes, and did not move or turn as Grosvenor sped by. The other man let out a yell, grabbed his vibrator, and fired it. The tracer beam flashed on the wall beside Grosvenor. Grosvenor whirled, and lunged forward, knocking the man to the floor. The man – a Kent supporter – glared at him malignantly. 'You damned spy!' he said harshly. 'We'll get you yet.' Grosvenor didn't pause. He reached his own department safely, and immediately took refuge in the film recording room. There he turned a barrage of flashing lights against the floors, the walls and the ceiling. The images were instantly eclipsed by the strong light superimposed upon them.

Quickly, Grosvenor set to work. One fact was already evident. This was mechanical visual hypnosis of such power that he had saved himself only by keeping his eyes averted, but what had happened was not limited to vision. The image had tried to control him by stimulating his brain through his eyes. He was up to date on most of the work that men had done in that field, and so he knew – though the attacker apparently did not – that control by an alien of a human nervous system was not possible except with an encephalo-adjuster or its equivalent.

He could only guess, from what had almost happened to him, that the other men had been precipitated into deep sleep trances, or else they were confused by hallucinations and were not responsible for their actions. His hope was that the woman-like beings – the enemy seemed to be feminine – were operating at a distance of several light years and so would be unable to refine their attempts at domination.

His job was to get to the control room and turn on the ship's energy screen. No matter where the attack was coming from, whether from another ship or actually from a planet, the energy screen should effectively cut off any carrier beams they might be sending.

With frantic fingers, Grosvenor worked to set up a mobile unit of lights. He needed something that would interfere with the images on his way to the control room. He was making the final connection when he felt an unmistakable sensation, a slight giddy feeling – that passed

251

almost instantly. Such feelings usually occurred during a considerable change of course and were a result of readjustment of the anti-accelerators. Had the course actually been changed? He couldn't stop to make sure. Hastily, Grosvenor carried his arrangement of lights to a power-driven loading vehicle in a nearby corridor, and placed it in the rear compartment. Then he climbed on and headed for the elevators.

He guessed that altogether ten minutes had gone by since he had first seen the image.

He took the turn into the elevator corridor at twenty-five miles an hour, which was fast for these comparatively narrow spaces. In the alcove opposite the elevators, two men were wrestling each other with a life and death concentration. They paid no attention to Grosvenor but swayed and strained and cursed. Their labored breathing was a loud sound in the confined area. Their single-minded hatred of each other was not affected by Grosvenor's arrangement of lights. Whatever world of hallucination they were in, it had 'taken' profoundly.

Grosvenor whirled his machine into the nearest elevator and started down. He was beginning to let himself hope that he might find the control room deserted. The hope died as he came to the main corridor. It swarmed with men. Barricades had been flung up, and there was an unmistakable odor of ozone. Vibrators fumed and fussed. Grosvenor peered cautiously out of the elevator, trying to size up the situation. It was visibly bad. The two approaches to the control room were blocked by scores of overturned loading-mules. Behind them crouched men in military uniform. Grosvenor caught a glimpse of Captain Leeth among the defenders and, on the far side, he saw Director Morton behind the barricade of one of the attacking groups. That clarified the picture slightly. Suppressed hostility had been stimulated by the images. The scientists were fighting the military whom they had always unconsciously hated. The

252

military, in turn, was suddenly freed to vent its contempt and fury upon the despised scientists.

It was, Grosvenor knew, not a true picture of their feeling for each other. The human mind normally balanced innumerable opposing impulses so that the average individual might live his life-span without letting one feeling gain important ascendancy over the others. That intricate balance had now been upset. The result threatened disaster to an entire expedition of human beings, and promised victory to an enemy whose purpose could only be conjectured. Whatever the reason, the way to the control room was blocked. Reluctantly, Grosvenor retreated again to his own department.

Carefully, but quickly, he tuned a wall communicator plate to the finely balanced steering devices in the fore part of the *Space Beagle*. The sending plate there was focused directly along a series of hair-line sights. The arrangement looked more intricate than it was. As he brought his eyes to the sights, Grosvenor saw that the ship was describing a slow curve which, at its climax, would bring it to bear directly on a bright white star. A servo-mechanism had been set up to make periodic adjustments that would hold it on its course.

Still he was more puzzled than alarmed. He shifted the viewer over to the bank of supplementary instruments. According to the star's special type, magnitude and luminosity, it was just over four light-years distant. The ship's speed was up to a light year every five hours. Since it was still accelerating, that would increase on a calculable curve. He estimated roughly that the vessel would reach the vicinity of the sun in approximately eleven hours. Grosvenor's thought suffered a pause at that point. With a jerky movement, he shut off the communicator. He stood there, shocked, but not incredulous. Destruction *could* be the purpose of the deluded person who had altered the ship's course. If so, there was just about ten hours in which to prevent catastrophe.

Even at that moment, when he had no clear plan, it seemed to Grosvenor that only an attack on the enemy, using hypnotic techniques, would effectively do the job. Meanwhile —

He stood up decisively. It was time for his second attempt to get into the control room.

He needed something that would cause direct stimulation to brain cells. There were several devices that could do that. Most of them were usable for medical purposes only. The exception was the encephalo-adjuster. Though important medically, it had other uses as well. It took Grosvenor several minutes to set up one of his adjusters. Testing it consumed still more time; and, because it was such a delicate machine, he had to fasten it to his loading vehicle with a cushion of springs around it. Altogether, the preparation required thirty-seven minutes.

The presence of the encephalo-adjuster made it necessary for him to keep down the speed of his vehicle as he headed for the control room. The enforced slow-down irked him, but it also gave him an opportunity to observe the changes that had taken place since the first moment of attack. He saw only an occasional unconscious body. Grosvenor guessed that most of the men who had fallen into deep trance sleeps had awakened spontaneously. Such awakenings were a common hypnotic phenomenon. Now they were responding to other stimuli on the same chance basis. Unfortunately – although that also was to be expected – it seemed to mean that long-suppressed impulses controlled their actions.

A highly developed mind – human or alien – was a built-up structure, an intricate balance of positive and negative excitations. The more superficial impulses, having considerable freedom of expression at all times, could not endanger the whole structure. The suppressed impulses, suddenly given free rein, acted like water breaking through a

254

dam. So men who, under normal circumstances merely disliked each other mildly, all in an instant had their dislike change to a murderous hatred. The deadly factor was that they would be unaware of the change. For the mind *could* be tangled without the individual being aware of it. It could be tangled by bad environmental association, or by the attack that was now being made against a ship-load of men. In either case, each person carried on as if his new beliefs were as soundly based as his old ones.

Grosvenor opened the elevator door on the control room level, and then drew back hastily. A heat projector was pouring flame along the corridor, the metal walls burning with a harsh, sizzling sound. Within his narrow field of vision, three men lay dead. As he waited, there was a thunderous explosion, and instantly, the flames stopped, blue smoke hazed the air, and there was a sense of suffocating heat. Within seconds, both the haze and the heat were gone. The ventilating system was still working.

He peered out cautiously. At first sight, the corridor seemed deserted. Then he saw Morton, half-hidden in a protective alcove less than a score of feet away, and at almost the same moment, the Director saw him and beckoned him over. Grosvenor hesitated, then realized he had to take the risk. He pushed his vehicle through the elevator doorway, and darted across the intervening space. The Director greeted him eagerly as he came up.

'You're just the man I want to see,' he said. 'We've got to get control of the ship away from Captain Leeth before Kent and his group organize their attack.'

Morton's gaze was calm and intelligent. He had the look of a man fighting for the right. Nor did it seem to occur to him that an explanation for his statement was required. The Director went on:

'We'll need your help, particularly against Kent. They're bringing up some chemical stuff I've never seen before. So far, our fans have blown it right back at them, but they're setting up fans of their own. Our big problem is, will we have time to defeat Leeth before Kent can bring his forces to bear?'

Time was also Grosvenor's problem. Unobtrusively, he brought his right hand up to his left wrist and touched the activating relay that controlled the directional sending plates of the adjuster. He pointed the plates at Morton as he said, 'I've got a plan, sir, and I think it might be effective against the enemy.'

He stopped. Morton was looking down. The Director said, 'You've brought along an adjuster, and it's on. What do you expect from that?'

Grosvenor's first tense reaction yielded to a need for a suitable answer. He had hoped that Morton would not be too familiar with adjusters. With that hope blasted, he could still try to use the instrument, though without the initial advantage of surprise. He said in a voice that was taut in spite of himself, 'That's it. It's this machine I want to use.'

Morton hesitated, then said, 'I gather from the thoughts coming into my mind that you're broadcasting —' He stopped. Interest quickened in his face. 'Say,' he said presently, 'that's good. If you can put over the notion that we're being attacked by aliens —' He broke off. His lips pursed. His eyes narrowed with calculation. He said, 'Captain Leeth has twice tried to make a deal with me. Now, we'll pretend to agree, and you go over with your machine. We'll attack the moment you signal us.' He explained with dignity, 'You understand, I would not consider dealing with either Kent or Captain Leeth except as a means to victory. You appreciate that, I hope?'

Grosvenor found Captain Leeth in the control room. The commander greeted him with stiff-backed friendliness. 'This fight among the scientists,' he said earnestly, 'has placed the military in an awkward position. We've got to defend the control room and the engine room and so perform our

256

minimum duty to the expedition as a whole.' He shook his head gravely. 'It's out of the question, of course, that either of them be allowed to win. In the final issue, we of the military are prepared to sacrifice ourselves to prevent the victory of either group.' The explanation startled Grosvenor out of his own purpose. He had been wondering if Captain Leeth was responsible for aiming the ship directly at a sun. Here was at least partial confirmation. The commander's motivation seemed to be that victory for any group but the military was unthinkable. With that beginning, it was probably only a tiny step to the concept that the whole expedition must be sacrificed. Unsuspected hypnosis had stimulated the step.

Casually, Grosvenor pointed the directional sender of the adjuster at Captain Leeth . . . . Brain waves, minute pulsations transmitted from axon to dendrite, from dendrite to axon, always following a previously established path depending on past associations – a process that operated endlessly among the ninety million neuron cells of a human brain. Each cell was in its own state of electro-colloidal balance, an intricate interplay of tension and impulse. Only gradually, over the years, had machines been developed that could detect with some degree of accuracy the meaning of the energy flow inside the brain.

The earliest encephalo-adjuster was an indirect descendant of the famous electro-encephalograph. But its function was the reverse of that first device. It manufactured artificial brain waves of any desired pattern. Using it, a skillful operator could stimulate any part of the brain, and so cause thoughts, emotions, and dreams, and bring up memories from the individual's past. It was not in itself a controlling instrument. The subject maintained his own ego. However, it could transmit the mind-impulses of one person to a second person. Since the impulses varied according to the sender's thoughts, the recipient was stimulated in a highly flexible fashion.

Unaware of the presence of the adjuster, Captain Leeth did not realize that his thoughts were no longer quite his own. He said, 'The attack being made on the ship by the images makes the quarrel of the scientists traitorous and unforgivable.' He paused, then said thoughtfully, 'Here's my plan.' The plan involved heat projectors, muscle-straining acceleration, and partial extermination of both groups of scientists. Captain Leeth failed even to mention the aliens, nor did it seem to occur to him that he was describing his intentions to an emissary of what he regarded as the enemy. He finished, 'Where your services will be important, Mr Grosvenor, is in the science department. As a Nexialist, with a coordinative knowledge of many sciences, you can play a decisive role against the other scientists —'

Weary and disheartened, Grosvenor gave up. The chaos was too great for one man to overcome. Everywhere he looked were armed men. Altogether, he had seen a score or more dead bodies. At any moment the uneasy truce between Captain Leeth and Director Morton would end in a burst of projector fire. And even now he could hear the roaring of the fans where Morton was holding off Kent's attack. He sighed as he turned back to the Captain. 'I'll need some equipment from my own department,' he said. 'Can you pass me through to the rear elevators? I can be back here in five minutes.'

As he guided his machine into the backdoor of his department a few minutes later, it seemed to Grosvenor that there was no longer any doubt about what he must do. What had seemed a far-fetched idea when he first thought of it was now the only plan he had left. He must attack the alien women through their myriad images, and with their own hypnotic weapons.

As he made his preparations, Grosvenor kept wiping the perspiration from his face, and yet it was not warm. The room temperature stood at normal. Unwillingly, he paused

258

finally to analyze his anxiety. He just didn't, he decided, know enough about the enemy. It was not sufficient that he had a theory about how they were operating. The great mystery was an enemy who had curiously woman-like faces and bodies, some partly doubled, some single. Uneasily, Grosvenor tried to imagine how Korita might analyze what was happening. In terms of cyclic history, what stage of culture could these beings be in? — The fellahin stage, he thought finally. It was actually an inevitable conclusion. A race that controlled hypnotic phenomena as did this one, would be able to stimulate each other's minds, and so would have naturally the kind of telepathy that human beings could obtain only through the encephalo-adjuster. Such beings would flash through the early stages of their culture, and arrive at the fellah stage in the swiftest possible time. *The ability to read minds without artificial aids would stultify any culture.*

Swiftly, Grosvenor went back mentally to the various civilizations of Earth history that had run their courses, apparently exhausted themselves, and then stagnated into fellahdom – Babylon, Egypt, China, Greece, Rome, and parts of west Europe. Then there were the Mayan, Toltec and Aztec cultures of early America, the East Indies, Ceylon and the mid-Pacific islanders, with their strange relics of by-gone glories – endlessly, the pattern repeated itself. Fellah folk resented newness and change, resisted it, and fought it blindly. The coming of this ship could have stirred these beings to just that kind of resistance. It seemed to Grosvenor that he had to act as if the analysis was correct. He had no other hypothesis. With such a theory as a starting point, he could try to obtain verification from one of the images. With pursed lips, he considered how it might be done. They wanted to conquer him also, of that he was sure, so accordingly, he must appear to play into their hands. A quick glance at the chronometer tensed him, as he saw he had less than seven hours to save the ship!

Hastily, he focused a beam of light through the encephalo-adjuster. With quick movements, he set a screen in front of the light, so that a small area of glass was thrown into shadow except for the intermittent light that played on it from the adjuster.

Instantly, an image appeared. It was one of the partially doubled ones, and because of the encephalo-adjuster, he was able to study it in safety. That first clear look astounded him. It was only vaguely humanoid, and yet it was understandable how his mind had leaped to the woman identification earlier. Its overlapping double face was crowned with a neat bun of golden feathers, but its head, though unmistakably bird-like now, did have a human appearance. There were no feathers on its face, which was covered with a lacework of what seemed to be veins. The human appearance resulted from the way those veins had formed into groups. They gave the effect of cheeks and nose. The second pair of eyes, and the second mouth, were in each case nearly two inches above the first. They almost made a second head, which was literally growing out of the first. There was also a second pair of shoulders, with a doubled pair of short arms that ended in beautifully delicate, amazingly long hands and fingers – and the over-all effect was still feminine. Grosvenor found himself thinking that the arms and fingers of the two bodies would be likely to separate first; then the second body would be able to help support its weight. Parthenogenesis, he thought. Here were genuine hymenopters.

The image in the wall before him showed vestigial wings, and tufts of feathers were visible at the wrists. It wore a bright blue tunic over an astonishingly straight and superficially human-like body. If there were other vestiges of a feathery past, they were hidden by the clothing. What was clear was that this bird didn't and couldn't fly under its own power.

Grosvenor completed his study swiftly. His first move

seemed as obvious as it was necessary. Somehow, he must convey to these beings that he would let himself be hypnotized in exchange for information. Tentatively, he drew a picture of the image and of himself on a blackboard. Forty-seven precious minutes and scores of drawings later, the 'bird' image suddenly faded from the wall. And a city scene appeared in its place. It was not a large community, and his first view of it was from a high vantage point. He had an impression of very tall, very narrow buildings clustered so close together that all the lower reaches must be lost in gloom for most of each day. Grosvenor wondered, in passing, if that might possibly reflect nocturnal habits in some primeval past. His mind leaped on. He ignored individual buildings in his desire to obtain a whole picture. Above everything else, he wanted to find out the extent of their machine culture, how they communicated, and if this was the city from which the attack on the ship was being launched.

He could see no machines, no aircraft, no cars, nor anything corresponding to the interstellar communication equipment used by human beings. On Earth, such communication required stations spaced over many square miles of land. It seemed likely, therefore, that this was not the origin of the attack. He had guessed, of course, that they would not show him anything vital. Even as he made his negative discovery, the view changed. He was no longer on a hill, but on a building near the center of the city. Whatever was taking that perfect color picture moved forward, and he looked down over the edge. His primary concern was with the whole scene. Yet he found himself wondering how they were showing it to him. The transition from one scene to another had been accomplished in the twinkling of an eye. Less than a minute had passed since his blackboard illustration had finally made known his desire for information.

That thought, like the others, was a flashing one. Even as he had it, he was gazing avidly down the side of the building.

261

The space separating it from the nearby structures seemed no more than ten feet. But now he saw something that had not been visible from the hillside. The buildings were connected on every level by walks only inches wide. Along these moved the pedestrian traffic of the bird city. Directly below Grosvenor, two individuals strode towards each other along the same narrow walk, seemingly unconcerned by the fact that it was a hundred feet or more to the ground. They passed casually, easily. Each swung his outside leg wide around the other, caught the walk, bent his inside leg far out, and then they were by, without having broken pace. There were other people on other levels going through the same intricate maneuvers in the same nonchalant manner. Watching them, Grosvenor guessed that their bones were thin and hollow, and that they were lightly built.

The scene changed again, and then again. It moved from one section of the street to another. He saw, it seemed to him, every possible variation of the reproductive condition. Some were so far advanced that the legs and arms and most of the body were free. Others were as he had already seen them. In every instance, the 'parent' seemed unaffected by the weight of the new body.

Grosvenor was trying to get a glimpse inside one of the dim interiors of a building when the picture began to fade from the wall. In a moment, the city had disappeared completely. In its place grew the double image. The image-fingers pointed at the encephalo-adjuster. Its motion was unmistakable. It had fulfilled its part of the bargain. It was time for him to fulfill his. Its naïve expectation that he would do so was typically fellah. Unfortunately, he had no alternative but to carry out his 'obligation'.

'I am calm and relaxed,' said Grosvenor's recorded voice. 'My thoughts are clear. What I see is not necessarily related to what I am looking at. What I hear may be meaningless to the interpretive centers of my brain, but I have seen their city as they think it is. Whether what I actually see and hear makes sense or nonsense, I remain calm, relaxed, and at ease . . . '

Grosvenor listened carefully to the words, and then nodded. The time might come, of course, when he would not consciously hear the message. But it would be there. Its patterns would impress ever more firmly on his mind. Still listening, he examined the adjuster for the last time, and all was as he wanted it. Carefully, he set the automatic cut-off for five hours. At the end of that time, unless he were dead, the limited cross connection would be broken. He would have preferred his first break to be in seconds, or minutes, but what he was about to do was not merely a scientific experiment – it was a life and death gamble. Ready for action, he put his hand on the control dial, and there he paused. For this was the moment. Within a few seconds the group mind of perhaps thousands of individual birdfolk would be in 'possession' of parts of his nervous system. They would undoubtedly try to control him as they were controlling the other men on the ship.

He was fairly positive that he would be up against a group of minds working together. He had seen no machines; not even a wheeled vehicle, that most primitive of mechanical devices. For a short time, he had taken it for granted that they were using television-type cameras. Now, he guessed that he had seen the city through the eyes of individuals, as with these beings, telepathy was a sensory process as sharp as vision itself. The enmassed mindpower of millions of bird-people could hurdle light years of distance. They didn't need machines.

On Earth, and elsewhere, nearly all lower order life forms that reproduced by parthenogenesis worked together in a curious unity of purpose. It suggested an interrelation that could dispense with actual physical contact.

Fellahdom must be a long standing condition of this race. There would be no doubt in the mind of the individual about the 'truth' of what it saw and heard and felt. It would be only too easy for them to settle into an inflexible pattern of existence. That pattern was now going to feel the sledge-hammer impact of new ideas. He couldn't hope to foresee the result.

Still listening to the recorder, Grosvenor manipulated the dial of the encephalo-adjuster, and slightly modified the rhythm of his own thoughts. It had to be slight. Even if he had wanted to, he could not offer the aliens complete attunement. In those rhythmic pulsations lay every variation of sanity, unsanity, and insanity. He had to restrict his reception to waves that would register 'sane' on a psychologist's graph.

The adjuster superimposed them on a beam of light which in turn shone directly on the image. If the individual 'behind' the image was affected by the pattern in the light, it didn't show it yet. Grosvenor did not expect overt evidence, and so he was not disappointed. He was convinced that the result would become apparent only in the changes that occurred in the patterns they were directing at him. And that, he was sure, he would have to experience with his own nervous system.

It was hard for him to concentrate on the image, but he persisted. The encephalo-adjuster began to interfere markedly with his vision, and still he stared steadily at the image.

'. . . I am calm and relaxed. My thoughts are clear . . .'

One instant the words were loud in his ears, and the next, they were gone. In their stead was a roaring sound as of distant thunder.

The noise faded slowly. It became a steady throbbing like the murmur in a large sea shell. Grosvenor was aware of a faint light. It was far away, and had the hazy dimness of a lamp seen through thick fog.

'I'm still in control,' he assured himself. 'I'm getting sense impressions through its nervous system. It's getting impressions through mine.'

He could wait. He could sit here and wait until the darkness cleared, until his brain started to make some kind of interpretation of the sense phenomena that were being telegraphed from that other nervous system. He could sit here and —

He stopped. 'Sit!' he thought. Was that what *it* was doing? He poised intent and alert. He heard a distant voice say, 'Whether what I actually see and hear makes sense or nonsense, I remain calm —' The sound of his recorded voice relieved him anew. The danger would come if his body were forced away from that reassuring sound, and away from the encephalo-adjuster. Until that threatened, he could let the alien impressions seep into him.

His nose began to itch. He thought: 'They don't have noses; at least I didn't see any. Therefore, it's either my own nose, or a random stimulation.' He started to reach up to scratch it, and felt a sharp pain in his stomach. He would have doubled up with the hurt of it if he had been able. He couldn't. He couldn't scratch his nose or put his hands on his abdomen.

He realized then that the itch and the pain stimuli did not derive from his own body, nor did they necessarily have any corresponding meaning in the other's nervous system. Two highly developed life forms were sending signals to each other – he hoped that he was sending signals to it also – which neither could interpret. His advantage was that he had expected it. The alien, if it was fellah, and if Korita's theory was valid, hadn't and couldn't expect it. Understanding that, *he* could hope for adjustment. *It* could only become more confused.

The itch went away, and the pain in his stomach became a feeling of satiation, as if he had eaten too much. A hot needle stabbed at his spine, digging at each vertebra. Half way down, the needle turned to ice, and the ice melted and ran in a freezing stream down his back. Something – a hand? a piece of metal? a pair of tongs? – snatched at a bundle of muscles in his arm, and almost tore them out by the roots. His mind shrieked with pain messages and he almost lost consciousness.

Grosvenor was a badly shaken man when that sensation faded into nothingness. These were all illusions. No such things were happening anywhere, not in his body, not in that of the bird-being. His brain was receiving a pattern of impulses through his eyes, and was misinterpreting them. In such a relationship, pleasure could become pain, any stimulus could produce any feeling. He hadn't counted on the misinterpretations being so violent.

He forgot that as his lips were caressed by something soft and squishy. A voice said, 'I am loved —' Grosvenor rejected the meaning. 'No, not loved.' It was, he believed, his own brain again trying to interpret sense phenomena from a nervous system that was experiencing a reaction different from any comparable human emotion. Consciously, he substituted the words: 'I am stimulated by . . . '– and then let the feeling run its course. In the end, he still didn't know what it was that he had felt. The stimulation was not unpleasant. His taste buds were titillated by a sense of sweetness, and his eyes watered. It was a relaxing process. A picture of a flower came into his mind. It was a lovely, red, Earth carnation, and thus could have no connection with the flora of the Riim world. 'Riim!' he thought. His mind poised in tense fascination. Had that come to him across the gulf of space? In some irrational way, the name seemed to fit. Yet no matter what came through, a doubt would remain in his mind.

The final series of sensations had all been pleasant. Nevertheless, he waited anxiously for the next manifestation. The light remained dim and hazy – then, once more his eyes seemed to water, his feet suddenly itched intensely. The sensation passed, leaving him unaccountably hot, and weighted by a suffocating lack of air.

'False!' he told himself. 'Nothing like that is happening.'

The stimulations ceased. Again there was only the steady throbbing sound, and the all-pervasive blur of light. It began to worry him. It was possible that his method was right and that, given time, he would eventually be able to exercise some control over a member, or a group of members of the enemy. Time was what he could not spare. Every passing second brought him a colossal distance nearer personal destruction. Out there – here (for an instant he was confused) – in space, one of the biggest and costliest ships ever built by men was devouring the miles at a velocity that had almost no meaning.

He knew which parts of his brain were being stimulated. He could hear a noise only when sensitive areas at the side of the cortex received sensations. The brain surface above the ear, when titillated, produced dreams and old memories. In the same way, every part of the human brain had long ago been mapped. The exact location of stimulation areas differed slightly for each individual, but the general structure, among humans, was always the same.

The normal human eye was a fairly objective mechanism. The lens focussed a real image on the retina. Judging by the pictures of their city, as transmitted by the Riim-folk, they also possessed objectively accurate eyes. If he could co-ordinate his visual centers with their eyes, he would receive dependable pictures.

More minutes went by. He thought, in sudden despair: 'Is it possible that I'm going to sit here the full five hours without ever making a useful contact?' For the first time, he questioned his good sense in committing himself so completely to this situation. When he tried to move his hand over to the control lever of the encephalo-adjuster, nothing seemed to happen. A number of vagrant sensations came, among them, unmistakably, the odor of burning rubber. For a third time, his eyes watered. And then, sharp and clear, a picture came. It flashed off as swiftly as it had flashed on. To Grosvenor, who had been trained by advanced tachistoscopic techniques, the after-image remained as vivid in his mind as if he had had a leisurely look. It seemed as if he were in one of the tall, narrow buildings. The interior was dimly lighted by the reflections from the sunlight that came through the open doors, as there were no windows. Instead of floors, the 'residence' was fitted with catwalks. A few bird people were sitting on these walks. The walls were lined with doors, indicating the existence of cabinets and storage areas.

The visualization both excited and disturbed him. Suppose he did establish a relationship whereby he was affected by its nervous system, and it by his. Suppose he reached the point where he could hear with its ears, see with its eyes, and feel to some degree what it felt. These were sensory impressions only. Could he hope to bridge the gap, and induce motor responses in the creature's muscles? Would he be able to force it to walk, turn its head, move its arms, and, generally, make it act as his body? The attack on the ship was being made by a group working together, thinking together, feeling together. By gaining control of one member of such a group, could he exercise some control over all?

His momentary vision must have come through the eyes of one individual. What he had experienced so far did not suggest any kind of group contact. He was like a man imprisoned in a dark room with a hole in the wall in front of him covered with layers of translucent material. Through this filtered a vague light. Occasionally, images penetrated the blur, and he had glimpses of the outside world. He could be fairly certain that the pictures were accurate, but that did not apply to the sounds that came through another hole on a side wall, or the sensations that came to him through still other holes in the ceiling and floor.

Humans could hear frequencies up to 20,000 a second. That was where some races started to hear. Under hypnosis, men could be conditioned to laugh uproariously when they were being tortured, and shriek with pain when tickled. Stimulation that meant pain to one life form, could mean nothing at all to another.

Mentally, Grosvenor let the tensions seep out of him. There was nothing for him to do but to relax and wait. He waited.

It occurred to him presently that there might be a connection between his own thoughts and the sensations he received. That picture of the inside of the building – what had he thought just before it came? Principally, he recalled, he had visualized the structure of the eye. The connection was so obvious that his mind trembled with excitement. There was another thing, also. Until now, he had concentrated on the notion of seeing and feeling with the nervous system of the individual. Still the realization of his hopes depended on his establishing contact with, and control of, the group of minds that had attacked the ship.

He saw his problem, suddenly, as one that would require control of his own brain. Certain areas would have to be virtually blacked out, kept at minimum performance levels. Others must be made extremely sensitive, so that all incoming sensations found it easier to seek expression through them. As a highly trained auto-hypnotic subject, he could accomplish both objectives by suggestion. Vision came first, of course. Then muscular control of the individual, through whom the group was working against him.

Flashes of colored light interrupted his concentration. Grosvenor regarded them as evidence of the effectiveness of his suggestions. He knew that he was on the right track when his vision cleared suddenly, and stayed clear. The scene was the same. His control still sat on one of the roosts inside one of the tall buildings. Hoping fervently that the vision was not going to fade, Grosvenor began to concentrate on moving the Riim's muscles. The trouble was that the ultimate explanation of why a movement could occur

269

at all was obscure. His visualization had to be on a level that was already gross. Nothing happened. Shocked but determined, Grosvenor tried symbol hypnosis, using a single cue word to cover the entire complex process.

Slowly, one of the attenuated arms came up. Another cue, and his control stood up cautiously. Then he made it turn its head. The act of looking reminded the bird-being that that drawer and that cabinet and that closet were 'mine'. The memory barely touched the conscious level. The creature knew its own possessions and accepted the fact without concern.

Grosvenor had a hard time fighting down his excitement. With tense patience, he had the bird-being get up from a sitting position, raise its arms, lower them, and walk back and forth along the roost. Finally, he made it sit down again. He must have been keyed up, his brain responsive to the slightest suggestion. Because he had barely started to concentrate again when his whole being was flooded by a message that seemed to affect every level of his thought and feeling. More or less automatically, Grosvenor translated the anguished thoughts into familiar verbalisms.

'. . . The cells are calling, calling. The cells are afraid. Oh, the cells know pain! There is darkness in the Riim world. Withdraw from the being – far from Riim . . . Shadows, darkness, turmoil . . . The cells must reject him . . . but they cannot. They were right to try to destroy the being who came out of the great dark. The night deepens. All cells withdraw . . . but they cannot . . .'

Grosvenor thought exultantly: 'I've got them!' After a minute of tremendous excitement, he grew sober. His problem was greater than theirs. If he broke his connection with them, they would be free. By avoiding him thereafter, they could go on to achieve the purpose of their disruptive attack . . . destruction of the *Space Beagle*. He would still have the problem of overcoming Morton and the others. He had no alternative but to go on with his plan.

He concentrated first on what seemed the most logical intermediate stage: – the transfer of control to another alien. The choice, in the case of these beings, was obvious.

'I am loved!' he told himself, deliberately producing the sensation which had confused him earlier. 'I am loved by my parent body, from which I am growing to wholeness. I share my parent's thoughts, but already I see with my own eyes, and know that I am one of the group . . .'

The transition came suddenly, as Grosvenor had expected it might. He moved the smaller, duplicate fingers. He arched the fragile shoulders. Then he oriented himself again to the parent Riim. The experiment was so completely satisfactory that he felt ready for the bigger jump that would take him into association with the nervous system of a more distant alien. That, also, proved to be a matter of stimulating the proper brain centers. Grosvenor came to awareness standing in a wilderness of brush and hill. Directly in front of him was a narrow stream, and beyond it, an orange sun rode low in a dark purple sky that was spotted with fleecy clouds. Grosvenor made his new control turn completely around. He saw that a small roost building, the only habitation in sight, nestled among the trees farther along the stream. He walked toward the building and looked inside. In the dim interior, he made out several roosts, one with two birds sitting on it, both with eyes closed. It was quite possible, he decided, that they were participating in the group assault on the *Space Beagle*.

From there, by a variation of the stimulus, he transferred his control to an individual on a part of the planet where it was night. The transition this time was even faster. He was in a lightless city, with ghostly buildings and catwalks. Swiftly, Grosvenor moved on to association with other nervous systems. He had no clear idea why the 'rapport' was established with one Riim, and not with another who fitted the same general requirement. It could be that the stimulations affected some individuals slightly faster than it

271

affected others. It was even possible that these were descendants or body-relatives of his original parent-control. When he had been associated with more than two dozen Riim all over the planet, it seemed to Grosvenor that he had a good, over-all impression.

It was a world of brick and stone and wood, and of a neuralogical community relationship that would probably never be surpassed. A race had by-passed the entire machine-age of man, with its penetration of the secrets of matter and energy. Now, he felt, he could safely take the next-to-the-last step of his counter-attack. He concentrated on a pattern which would characterize one of the beings who had projected an image to the *Space Beagle*. (He had, then, a sense of a small but noticeable lapse of time.) Then he was looking forth from one of the images, seeing the ship through an image.

His first concern was with how the battle was progressing, but he had to restrain his will to know because to come aboard was only part of his necessary pre-conditioning. He wanted to affect a group of perhaps millions of individuals, and had to affect them so powerfully that they would have to withdraw from the *Space Beagle*, and have no recourse but to stay away from it.

He had proved that he could receive their thoughts, and that they could receive his. His association with one nervous system after another would not have been possible unless that was so. Now he was ready. He thought into the darkness:

'You live in a Universe; and within you, you form pictures of the Universe as it seems to you. Of that Universe you know nothing and can know nothing except for the pictures, but the pictures within you of the Universe are not the Universe . . .'

How could you influence another's mind? — By changing his assumptions. How could you alter another's actions? — By changing his basic beliefs, his emotional certainties.

Carefully, Grosvenor went on: 'And the pictures within you do not show all about the Universe, for there are many things which you cannot know directly, not having senses to know. Within the Universe there is an order, and if the order of the pictures within you is not as the order of the Universe, then you are deceived . . .'

In the history of life, few thinking beings had ever done anything illogical – within their frame of reference. If the frame was falsely based, if the assumptions were untrue to reality, then the individual's automatic logic could lead him to disastrous conclusions.

The assumptions had to be changed. Grosvenor changed them, deliberately, coolly, honestly. His own basic hypothesis behind what he was doing was that the Riim had no defense. These were the first new ideas they had had in countless generations and he did not doubt that the impact would be colossal. This was a fellah civilization, rooted in certainties that had never before been challenged. There was ample historical evidence that a tiny intruder could influence decisively the future of entire fellahin races.

Huge old India had crumbled before a few thousand Englishmen. Similarly, all the fellah peoples of ancient Earth were taken over with ease, and did not revive till the core of their inflexible attitudes was forever shattered by the dawning realization that there was more to life than they had been taught under their rigid systems. The Riim were peculiarly vulnerable. Their method of communication, unique and wonderful though it was, made it possible to influence them all in a single intensive operation. Over and over, Grosvenor repeated his message, adding, each time, one instruction that had to do with the ship. The instruction was:

'Change the pattern you are using against those on the ship, and then withdraw it. Change the pattern, so that they can relax, and sleep . . . then withdraw it . . . do not attack again . . .'

273

He had only a vague notion as to how long he actually poured his commands into that tremendous neural circuit. He guessed about two hours. Whatever the time involved, it ended as the relay switch on the encephalo-adjuster automatically broke the connection between himself and the image in the wall of his department. Abruptly, he was aware of the familiar surroundings of his own department. He glanced at where the image had been and tensed as he saw that it was still there, but shook his head slightly. He could hardly expect a definite reaction this soon. The Riim, also, were recovering from a connection that had just been broken.

As Grosvenor watched, the pattern of light from the image changed subtly. Grosvenor's head drooped sleepily. He sat up jerkily, remembering. The instructions he had given – to relax and sleep – this was the result. All over the ship, men would be sleeping as the new hypnotic pattern extended its inhibitory paralysis over the hemispheres of the brain.

About three minutes went by. Suddenly, the double image of the Riim vanished from the glistening wall in front of him. A moment later, Grosvenor was out in the corridor. As he raced along, he saw that unconscious men lay everywhere but that the walls were bright and clear. Not once on his journey to the control room did he see an image.

Inside the control room, he stepped gingerly over the sleeping form of Captain Leeth, who lay on the floor near the control panel. With a sigh of relief, Grosvenor threw the switch that energized the outer screen of the ship.

Seconds later, Elliott Grosvenor was in the control chair, altering the course of the *Space Beagle*.

THE EXPENDABLES

1

ONE HUNDRED and nine years after leaving Earth, the spaceship, *Hope of Man*, went into orbit around Alta III.

The following 'morning' Captain Browne informed the shipload of fourth and fifth generation colonists that a manned lifeboat would be dropped to the planet's surface.

'Every member of the crew must consider himself expendable,' he said earnestly. 'This is the day that our great grandparents, our forefathers, who boldly set out for the new space frontier so long ago, looked forward to with unfaltering courage. We must not fail them.'

He concluded his announcement over the intercom system of the big ship by saying that the names of the crew members of the lifeboat would be given out within the hour. 'And I know that every real man aboard will want to see his name there.'

John Lesbee, the fifth of his line aboard, had a sinking sensation as he heard those words – and he was not mistaken.

Even as he tried to decide if he should give the signal for a desperate act of rebellion, Captain Browne made the expected announcement.

The commander said, 'And I know you will all join him in his moment of pride and courage when I tell you that John Lesbee will lead the crew that carries the hopes of man in this remote area of space. And now the others —'

He thereupon named seven of the nine persons with whom Lesbee had been conspiring to seize control of the ship.

Since the lifeboat would only hold eight persons, Lesbee recognized that Browne was dispatching as many of his enemies as he could. He listened with a developing dismay, as the commander ordered all persons on the ship to come to the recreation room. 'Here I request that the crew of the lifeboat join me and the other officers on stage. Their instructions are to surrender themselves to any craft which seeks to intercept them. They will be equipped with instruments whereby we here can watch, and determine the stage of scientific attainments of the dominant race on the planet below.'

Lesbee hurried to his room on the technicians' deck, hoping that perhaps Tellier or Cantlin would seek him out there. He felt himself in need of a council of war, however brief. He waited five minutes, but not one member of his conspiratorial group showed.

Nonetheless, he had time to grow calm. Peculiarly, it was the smell of the ship that soothed him most. From the earliest days of his life, the odor of energy and the scent of metal under stress had been perpetual companions. At the moment, with the ship in orbit, there was a letting up of stress. The smell was of old energies rather than new. But the effect was similar.

He sat in the chair he used for reading, eyes closed, breathing in that complex of odors, product of so many titanic energies. Sitting there, he felt the fear leave his mind and body. He grew brave again, and strong.

Lesbee recognized soberly that his plan to seize power had involved risks. Worse, no one would question Browne's choice of him, as the leader of the mission. 'I am,' thought Lesbee, 'probably the most highly trained technician ever to be on this ship.' Browne Three had taken him when he was ten, and started him on the long grind of learning that led him, one after the other, to master the mechanical skills of all the various technical departments. And Browne Four had continued his training.

He was taught how to repair relay systems. He gradually

came to understand the purposes of countless analogs. The time came when he could visualize the entire automation. Long ago, the colossal cobweb of electronic instruments within the walls had become almost an extension of his nervous system.

During those years of work and study, each daily apprenticeship chore left his slim body exhausted. After he came off duty, he sought a brief relaxation and usually retired to an early rest.

He never did find the time to learn the intricate theory that underlay the ship's many operations.

His father, while he was alive, had made numerous attempts to pass his knowledge on to his son. But it was hard to teach complexities to a tired and sleepy boy. Lesbee even felt slightly relieved when his parent died. It took the pressure off him. Since then, however, he had come to realize that the Browne family, by forcing a lesser skill on the descendant of the original commander of the ship, had won their greatest victory.

As he headed finally for the recreation room, Lesbee found himself wondering: Had the Brownes trained him with the intention of preparing him for such a mission as this?

His eyes widened. If that was true, then his own conspiracy was merely an excuse. The decision to kill him might actually have been made more than a decade ago, and light years away . . .

As the lifeboat fell toward Alta III, Lesbee and Tellier sat in the twin control chairs and watched on the forward screen the vast, misty atmosphere of the planet.

Tellier was thin and intellectual, a descendant of the physicist Dr Tellier who had made many speed experiments in the early days of the voyage. It had never been understood why spaceships could not attain even a good fraction of the speed of light, let alone velocities greater than light. When the scientist met his untimely death, there was no one with the training to carry on a testing program.

It was vaguely believed by the trained personnel who succeeded Tellier that the ship had run into one of the paradoxes implicit in the Lorenz-Fitzgerald Contraction theory.

Whatever the explanation, it was never solved.

Watching Tellier, Lesbee wondered if his companion and best friend felt as empty inside as he did. Incredibly, this was the first time he – or anyone – had been outside the big ship. 'We're actually heading down,' he thought, 'to one of those great masses of land and water, a planet.'

As he watched, fascinated, the massive ball grew visibly bigger.

They came in at a slant, a long, swift, angling approach, ready to jet away if any of the natural radiation belts proved too much for their defense systems. But as each stage of radiation registered in turn, the dials showed that the lifeboat machinery made the proper responses automatically.

The silence was shattered suddenly by an alarm bell.

Simultaneously, one of the screens focused on a point of rapidly moving light far below. The light darted toward them.

A missile!

Lesbee caught his breath.

But the shining projectile veered off, turned completely around, took up position several miles away, and began to fall with them.

His first thought was: 'They'll never let us land,' and he experienced an intense disappointment.

Another signal brrred from the control board.

'They're probing us,' said Tellier, tensely.

An instant after the words were uttered, the lifeboat seemed to shudder and to stiffen under them. It was the

278

unmistakable feel of a tractor beam. Its field clutched the lifeboat, drew it, held it.

The science of the Alta III inhabitants was already proving itself formidable.

Underneath him the lifeboat continued its movement.

The entire crew gathered around and watched as the point of brightness resolved into an object, which rapidly grew larger. It loomed up close, bigger than they.

There was a metallic bump. The lifeboat shuddered from stem to stern.

Even before the vibrations ceased Tellier said, 'Notice they put our airlock against theirs.'

Behind Lesbee, his companions began that peculiar joking of the threatened. It was a coarse comedy, but it had enough actual humor suddenly to break through his fear. Involuntarily he found himself laughing.

Then, momentarily free of anxiety, aware that Browne was watching and that there was no escape, he said, 'Open the airlock! Let the aliens capture us as ordered.'

2

A few minutes after the outer airlock was opened, the airlock of the alien ship folded back also. Rubberized devices rolled out and contacted the Earth lifeboat, sealing off both entrances from the vacuum of space.

Air hissed into the interlocking passageway between the two craft. In the alien craft's lock, an inner door opened.

Again Lesbee held his breath.

There was a movement in the passageway. A creature ambled into view. The being came forward with complete assurance, and pounded with something he held at the end of one of his four leathery arms on the hull.

The creature had four legs and four arms, and a long thin body held straight up. It had almost no neck, yet the many skin folds between the head and the body indicated great flexibility was possible.

Even as Lesbee noted the details of its appearance, the being turned his head slightly, and its two large expressionless eyes gazed straight at the hidden wall receptor that was photographing the scene, and therefore straight into Lesbee's eyes.

Lesbee blinked at the creature, then tore his gaze away, swallowed hard, and nodded at Tellier. 'Open up!' he commanded.

The moment the inner door of the Earth lifeboat opened, six more of the four-legged beings appeared one after another in the passageway, and walked forward in the same confident way as had the first.

All seven creatures entered the open door of the lifeboat.

As they entered, their thoughts came instantly into Lesbee's mind . . .

As Dzing and his boarding party trotted from the small Karn ship through the connecting airlock, his chief officer thought a message to him.

'Air pressure and oxygen content are within a tiny percentage of what exists at ground level on Karn. They can certainly live on our planet.'

Dzing moved forward into the Earth ship, and realized that he was in the craft's control chamber. There, for the first time, he saw the men. He and his crew ceased their forward motion; and the two groups of beings – the humans and the Karn – gazed at each other.

The appearance of the two-legged beings did not surprise Dzing. Pulse viewers had, earlier, penetrated the metal walls of the lifeboat and had accurately photographed the shape and dimension of those aboard.

His first instruction to his crew was designed to test if the strangers were, in fact, surrendering. He commanded: 'Convey to the prisoners that we require them as a precaution to remove their clothing.'

. . . Until that direction was given, Lesbee was still un-

280

certain as to whether or not these beings could receive human thoughts as he was receiving theirs. From the first moment, the aliens had conducted their mental conversations *as if* they were unaware of the thoughts of the human beings. Now he watched the Karn come forward. One tugged suggestively at his clothing. And there was no doubt.

The mental telepathy was a one-way flow only – from the Karn to the humans.

He was already savoring the implications of that as he hastily undressed . . . It was absolutely vital that Browne do not find it out.

Lesbee removed all his clothes; then, before laying them down, took out his notebook and pen. Standing there naked he wrote hurriedly:

'Don't let on that we can read the minds of these beings.'

He handed the notebook around, and he felt a lot better as each of the men read it, and nodded at him silently.

Dzing communicated telepathically with someone on the ground. 'These strangers,' he reported, 'clearly acted under command to surrender. The problem is, how can we now let them overcome us without arousing their suspicion that this is what we want them to do?'

Lesbee did not receive the answer directly. But he picked it up from Dzing's mind: 'Start tearing the lifeboat apart. See if that brings a reaction.'

The members of the Karn boarding party went to work at once. Off came the control panels; floor plates were melted and ripped up. Soon instruments, wiring, controls were exposed for examination. Most interesting of all to the aliens were the numerous computers and their accessories.

Browne must have watched the destruction; for now, before the Karn could start wrecking the automatic machinery, his voice interjected:

'Watch out, you men! I'm going to shut your airlock

and cause your boat to make a sharp right turn in exactly twenty seconds.'

For Lesbee and Tellier that simply meant sitting down in their chairs, and turning them so that the acceleration pressure would press them against the backs. The other men sank to the ripped-up floor, and braced themselves.

Underneath Dzing, the ship swerved. The turn began slowly, but it propelled him and his fellows over to one wall of the control room. There he grabbed with his numerous hands at some handholds that had suddenly moved out from the smooth metal. By the time the turn grew sharper, he had his four short legs braced, and he took the rest of the wide swing around with every part of his long, sleek body taut. His companions did the same.

Presently, the awful pressure eased up, and he was able to estimate that their new direction was almost at right angles to what it had been.

He had reported what was happening while it was going on. Now, the answer came: 'Keep on destroying. See what they do, and be prepared to succumb to anything that looks like a lethal attack.'

Lesbee wrote quickly in his notebook: 'Our method of capturing them doesn't have to be subtle. They'll make it easy for us – so we can't lose.'

Lesbee waited tensely as the notebook was passed around. It was still hard for him to believe that no one else had noticed what he had about this boarding party.

Tellier added a note of his own: 'It's obvious now that these beings were also instructed to consider themselves expendable.'

And that settled it for Lesbee. The others hadn't noticed what he had. He sighed with relief at the false analysis, for it gave him that most perfect of all advantages: that which derived from his special education.

Apparently, he alone knew enough to have analyzed what these creatures were.

The proof was in the immense clarity of their thoughts. Long ago, on earth, it had been established that man had a faltering telepathic ability, which could be utilized consistently only by electronic amplification *outside* his brain. The amount of energy needed for the step-up process was enough to burn out brain nerves, if applied directly.

Since the Karn were utilizing it directly, they couldn't be living beings.

Therefore, Dzing and his fellows were an advanced robot type.

The true inhabitants of Alta III were not risking their own skins at all.

Far more important to Lesbee, he could see how he might use these marvellous mechanisms to defeat Browne, take over the *Hope of Man*, and start the long journey back to Earth.

3

He had been watching the Karn at their work of destruction, while he had these thoughts. Now, he said aloud: 'Hainker, Graves.'

'Yes?' The two men spoke together.

'In a few moments I'm going to ask Captain Browne to turn the ship again. When he does, use our specimen gas guns!'

The men grinned with relief. 'Consider it done,' said Hainker.

Lesbee ordered the other four crewmen to be ready to use the specimen-holding devices at top speed. To Tellier he said, 'You take charge if anything happens to me.'

Then he wrote one more message in the notebook: 'These beings will probably continue their mental intercommunication after they are apparently rendered unconscious. Pay no attention, and do not comment on it in any way.'

He felt a lot better when that statement also had been

283

read by the others, and the notebook was once more in his possession. Quickly, he spoke to the screen:

'Captain Browne! Make another turn, just enough to pin them.'

And so they captured Dzing and his crew.

As he had expected, the Karn continued their telepathic conversation. Dzing reported to his ground contact: 'I think we did that rather well.'

There must have been an answering message from below, because he went on, 'Yes, commander. We are now prisoners as per your instructions, and shall await events . . . The imprisoning method? Each of us is pinned down by a machine which has been placed astride us, with the main section adjusted to the contour of our bodies. A series of rigid metal appendages fasten our arms and legs. All these devices are electronically controlled, and we can of course escape at any time. Naturally, such action is for later . . .'

Lesbee was chilled by the analysis; but for expendables there was no turning back.

He ordered his men: 'Get dressed. Then start repairing the ship. Put all the floor plates back except the section at G-8. They removed some of the analogs, and I'd better make sure myself that it all goes back all right.'

When he had dressed, he reset the course of the lifeboat, and called Browne. The screen lit up after a moment, and there staring back at him was the unhappy countenance of the forty-year-old officer.

Browne said glumly: 'I want to congratulate you and your crew on your accomplishments. It would seem that we have a small scientific superiority over this race, and that we can attempt a limited landing.'

Since there would never be a landing on Alta III, Lesbee simply waited without comment as Browne seemed lost in thought.

The officer stirred finally. He still seemed uncertain. 'Mr Lesbee,' he said, 'as you must understand, this is an extremely dangerous situation for me – and – ' he added hastily – 'for this entire expedition.'

What struck Lesbee, as he heard those words, was that Browne was not going to let him back on the ship. But he had to get aboard to accomplish his own purpose. He thought: 'I'll have to bring this whole conspiracy out into the open, and apparently make a compromise offer.'

He drew a deep breath, gazed straight into the eyes of Browne's image on the screen and said with the complete courage of a man for whom there is no turning back: 'It seems to me, sir, that we have two alternatives. We can resolve all these personal problems either through a democratic election or by a joint captaincy, you being one of the captains and I being the other.'

To any other person who might have been listening the remark must have seemed a complete non sequitur. Browne, however, understood its relevance. He said with a sneer, 'So you're out in the open. Well, let me tell you, Mr Lesbee, there was never any talk of elections when the Lesbees were in power. And for a very good reason. A spaceship requires a technical aristocracy to command it. As for a joint captaincy, it wouldn't work.'

Lesbee urged his lie: 'If we're going to stay here, we'll need at least two people of equal authority – one on the ground, one on the ship.'

'I couldn't trust you on the ship!' said Browne flatly.

'Then you be on the ship,' Lesbee proposed. 'All such practical details can be arranged.'

The older man must have been almost beside himself with the intensity of his own feelings on this subject. He flashed, 'Your family has been out of power for over fifty years! How can you still feel that you have any rights?'

Lesbee countered, 'How come you still know what I'm talking about?'

Browne said, a grinding rage in his tone, 'The concept

of inherited power was introduced by the first Lesbee. It was never planned.'

'But here you are,' said Lesbee, 'yourself a beneficiary of inherited power.'

Browne said from between clenched teeth: 'It's absolutely ridiculous that the Earth government which was in power when the ship left – and every member of which has been long dead – should appoint somebody to a command position . . . and that now his descendant think that command post should be his, and his family's, for all time!'

Lesbee was silent, startled by the dark emotions he had uncovered in the man. He felt even more justified, if that were possible, and advanced his next suggestion without a qualm.

'Captain, this is a crisis. We should postpone our private struggle. Why don't we bring one of these prisoners aboard so that we can question him by use of films, or play acting? Later, we can discuss your situation and mine.'

He saw from the look on Browne's face that the reasonableness of the suggestion, *and its potentialities*, were penetrating.

Browne said quickly, 'Only you come aboard – and with one prisoner only. No one else!'

Lesbee felt a dizzying thrill as the man responded to his bait. He thought: 'It's like an exercise in logic. He'll try to murder me as soon as he gets me alone and is satisfied that he can attack without danger to himself. But that very scheme is what will get me aboard. And I've got to get on the ship to carry out *my* plan.'

Browne was frowning. He said in a concerned tone: 'Mr Lesbee, can you think of any reason why we should not bring one of these beings aboard?'

Lesbee shook his head. 'No reason, sir,' he lied.

Browne seemed to come to a decision. 'Very well. I'll see you shortly, and we can then discuss additional details.'

Lesbee dared not say another word. He nodded, and

broke the connection, shuddering, disturbed, uneasy.

'But,' he thought, 'what else can we do?'

He turned his attention to the part of the floor that had been left open for him. Quickly, he bent down and studied the codes on each of the programming units, as if he were seeking exactly the right ones that had originally been in those slots.

He found the series he wanted: an intricate system of cross-connected units that had originally been designed to program a remote-control landing system, an advanced Waldo mechanism capable of landing the craft on a planet and taking off again, all directed on the pulse level of human thought.

He slid each unit of the series into its sequential position and locked it in.

Then, that important task completed, he picked up the remote control attachment for the series and casually put it in his pocket.

He returned to the control board and spent several minutes examining the wiring and comparing it with a wall chart. A number of wires had been torn loose. These he now re-connected, and at the same time he managed with a twist of his pliers to short-circuit a key relay of the remote control pilot.

Lesbee replaced the panel itself loosely. There was no time to connect it properly. And, since he could easily justify his next move, he pulled a cage out of the storeroom. Into this he hoisted Dzing, manacles and all.

Before lowering the lid he rigged into the cage a simple resistor that would prevent the Karn from broadcasting on the human thought level. The device was simple merely in that it was not selective. It had an on-off switch which triggered, or stopped, energy flow in the metal walls on the thought level.

When the device was installed, Lesbee slipped the tiny

remote control for *it* into his other pocket. He did not activate the control. Not yet.

From the cage Dzing telepathed: 'It is significant that these beings have selected me for this special attention. We might conclude that it is a matter of mathematical accident, or else that they are very observant and so noticed that I was the one who directed activities. Whatever the reason, it would be foolish to turn back now.'

A bell began to ring. As Lesbee watched, a spot of light appeared high on one of the screens. It moved rapidly toward some crossed lines in the exact center of the screen. Inexorably, then, the *Hope of Man*, as represented by the light, and the lifeboat moved toward their fateful rendezvous.

4

Browne's instructions were: 'Come to Control Room Below!'

Lesbee guided his powered dolly with the cage on it out of the big ship's airlock P – and saw that the man in the control room of the lock was Second Officer Selwyn. Heavy brass for such a routine task. Selwyn waved at him with a twisted smile as Lesbee wheeled his cargo along the silent corridor.

He saw no one else on his route. Other personnel had evidently been cleared from this part of the vessel. A little later, grim and determined, he set the cage down in the center of the big room and anchored it magnetically to the floor.

As Lesbee entered the captain's office, Browne looked up from one of the two control chairs and stepped down from the rubber-sheathed dais to the same level as Lesbee. He came forward, smiling, and held out his hand. He was a big man, as all the Brownes had been, bigger by a head than Lesbee, good-looking in a clean-cut way. The two men were alone.

'I'm glad you were so frank,' he said. 'I doubt if I could have spoken so bluntly to you without your initiative as an example.'

But as they shook hands, Lesbee was wary and suspicious. Lesbee thought: 'He's trying to recover from the insanity of his reaction. I really blew him wide open.'

Browne continued in the same hearty tone: 'I've made up my mind. An election is out of the question. The ship is swarming with untrained dissident groups, most of which simply want to go back to Earth.'

Lesbee, who had the same desire, was discreetly silent.

Browne said, 'You'll be ground captain; I'll be ship captain. Why don't we sit down right now and work out a communique on which we can agree and that I can read over the intercom to the others?'

As Lesbee seated himself in the chair beside Browne, he was thinking: 'What can be gained from publicly naming me ground captain?'

He concluded finally, cynically, that the older man could gain the confidence of John Lesbee – lull him, lead him on, delude him, destroy him.

Surreptitiously Lesbee examined the room. Control Room Below was a large square chamber adjoining the massive central engines. Its control board was a duplicate of the one on the bridge located at the top of the ship. The great vessel could be guided equally from either board, except that pre-emptive power was on the bridge. The officer of the watch was given the right to make Merit decisions in an emergency.

Lesbee made a quick mental calculation, and deduced that it was First Officer Miller's watch on the bridge. Miller was a staunch supporter of Browne. The man was probably watching them on one of his screens, ready to come to Browne's aid at a moment's notice.

A few minutes later, Lesbee listened thoughtfully as Browne

read their joint communique over the intercom, designating him as ground captain. He found himself a little amazed, and considerably dismayed, at the absolute confidence the older man must feel about his own power and position on the ship. It was a big step, naming his chief rival to so high a rank.

Browne's next act was equally surprising. While they were still on the viewers, Browne reached over, clapped Lesbee affectionately on the shoulders and said to the watching audience:

'As you all know, John is the only direct descendant of the original captain. No one knows exactly what happened half a hundred years ago when my grandfather first took command. But I remember the old man always felt that only he understood how things should be. I doubt if he had any confidence in *any* young whippersnapper over whom he did not have complete control. I often felt that my father was the victim rather than the beneficiary of my grandfather's temper and feelings of superiority.'

Browne smiled engagingly. 'Anyway, good people, though we can't unbreak the eggs that were broken then, we can certainly start healing the wounds, without – ' his tone was suddenly firm – 'negating the fact that my own training and experience make me the proper commander of the ship itself.'

He broke off. 'Captain Lesbee and I shall now jointly attempt to communicate with the captured intelligent life form from the planet below. You may watch, though we reserve the right to cut you off for good reason.' He turned to Lesbee. 'What do you think we should do first, John?'

Lesbee was in a dilemma. The first large doubt had come to him, the possibility that perhaps the other was sincere. The possibility was especially disturbing because in a few moments a part of his own plan would be revealed.

He sighed, and realized that there was no turning back at this stage. He thought: 'We'll have to bring the entire

290

madness out into the open, and only then can we begin to consider agreement as real.'

Aloud, he said in a steady voice, 'Why not bring the prisoner out where we can see him?'

As the tractor beam lifted Dzing out of the cage, and thus away from the energies that had suppressed his thought waves, the Karn telepathed to his contact on Alta III:

'Have been held in a confined space, the metal of which was energized against communication. I shall now attempt to perceive and evaluate the condition and performance of this ship —'

At that point, Browne reached over and clicked off the intercom. Having shut off the audience, he turned accusingly to Lesbee, and said, 'Explain your failure to inform me that these beings communicated by telepathy.'

The tone of his voice was threatening. There was a hint of angry color in his face.

It was the moment of discovery.

Lesbee hesitated, and then simply pointed out how precarious their relationship had been. He finished frankly, 'I thought by keeping it a secret I might be able to stay alive a little longer, which was certainly not what you intended when you sent me out as an expendable.'

Browne snapped, 'But how did you hope to utilize —?'

He stopped. 'Never mind,' he muttered.

Dzing was telepathing again:

'In many ways this is mechanically a very advanced type ship. Atomic energy drives are correctly installed. The automatic machinery performs magnificently. There is massive energy screen equipment, and they can put out a tractor beam to match anything we have that's mobile. But there is a wrongness in the energy flows of this ship, which I lack the experience to interpret. Let me furnish you some data . . .'

The data consisted of variable wave measurements,

evidently – so Lesbee deduced – the wavelengths of the energy flows involved in the 'wrongness'.

He said in alarm at that point, 'Better drop him into the cage while *we* analyze what he could be talking about.'

Browne did so – as Dzing telepathed: 'If what you suggest is true, then these beings are completely at our mercy —'

Cut off!

Browne was turning on the intercom. 'Sorry I had to cut you good people off,' he said. 'You'll be interested to know that we have managed to tune in on the thought pulses of the prisoner and have intercepted his calls to someone on the planet below. This gives us an advantage.' He turned to Lesbee. 'Don't you agree?'

Browne visibly showed no anxiety, whereas Dzing's final statement flabbergasted Lesbee. '. . . *completely at our mercy . . .*' surely meant exactly that. He was staggered that Browne could have missed the momentous meaning.

Browne addressed him enthusiastically. 'I'm excited by this telepathy! It's a marvelous short-cut to communication, if we could build up our own thought pulses. Maybe we could use the principle of the remote-control landing device which, as you know, can project human thoughts on a simple, gross level, where ordinary energies get confused by the intense field needed for the landing.'

What interested Lesbee in the suggestion was that he had in his pocket a remote control for precisely such mechanically produced thought pulses. Unfortunately, the control was for the lifeboat. It probably would be advisable to tune the control to the ship landing system also. It was a problem he had thought of earlier, and now Browne had opened the way for an easy solution.

He held his voice steady as he said, 'Captain, let me program those landing analogs while you prepare the film communication project. That way we can be ready for him either way.'

292

Browne seemed to be completely trusting, for he agreed at once.

At Browne's direction, a film projector was wheeled in. It was swiftly mounted on solid connections at one end of the room. The cameraman and Third Officer Mindel – who had come in with him – strapped themselves into two adjoining chairs attached to the projector, and were evidently ready.

While this was going on, Lesbee called various technical personnel. Only one technician protested. 'But, John,' he said, 'that way we have a double control – with the lifeboat control having pre-emption over the ship. That's very unusual.'

It was unusual. But it was the lifeboat control that was in his pocket where he could reach it quickly; and so he said adamantly, 'Do you want to talk to Captain Browne? Do you want his okay?'

'No, no.' The technician's doubts seemed to subside. 'I heard you being named joint captain. You're the boss. It shall be done.'

Lesbee put down the closed-circuit phone into which he had been talking, and turned. It was then he saw that the film was ready to roll, and that Browne had his fingers on the controls of the tractor beam. The older man stared at him questioningly.

'Shall I go ahead?' he asked.

At this penultimate moment, Lesbee had a qualm.

Almost immediately he realized that the only alternative to what Browne planned was that he reveal his own secret knowledge.

He hesitated, torn by doubts. Then: 'Will you turn that off?' He indicated the intercom.

Browne said to the audience, 'We'll bring you in again on this in a minute, good people.' He broke the connection and gazed questioningly at Lesbee.

Whereupon Lesbee said in a low voice, 'Captain, I should inform you that I brought the Karn aboard in the hope of using him against you.'

'Well, that is a frank and open admission,' the officer replied very softly.

'I mention this,' said Lesbee, 'because if you had similar ulterior motives, we should clear the air completely before proceeding with this attempt at communication.'

A blossom of color spread from Browne's neck over his face. At last he said slowly, 'I don't know how I can convince you, but I had no schemes.'

Lesbee gazed at Browne's open countenance, and suddenly he realized that the officer was sincere. Browne had accepted the compromise. The solution of a joint captaincy was agreeable to him.

Sitting there, Lesbee experienced an enormous joy. Seconds went by before he realized what underlay the intense pleasurable excitement. It was simply the discovery that – communication worked. You could tell your truth and get a hearing . . . if it made sense.

It seemed to him that his truth made a lot of sense. He was offering Browne peace aboard the ship. Peace at a price, of course; but still peace. And in this severe emergency Browne recognized the entire validity of the solution.

So it was now evident to Lesbee.

Without further hesitation he told Browne that the creatures who had boarded the lifeboat, were robots – not alive at all.

Browne was nodding thoughtfully. Finally he said: 'But I don't see how this could be utilized to take over the ship.'

Lesbee said patiently, 'As you know, sir, the remote landing control system includes five principal ideas which are projected very forcibly on the thought level. Three of these are for guidance – up, down and sideways. Intense magnetic fields, any one of which could partially jam a

294

complex robot's thinking process. The fourth and fifth are instructions to blast either up or down. The force of the blast depends on how far the control is turned on. Since the energy used is overwhelming, those simple commands would take pre-emption over the robot. When that first one came aboard the lifeboat, I had a scan receiver – nondetectable – on him. This registered two power sources, one pointing forward, one backward, from the chest level. That's why I had him on his back when I brought him in here. But the fact is I could have had him tilted and pointing at a target, and activated either control four or five, thus destroying whatever was in the path of the resulting blast. Naturally, I took all possible precautions to make sure that this did not happen until you had indicated what you intended to do. One of these precautions would enable us to catch this creature's thoughts without —'

As he was speaking, he eagerly put his hand into his pocket, intending to show the older man the tiny on-off control device by which – when it was off – they would be able to read Dzing's thoughts without removing him from the cage.

He stopped short in his explanation, because an ugly expression had come suddenly into Browne's face.

The big man glanced at Third Officer Mindel. 'Well, Dan,' he said, 'do you think that's it?'

Lesbee noticed with shock that Mindel had on sound amplifying earphones. He must have overheard every word that Browne and he had spoken to each other.

Mindel nodded. 'Yes, Captain,' he said. 'I very definitely think he has now told us what we wanted to find out.'

Lesbee grew aware that Browne had released himself from his acceleration safety belt and was stepping away from his seat. The officer turned and, standing very straight, said in a formal tone:

'Technician Lesbee, we have heard your admission of gross dereliction of duty, conspiracy to overthrow the lawful government of this ship, scheme to utilize alien creatures to destroy human beings, and confession of other unspeakable crimes. In this extremely dangerous situation, summary execution without formal trial is justified. I therefore sentence you to death and order Third Officer Dan Mindel to —'

He faltered, and came to a stop.

5

Two things had been happening as he talked. Lesbee squeezed the 'off' switch of the cage control, an entirely automatic gesture, convulsive, a spasmodic movement, result of his dismay. It was a mindless gesture. So far as he knew consciously, freeing Dzing's thoughts had no useful possibility for him. His only real hope – as he realized almost immediately – was to get his other hand into his remaining coat pocket and with it manipulate the remote-control landing device, the secret of which he had so naïvely revealed to Browne.

The second thing that happened was that Dzing, released from mental control, telepathed:

'Free again – and this time of course permanently! I have just now activated by remote control the relays that will in a few moments start the engines of this ship, and I have naturally re-set the mechanism for controlling the rate of acceleration —'

His thoughts must have impinged progressively on Browne, for it was at that point that the officer paused uncertainly.

Dzing continued: 'I verified your analysis. This vessel does not have the internal energy flows of an interstellar ship. These two-legged beings have therefore failed to achieve the Light Speed Effect which alone makes possible trans-light velocities. I suspect they have taken many generations to make this journey, are far indeed from their home base, and I'm sure I can capture them all.'

Lesbee reached over, tripped on the intercom and yelled at the screen: 'All stations prepare for emergency acceleration! Grab anything!'

To Browne he shouted: 'Get to your seat – *quick!*'

His actions were automatic responses to danger. Only after the words were spoken did it occur to him that he had no interest in the survival of Captain Browne. And that in fact the only reason the man was in danger was because he had stepped away from his safety belt, so that Mindel's blaster would kill Lesbee without damaging Browne.

Browne evidently understood his danger. He started toward the control chair from which he had released himself only moments before. His reaching hands were still a foot or more from it when the impact of Accleration One stopped him. He stood there trembling like a man who had struck an invisible but palpable wall. The next instant Acceleration Two caught him and thrust him on his back to the floor. He began to slide toward the rear of the room, faster and faster, and because he was quick and understanding he pressed the palms of his hands and his rubber shoes hard against the floor and so tried to slow the movement of his body.

Lesbee was picturing other people elsewhere in the ship desperately trying to save themselves. He groaned, for the commander's failure was probably being duplicated everywhere.

Even as he had that thought, Acceleration Three caught Browne. Like a rock propelled by a catapult he shot toward the rear wall. It was cushioned to protect human beings, and so it reacted like rubber, bouncing him a little. But the stuff had only momentary resilience.

Acceleration Four pinned Browne halfway into the cushioned wall. From its imprisoning depths, he managed a strangled yell.

'Lesbee, put a tractor beam on me! Save me! I'll make it up to you. I —'

Acceleration Five choked off the words.

The man's appeal brought momentary wonder to Lesbee. He was amazed that Browne hoped for mercy . . . after what had happened.

Browne's anguished words did produce one effect in him. They reminded him that there was something he must do. He forced his hand and his arm to the control board and focussed a tractor beam that firmly captured Third Officer Mindel and the cameraman. His intense effort was barely in time. Acceleration followed acceleration, making movement impossible. The time between each surge of increased speed grew longer. The slow minutes lengthened into what seemed an hour, then many hours. Lesbee was held in his chair as if he were gripped by hands of steel. His eyes felt glassy; his body had long since lost all feeling.

He noticed something.

The rate of acceleration was different from what the original Tellier had prescribed long ago. The actual increase in forward pressure each time was less.

He realized something else. For a long time, no thoughts had come from the Karn.

Suddenly, he felt an odd shift in speed. A physical sensation of slight, very slight, angular movement accompanied the maneuver.

Slowly, the metal-like bands let go of his body. The numb feeling was replaced by the pricking as of thousands of tiny needles. Instead of muscle-compressing acceleration there was only a steady pressure.

It was the pressure that he had in the past equated with gravity.

Lesbee stirred hopefully, and when he felt himself move, realized what had happened. The artificial gravity had been shut off. Simultaneously, the ship had made a half turn within its outer shell. The drive power was now coming from below, a constant one gravity thrust.

At this late, late moment, he plunged his hand into the

298

pocket which held the remote control for the pilotless landing mechanism – and activated it.

'That ought to turn on his thoughts,' he told himself savagely.

But if Dzing was telepathing to his masters, it was no longer on the human thought level. So Lesbee concluded unhappily.

The ether was silent.

He now grew aware of something more. The ship smelled different: better, cleaner, purer.

Lesbee's gaze snapped over to the speed dials on the control board. The figures registering there were unbelievable. They indicated that the spaceship was traveling at a solid fraction of the speed of light.

Lesbee stared at the numbers incredulously. 'We didn't have time!' he thought. 'How could we go so fast so quickly – in hours only to near the speed of light!'

Sitting there, breathing hard, fighting to recover from the effects of that prolonged speed-up, he felt the fantastic reality of the universe. During all this slow century of flight through space, the *Hope of Man* had had the potential for this vastly greater velocity.

He visualized the acceleration series so expertly programmed by Dzing as having achieved a shift to a new state of matter in motion. The 'light speed effect', the Karn robot had called it.

'And Tellier missed it,' he thought.

All those experiments the physicist had performed so painstakingly, and left a record of, had missed the great discovery.

Missed it! And so a shipload of human beings had wandered for generations through the black deeps of interstellar space.

Across the room Browne was climbing groggily to his feet. He muttered, '. . . Better get back to . . . control chair.'

He had taken only a few uncertain steps when a realization seemed to strike him. He looked up then, and stared wildly at Lesbee. 'Oh!' he said. The sound came from the gut level, a gasp of horrified understanding.

As he slapped a complex of tractor beams on Browne, Lesbee said, 'That's right, you're looking at your enemy. Better start talking. We haven't much time.'

Browne was pale now. But his mouth had been left free and so he was able to say huskily, 'I did what any lawful government does in an emergency. I dealt with treason summarily, taking time only to find out what it consisted of.'

Lesbee had had another thought, this time about Miller on the bridge. Hastily, he swung Browne over in front of him. 'Hand me your blaster,' he said. 'Stock first.'

He freed the other's arm, so that he could reach into the holster and take it out.

Lesbee felt a lot better when he had the weapon. But still another idea had come to him. He said harshly, 'I want to lift you over to the cage, and I don't want First Officer Miller to interfere. Get that, *Mister* Miller!'

There was no answer from the screen.

Browne said uneasily, 'Why over to the cage?'

Lesbee did not answer right away. Silently he manipulated the tractor beam control until Browne was in position. Having gotten him there, Lesbee hesitated. What bothered him was, why had the Karn's thought impulses ceased? He had an awful feeling that something was very wrong indeed.

He gulped, and said, 'Raise the lid!'

Again, he freed Browne's arm. The big man reached over gingerly, unfastened the catch, and then drew back and glanced questioningly at Lesbee.

'Look inside!' Lesbee commanded.

Browne said scathingly, 'You don't think for one second that —' He stopped, for he was peering into the cage. He uttered a cry: 'He's gone!'

Lesbee discussed the disappearance with Browne.

It was an abrupt decision on his part to do so. The question of where Dzing might have got to was not something he should merely turn over in his own head.

He began by pointing at the dials from which the immense speed of the ship could be computed, and then, when that meaning was absorbed by the older man, said simply, 'What happened? Where did he go? And how could we speed up to just under 186,000 miles a second in so short a time?'

He had lowered the big man to the floor, and now he took some of the tension from the tractor beam but did not release the power. Browne stood in apparent deep thought. Finally, he nodded. 'All right,' he said, 'I know what happened.'

'Tell me.'

Browne changed the subject, said in a deliberate tone, 'What are you going to do with me?'

Lesbee stared at him for a moment unbelievingly. 'You're going to withhold this information?' he demanded.

Browne spread his hands. 'What else can I do? Till I know my fate, I have nothing to lose.'

Lesbee suppressed a strong impulse to rush over and strike his prisoner. He said finally, 'In your judgment is this delay dangerous?'

Browne was silent, but a bead of sweat trickled down his cheek. '*I* have nothing to lose,' he repeated.

The expression in Lesbee's face must have alarmed him, for he went on quickly, 'Look, there's no need for you to conspire any more. What you really want is to go home, isn't it? Don't you see, with this new method of acceleration, we can make it to Earth in a few *months!*'

He stopped. He seemed momentarily uncertain.

Lesbee snapped angrily, 'Who are you trying to fool?

Months! We're a dozen light years in actual distance from Earth. You mean years, not months.'

Browne hesitated then: 'All right, a few years. But at least not a lifetime. So if you'll promise not to scheme against me further, I'll promise —'

'*You'll* promise!' Lesbee spoke savagely. He had been taken aback by Browne's instant attempt at blackmail. But the momentary sense of defeat was gone. He knew with a stubborn rage that he would stand for no nonsense.

He said in an uncompromising voice, 'Mister Browne, twenty seconds after I stop speaking, you start talking. If you don't, I'll batter you against these walls. I mean it!'

Browne was pale. 'Are you going to kill me? That's all I want to know. Look –' his tone was urgent – 'we don't have to fight any more. We can go home. Don't you see? The long madness is just about over. Nobody has to die.'

Lesbee hesitated. What the big man said was at least partly true. There was an attempt here to make twelve years sound like twelve days, or at most twelve weeks. But the fact was, it *was* a short period compared to the century-long journey which, at one time, had been the only possibility.

He thought: 'Am I going to kill him?'

It was hard to believe that he would, under the circumstances. All right. If not death, then what? He sat there uncertain. The vital seconds went by, and he could see no solution. He thought finally, in desperation: 'I'll have to give in for the moment. Even a minute thinking about this is absolutely crazy.'

He said aloud in utter frustration, 'I'll promise you this. If you can figure out how I can feel safe in a ship commanded by you I'll give your plan consideration. And now, mister, start talking.'

Browne nodded. 'I accept that promise,' he said. 'What we've run into here is the Lorenz-Fitzgerald Contraction

302

Theory. Only it's not a theory any more. We're living the reality of it.'

Lesbee argued, 'But it only took us a few hours to get to the speed of light.'

Browne said, 'As we approach light speed, space foreshortens and time compresses. What seemed like a few hours would be days in normal time and space.'

What Browne explained then was different rather than difficult. Lesbee had to blink his mind to shut out the glare of his old ideas and habits of thought, so that the more subtle shades of super-speed phenomena could shine through into his awareness.

The time compression – as Browne explained it – was gradational. The rapid initial series of accelerations were obviously designed to pin down the personnel of the ship. Subsequent increments would be according to what was necessary to attain the ultra-speed finally achieved.

Since the drive was still on, it was clear that some resistance was being encountered, perhaps from the fabric of space itself.

It was no time to discuss technical details. Lesbee accepted the remarkable reality and said quickly, 'Yes, but where is Dzing?'

'My guess,' said Browne, 'is that he did not come along.'

'How do you mean?'

'The space-time foreshortening did not affect him.'

'But —' Lesbee began blankly.

'Look,' said Browne harshly, 'don't ask me how he did it. My picture is, he stayed in the cage till after the acceleration stopped. Then, in a leisurely fashion, he released himself from the electrically locked manacles, climbed out, and went off to some other part of the ship. He wouldn't have to hurry since by this time he was operating at a rate of, say, five hundred times faster than our living pace.'

Lesbee said, 'But that means he's been out there for hours – his time. What's he been up to?'

Browne admitted that he had no answer for that.

'But you can see,' he pointed out anxiously, 'that I meant what I said about going back to Earth. We have no business in this part of space. These beings are far ahead of us scientifically.'

His purpose was obviously to persuade. Lesbee thought: 'He's back to *our* fight. That's more important to him than any damage the real enemy is causing.'

A vague recollection came of the things he had read about the struggle for power throughout Earth history. How men intrigued for supremacy while vast hordes of the invader battered down the gates. Browne was a true spiritual descendant of all those mad people.

Slowly, Lesbee turned and faced the big board. What was baffling to him was, what could you do against a being who moved five hundred times as fast as you did?

7

He had a sudden sense of awe, a picture . . . At any given instant Dzing was a blur. A spot of light. A movement so rapid that, even as the gaze lighted on him, he was gone to the other end of the ship – and back.

Yet Lesbee knew it took time to traverse the great ship from end to end. Twenty, even twenty-five minutes, was normal walking time for a human being going along the corridor known as Center A.

It would take the Karn a full six seconds there and back. In its way that was a significant span of time, but after Lesbee had considered it for a moment he felt appalled.

What could they do against a creature who had so great a time differential in his favor?

From behind him, Browne said, 'Why don't you use against him that remote landing control system that you set up with my permission?'

Lesbee confessed: 'I did that, as soon as the acceleration

ceased. But he must have been – back – in the faster time by then.'

'That wouldn't make any difference,' said Browne.

'Eh!' Lesbee was startled.

Browne parted his lips evidently intending to explain, and then he closed them again. Finally he said, 'Make sure the intercom is off.'

Lesbee did so. But he was realizing that Browne was up to something again. He said, and there was rage in his tone, 'I don't get it, and you do. Is that right?'

'Yes,' said Browne. He spoke deliberately, but he was visibly suppressing excitement. 'I know how to defeat this creature. That puts me in a bargaining position.'

Lesbee's eyes were narrowed to slits. 'Damn you, no bargain. Tell me, or else!'

Browne said, 'I'm not really trying to be difficult. You either have to kill me, or come to some agreement. I want to know what that agreement is, because of course I'll do it.'

Lesbee said, 'I think we ought to have an election.'

'I agree!' Browne spoke instantly. 'You set it up.' He broke of. 'And now release me from these tractors and I'll show you the neatest space-time trick you've ever seen, and that'll be the end of Dzing.'

Lesbee gazed at the man's face, saw there the same openness of countenance, the same frank honesty that had preceded the execution order, and he thought, 'What can he do?'

He considered many possibilities, and thought finally, desperately: 'He's got the advantage over me of superior knowledge – the most undefeatable weapon in the world. The only thing I can really hope to use against it in the final issue is *my* knowledge of a multitude of technician-level details.'

But – what could Browne do against Lesbee?

He said unhappily to the other, 'Before I free you, I want to lift you over to Mindel. When I do, you get his blaster for me.'

'Sure,' said Browne casually.

A few moments later he handed Mindel's gun over to Lesbee. So that wasn't it.

Lesbee thought: 'There's Miller on the bridge – can it be that Miller flashed him a ready signal when my back was turned to the board?'

Perhaps, like Browne, Miller had been temporarily incapacitated during the period of acceleration. It was vital that he find out Miller's present capability.

Lesbee tripped the intercom between the two boards. The rugged, lined face of the first officer showed large on the screen. Lesbee could see the outlines of the bridge behind the man and, beyond, the starry blackness of space. Lesbee said courteously, 'Mr Miller, how did you make out during the acceleration?'

'It caught me by surprise, Captain. I really got a battering. I think I was out for a while. But I'm all right now.'

'Good,' said Lesbee. 'As you probably heard, Captain Browne and I have come to an agreement, and we are now going to destroy the creature that is loose on the ship. Stand by!'

Cynically, he broke the connection.

Miller was there all right, waiting. But the question was still, what could Miller do? The answer of course was that Miller could pre-empt. And – Lesbee asked himself – what could *that* do?

Abruptly, it seemed to him, he had the answer.

It was the technician's answer that he had been mentally straining for.

He now understood Browne's plan. They were waiting for Lesbee to let down his guard for a moment. Then Miller would pre-empt, cut off the tractor beam from Browne and seize Lesbee with it.

For the two officers it was vital that Lesbee not have time to fire the blaster at Browne. Lesbee thought: 'It's the only

306

thing they can be worried about. The truth is, there's nothing else to stop them.'

The solution was, Lesbee realized with a savage glee, to let the two men achieve their desire. But first —

'Mr Browne,' he said quietly, 'I think you should give your information. If I agree that it is indeed the correct solution, I shall release you and we shall have an election. You and I will stay right here till the election is over.'

Browne said, 'I accept your promise. The speed of light is a constant, and does not change in relation to moving objects. That would also apply to electromagnetic fields.'

Lesbee said, 'Then Dzing was affected by the remote-control device I turned on.'

'Instantly,' said Browne. 'He never got a chance to do anything. How much power did you use?'

'Only first stage,' said Lesbee. 'But the machine-driven thought pulses in that would interfere with just about every magnetic field in his body. He couldn't do another coherent thing.'

Browne said in a hushed tone, 'It's got to be. He'll be out of control in one of the corridors, completely at our mercy.' He grinned. 'I told you I knew how to defeat him – because, of course, he was already defeated.'

Lesbee considered that for a long moment, eyes narrowed. He realized that he accepted the explanation, but that he had preparations to make, and quickly – before Browne got suspicious of his delay.

He turned to the board and switched on the intercom. 'People,' he said, 'strap yourselves in again. Help those who were injured to do the same. We may have another emergency. You have several minutes, I think, but don't waste any of them.'

He cut off the intercom, and he activated the closed-circuit intercom of the technical stations. He said urgently, 'Special instruction to Technical personnel. Report anything unusual, particularly if strange thought forms are going through your mind.'

He had an answer to that within moments after he finished speaking. A man's twangy voice came over: 'I keep thinking I'm somebody named Dzing, and I'm trying to report to my owners. Boy, am I incoherent!'

'Where is this?'

'D – 4 – 19.'

Lesbee punched the buttons that gave them a TV view of that particular ship location. Almost immediately he spotted a shimmer near the floor.

After a moment's survey he ordered a heavy-duty mobile blaster brought to the corridor. By the time its colossal energies ceased, Dzing was only a darkened area on the flat surface.

While these events were progressing, Lesbee had kept one eye on Browne and Mindel's blaster firmly gripped in his left hand. Now he said, 'Well, sir, you certainly did what you promised. Wait a moment while I put this gun away, and then I'll carry out my part of the bargain.'

He started to do so, then, out of pity, paused.

He had been thinking in the back of his mind about what Browne had said earlier: that the trip to Earth might only take a few months. The officer had backed away from that statement, but it had been bothering Lesbee ever since.

If it were true, then it was indeed a fact that nobody need die!

He said quickly, 'What was your reason for saying that the journey home would only take – well – less than a year?'

'It's the tremendous time compression,' Browne explained eagerly. 'The distance as you pointed out is over 12 light-years. But with a time ratio of 3, 4 or 500 to one, we'll make it in less than a month. When I first started to say that, I could see that the figures were incomprehensible to you in your tense mood. In fact, I could scarcely believe them myself.'

Lesbee said, staggered, 'We can get back to Earth in a couple of weeks – my God!' He broke off, said urgently, 'Look, I accept you as commander. We don't need an election. The status quo is good enough for any short period of time. Do you agree?'

'Of course,' said Browne. 'That's the point I've been trying to make.'

As he spoke, his face was utterly guileless.

Lesbee gazed at that mask of innocence, and he thought hopelessly: 'What's wrong? Why isn't he really agreeing? Is it because he doesn't want to lose his command so quickly?'

Sitting there, unhappily fighting for the other's life, he tried to place himself mentally in the position of the commander of a vessel, tried to look at the prospect of a return to view. It was hard to picture such a reality. But presently it seemed to him that he understood.

He said gently, feeling his way, 'It would be kind of a shame to return without having made a successful landing anywhere. With this new speed, we could visit a dozen sun systems, and still get home in a year.'

The look that came into Browne's face for a fleeting moment told Lesbee that he had penetrated to the thought in the man's mind.

The next instant, Browne was shaking his head vigorously. 'This is no time for side excursions,' he said. 'We'll leave explorations of new star systems to future expeditions. The people of this ship have served their term. We go straight home.'

Browne's face was now completely relaxed. His blue eyes shone with truth and sincerity.

There was nothing further that Lesbee could say. The gulf between Browne and himself could not be bridged.

The commander had to kill his rival, so that he might

finally return to Earth and report that the mission of the *Hope of Man* was accomplished.

8

In the most deliberate fashion Lesbee shoved the blaster into the inner pocket of his coat. Then, as if he were being careful, he used the tractor beam to push Browne about four feet away. There he set him down, released him from the beam, and – with the same deliberateness – drew his hand away from the tractor controls. Thus he made himself completely defenseless.

It was the moment of vulnerability.

Browne leaped at him, yelling: 'Miller – pre-empt!'

First Officer Miller obeyed the command of his captain.

What happened then, only Lesbee, the technician with a thousand bits of detailed knowledge, expected.

For years it had been observed that when Control Room Below took over from Bridge, the ship speeded up slightly. and when Bridge took over from Control Room Below, the ship slowed instantly by the same amount – in each instance, something less then half a mile an hour.

The two boards were not completely synchronized. The technicians often joked about it, and Lesbee had once read an obscure technical explanation for the discrepancy. It had to do with the impossibility of ever getting two metals refined to the same precision of internal structure.

It was the age-old story of no two objects in the universe are alike. But in times past, the differential had meant nothing. It was a technical curiosity, an interesting phenomenon of the science of metallurgy, a practical problem that caused machinists to curse good-naturedly when technicians like Lesbee required them to make a replacement part.

Unfortunately for Browne, the ship was now traveling near the speed of light.

His strong hands, reaching towards Lesbee's slighter body, were actually touching the latter's arm when the

310

momentary deceleration occurred as Bridge took over. The sudden slow-down was at a much faster rate than even Lesbee expected. The resistance of space to the forward movement of the ship must be using up more engine power than he had realized; it was taking a lot of thrust to maintain a one gravity acceleration.

The great vessel slowed about 150 miles per hour in the space of a second.

Lesbee took the blow of that deceleration partly against his back, partly against one side – for he had half-turned to defend himself from the bigger man's attack.

Browne, who had nothing to grab on to, was flung forward at the full 150 miles per hour. He struck the control board with an audible thud, stuck to it as if he were glued there; and then, when the adjustment was over – when the *Hope of Man* was again speeding along at one gravity – his body slid down the face of the board, and crumpled into a twisted position on the rubberized dais.

His uniform was discolored. As Lesbee watched, blood seeped through and dripped to the floor.

'Are you going to hold an election?' Tellier asked.

The big ship had turned back under Lesbee's command, and had picked up his friends. The lifeboat itself, with the remaining Karn still aboard, was put into an orbit around Alta III and abandoned.

The two young men were sitting now in the Captain's cabin.

After the question was asked, Lesbee leaned back in his chair, and closed his eyes. He didn't need to examine his total resistance to the suggestion. He had already savored the feeling that command brought.

Almost from the moment of Browne's death, he had observed himself having the same thoughts that Browne had voiced – among many others, the reasons why elections were not advisable aboard a spaceship. He waited now while

311

Eleesa, one of his three wives – she being the younger of the two young widows of Browne – poured wine for them, and went softly out. Then he laughed grimly.

'My good friend,' he said, 'we're all lucky that time is so compressed at the speed of light. At 500-times compression, any further exploration we do will require only a few months, or years at most. And so I don't think we can afford to take the chance of defeating at an election the only person who understands the details of the new acceleration method. Until I decide exactly how much exploration we shall do, I shall keep our speed capabilities a secret. But I did, and do, think one other person should know where I have this information documented. Naturally, I selected First Officer Tellier.'

'Thank you, sir,' the youth said. But he was visibly thoughtful as he sipped his wine. He went on finally, 'Captain, I think you'd feel a lot better if you held an election. I'm sure you could win it.'

Lesbee laughed tolerantly, shook his head. 'I'm afraid you don't understand the dynamics of government,' he said. 'There's no record in history of a person who actually had control, handing it over.'

He finished with the casual confidence of absolute power. 'I'm not going to be presumptuous enough to fight a precedent like that!'

SILKIES IN SPACE

1

NAT CEMP, walking along the street, passed the man – and stopped.

Something about the other triggered a signal in that portion of his nervous system which, even in his human state, retained a portion of his Silkie ability. He couldn't remember, hard as he tried, ever having felt that particular signal before.

Cemp turned in the street and looked back. The stranger had paused at the near corner. Then, as the light became green, he walked briskly toward the far sidewalk. He was about Cemp's height of slightly over six feet and seemed about the same build – about a hundred and ninety pounds.

His hair was dark brown, like Cemp's, and he wore a dark gray suit, as did Cemp. Now that they were several hundred feet apart, the initial impression he had had of somebody familiar was not so clear.

Yet after only a slight hesitation, Cemp rapidly walked after the man, presently came up to him, and said courteously, 'May I speak to you?'

The man stopped. At close range, the resemblance between them was truly remarkable, suggesting consanguinity. Blue-gray eyes, straight nose, firm mouth, strong neck, shape of ears, and the very way they held themselves were similar.

Cemp said, 'I wonder if you are aware that you and I are practically twins.'

The man's face twisted slightly. His lips curled into a faint sneer, and his eyes gazed scornfully at Cemp. He said in an exact replica of Cemp's baritone voice, 'It was my intent that you notice. If you hadn't this first time, then I would have approached you again. My name is U-Brem.'

Cemp was silent, startled. He was surprised at the hostility in the stranger's tone and manner. Contempt, he analyzed wonderingly.

Had the man been merely a human being who had somehow recognized a Silkie in human form, Cemp would have considered it one of those occasional incidents. Known Silkies were sometimes sought out by humans and insulted. Usually the human who committed such a foolish act could be evaded or good-naturedly parried or won over. But once in a while a Silkie had to fight. However, the man's resemblance to Cemp indicated that this encounter was different.

As he had these thoughts, the stranger's cynical gray-blue eyes were gazing into Cemp's. The man's lips parted in a derisive smile, showing even white teeth. 'At approximately this moment,' he said, 'every Silkie in the solar system is receiving a communication from his alter ego.'

He paused; again the insolent smile. 'I can see that has alerted you, and you're bracing yourself . . .'

It was true. Cemp had abruptly decided that whether the other's statement was true or not, he could not let him get away.

The man continued, '. . . bracing yourself to try to seize me. It can't be done, for I match you in every way.'

'You're a Silkie?' Cemp asked.

'I'm a Silkie.'

By all the logic of Silkie history, that had to be a false claim. And yet there was the unmistakable, sensational resemblance to himself.

But Cemp did not change his mind. Even if this was a Silkie, Cemp had a superiority over all other Silkies. In his struggle with the Kibmadine the year before, he had learned things about body control that were known to no other Silkie, since it had been decided by the Silkie Authority that he must not communicate to other Silkies the newly gained abilities. And he hadn't.

That extra knowledge would now be to his advantage – if the other was indeed a Silkie.

'Ready for the message?' asked the man insolently.

Cemp, who was ready for the battle of his life, nodded curtly.

'It's an ultimatum.'

'I'm waiting,' said Cemp.

'You are to cease and desist from your association with human beings. You are commanded to return to the nation of Silkies. You have a week to make up your mind. After that date you will be considered a traitor and will be treated as traitors have always been treated, without mercy.'

Since there was no 'nation' of Silkies and never had been, Cemp, after considering the unexpected 'ultimatum' for a moment, made his attack.

He still didn't quite believe that his 'twin' was a Silkie. So he launched a minimum electric charge on one of the magnetic bands that he could use as a human – enough to render unconsciousness but not damage.

To his dismay, a Silkie magnetic screen as powerful as anything he could muster warded off the energy blow. So the man was a Silkie.

The stranger stared at him, teeth showing, eyes glinting with sudden rage. 'I'll remember this!' he snarled. 'You'd have hurt me if I hadn't had a defense.'

Cemp hesitated, questioning his own purpose. It didn't have to be capture. 'Look,' he urged, 'why don't you come with me to the Silkie Authority? If there is a Silkie nation, normal communication is the best way of proving it.'

The strange Silkie began to back away. 'I've done my duty,' he muttered. 'I'm not accustomed to fighting. You tried to kill me.'

He seemed to be in a state of shock. His eyes had changed again, and they looked dazed now. All the man's initial cocksureness was gone as he continued backing away.

Cemp followed, uncertain. He was himself a highly trained

fighter; it was hard to grasp that here might be a Silkie who was actually not versed in battle.

He soothed, 'We don't have to fight. But you can't expect to deliver an ultimatum and then go off into nowhere, as if you've done your part. You say your name is U-Brem. Where do you come from?'

He was aware, as he spoke, that people had stopped in the street and were watching the strange drama of two men, one retreating, the other pursuing, a slow step at a time.

'First, if there's a Silkie nation, where has it – where have you – been hiding all these years?' Cemp persisted.

'Damn you, stop badgering me. You've got your ultimatum. You've got a week to think about it. Now leave me alone!'

The alter ego had clearly not considered what he would do after delivering his message. His unpreparedness made the whole incident even more fantastic. But he was showing anger again, recovering his nerve.

An electric discharge, in the jagged form of lightning, rode a magnetic beam of U-Brem's creation and struck at Cemp, crackling against the magnetic screen he kept ready to be triggered into instant existence.

The lightning bolt bounced away from Cemp, caromed off a building, flashed across the sidewalk past several startled people, and grounded itself on the metal grill of a street drain.

'Two can play that game,' said U-Brem in a savage tone.

Cemp made no reply. The other's electric beam had been maximum for a Silkie in human form – death-level potency. Somewhere nearby, a woman screamed. The street was clearing. People were running away, seeking shelter.

The time had come to end this madness, or someone might be killed. Cemp acted on his evaluation that for some reason that was not clear, this Silkie was not properly trained and was therefore vulnerable to a nonlethal attack by a technique involving a simple version of levels of logic.

316

He wouldn't even have to use the secret ability he had learned from the Kibmadine the year before.

The moment he made up his mind, he did a subtle energy thing. He modified a specific set of low-energy force lines passing through his brain and going in the direction of U-Brem.

Instantly, there was manifested a strange logic implicit in the very structure and makeup of life. The logic of levels! The science that had been derived by human scientific methods from the great Silkie ability for changing form.

Each life cell had its own rigidity. Each gestalt of cells did a specific action, could do no other. Once stimulated, the 'thought' in that particular nerve bundle went through its exact cycle, and if there was an accompanying motion or emotion, that also manifested itself precisely and exactly and without qualification.

Even more meaningful, more important – a number of cell colonies could be joined together to form a new gestalt, and groups of such clusters had *their* special action. One such colony gestalt was the sleep center in human beings.

The method Cemp used wouldn't work on a Silkie in his class-C form. Even a B Silkie could fight off sleep. But this Silkie in human form began to stagger. His eyes were suddenly heavy lidded, and the uncontrolled appearance of his body showed that he was asleep on his feet.

As the man fell, Cemp stepped forward and caught his body, preventing an injurious crash to the concrete sidewalk. Simultaneously, he did a second, subtle thing. On another force line, he put a message that manipulated the unconsciousness gestalt in the other's brain. It was an attempt at complete control. Sleep cut off U-Brem's perception of his environment. Cemp's manipulation of his unconsciousness mechanism eliminated those messages from the brain's stored memory which would normally stimulate to wakefulness someone who was not really sleepy.

Cemp was congratulating himself on his surprisingly easy

capture – when the body he held stiffened. Cemp, sensing an outside force, drew back. To his complete astonishment, the unconscious man rose straight up into the sky.

In his human form, Cemp was not able to determine the nature of the energy that could accomplish such an improbable feat. He should he realized, transform to Silkie. He found himself hesitating. There was a rule against changing in full view of human beings. Abruptly, he recognized that this situation was unique, a never-before-encountered emergency. He transformed to Silkie and cut off gravity.

The ten-foot body, shaped a little like a projectile, rose from the ground at missile speed. Most of his clothes, completely torn away, fell to the ground. A few tattered remnants remained but were swept away by the gale winds created by his passage.

Unfortunately, all of five seconds had gone by while he made the transformation, and since several seconds had already passed before he acted, he found himself pursuing a speck that was continuing to go straight up.

What amazed him anew was that even with his Silkie perception, he could detect no energy from it, below it, or around it. Yet its speed was as great as anything he could manage. Accordingly, after only moments, he realized that his pursuit was not swift enough to overtake the man and that the body of U-Brem would reach an atmosphere height too rarefied for human survival unless he acted promptly. He therefore mercifully removed the pressure from the sleep and unconsciousness center of the other's body.

Moments later, he was disappointed, but not surprised, he sensed from the other a shift to Silkie form; proof that he had awakened and could now be responsible for himself.

U-Brem continued straight up, as a full-grown Silkie now, and it was presently obvious that he intended to risk going through the Van Allen belt. Cemp had no such foolhardy purpose.

As the two of them approached the outer limits of the atmosphere, Cemp put a thought on a beam to a manned Telstar unit in orbit around Earth. The thought contained simply the data about what had happened.

The message sent, he turned back. Greatly disturbed by his experience – and being without clothes for human wear – he flew straight to the Silkie Authority.

2

Cemp, descending from the sky down to the vast building complex that comprised the central administration for dealing with Silkies, saw that other Silkies were also coming in. He presumed, grimly, that they were there for the same reason as he was.

As the realization came, he scanned the heavens behind him with his Silkie senses and perceived that scores more of black spots were out there, hurtling closer. Divining imminent confusion, he slowed and stopped. Then, from his position in the sky, he telepathed Charley Baxter, proposing a special plan to handle the emergency.

Baxter was in a distracted state, but presently his return thought came. 'Nat, yours is just about the best idea we've had. And you're right. This could be dangerous.'

There was a pause. Baxter must have got his message through to other of the Special People, for Cemp began to record a general Silkie warning. 'To all Silkies: It would be unwise for too many of you to concentrate at one time in one place. So divide into ten groups on the secret-number system, plan G. Group One only, approach and land. All others disperse until called.'

In the sky near Cemp, Silkies began to mill around. Cemp, who, by the designated number system, was in group three, veered off, climbed to the upper atmosphere, and darted a thousand miles over, to his home in Florida.

En route, he talked mentally to his wife, Joanne. And so by the time he walked naked into the house, she had clothes laid out for him and knew as much as he about what had happened.

As Cemp dressed, he saw that she was in a womanly state of alarm, more concerned than he. She accepted that there was a Silkie nation and that this meant there would also be Silkie women.

'Admit it!' she said tearfully. 'That thought has already crossed your mind, hasn't it?'

'I'm a logical person,' Cemp defended. 'So I've had fleeting thoughts about all possibilities. But being sensible, I feel that a lot of things have to be explained before I can reject what we know of Silkie history. And so until we have proof of something different, I shall go on believing that Silkies are the result of biological experiments with DNA and DNP and that old Sawyer did it there on Echo Island.'

'What's going to become of our marriage?' Joanne said in an anguished voice.

'Nothing will change.'

She sobbed. 'I'm going to seem to you like a native woman of three hundred years ago who is married to a white man on a South Sea Island – and then white women begin arriving on the island.'

The wildness of her fantasying astounded Cemp. 'It's not the same,' he said. 'I promise complete loyalty and devotion for the rest of our lives.'

'Nobody can promise anything in personal relations,' she said. But his words seemed to reassure her after a moment. She dried her eyes and came over to him and allowed herself to be kissed.

It was an hour before a phone call came from Charley Baxter. The man was apologetic for the delay but explained that it was the result of a conference on Cemp's future actions.

'It was a discussion just about you in all this,' Baxter said. Cemp waited.

The final decision was to continue to not let Cemp intermingle with other Silkies – 'for reasons that you know,' Baxter said significantly.

Cemp surmised that the reference was to the secret knowledge he had gained from the Kibmadine Di-isarinn and that this meant they would continue to send him on special missions that kept him away from other Silkies.

Baxter now produced the information that only four hundred Silkies had been approached by alter egos. 'The number actually reported in,' he said, 'is three hundred and ninety-six.'

Cemp was vaguely relieved, vaguely contemptuous. U-Brem's claim that all Silkies were targets was now proved to be propaganda. He had already shown himself to be an inept Silkie. The lie added one more degrading touch.

'Some of them were pretty poor duplicates,' said Baxter. 'Apparently, mimicking another body is not a great skill with them.'

However, he admitted, even four hundred was more than enough to establish the existence of a hitherto unknown group of Silkies.

'Even if they are untrained,' he said, 'we've absolutely got to find out who they are and where they come from.'

'Is there no clue?' Cemp asked.

No more than he already knew.

'They all got away?' Cemp said, astounded. 'No one did any better than I did?'

'On the average, not as well,' said Baxter.

It seemed that most Silkies had made no effort to hold the strange Silkies who confronted them; they had simply reported in and asked for instructions.

'Can't blame them,' said Baxter.

He continued, 'But I might as well tell you that your fight and your reasons for fighting make you one of the two dozen Silkies we feel we can depend on in this matter. So here are your instructions . . .'

He talked for several minutes and concluded, 'Take Joanne with you, but go at once!'

The sign said, ALL THE MUSIC IN THIS BUILDING IS SILKIE MUSIC.

Cemp, who had never listened for long to any other kind, saw the faint distaste come into his wife's face. She caught his look and evidently his thought, for she said, 'All right, so it sounds dead level to me, as if it's all the same note – well, anyway, the same few notes, close together, repeated in various sickening combinations.'

She stopped, shook her beautiful blonde head, and said, 'I guess I'm tense and afraid and need something wild and clashy.'

To Cemp, who could hear harmonies in the music that were beyond the reach of ordinary human ears, her outburst was but a part of the severe emotional reactions to things that Silkies married to human women had to become accustomed to. The wives of Silkies had a hard time making their peace with the realities of the relationship.

As Joanne had put it more than once, 'There you are with this physically perfect, beautiful male. But all the time you're thinking, "This is not really a man. It's a monster that can change in a flash into either a fishlike being or a creature of space." But of course, I wouldn't part with him for anything.'

The music sign was soon behind them, and they walked on into the interior of the museum. Their destination was the original laboratory, in which the first Silkie was supposed to have been produced. The lab occupied the center of the building; it had been moved there from the West Indies a hundred and ten years before, according to a date on a wall plaque at the entrance.

It had seemed to Baxter that a sharper study should be made of the artifacts of Silkie history. The entire structure of that history was now being questioned for the very first time.

This task, of reevaluating the past data, had been assigned to Cemp and Joanne.

The lab was brightly lighted. It had only one visitor; a rather plain young woman with jet-black hair but no makeup, wearing ill-fitting clothes, was standing at one of the tables beside the far doorway.

As Cemp came in, a thought not his own touched his mind. He started to turn to Joanne, taking it for granted that she had communicated with him on that level. He took it for granted, that is, for several seconds.

Belatedly, realization came that the thought had arrived on a magnetic carrier wave – Silkie level.

Cemp swung around and stared at the black-haired woman. She smiled at him, somewhat tensely, he noted, and then her thought came, unmistakably: 'Please don't give me away. I was stationed here to convince any doubting Silkie.'

She didn't have to explain what she meant. The thunder of it was pouring through Cemp's mind.

According to his knowledge, there had never been any female Silkies. All Silkies on Earth were males, married to women of the Special People – like Joanne.

But this black-haired, farm-woman type was a female Silkie! That was what she was letting him know by her presence. In effect, by being here, she was saying, 'Don't bother to search dusty old files. I'm living proof that Silkies were not produced in somebody's laboratory two hundred and thirty years ago.'

Suddenly Cemp was confused. He was aware that Joanne had come up beside him, that she must have caught his thought, that she was herself dismayed. The one glimpse he had of her face showed that she had become very pale.

'Nat!' her voice came sharply. 'You've got to capture her!'

Cemp started forward, but it was a half-hearted movement. Yet in spite of the uncertainty in his actions, he was already having logical thoughts.

Since only hours had gone by since the moment he first

saw U-Brem, she must have been stationed here in advance. She would therefore have had no contact with the others. And so she wouldn't know that to a trained Silkie like himself, she was as vulnerable as an unarmed civilian opposed by a soldier.

The black-haired woman must have suddenly had some doubt of her own. Abruptly she stepped through the door near which she had been standing and closed it after her.

'Nat!' Joanne's voice, high-pitched, sounded mere inches behind him. 'You can't let her get away!'

Cemp, who had emerged from his brief stasis, projected a thought after the female Silkie. 'I'm not going to fight you, but I'm going to stay close to you until I have all the information we want.'

'Too late!' A magnetic carrier wave, human-Silkie level, brought her thought. 'You're already too late.'

Cemp didn't think so. He arrived at the door through which she had disappeared, was slightly disconcerted to find that it was locked, smashed it with a single jagged lightning thrust of electrical force, stepped through its smoking remains – and saw the woman in the act of entering a gap in the wall made by a sliding door.

She was not more than three dozen feet away, and she had half-turned to look back in his direction. What she saw was evidently a surprise, for a startled look came into her face.

Hastily, her hand came up to something inside the aperture, and the door slid shut. As it closed, Cemp, who was running toward it, had a glimpse of a gleaming corridor beyond. The existence of such a secret passageway had too many implications for Cemp to consider immediately.

He was at the wall, fumbling for the hidden door. When he could not find it after several long moments, he stepped back and burned it down with the two energy flows from his brain, which, when they came together outside his body, created an intense electrical arc. It was the only energy weapon available to him as a human being, but it was enough.

A minute later, he stepped through the smoking opening into a narrow corridor.

3

The corridor in which Cemp found himself was made of concrete and slanted gently downward. It was dimly lighted and straight, and he could see the young woman in the near distance ahead – about two hundred feet away.

She was running, but as a woman wearing a dress runs – not very fast. Cemp broke into his own high-speed lope and in a minute had cut the distance between them in half. Abruptly, the concrete ended. Ahead was a dirt cave, still lighted, but the lights were set farther apart.

As she reached this point, the young woman sent him a message on a magnetic force line. 'If you don't stop chasing me, I'll have to use the (something not clear to Cemp) power.'

Cemp remembered the energy that had lifted U-Brem into the sky. He took the threat seriously and instantly modified a magnetic wave to render her unconscious.

It was not so cruel an act as it would have been earlier. Now she fell like a stone – which was the unfortunate characteristic of the unconsciousness gestalt – but she fell on dirt and not on cement. The motion of her body was such that she pitched forward on her knees, then slid down on her right shoulder. It didn't look too severe for her – so it seemed to Cemp as he came closer to where she was lying.

He had slowed to a walk. Now, still wary, he approached the prostrate body, determined not to let any special 'power' remove her from him. He felt only slightly guilty at the violent method he had used. His reasoning had permitted no less control over her. The 'sleep' shut-off on U-Brem had not prevented that individual from turning on the force field – so Cemp considered it to be – that had saved him. Quite simply, he couldn't let her get away.

Because it was an untried situation, he acted at once. At this moment, he had her; there were too many unknowns for him to risk any delay. He knelt beside her. Since she was unconscious and not asleep, her sensory system was open to exterior stimulation. But for her to answer, she would have to be switched to sleep, so that the shut-off interior perception could flow.

So he sat there, alternately manipulating her unconsciousness center, when he wanted to ask a question, and her sleep center, for her reply. It was like ancient ham radio with each party saying 'over' when his message was completed.

And of course, in addition, he had to make sure that she did reply to his queries. So he asked one question after another, and with each question he modified a magnetic wave with a message to the brain-cell gestalt that responded to hypnotic drugs. The result was a steady mental conversation.

'What is your name?'

'B-Roth.'

'Where do you come from?'

'From home.'

'Where is home?'

'In the sky.' A mental image came of a small stone body in space; Cemp's impression was of a meteorite less than twenty miles in diameter. 'About to go around the sun, inside the first planet's orbit.'

So she *had* come to Earth in advance. So they *were* all far from 'home' and had apparently had no preliminary knowledge that they were outskilled by Earth Silkies. As a result, he was now obtaining this decisive information.

'What is its orbit?' Cemp asked.

'It goes as far out as the eighth planet.'

Neptune! What a tremendous distance – nearly thirty astronomical units.

Cemp asked quickly, 'What is its mean speed?'

326

Her answer was in terms of Mercury's year. Converted to Earth time, it came to a hundred and ten years per orbit.

Cemp whistled softly. An immediate association had leaped into his mind. The first Silkie baby had been born to Marie Ederle slightly more than two hundred and twenty years before, according to the official history. The time involved was approximately twice as long as the orbital period of the little Silkie planetoid.

Cemp ended that train of speculation abruptly and demanded from B-Roth exactly how she would again find the planetoid, which surely must be one of thousands of similar bodies.

The answer was one that only a Silkie could operate from. She had in her brain a set of relationships and signal-recognition images that identified for her the location of the Silkie home.

Cemp made an exact mental copy of these images. He was about to begin questioning her for details on other matters – when an inertia phenomenon effected his body.

He was flung backward. . . . It was as if he were in a vehicle, his back to the forward motion, and the vehicle stopped suddenly, but he went on.

Because he always had protection against sudden falls, he had been moved less than eight feet before he triggered his magnetic field, his only screening mechanism as a human.

The field he set up could not stop the pull of gravity directly, but it derived from the Earth's magnetic force and gained its power from the force lines that passed through this exact space.

As Cemp modulated the lines now, they attached themselves to flexible metal bands that were woven into his clothes, and they held him. He hung there a few feet above the floor. From this vantage point he was able to examine his situation.

At once, the phenomenon was shown as completely fantastic. He detected in the heart of the gravity field a tiny molecule complex. What was fantastic about it was this: Gravity was an invariable, solely dependent on mass and square of distance. Cemp had already calculated the gravity pull on him to be the equivalent of three times that of Earth at sea level. And so, by all the laws of physics, that incredibly small particle must have an equivalent mass to three Earths!

Impossible, of course.

It was by no means a complex of one of the large molecules, as far as Cemp could determine, and it was not radioactive.

He was about to abandon his study of it and to turn his attention to his own situation, when he noticed that the gravity field had an even more improbable quality. Its pull was limited to organic matter. It had no effect on the surrounding dirt walls, and in fact – his mind poised in a final amazement – the woman's body was not influenced by it.

The gravity was limited to one particular organic configuration – himself! One body, one human being only – Nat Cemp – was the sole object toward which it was oriented.

He found himself remembering how he had been untouched by the field that had lifted U-Brem. He had sensed the presence of a field but only by the way the magnetic lines that passed through his head were affected by it. Even in his Silkie form, as he pursued the hurtling body of his alter ego, that, and merely that, had been true.

This was for him a personal gravitational field, a small group of molecules that 'knew' him.

As these flashing awarenesses came to him, Cemp turned his head and gazed back at the young woman. He was not surprised at what he saw. His attention had been forcibly removed from her, so the pressure on the unconsciousness valve in her brain was released. She was stirring, coming to.

She sat up, looked around, and saw him.

She came to her feet quickly, with an athletic ease. She evidently did not remember what had happened while she was unconscious, did not realize how completely she had given away basic secrets, for her face broke into a smile.

'You see?' she said. 'I told you what would happen. Well, goodbye.'

Her spirits visibly high, she turned, walked off into the cave, and presently disappeared as it gradually curved off to the left.

After she was gone, Cemp turned his attention back to the gravity field. He assumed that it would eventually be withdrawn or fade out, and he would be free. He had the distinct conviction that he might have only minutes in which to examine it and discover its nature.

He thought unhappily, *If I could change into my Silkie form, I could really examine it.*

But he dared not, could not. At least, he couldn't do it and simultaneously maintain his safe position.

Silkies had one weakness, if it could be called that. They were vulnerable when they changed from one form to another. Considering this, Cemp now conducted his first mental conversation with Joanne. He explained his predicament, described what he had learned, and ended, 'I think I can stay here all day and see what comes of this, but I should probably have another Silkie stand by for emergencies.'

Her anxious reply was, 'I'll have Charley Baxter contact you.'

4

She phoned Baxter and passed the conversation on to Cemp in thought form.

Baxter was enormously excited by the information that Cemp had obtained about the alien Silkies. He regarded the gravity field as a new energy application, but he was reluctant to send in another Silkie.

'Let's face it, Joanne,' he said. 'Your husband learned something last year which, if other Silkies understood it, might wreck the delicate balance by which we are maintaining our present Silkie-human civilization. Nat understands our concern about that. So tell him I'll send a machine in there to act as a barrier for him while he makes his change-over into Silkie.'

It occurred to Cemp that the appearance of new, hitherto unknown Silkies would alter the Silkie-human relationship even more. But he did not permit that thought to go out to Joanne.

Baxter's conversation concluded with the statement that it would probably take a while before the machine could be got to him. 'So tell him to hold on.'

After Baxter had hung up, Joanne thought at Cemp, 'I should tell you that I am relieved about one thing.'

'What's that?'

'If the Silkie women are all as plain in human form as B-Roth, then I'm not going to worry.'

An hour went by. Two . . . ten.

In the world outside, the skies would be dark, the sun long gone, the stars signaling in their tiny brilliant fashion.

Charley Baxter's machine had come and gone, and Cemp, safe in the Silkie form, remained close to the most remarkable energy field that had ever been seen in the solar system. What was astounding was that it showed no diminution of its colossal gravity effect. His hope had been that with his supersensitive Silkie perception he would be able to perceive any feeder lines that might be flowing power to it from an outside source. But there was nothing like that; nothing to trace. The power came from the single small group of molecules. It had no other origin.

The minutes and the hours lengthened. The watch became long, and he had time to feel the emotional impact of the problem that now confronted every Silkie on Earth – the need to make a decision about the Space Silkies.

Morning.

Shortly after the sun came up outside, the field manifested an independent quality. It began to move along the corridor, heading deeper into the cave. Cemp floated along after it, letting a portion of its gravitational pull draw him. He was wary but curious, hopeful that now he would find out more.

The cave ended abruptly in a deep sewer, which had the look of long abandonment. The concrete was cracked, and there were innumerable deep fissures in the walls. But to the group of molecules and their field, it seemed to be a familiar area, for they went forward more rapidly. Suddenly, there was water below them. It was not stagnant, but rippled and swirled. A tidal pool, Cemp analyzed.

The water grew deeper, and presently they were in it, traveling at undiminished speed. Ahead, the murky depths grew less murky. They emerged into sunlit waters in a canyon about a hundred feet below the surface of the ocean.

As they broke surface a moment later, the strange energy complex accelerated. Cemp, suspecting that it would now try to get away from him, made a final effort to perceive its characteristics.

But nothing came back to him. No message, no sign of energy flow. For a split second, he did have the impression that the atoms making up the molecule group were some-how . . . not right. But when he switched his attention to the band involved, either the molecules became aware of his momentary awareness and closed themselves off or he imagined it.

Even as he made the analysis, his feeling that he was about to be discarded was borne out. The particle's speed increased rapidly. In seconds, its velocity approached the limits of what he could permit himself to endure inside an atmosphere. The outer chitin of his Silkie body grew hot, then hotter.

Reluctantly, Cemp adjusted his own atomic structure, so that the gravity of the alien field no longer affected him. As he fell away, it continued to pursue a course that took an easterly direction, where the sun was now about an hour above the horizon. Within mere seconds of his separation from it, it left the atmosphere and, traveling at many miles a second, headed seemingly straight for the sun.

Cemp came to the atmosphere's edge. 'Gazing' by means of his Silkie perceptors out upon the vast, dark ocean of space beyond, he contacted the nearest Telstar unit. To the scientists aboard, he gave a fix on the speeding molecule group. Then he waited hopefully while they tried to put a tracer on it.

But the word finally came, 'Sorry, we get no reaction.'

Baffled, Cemp let himself be drawn by Earth's gravity. Then, by a series of controlled adjustments to the magnetic and gravity fields of the planet, he guided himself to the Silkie Authority.

5

Three hours of talk . . .

Cemp, who, as the only Silkie present, occupied a seat near the foot of the long table, found the discussion boring.

It had early seemed to him that he or some other Silkie ought to be sent to the Silkie planetoid to learn the facts, handle the matter in a strictly logical but humanitarian fashion, and report back to the Authority.

If, for some reason, the so-called Silkie nation proved unamenable to reason, then a further discussion would be in order.

As he waited for the three dozen human conferees to reach the same decision, he couldn't help but notice the order of importance at the table.

The Special People, including Charley Baxter, were at the head of the long table. Next, ranging down on either side, were the ordinary human beings. Then, on one side, himself, and below him, three minor aides and the official secretary of the three-man Silkie Authority.

It was not a new observation for him. He had discussed it with other Silkies, and it had been pointed out to him that here was a reversal of the power role that was new in history. The strongest individuals in the solar system – the Silkies – were still relegated to secondary status.

He emerged from his reverie to realize that silence had fallen. Charley Baxter, slim, gray-eyed, intense, was coming around the long table. He stopped across from Cemp.

'Well, Nat,' said Baxter, 'there's the picture as we see it.' He seemed embarrassed.

Cemp did a lightning mental backtrack on the discussion and realized that they had indeed arrived at the inevitable conclusion. But he noted also that they considered it a weighty decision. It was a lot to ask of any person, that was the attitude. The result could be personal disaster. They wouldn't be critical if he refused.

'I feel ashamed to ask it,' said Baxter, 'but this is almost a war situation.'

Cemp could see that they were not sure of themselves. There had been no war on Earth for a hundred and fifty years. No one was an expert in it any more.

He climbed to his feet as these awarenesses touched him. Now he looked around at the faces turned to him and said, 'Calm yourselves, gentlemen. Naturally I'll do it.'

They all looked relieved. The discussion turned quickly to details – the difficulty of locating a single meteorite in space, particularly one that had such a long sidereal period.

It was well known that there were about fifteen hundred large meteorites and planetoids and tens of thousands of smaller objects orbiting the sun. All these had orbits or motions that, though subject to the laws of celestial mechanics, were often very eccentric. A few of them, like comets, periodically came in close to the sun, then shot off into space again, returning for another hectic go-round fifty to a hundred years later. There were so many of these intermediate-sized rocks that they were identified and their courses plotted only for special reasons. There had simply never been any point in tracking them all.

Cemp had matched course with and landed on scores of lone meteorites. His recollections of those experiences were

333

among the bleaker memories of his numerous space flights – the darkness, the sense of utterly barren rock, the profound lack of sensory stimulation. Oddly, the larger they were, the worse the feeling was.

He had discovered that he could have a kind of intellectual affinity with a rock less than a thousand feet in diameter. This was particularly true when he encountered an inarticulate mass that had finally been precipitated into a hyperbolic orbit. When he computed that it was thus destined to leave the solar system forever, he would find himself imagining how long it had been in space, how far it had gone, and how it would now hurtle away from the solar system and spend eons between the stars, and he could not help feeling a sense of loss.

A government representative – a human being named John Mathews – interrupted his thought. 'Mr Cemp, I'd like to ask you a very personal question.'

Cemp looked at him and nodded.

The man went on, 'According to reports, several hundred Earth Silkies have already defected to these native Silkies. Evidently, you don't feel as they do, that the Silkie planetoid is home. Why not?'

Cemp smiled. 'Well, first of all,' he said, 'I would never buy a pig in a poke the way they have done.'

He hesitated. Then, in a serious tone, he continued, 'Entirely apart from my feelings of loyalty to Earth, I do not believe the future of life forms will be helped or advanced by any rigid adherence to the idea that I am a lion, or I am a bear. Intelligent life is, or should be, moving toward a common civilization. Maybe I'm like the farm boy who went to the city – Earth. Now my folks want me to come back to the farm. They'll never understand why I can't, so I don't even try to explain it to them.'

'Maybe,' said Mathews, 'the planetoid is actually the big city and Earth the farm. What then?'

Cemp smiled politely but merely shook his head.

334

Mathews persisted, 'One more question. How should Silkies be treated?'

Cemp spread his hands. 'I can't think of a single change that would be of value.'

He meant it. He had never been able to get excited about the pecking order. Yet he had known for a long time that some Silkies felt strongly about their inferior – as it seemed to them – role. Others, like himself, did their duty, were faithful to their human wives, and tried to enjoy the somewhat limited possibilities of human civilization – limited for Silkies, who had so many additional senses for which there was no real creative stimulation.

Presumably, things could be better. But meanwhile, they were what they were. Cemp recognized that any attempt to alter them would cause fear and disturbance among human beings. And why do that merely to satisfy the egos of somewhat fewer than two thousand Silkies?

At least, that had been the problem until now. The coming of the space Silkies would add an indefinite number of new egos to the scene, yet, Cemp reasoned, not enough to change the statistics meaningfully.

Aloud, he said, 'As far as I can see, under all conceivable circumstances, there is no better solution to the Silkie problem than that which exists right now.'

Charley Baxter chose that moment to end the discussion, saying, 'Nat, you have our best, our very best, wishes. And our complete confidence. A spaceship will rush you to Mercury's orbit and give you a head start. Good luck.'

6

The scene ahead was absolutely fantastic.

The Silkie planetoid would make its circuit of the sun far inside Mercury's eccentric orbit, and the appearance was that it might brush the edges of the great clouds of hot gas that seemed to poke out like streamers or shapeless arms from the sun's hot surface.

Cemp doubted if such a calamity would actually occur, but as he periodically subjected his steel-hard chitinous Silkie body to the sun's gravity, he sensed the enormous pull of it at this near distance. The circle of white fire filled almost the entire sky ahead. The light was so intense and came in on him on so many bands that it overwhelmed his receptor system whenever he let it in. And he had to open up at intervals in order to make readjustments in his course.

The two hurtling bodies – his own and that of the planetoid – were presently on a collision course. The actual moment of 'collision' was still hours away. So Cemp shut off his entire perception system. Thus, instantly, he sank into the deep sleep that Silkies so rarely allowed themselves.

He awoke in stages and saw that his timing had been exact. The planetoid was now 'visible' on one of the tiny neural screens inside the forward part of his body. It showed as a radar-type image, and at the beginning it was the size of a pea.

In less than thirty minutes it grew to an apparent size of five miles, which was half its diameter, he estimated.

At this point, Cemp performed his only dangerous maneuver. He allowed the sun's gravity to draw him between the sun and the planetoid. Then he cut off the sun's gravity and, using a few bursts of energy manufactured at the edge of a field behind his body, darted toward the planetoid's surface.

What was dangerous about this action was that it brought him in on the dayside. With the superbrilliant sunlight behind him, he was clearly visible to anyone in or on or around the planetoid. But his theory was that no Silkie would normally be exposing himself to the sun, that in fact, every sensible Silkie would be inside the big stone ball or on its night side.

At close range in that ultrabright light, the planetoid looked like the wrinkled head and face of a bald old Amerind. It was reddish-gray and pock marked and lined and not quite round. The pock marks turned out to be actual caves. Into one of these, Cemp floated. He went down into what to human eyes would have been pitch darkness, but the interior was visible to him as a Silkie on many bands.

He found himself in a corridor with smooth granite walls that led slantingly downward. After about twenty minutes he came to a turn in the passageway. As he rounded it, he saw a shimmering, almost opaque energy screen in front of him.

Cemp decided at once not to regard it as a problem. He doubted if it had been put up to catch anyone. In fact, his lightning analysis of it indicated that it was a wall, with the equivalent solidity of a large spaceship's outer skin.

As a screen it was strong enough to keep out the most massive armor-piercing shells. Going through such a screen was an exercise in Silkie energy control. First, he put up a matching field and started it oscillating. The oscillation unstabilized the opposing screen and started it in a sympathetic vibration. As the process continued, the screen and the field began to merge. But it was the screen that became part of Cemp's field, not the reverse.

Thus, his field was within minutes a part of the barrier. Safely inside his field, he crossed the barrier space. Once past it, disengagement was a matter of slowing down the oscillation until the field and the screen abruptly became separate entities.

The sound of the separation was like the crack of a whip, and the presence of sound indicated he had come into air space. Quickly, he discovered that it was air of an unearthly mixture – thirty percent oxygen, twenty percent helium, and most of the rest gaseous sulphur compounds.

The pressure was about twice that of sea level on Earth, but it was air, and it undoubtedly had a purpose.

From where he had floated through the energy barrier, he saw a large chamber the floor of which was about a hundred feet below him.

Soft lights shone down. Seen in their light, the room was

a jewel. The walls were inlaid with precious stones, fine metals, and vari-colored rock cunningly cut into a design. The design was a continuing story picture of a race of four-legged centaur-type beings with a proud bearing and – wherever there were close-ups – sensitive though nonhuman faces.

On the floor was a picture of a planet inset in some kind of glowing substance that showed the curving, mountainous surface, with sparkling lines where rivers flowed, likenesses of forests and other growth, glinting oceans and lakes, and thousands of bright spots marking cities and towns.

The sides of the planet curved away in proper proportion, and Cemp had the feeling that the globe continued on down and that the bottom was probably visible in some lower room.

The overall effect was completely and totally *beautiful*.

Cemp surmised that the life scenes and the planet picture were an accurate eidolon of a race and a place with which the Silkies had at some time in their past been associated.

He was mentally staggered by the artistic perfection of the room.

He had already, as he floated down, noticed that there were large archways leading to adjoining chambers. He had glimpses of furniture, machines, objects, shining bright and new. He surmised they were artifacts of either the centaur or other civilizations. But he could not take time to explore. His attention fastened on a stairway that led down to the next level.

He went down it and presently found himself facing another energy barrier. Penetrating it exactly as he had the other, he moved on and into a chamber filled with sea water. Inset in the floor of that huge room was a planet that glimmered with the green-blue of an under-sea civilization.

And that was only the beginning. Cemp went down from one level to another, each time through an energy screen and through a similarly decorated chamber. Each was inlaid in the same way with precious stones and glinting metals. Each had breathtaking scenes from what he presumed were habitable planets of far stars, and each had a different atmosphere.

After a dozen such chambers, Cemp found that the impact was cumulative. Realization came to him that here, inside this planetoid, had been gathered such treasure as probably did not exist anywhere else. Cemp visualized the seven-hundred-odd cubic miles that comprised the interior of the most fantastic asteroid in the galaxy, and he remembered what Mathews had said – that perhaps the planetoid was the 'city' and Earth was the 'farm'.

It began to seem that the man's speculation might be truth.

He had been expecting to collide momentarily with an inhabitant of the planetoid. After passing three more chambers, each with its glowing duplicate in miniature of a planet of long ago and far away, Cemp paused and reconsidered.

He had a strong feeling that in learning of these treasures, he had gained an advantage – which he must not lose – and that the Silkies did indeed have their living quarters on the side away from the sun and that they did not expect anyone to arrive in this surprise fashion.

The idea continued to seem correct, and so he turned back and was presently dropping directly toward the dark side. Again the cave openings and, a few score feet inside, the energy barrier. Beyond that were air and gravitation exactly like those at sea level on Earth.

Cemp floated down into a smoothly polished granite chamber. It was furnished with settees, chairs, and tables, and there was a long, low-built bookcase at one end. But the arrangement was like that in an anteroom – formal and unlived in. It gave him an eerie feeling.

Still in his Silkie form, he went down a staircase and into another chamber. It had soil in it, and there was vegetation, which consisted of temperate-zone Earth shrubs and flowers. Once more, the arrangement was formal.

On the third level down were Earthlike offices, with information computers. Cemp, who understood such matters, recorded what they were. He observed also that no one was using this particular source of data.

He was about to go down to the next level, when an energy beam of enormous power triggered the superfast defense screen he had learned from the Kibmadine.

The coruscation as the beam interacted, in an ever-vaster intensity, with Cemp's barrier screen lit the chamber as if sunlight had suddenly been let in. It stayed lit as whoever was directing the beam tested the screen's durability in a sustained power thrust.

For Cemp, it was a fight that moved at lightning speed down the entire line of his defenses and came finally up against the hard core of the second method the Kibmadine had taught him.

There, and only there, he held his own.

7

A minute went by before the attacker finally seemed to accept that Cemp simply used the beam itself to maintain the barrier. Hence, it took nothing out of him, and the barrier would last as long as the beam did, reforming as often as necessary.

As suddenly as it had begun, the attacking energy ceased.

Cemp stared around him, dismayed. The entire chamber was a shambles of twisted, white-hot machinery and debris. The granite walls had crumbled, exposing raw meteorite rock. Molten rock dripped in a score of flowing rivers from the shattered ceiling and walls. Great sections were still tumbling and sliding.

What had been a modern office had become in a matter of minutes a gutted desolation of blackened metal and rock.

For Cemp, the initial staggering reality was that only the

high-speed Kibmadine screen had saved him. The assault had been gauged to overwhelm and overspeed the entire Silkie defense and attack system.

The intent had been death. No bargaining, no discussion, no questions.

The hard fight had driven him down to a special logic of levels. He felt an automatic outflow of hatred.

Yet after a little, another realization penetrated. *I won!* he thought.

Calm again but savage, he went down five more levels and emerged abruptly at the upper level of a great vista, a huge open space. The city of the space Silkies spread below him.

It was precisely and exactly a small Earth city – apartment buildings, private residences, tree-lined streets. Cemp was bemused, for here, too, the native Silkies had clearly attempted to create a human atmosphere.

He could make out figures on a sidewalk far below. He started down. When he was a hundred feet above them, the people stopped and looked up at him. One – a woman – directed a startled thought at him. 'Who are you?'

Cemp told her.

The reaction of the four nearest people was astonishment. But they were not afraid or hostile.

The little group, three women and one man, waited for him. As Cemp came down, he was aware that they were signaling to others. Soon a crowd had gathered, mostly in human bodies, mostly women, but an even dozen arrived in Silkie form.

Guards? he wondered. But they were not antagonistic either. Everybody was mentally open, and what was disconcerting about that was, no one showed any awareness of the attack that had been made on him in the office section near the surface.

Instantly, he saw their unawareness as an opportunity. By keeping silent and alert, he would be able to spot his vicious assailant. He presumed that the violence had been planned and carried out at the administrative level.

I'll find those so and sos! he thought grimly.

To his audience of innocent citizens, he said, 'I'm acting as an emissary of the Earth Government. My purpose here is to discover what binding agreements are possible.'

A woman called up to him, 'We can't seem to change into attractive females, Earth-style. What do you suggest?'

A gale of laughter greeted her remark. Cemp was taken aback. He hadn't expected such easy friendliness from the crowd. But his determination did not waver. 'I presume we can discuss that at government level,' he said, 'but it won't be first on the agenda.'

Some remnants of his hate flow must have gone out to them with this thought, for a man said sharply, 'He doesn't sound very friendly.'

A woman added quickly, 'Come now, Mr Cemp. This is your real home.'

Cemp had recovered. He replied in a steady, level thought, 'You'll get what you give. Right now, you're giving good. But the agents your government sent to Earth made bloodthirsty threats.'

His thought paused there, puzzled. For these people as they were right now did not seem to have any of that threat in them. It struck him that that should be very significant.

After a moment's hesitation, he finished, 'I'm here to discover what it's all about, so why not direct me to someone in authority?'

'We don't have authorities.' That was a woman.

A man said, 'Mr Cemp, we live a completely free existence here, and you and other Earth Silkies are invited to join us.'

Cemp persisted, 'Who decided to send those four hundred messengers to Earth?'

'We always do that, when the time comes,' another woman replied.

'Complete with threats?' asked Cemp. 'Threats of death?'

The woman seemed suddenly uncertain. She turned to one of the men. 'You were down there,' she said. 'Did you threaten violence?'

The man hesitated. 'It's a little vague,' he said, 'but I guess so.' He added quickly, 'It's always been this way when E-Lerd conditions us in connection with the Power. Memory tends to fade very quickly. In fact, I hadn't recalled that threat aspect until now.' He seemed astonished. 'I'll be damned. I think we'd better speak to E-Lerd and find the reason for it.'

Cemp telepathed directly to the man, 'What was your afterfeeling about what you had done?'

'Just that I communicated that we space Silkies were here and that it was time for the Earth Silkies to become aware of their true origin.'

He turned to the others. 'This is incredible,' he said. 'I'm astounded. We need to look into E-Lerd's administration of the Power. I uttered murderous words when I was on Earth! That's not like me at all.'

His complete amazement was more convincing than anything else could possibly have been.

Cemp said firmly, 'I gather, then, that contrary to your earlier statements, you do have a leader and his name is E-Lerd.'

One of the Silkies answered that. 'No, he's not a leader, but I can see how that might be understood. We're free. No one tells us what to do. But we do delegate responsibilities. For example, E-Lerd is in charge of the Power, and we get its use through him. Would you like to talk to him, Mr Cemp?'

'Indeed I would,' said Cemp with intense satisfaction.

He was thinking, *The Power! Of course. Who else? The person who has control of the Power is the only one who could have attacked me!*

'My name is O-Vedd,' said the space Silkie. 'Come with me.'

His long, bulletlike body detached itself from the group of similar bodies and darted off over the heads of the crowd. Cemp followed. They came down to a small entrance and into a narrow, smooth-walled granite corridor. After a hundred feet this opened out to another huge space. Here was a second city.

At least, for a moment that was what it looked like.

Then Cemp saw that the buildings were of a different character – not dwellings at all. For him, who was familiar with most of the paraphernalia of manufactured energy, there was no question. Some of the massive structures below were the kind that housed atomic power. Others were distributing plants for electricity. Still others had the unmistakable shape of the Ylem transformation systems.

None of these, of course, was *the* Power, but here indeed was power in abundance.

Cemp followed O-Vedd down to the courtyard of a building complex that, despite all its shields, he had no difficulty in identifying as a source of magnetic beams.

The space Silkie landed and transformed to human form, then stood and waited for Cemp to do likewise.

'Nothing doing!' said Cemp curtly. 'Ask him to come out here.'

O-Vedd shrugged. As a human he was short and dark. He walked off and vanished into a doorway.

Cemp waited amid a silence that was broken only by the faint hum of power from the buildings. A breeze touched the supersensitive spy-ray extensions that he maintained in operation under all circumstances. The little wind registered through the spy mechanism but did not trigger the defense screens behind it.

It was only a breeze, after all, and he had never programmed himself to respond to such minor signals. He was about to dismiss it from his mind, about to contemplate his reaction to the space Silkies – he liked the crowd he had seen – when he thought sharply, A *breeze* here!

Up went his screen. Out projected his perceptors. He had time to notice, then, that it was indeed a breeze but that it was being stirred by a blankness in the surrounding space. Around Cemp, the courtyard grew hazy; then it faded.

There was no planetoid.

Cemp increased all signal sensitivity to maximum. He continued to float in the vacuum of space, and off to one side was the colossal white circle that was the sun. Suddenly, he felt energy drain from his body. The sensation was of his Silkie screens going up, of his system resisting outside energy at many levels.

He thought in tense dismay, *I'm in a fight. It's another attempt to kill me.*

Whatever it was, it was automatic. His own perception remained cut off, and he was impelled to experience what the attacker wanted him to.

Cemp felt like a man suddenly set upon in pitch darkness. But what was appalling about it was that his senses were being held by other forces, preventing awareness of the nature of the attack. What he saw was —

Distance disappeared!

There, spread over many miles of space, was a group of Silkies. Cemp saw them clearly, counted in his lightning fashion two hundred and eighty-eight, caught their thoughts, and recognized that these were the renegade Silkies from Earth.

Suddenly, he understood that they had been told where the Silkie planetoid was and were on their way 'home'.

Time was telescoped.

The entire group of Silkies was transported in what seemed an instant to within a short distance of the planetoid. Cemp could see the planetoid in the near distance – only a few miles away, twenty at the maximum.

But to him the baffling, deadly, fantastic thing was that as these marvelous events ran their course at one level of his perception, at another level the feeling remained that a determined attempt was being made to kill him.

He could see, feel, be aware of almost nothing. But throughout, the shadowy sensations continued. His energy fields were going through defensive motions. But it was all far away from his awareness, like a human dream.

Being a fully trained Silkie, Cemp watched the internal as well as the external developments with keen observation, strove instant by instant to grasp the reality, monitored incoming signals by the thousands.

He began to sense meaning and to formulate initial speculations about the nature of the physical-world phenomenon involved. And he had the feeling of being on the verge of his first computation, when, as suddenly as it had begun, it ended.

The space scene began to fade. Abruptly, it winked out.

He was back in the courtyard of the buildings that housed the magnetic-power complex. Coming toward him from the open doorway of the main building was O-Vedd. He was accompanied by a man who was of Cemp's general human build – over six feet and strongly muscled. His face was heavier than Cemp's, and his eyes were brown instead of gray.

As he came near, he said, 'I am E-Lerd. Let's talk.'

8

'To begin with, I want to tell you the history of the Silkies,' E-Lerd said.

Cemp was electrified by the statement. He had been braced for a bitter quarrel, and he could feel in himself a multitude of readjusting energy flows . . . proof of the severity of the second all-out fight he had been in. And he absolutely required a complete explanation for the attacks on him.

At that moment, caught up as he was in a steely rage, nothing else could have diverted his attention. But . . . the history of the Silkies! To Cemp, it was instantly the most important subject in the universe.

The Silkie planetoid, E-Lerd began, had entered the solar

system from outer space nearly three hundred years before It had, in due course, been drawn into a Sol-Neptunian orbit. On its first encirclement of the Sun, Silkies visited the inner planets and found that Earth alone was inhabited.

Since they could change form, they studied the biological structure necessary to function in the two atmospheres of Earth – air and water – and set up an internal programming for that purpose.

Unfortunately, a small percentage of the human population, it was soon discovered, could tune in on the thoughts of Silkies. All those who did so in this first visit were quickly hunted down and their memories of the experience blotted out.

But because of these sensitive humans, it became necessary for Silkies to seem to be the product of human biological experiments. An interrelationship with human females was accordingly programmed into Silkies, so that the human female ovum and the male Silkie sperm would produce a Silkie who knew nothing of Silkie history.

In order to maintain this process on an automatic level, the Special People – those persons who could read Silkie minds – were maneuvered into being in charge of it.

Thereupon, all but one of the adult Silkies returned to their planetoid, which now went to the remote end of its orbit. When it came again into the vicinity of Earth, more than a hundred years later, cautious visits were made.

It became apparent that several unplanned things had happened. Human biologists had experimented with the process. As a result, in the early stages, variants had been born. These had propagated their twisted traits and were continuing to do so, growing ever more numerous.

The actual consequences were: a number of true Silkies, capable of making the three-fold transformation at will; class-B Silkies, who could transform from human to fish state, but could not become space people; and a stable form, Variants!

The last two groups had largely taken to the oceans. Accordingly it was decided to leave the class-B Silkies alone but to make an effort to inveigle Variants into gigantic spaceships filled with water where they would be isolated and prevented from interbreeding.

This plan was already underway by the time the Silkie planetoid made its round of the sun and again headed out toward far Neptune.

Now they were back, and they had found an unfortunate situation. Somehow, Earth science, virtually ignored by the early visitors, had achieved a method for training the Silkie perception system.

The Earth Silkies had become a loyal-to-Earth, tight-knit, masterful group of beings, lacking only the Power.

Cemp 'read' all this in E-Lerd's thought, and then, because he was amazed, he questioned him about what seemed a major omission in his story. Where had the Silkie planetoid come from?

E-Lerd showed his first impatience. 'These journeys are too far,' he telepathed. 'They take too long. Nobody remembers origins. Some other star system, obviously.'

'Are you serious?' Cemp was astounded. 'You don't know?'

But that was the story. Pry at it as he might, it did not change. Although E-Lerd's mind remained closed except for his telepathed thoughts, O-Vedd's mind was open. In it Cemp saw the same beliefs and the same lack of information.

But why the tampering with human biology and the inter-mixing of the two breeds?

'We always do that. That's how we live – in a relationship with the inhabitants of a system.'

'How do you know you always do that? You just told me you can't remember where you came from this time or where you were before that.'

'Well . . . it's obvious from the artifacts we brought along.'

E-Lerd's attitude dismissed the questions as being ir-

348

relevant. Cemp detected a mind phenomenon in the other that explained the attitude. To space Silkies, the past was unimportant. Silkies *always* did certain things, because that was the way they were mentally, emotionally, and physically constructed.

A Silkie didn't have to know from past experience. He simply had to *be* what was innate in Silkies.

It was, Cemp realized, a basic explanation for much that he had observed. This was why these Silkies had never been trained scientifically. Training was an alien concept in the cosmos of the space Silkies.

'You mean,' he protested, incredulous, 'you have no idea why you left the last system where you had this interrelationship with the race there? Why not stay forever in some system where you have located yourself?'

'Probably,' said E-Lerd, 'somebody got too close to the secret of the Power. That could not be permitted.'

That was the reason, he continued, why Cemp and other Silkies had to come back into the fold. As Silkies, they might learn about the Power.

The discussion had naturally come around to *that* urgent subject.

'What,' said Cemp, 'is the Power?'

E-Lerd stated formally that that was a forbidden subject.

'Then I shall have to force the secret from you,' said Cemp. 'There can be no agreement without it.'

E-Lerd replied stiffly that any attempt at force would require him to use the Power as a defense.

Cemp lost patience. 'After your two attempts to kill me,' he telepathed in a steely rage, 'I'll give you thirty seconds —'

'What attempts to kill you?' said E-Lerd, surprised.

At that precise moment, as Cemp was bracing himself to use logic of levels, there was an interruption.

An 'impulse' band – a very low, slow vibration – touched one of the receptors in the forward part of his brain. It operated at mere multiples of the audible sound range directly on his sound-receiving system.

What was new was that the sound acted as a carrier for the accompanying thought. The result was as if a voice spoke clearly and loudly into his ears.

'You win,' said the voice. 'You have forced me. I shall talk to you myself – bypassing my unknowing servants.'

9

Cemp identified the incoming thought formation as a direct contact. Accordingly, his brain, which was programmed to respond instantaneously to a multitude of signals, was triggered into an instant effort to suction more impulses from the sending brain . . . and he got a picture. A momentary glimpse, so brief that even after a few seconds it was hard to be sure that it was real and not a figment of fantasy.

Something huge lay in the darkness deep inside the planetoid. It lay there and gave forth with an impression of vast power. It had been withholding itself, watching him with some tiny portion of itself. The larger whole understood the universe and could manipulate massive sections of space-time.

'Say nothing to these others.' Again the statement was a direct contact that sounded like spoken words.

The dismay that had seized on Cemp in the last few moments was on the level of desperation. He had entered the Silkie stronghold in the belief that his human training and Kibmadine knowledge gave him a temporary advantage over the space Silkies and that if he did not delay, he could win a battle that might resolve the entire threat from these natural Silkies.

Instead, he had come unsuspecting into the lair of a cosmic giant. He thought, appalled, *Here is what has been called 'the Power'*.

And if the glimpse he had had was real, then it was such a

colossal power that all his own ability and strength were as nothing.

He deduced now that this was what had attacked him twice. 'Is that true?' he telepathed on the same band as the incoming thoughts had been on.

'Yes. I admit it.'

'Why?' Cemp flashed the question. 'Why did you do it?'

'So that I would not have to reveal my existence. My fear is always that if other life forms find out about me, they will analyze how to destroy me.'

The direction of the alien thought altered. 'But now, listen; do as follows. . . .'

The confession had again stirred Cemp's emotions. The hatred that had been aroused in him had a sustained force deriving from the logic-of-levels stimulation – in this instance the body's response to an attempt at total destruction. Therefore, he had difficulty now restraining additional automatic reactions.

But the pieces of the puzzle were falling into place. So, presently he was able, at the request of the monster, to say to E-Lerd and the other Silkies, 'You take a while to think this over. And when the Silkies who have defected arrive from Earth, I'll talk to them. We can then have another discussion.'

It was such a complete change of attitude that the two Silkies showed their surprise. But he saw that to them the change had the look of weakness and that they were relieved.

'I'll be back here in one hour!' he telepathed to E-Lerd. Whereupon he turned and climbed up and out of the courtyard, darting to an opening that led by a roundabout route deeper into the planetoid.

Again the low, slow vibration touched his receptors. 'Come closer!' the creature urged.

Cemp obeyed, on the hard-core principle that either he could defend himself – or he couldn't. Down he went, past a dozen screens, to a barren cave, a chamber that had been carved out of the original meteorite stuff. It was not even lighted. As he entered, the direct thought touched his mind again: 'Now we can talk.'

Cemp had been thinking at furious speed, striving to adjust to a danger so tremendous that he had no way of evaluating it. Yet the Power had revealed itself to him rather than let E-Lerd find out anything. That seemed to be his one hold on it; and he had the tense conviction that even that was true only as long as he was inside the planetoid.

He thought . . . *Take full advantage!*

He telepathed, 'After those attacks, you'll have to give me some straight answers, if you expect to deal with me.'

'What do you want to know?'

'Who are you? Where do you come from? What do you want?'

It didn't know who it was. 'I have a name,' it said. 'I am the Glis. There used to be many like me long ago. I don't know what happened to them.'

'But *what* are you?'

It had no knowledge. An energy life form of unknown origin, traveling from one star system to another, remaining for a while, then leaving.

'But why leave? Why not stay?' sharply.

'The time comes when I have done what I can for a particular system.'

By using its enormous power, it transported large ice-and-air meteorites to airless planets and made them habitable, cleared away dangerous space debris, altered poisonous atmospheres into nonpoisonous ones. . . .

'Presently the job is done, and I realize it's time to go on to explore the infinite cosmos. So I make my pretty picture of the inhabited planets, as you saw, and head for outer space.'

'And the Silkies?'

They were an old meteorite life form.

'I found them long ago, and because I needed mobile units

352

that could think, I persuaded them into a permanent relationship.'

Cemp did not ask what persuasive methods had been used. In view of the Silkies' ignorance of what they had a relationship with, he divined that a sly method had been used. But still, what he had seen showed an outwardly peaceful arrangement. The Glis had agents – the Silkies – who acted for it in the world of tiny movements. They, in turn, had at their disposal bits and pieces of the Glis's own 'body', which could apparently be programmed for specific tasks beyond the Silkies' ability to perform.

'I am willing,' said the Glis, 'to make the same arrangement with your government for as long as I remain in the solar system.'

But absolute secrecy would be necessary.

'Why?'

There was no immediate reply, but the communication band remained open. And along the line of communication there flowed an essence of the reaction from the Glis – an impression of unmatched power, of a being so mighty that all other individuals in the universe were less by some enormous percentage.

Cemp felt staggered anew. But he telepathed, 'I must tell someone. Somebody has to know.'

'No other Silkies – absolutely.'

Cemp didn't argue. All these millennia, the Glis had kept its identity hidden from the space Silkies. He had a total conviction that it would wreck the entire planetoid to prevent them from learning it.

He had been lucky. It had fought him at a level where only a single chamber of the meteorite had been destroyed. It had restricted itself.

'Only the top government leaders and the Silkie Council may know,' the Glis continued.

It seemed an adequate concession; yet Cemp had an awful

353

suspicion that in the long past of this creature every person who uncovered its secret had been murdered.

Thinking thus, he could not compromise. He demanded, 'Let me have a complete view of you – what I caught a fleeting glimpse of earlier.'

He sensed, then, that the Glis hesitated.

Cemp urged, 'I promise that only the persons you named will be told about this – but we *must* know!'

Floating there in the cave in his Silkie form, Cemp felt a change of energy tension in the air and in the ground. Although he put forth no additional probing energies, he recognized that barriers were going down. And presently he began to record.

His first impression was of hugeness. Cemp estimated, after a long, measuring look, that the creature, a circular rocklike structure, was about a thousand feet in diameter. It was alive, but it was not a thing of flesh and blood. It 'fed' from some inner energy that rivaled what existed in the heart of the sun.

And Cemp noticed a remarkable phenomenon. Magnetic impulses that passed through the creature and impinged on his senses were altered in a fashion that he had never observed before – as if they had passed through atoms of a different structure than anything he knew.

He remembered the fleeting impression he had had from the molecule. This was the same but on a massive scale. What startled him was that all his enormous training in such matters gave no clue to what the structure might be.

'Enough?' asked the creature.

Doubtfully, Cemp said, 'Yes.'

Glis accepted his reluctant agreement as a complete authorization. What had been a view through and past the cave wall disappeared abruptly.

The alien thought spoke into his mind, 'I have done a very dangerous thing for me in thus revealing myself. Therefore, I again earnestly impress on you the importance of a limited number of people being told what you have just witnessed.

In secrecy, it continued, lay the greatest safety, not only for it, but for Cemp.

'I believe,' said the creature, 'that what I can do is overwhelming. But I could be wrong. What disturbs me is, there is only one of me. I would hate to suddenly feel the kind of fear that might motivate me to destroy an entire system.'

The implied threat was as deadly – and as possible – as anything Cemp had ever heard. Cemp hesitated, feeling overwhelmed, desperate for more information.

He flashed, 'How old do Silkies get?' and added quickly, 'We've had no experience, since none has yet died a natural death.'

'About a thousand of your Earth years,' was the answer.

'What have you in mind for Earth-born Silkies? Why did you want us to return here?'

Again there was a pause; once more the sense of colossal power. But presently with it there came a reluctant admission that new Silkies, born on planets, normally had less direct knowledge of the Glis than those who had made the latest trip.

Thus, the Glis had a great interest in ensuring that plenty of time was allowed for a good replacement crop of unknowing young Silkies.

It finished, 'You and I shall have to make a special agreement. Perhaps you can have E-Lerd's position and be my contact.'

Since E-Lerd no longer remembered that he was the contact, Cemp had no sense of having being offered anything but . . . danger.

He thought soberly, *I'll never be permitted to come back here, once I leave.*

But that didn't matter. The important thing was – get away! At once!

10

At the Silkie Authority, the computer gave four answers.

Cemp rejected two of them at once. They were, in the parlance of computer technology, 'trials'. The machine simply presented all the bits of information, strung out in two lookovers. By this means a living brain could examine the data in segments. But Cemp did not need such data – not now.

Of the remaining two answers, one postulated a being akin to a god. But Cemp had experienced the less-than-godlike powers of the Glis, in that it had twice failed to defeat him. True, he believed that it had failed to destroy him because it did not wish to destroy the planetoid. But an omnipotent god would not have found that a limitation.

He had to act as if the amazing fourth possibility were true. The picture that had come through in that possibility was one of ancientness. The mighty being hidden in the planetoid predated most planetary systems.

'In the time from which it derives,' said the computer, 'there were, of course, stars and star systems, but they were different. The natural laws were not what they are today. Space and time have made adjustments since then, grown older; therefore, the present appearance of the universe is different from that which the Glis knew at its beginnings. This seems to give it an advantage, for it knows some of the older shapes of atoms and molecules and can re-create them. Certain of these combinations reflect the state of matter when it was – the best comparison – younger.'

The human government group, to whom Cemp presented this data, was stunned. Like himself, they had been basing their entire plan on working out a compromise with the space Silkies. Now, suddenly, here was a colossal being with unknown power.

'Would you say,' asked one man huskily, 'that to a degree the Silkies are slaves of this creature?'

Cemp said, 'E-Lerd definitely didn't know what he was dealing with. He simply had what he conceived to be a scientific system for utilizing a force of nature. The Glis responded to his manipulation of this system, as if it were simply another form of energy. But I would guess that it controlled him, perhaps through preconditioning installed long ago.'

As he pointed out, such a giant life form would not be concerned with the everyday living details of its subjects. It would be satisfied with having a way of invariably getting them to do what it wanted.

'But what *does* it want?' That came from another man.

'It goes around doing good,' said Cemp with a tight smile. 'That's the public image it tried to give me. I have the impression that it's willing to make over the solar system to our specifications.'

At this point Mathews spoke. 'Mr Cemp,' he said, 'what does all this do to the Silkie situation?'

Cemp said that the Silkies who had defected had clearly acted hastily. 'But,' he finished, 'I should tell you that I find the space Silkies a very likeable group. In my opinion, they are not the problem. They have the same problem, in another way, that we have.'

'Nat,' said Charley Baxter, 'do you trust this monster?'

Cemp hesitated, remembering the deadly attacks, remembering that only the Kibmadine defense screen and energy-reversal process had saved him. He remembered, too, that the great being had been compelled to reveal its presence to prevent him from forcing E-Lerd to open his mind – which would have informed the space Silkies of the nature of the Power.

'No!' he said.

Having spoken, he realized that a simple negative was not answer enough. It could not convey the reality of the terrifying danger that was out there in space.

He said slowly, 'I realize that my own motives may be

suspect in what I am about to say, but it's my true opinion. I think all Earth Silkies should be given full knowledge of the Kibmadine attack-and-defense system at once and that they should be assigned to work in teams to keep a constant watch on the Glis, permitting no one to leave the planetoid – except to surrender.'

There was a pregnant silence. Then a scientist said in a small voice, 'Any chance of logic of levels applying?'

'I don't see how,' said Cemp.

'I don't either,' said the man unhappily.

Cemp addressed the group again. 'I believe we should gird ourselves to drive this thing from the solar system. We're not safe until it's gone.'

As he finished speaking, he sensed an energy tension . . . familiar! He had a sensation, then, of cosmic distance and cosmic time – opening. Power unlimited!

It was the same feeling he had had in the second attack, when his senses had been confused.

The fear that came to Cemp in that moment had no parallel in his experience. It was the fear of a man who suddenly has a fleeting glimpse of death and destruction for all his own kind and for his planet.

As he had that awful consciousness, Cemp whirled from where he was standing. He ran headlong toward the great window behind him, shattering it with an arc of lightning as he did so. And with eyes closed against the flying glass, he plunged out into the empty air seventy stories above the ground.

As he fell, the fabric of space and time collapsed around him like a house of cards tumbling. Cemp transformed into class-C Silkie and became immensely more perceptive. Now he sensed the nature of the colossal energy at work – a gravitational field so intense that it actually closed in upon itself. Encompassing all things, organic and inorganic, it squeezed with irresistible power. . . .

Defensively, Cemp put up, first, his inverter system . . .

and perceived that that was not the answer.

Instantly, he triggered gravity transformation – an infinitely variable system that converted the encroaching superfield to a harmless energy in relation to himself.

With that, he felt the change slow. It did not stop. He was no longer so involved, so enveloped; yet he was not completely free.

He realized what held him. He was oriented to this massive segment of space-time. To an extent, anything that happened here happened to him. To that extent, he could not get away.

The world grew dim. The sun disappeared.

Cemp saw with a start that he was inside a chamber and realized that his automatic screens had protected him from striking the hard, glittering walls.

And he became aware of three other realities. The chamber was familiar, in that there below him was one of the glowing images of a planet. The image showed the oceans and the continents, and since he was looking down at it, he felt that he was somehow back inside the Silkie planetoid, in one of the 'art' rooms.

What was different was that as he looked down at the planetary image, he saw the familiar outlines of the continents and oceans of Earth. And he realized that the feeling of a virtually unlimited force pressing in was a true explanation of what was happening.

The ancient monster that lived at the core of the planetoid had taken Earth, compressed it and everything on it from an 8,000-mile-in-diameter planet into a hundred-foot ball, and added the ball to its fabulous collection.

It was not a jewel-like image of Earth there in the floor – it was Earth itself.

Even as he had the thought, Cemp sensed that the planetoid was increasing its speed.

He thought, *We're leaving the solar system.*

In a matter of minutes, as he hovered there, helpless to act, the speed of the planetoid became hundreds, then thousands of miles a second.

After about an hour of continuing acceleration, the velocity of the tiny planetoid, in its ever-widening hyperbolic orbit, was nearly half that of light.

A few hours later, the planetoid was beyond the orbit of Pluto, and it was traveling at near light speed.

And still accelerating . . .

11

Cemp began to brace himself. Anger spilled through him like a torrent down a rocky decline.

'You incredible monster!' he telepathed.

No answer.

Cemp raged on, 'You're the most vicious creature that ever existed. I'm going to see that you get what's coming to you!'

This time he got a reply. 'I'm leaving the solar system forever,' said the Glis. 'Why don't you get off before it's too late? I'll let you get away.'

Cemp had no doubt of that. He was its most dangerous enemy, and his escape and unexpected appearance must have come as a hideous shock to the Glis.

'I'm not leaving,' he retorted, 'until you undo what you've done to Earth.'

There was silence.

'Can you and will you?' Cemp demanded.

'No. It's impossible.' The response came reluctantly.

'But you could, if you wanted to, bring Earth back to size.'

'No. But I now wish I had not taken your planet,' said the Glis unhappily. 'It has been my policy to leave alone inhabited worlds that are protected by powerful life forms. I simply could not bring myself to believe that any Silkie was really dangerous to me. I was mistaken.'

It was not the kind of repentance that Cemp respected. 'Why can't you . . . unsqueeze it?' he persisted.

360

It seemed that the Glis could create a gravity field, but it could not reverse such a field. It said apologetically, 'It would take as much power to undo it as it took to do it. Where is there such power?'

Where, indeed? But still he could not give up. 'I'll teach you what antigravity is like,' Cemp offered, 'from what I can do in my own energy-control system.'

But the Glis pointed out that it had had the opportunity to study such systems in other Silkies. 'Don't think I didn't try. Evidently antigravity is a late manifestation of matter and energy. And I'm an early form – as you, and only you, know.'

Cemp's hope faded suddenly. Somehow, he had kept believing that there was a possibility. There wasn't.

The first grief touched him, the first real acceptance of the end of Earth.

The Glis was communicating again. 'I can see that you and I now have a serious situation between us. So we must arrive at an agreement. I'll make you the leader of the Silkie nation. I'll subtly influence everything and everyone to fit your wishes. Women – as many as you desire. Control – as much as you want. Future actions of the planetoid, you and I shall decide.'

Cemp did not even consider the offer. He said grimly, 'You and I don't think alike. I can just imagine trusting you to leave me alone if I ever took the chance of changing to human form.' He broke off, then said curtly, 'The deal as I see it is a limited truce while I consider what I can do against you and you figure out what you can do to me.'

'Since that's the way you feel,' was the harsh reply, 'let me make my position clear. If you begin any action against me, I shall first destroy Earth and the Silkie nation and then give you my attention.'

Cemp replied in his own steely fashion, 'If you ever damage anything I value – and that includes all Silkies and what's left of Earth – I'll attack you with everything I've got.'

The Glis said scornfully, 'You have nothing that can touch me – except those defense screens that reverse the attack flow. That way, you can use my own force against me. So I won't attack. Therefore – permanent stalemate.'

Cemp said, 'We'll see.'

The Glis said, 'You yourself stated that your levels of logic wouldn't work on me.'

'I meant not directly,' said Cemp. 'There are many indirect approaches to the mind.'

'I don't see how anything like that can work on me,' was the reply.

At that moment, Cemp didn't either.

12

Through miles of passageways, up as well as down and roundabout, Cemp made his way. The journey took him through long chambers filled with furniture and art objects from other planets.

En route he saw strange and wonderful scenes in bas-relief and brilliant color on one wall after another. And always there were the planets themselves, glowingly beautiful, but horrifying too, in his awareness that each one represented a hideous crime.

His destination was the city of the Silkies. He followed the internal pathway to it because he dared not leave the planet-oid to take an external route. The Glis had virtually admitted that it had not anticipated that he, its most dangerous enemy, would survive. So if he ever left these caves, he would have no further choice, no chance to decide on what the penalty – if any – or the outcome should be and no part at all in the Silkie future. For he would surely never be allowed to return.

Not that there was any purpose in him – his grief was too deep and terrible. He had failed to protect, failed to realize, failed in his duty.

Earth was lost. It was lost quickly, completely, a disaster

so great that it could not even be contemplated for more than instants at a time.

At intervals, he mourned Joanne and Charley Baxter and other friends among the Special People and the human race.

By the time he was sunk into these miseries, he had taken up an observation position on top of a tree overlooking the main street of the Silkie city. There he waited, with all his signal systems constantly at peak alert.

While he maintained his tireless vigil, the life of the Silkie community had its being around him. The Silkies continued to live mostly as humans, and this began to seem significant.

Cemp thought, shocked, *They're being kept vulnerable!*

In human form, they could all be killed in a single flash of intolerable flame.

He telepathed on the Glis band: 'Free them from that compulsion or I'll tell them the truth about what you are.'

An immediate, ferocious answer came: 'You say one word, and I shall wipe out the entire nest.'

Cemp commanded, 'Release them from that compulsion, or we come to our crisis right now.'

His statement must have given the Glis pause, for there was a brief silence. Then, 'I'll release half of them. No more. I must retain some hold over you.'

Cemp considered that and realized its truth. 'But it has to be on an alternating basis. Half are free for twelve hours, then the other half.'

The Glis accepted the compromise without further argument. Clearly, it was prepared to recognize the balance of power.

'Where are we heading?' asked Cemp.

'To another star system.'

The answer did not satisfy Cemp. Surely the Glis didn't expect to go on with its malignant game of collecting inhabited planets.

He challenged, 'I feel that you have some secret purpose.'

'Don't be ridiculous, and don't bother me any more.'

Stalemate.

As the days and the weeks went by, Cemp tried to keep track of the distance the planetoid was covering and the direction it was going. The speed of the meteorite had reached nearly a light-year per day, Earth time.

Eighty-two of those days passed. And then there was the feel of slowing down. The deceleration continued all that day and the next. And for Cemp, there was finally no question – he could not permit this strange craft which was now his home to arrive at a destination about which he knew nothing.

'Stop this ship!' he ordered.

The Glis replied angrily, 'You can't expect to control such minor things as this!'

Since it could be a deadly dangerous scheme, Cemp replied, 'Then open yourself to me. Show me everything you know about this system.'

'I've never been here before.'

'All right, then that's what I'll see when you open up.'

'I can't possibly let you look inside me. You may see something this time that will make me vulnerable to your techniques.'

'Then change course.'

'No. That would mean I can't go anywhere until you die about a thousand years from now. I refuse to accept such a limitation.'

The second reference to Silkie age gave Cemp great pause. On Earth no one had known how long Silkies could live, since none born there had died a natural death. He himself was only thirty-eight years of age.

'Look,' he said finally, 'if I have only a thousand years, why don't you just sit me out? That must be only a pinpoint in time compared with your lifespan.'

'All right, we'll do that!' replied the Glis. But the deceleration continued.

364

Cemp telepathed, 'If you don't turn aside, I must take action.'

'What can you do?' was the contemptuous response.

It was a good question. What, indeed?

'I warn you,' said Cemp.

'Just don't tell anyone about me. Other than that, do anything you please.'

Cemp said, 'I gather you've decided I'm not dangerous. And this is the way you act with those you consider harmless.'

The Glis said that had Cemp been able to do something, he would already have done it. It finished, 'And so I tell you flatly, I'm going to do as *I* please; and the only restriction on you is, don't violate my need for secrecy. Now, don't bother me again.'

The meaning of the dismissal was clear. He had been judged helpless, categorized as someone whose desires need not be considered. The eighty days of inaction had stood against him. He hadn't attacked; therefore, he couldn't. That was palpably the other's logic.

Well . . . what could he do?

He could make an energy assault. But that would take time to mount, and he could expect that the Silkie nation would be wiped out in retaliation and Earth destroyed.

Cemp decided that he was not ready to force such a calamity.

He was presently dismayed to realize that the Glis's analysis was correct. He could keep his mind shut and respect its need for secrecy – and nothing more.

He ought, it seemed to him, to point out to the Glis that there were different types of secrecy. Gradations. Secrecy about itself was one type. But secrecy about the star system ahead was quite another. The whole subject of secrecy –

Cemp's mind poised. Then he thought, *How could I have missed it?*

Yet, even as he wondered, he realized how it had hap-

365

pened. The Glis's need to withhold knowledge of itself had seemed understandable, and somehow the naturalness of it had made him bypass its implications. But now . . .

Secrecy, he thought. *Of course! That's it!*

To Silkies, secrecy was an understood phenomenon.

After a few more seconds of thinking about it, Cemp took his first action. He reversed gravity in relation to the planetoid mass below him. Light as a thistledown, he floated up and away from the treetop that had been his observation post for so long. Soon he was speeding along granite corridors.

13

Without incident, Cemp reached the chamber containing Earth.

As he set his signals so that all his screens would protect that precious round ball, Cemp permitted himself another increment of hope.

Secrets! he thought again, and his mind soared.

Life, in its natural impulse, had no secrets.

Baby gurgled or cried or manifested needs instant by instant as each feeling was experienced. But the child, growing older, was progressively admonished and inhibited, subjected to a thousand restraints. Yet all his life the growing being would want openness and unrestraint, would struggle to free himself from childhood conditioning.

Conditioning was not of itself logic of levels, but it was related – a step lower. The appearance was of a control center; that is, a rigidity. But it was a created center and could be repeatedly mobilized by the correct stimulus. That part was automatic.

The decisive fact was that, since the Glis had conditioned itself to secrecy – it was conditionable.

Having reached this penultimate point in his analysis, Cemp hesitated. As a Silkie, he was conditioned to incapacitate rather than kill, to negotiate rather than incapacitate, and to promote well-being everywhere.

366

Even for the Glis, death should be the final consideration not the first.

So he telepathed, 'In all your long span, you have feared that someone would one day learn how to destroy you. I have to tell you that I am that feared person. So unless you are prepared to back down from those insolent statements of a little while ago, you must die.'

The answer came coldly. 'I let you go to your planet Earth because I have the real hostages under my complete control – the Silkie nation!'

'That is your final statement?' Cemp questioned.

'Yes. Cease these foolish threats. They are beginning to irritate me.'

Cemp now said, 'I know where you come from, what you are, and what happened to others like you.'

Of course, he knew nothing of the kind. But it was the technique. By stating the generalization, he would evoke from the Glis's perception and memory network, first, the truth. Then, like all living things, the Glis would immediately have the automatic impulse to give forth the information as it actually was.

Yet before it could do so, it would exercise the restraint of secrecy. And that would be an exact pattern, a reaffirmation of similar precise restraints in its long, long past. His problem was to utilize it before it destimulated, because as long as it held, it was the equivalent of a logic-of-levels gestalt.

Having, according to the theory, mobilized it, Cemp transmitted the triggering signal.

A startled thought came from the Glis: 'What have you done?'

It was Cemp's turn to be sly, covert, scheming. He said, 'I had to call to your attention that you had better deal with me.'

It was too late for the Glis to help itself, but the pretense – if successful – might save many lives.

367

'I wish to point out,' said the Glis, 'that I have not yet damaged anything of value.'

Cemp was profoundly relieved to hear the statement. But he had no regrets. With such a creature as this, he could not hope to repeat what he was doing against it. Once the process was started, it was all or nothing.

'What was it you said before about bargaining?' the Glis asked urgently.

Cemp steeled himself against sympathy.

The Glis continued, 'I'll give you all my secrets in exchange for your telling me what you're doing to me. I'm experiencing severe internal disturbance, and I don't know why.'

Cemp hesitated. It was a tremendous offer. But he divined that once he made such a promise, he would have to keep it.

What had happened was this: As he had hoped, his final signal had triggered the equivalent of a colony gestalt, in this instance the process by which life forms slowly over the millennia adjusted to exterior change.

And the cycle-completing control centers, the growth-change mechanisms in the great being, were stimulated.

Silkies understood the nature of growth, and of change they knew much from their own bodies. But Silkies were late indeed in the scheme of life. In terms of evolution, their cells were as old as the rocks and the planets. The entire history of life's progression was in every cell of a Silkie.

That could not be true of the Glis. It was from an ancient eon, and it had stopped time within itself. Or at least, it had not passed on its seed, which was the way of change through time. In itself, it manifested old, primitive forms. Great forms they were, but the memory in each cell would be limited to what had gone before. Therefore, it couldn't know what, in holding back as it had, it was holding back from.

'I promise not to go on to the Nijjan system,' said the Glis. 'Observe – I'm already stopping.'

Cemp sensed a cessation of the motion of the planetoid, but it seemed a minor act, not meaningful.

He merely noted, in passing, the identity of the star the Glis had named, observing that since it knew the name, it *had* been there before. This seemed to imply that the Glis had a purpose in going there.

It didn't matter; they were turning away from it, would never reach it. If there was a threat there for Cemp or for Silkies, it was now diverted and had been useful only in that it had forced him to action regardless of the consequences.

The Glis's willingness to make amends when it no longer had any choice was merely a sad commentary on its character, but much too late. Many planets too late, Cemp thought.

How many? he wondered. And because he was in the strange emotional condition of someone whose whole thought and effort are concentrated on a single intensely felt purpose, he asked the question aloud automatically, as it came into his mind.

'I don't think I should tell you; you might hold it against me,' the Glis replied.

It must have sensed Cemp's adamant state, for it said quickly, 'Eighteen hundred and twenty-three.'

So many!

The total of them did not shock Cemp – it hurt him. For one of that countless number of unnecessary dead on those planets was Joanne. Another was Charley Baxter.

'Why have you done all this?' Cemp asked. 'Why destroy all those planets?'

'They were so beautiful.'

True. Cemp had a sudden mental vision of a great planet hanging in space, its amosphere ballooning up above the oceans and mountains and plains. He had seen that sight often, yet found it always a thing of splendor beyond all the visual delights of the universe.

The feeling passed, for a planet was beautiful when it was

brooded over by its parent sun and not as a shrunken museum piece.

The Glis with its planets was like a head hunter of old. Skillfully, he had murdered each victim. Patiently, he had reduced the head to its small size. Lovingly, he had placed it in his collection.

For the head hunter, each perfect miniature head was a symbol of his manhood. For the Glis, the planets were . . . what?

Cemp couldn't imagine.

But he had delayed long enough. He sensed incipient violence on the communication band. He said hastily, 'All right, I agree – as soon as you do what I want, I'll tell you exactly how I'm attacking you.'

'What do you want?'

Cemp said, 'First, let the other Silkies go outside.'

'But you'll do as I've asked?'

'Yes. When you've released them, put me and the Earth outside, safely.'

'Then you'll tell me?'

'Yes.'

The Glis threatened, 'If you don't, I'll smash your little planet. I will not let you or it escape, if you don't tell me.'

'I'll tell you.'

14

The method that was used was, the entire section of the planetoid surrounding Cemp simply lifted up and shot off into the sky. Cemp found himself floating in black, empty space, surrounded by meteorite debris.

The Glis's thought came to him, 'I have done my part. Now tell me!'

Even as Cemp complied, he began to wonder if he really understood what was happening.

Uneasiness came. In setting in motion a cycle-completion process, he had taken it for granted that Nature would strike a balance. An old life form had somehow been preserved here, and in its body, evolution was now proceeding at lightning speed. Millions of years of change had already been compressed into minutes of time. Since none other of its kind remained alive, he had assumed that the species had long since evolved to . . . what?

What was this creature? A chrysalis? An egg? Would it become a butterfly of space, a great worm, a gigantic bird?

Such possibilities had not occurred to him before. He had thought only of the possibility of extinction. But – it struck him keenly – he hadn't considered seriously enough what extinction might consist of in its end product.

Indeed, he hadn't thought about the existence of an end product.

Unhappily, Cemp remembered what the computer had reported – that the atomic structure of this giant being reflected a younger state of matter.

Could it be that, as the particles 'adjusted' and changed to current norm, energy would be released on a hitherto unknown scale?

Below, a titanic thing happened.

Part of the planetoid lifted, and a solid ball of red-hot matter, at least a mile thick, lifted slowly out of it. As Cemp drew aside to let the improbable thing past him, he saw that an even more unlikely phenomenon was taking place. The 'up' speed of the chunk of now white-hot rock and dirt was increasing – and the mass was growing.

It was well past him, and it was at least a hundred miles in diameter. A minute later, it was five hundred miles thick, and it was still expanding, still increasing in speed.

It expanded to a burning, incredible mass.

Suddenly, it was ten thousand miles in diameter and was still going away, still growing.

Cemp sent out a general alarm: 'Get away – as fast as you can. Away!'

As he himself fled, using a reversal of the gravity of the

monstrous body behind him, he saw that in those few minutes it had grown more than 100,000 miles in diameter.

It was quite pink at this point – strangely, beautifully pink.

The color altered even as he watched, turning faintly yellow. And the body that emitted the beautiful ocher light was now more than 1,000,000 miles in diameter.

As big as Earth's sun.

In minutes more, it grew to the size of a giant blue sun, ten times the diameter of Sol.

It began to turn pink again, and it grew *one hundred times* in ten minutes. Brighter than Mira the Wonderful, bigger than glorious Ras Algethi.

But pink, not red. A deeper pink than before; not red, so definitely not a variable.

All around was the starry universe, bright with unfamiliar objects that glowed near and far – hundreds of them, strung out like a long line of jack-o'-lanterns.

Below was Earth.

Cemp looked at that scene in the heavens and then at the near, familiar planet, and an awful excitement seized him.

He thought, *Is it possible that everything had to grow, that the Glis's change altered this entire area of space-time?*

Old forms could not keep their suppressed state once the supercolossal pink giant completed the growth that had somehow been arrested from time's beginning.

And so the Glis was now a sun in its prime, but with eighteen hundred and twenty-three planets strung out like so many starry brilliants over the whole near sky.

Everywhere he looked were planets so close to him that they looked like moons. He made a quick, anxious calculation and realized with great relief that all those planets were still within the warming area of the monstrous sun that hung out there, half a light-year away.

As Cemp descended, at the top speed his Silkie body could

withstand, into the huge atmosphere blanket that surrounded Earth, everything seemed the same – the land, the sea, the cities. . . .

He swooped low over one highway and observed cars going along it.

He headed for the Silkie Authority in a haze of wonder and saw the shattered window from which he had leaped so dramatically – not yet repaired!

When, moments later, he landed among the same group of men who had been there at his departure, he realized there had been some kind of a time stasis, related to size.

For Earth and its people, that eighty days had been . . . eighty seconds.

Afterwards, he would hear how people had experienced what seemed like an earthquake, tension in their bodies, momentary sensory blackout, a brief feeling that it was dark. . . .

Now, as he entered, Cemp transformed to human form and said in a piercing voice, 'Gentlemen, prepare for the most remarkable piece of information in the history of the universe. That pink sun out there is not the result of an atmospheric distortion.

'And, gentlemen, Earth now has eighteen hundred inhabited sister planets. Let's begin to organize for a fantastic future!'

Later, comfortably back in his Florida home, Cemp said to Joanne, 'Now we can see why the Silkie problem didn't have a solution as things stood. For Earth, two thousand of us was saturation. But in this new sun system . . .'

It was no longer a question of what to do with the 6,000 members of the Silkie nation but of how they could get a hundred such groups to cope with the work to be done.

Quickly!

THE PROXY INTELLIGENCE

1

Take a sentient being —

Even Steve Hanardy could fit that description. He was a short, stocky man, with the look about him of someone who had lived too close to the animal stage. His eyes were perpetually narrowed, as if he were peering against a bright light. His face was broad and fleshy. But he was human. He could think and act, and he was a giver and not a taker.

– Put this sentient person in a solar system surrounded by a two billion light-year ocean of virtual nothingness beyond which, apparently, is more nothingness —

Hanardy, a product of the Earth's migration to the moon and to the planets of the solar system, was born on Europa, one of the moons of Jupiter, before the educational system caught up to the colonists. He grew up an incoherent roustabout and a spacehand on the freighters and passenger liners that sped about among the immense amount of debris – from moons to habitable meteorites – that surrounded the massive Jupiter. It was a rich and ever-growing trade area, and so presently even the stolid, unimaginative Hanardy had a freighter of his own. Almost from the beginning, his most fruitful journeys were occasional trips to the meteorite where a scientist, Professor Ungarn, lived with his daughter, Patricia. For years, it was a lucrative, routine voyage, without incident.

– Confront this sentient individual with this enigma of being —

The last voyage had been different.

To begin with, he accepted a passenger – a reporter named William Leigh, who ostensibly wanted to write up the lonely route for his news syndicate. But almost as soon as the

374

freighter reached the Ungarn meteorite and entered the airlock, the meteorite was attacked by strange space vessels,
which were capable of far greater speeds than anything
Hanardy had ever seen. And William Leigh was not who
he seemed.

It was hard to know just who he was. What actually happened as far as Hanardy was concerned, was quite simple:
One of the defensive energy screens had gone down before
the attack of the strange ships; and Professor Ungarn sent
Hanardy to machine a new part for the screen's drive unit.
While he was engaged in this, Leigh came upon him by
surprise, attacked him, and tied him up.

Lying there on the floor, bound hand and foot, Hanardy
thought in anguish: 'If I ever get loose, I'm gonna hightail it
out of here!'

He tested the rope that held him and groaned at its un-
yielding toughness. He lay, then, for a while, accepting the
confinement of the bonds, but underneath was a great grief
and a great fear.

He suspected that Professor Ungarn and the professor's
daughter, Patricia, were equally helpless, or they would have
tried during the past hour to find out what had happened to
him.

He listened again, intently, holding himself still. But only
the steady throbbing of the distant dynamos was audible.
No footsteps approached; there was no other movement.

He was still listening when he felt an odd tugging inside
his body.

Shivering a little, Hanardy shook his head as if to clear it
of mental fog – and climbed to his feet.

He didn't notice that the cords that had bound him fell
away.

Out in the corridor, he paused tensely. The place looked
deserted, empty. Except for the vague vibration from the
dynamos, a great silence pressed in upon him. The place

had the look and feel of being on a planet. The artificial gravity made him somewhat lighter than on Earth, but he was used to such changes. It was hard to grasp that he was inside a meteorite, hundreds of thousands of miles from the nearest moon or inhabited planet. Being here was like being inside a big building, on an upper floor.

Hanardy headed for the nearest elevator shaft. He thought: I'd better untie Miss Pat, then her pop, and then get.

It was an automatic decision, to go to the girl first. Despite her sharp tongue, he admired her. He had seen her use weapons to injure, but that didn't change his feeling. He guessed that she'd be very angry – very possibly she'd blame him for the whole mess.

Presently he was knocking hesitantly on the door to Patricia's apartment. Hesitantly, because he was certain that she was not in a position to answer.

When, after a reasonable pause, there was no reply, he pressed gently on the latch. The door swung open.

He entered pure enchantment.

The apartment was a physical delight. There were French-type windows that opened onto a sunlit window. The French doors were open, and the sound of birds singing wafted in through them. There were other doors leading to the inner world of the girl's home, and Hanardy, who had occasionally been in the other rooms to do minor repair work, knew that there also everything was as costly as it was here in this large room that he could see.

Then he saw the girl. She was lying on the floor, half-hidden behind her favorite chair, and she was bound hand and foot with wire.

Hanardy walked toward her unhappily. It was he who had brought William Leigh, and he wasn't quite sure just how he would argue himself out of any accusation she might make about that. His guilt showed in the way he held his thick-set body, in the shuffling of his legs, in the awkward way he knelt beside her. He began gingerly to deal with the thin wire that enlaced and interlaced her limbs.

The girl was patient. She waited till he had taken all the wire off her and then, without moving from the floor, began to rub the circulation back into her wrists and ankles.

She looked up at him and made her first comment: 'How did you avoid being tied up?'

'I didn't. He got me, too,' said Hanardy. He spoke eagerly, anxious to be one of the injured, along with her. He already felt better. She didn't seem to be angry.

'Then how did you get free?' Patricia Ungarn asked.

'Why, I just —' Hanardy began.

He stopped, thunderstruck. He thought back, then over what had happened. He had been lying there, tied. And then ... and then ...

What?

He stood blank, scarcely daring to think. Realizing that an answer was expected, he began apologetically, 'I guess he didn't tie me up so good, and I was in a kind of a hurry, figuring you were here, and so I just —'

Even as he spoke, his whole being rocked with the remembrance of how tough those ropes had been a few minutes before he freed himself.

He stopped his mumbling explanation because the girl wasn't listening, wasn't even looking. She had climbed to her feet, and she was continuing to rub her hands. She was small of build and good-looking in a bitter way. Her lips were pressed too tightly together; her eyes were slightly narrowed with a kind of permanent anxiety. Except for that, she looked like a girl in her teens, but cleverer and more sophisticated than most girls her age.

Even as Hanardy, in his heavy way, was aware of the complexity of her, she faced him again. She said with an un-girl-like decisiveness, 'Tell me everything that happened to you.'

377

Hanardy was glad to let go of the unsatisfactory recollection of his own escape. He said, 'First thing I know, this guy comes in there while I'm working at the lathe. And is he strong, and is he fast! I never would've thought he had that kind of muscle and that fast way of moving. I'm pretty chunky, y'understand —'

'What then?' She was patient, but there was a pointedness about her question that channeled his attention back to the main line of events.

'Then he ties me up, and then he goes out, and then he takes those Dreeghs from the spaceship and disappears into space.' Hanardy shook his head, wonderingly. 'That's what gets me. How did he do that?'

He paused, in a brown study; but he came from the distance of his thought back into the room, to realize guiltily that the girl had spoken to him twice.

'Sorry,' he muttered. 'I was thinking about how he did that, and it's kind of hard to get the idea.' He finished, almost accusingly: 'Do you know what he does?'

The girl looked at him, a startled expression on her face. Hanardy thought she was angry at his inattention and said hastily: 'I didn't hear what you wanted me to do. Tell me again, huh!'

She seemed unaware that he had spoken. 'What *does* he do, Steve?'

'Why, he just —'

At that point, Hanardy stopped short and glanced back mentally over the glib words he had been using. It was such a fantastic dialogue, that he could feel the blood draining from his cheeks.

'Huh!' he said.

'What does he do, Steve?' He saw that she was looking at him, as if she understood something that he didn't. It irritated him.

He said unhappily: 'I'd better go and untie your father before that last bunch of Dreeghs shows up.'

Having spoken, he stopped again, his mouth open in amazement. He thought: 'I must be nuts. What am I saying?'

He turned and started for the door.

'Come back here!'

Her voice, sharp and commanding, cut into him. Defensively, he put up between himself and her the thick barrier of stolidity which had served him for so many years in his relations with other people. He swung awkwardly around to face her again. Before he could speak, she said with intensity: 'How did he do it, Steve?'

The question ran up against a great stubbornness in him. He had no feeling of deliberately resisting her. But the mental fog seemed to settle down upon his being, and he said: 'Do what, Miss?'

'Leave?'

'Who?' He felt stupid before her questions, but he felt even more stupid for having had meaningless thoughts and said meaningless things.

'Leigh – you fool! That's who.'

'I thought he took that spaceboat of yours that looks like an automobile.'

There was a long pause. The girl clenched and unclenched her hands. Now she seemed very unchildlike indeed. Hanardy, who had seen her angry before, cringed and waited for the thunder and lightning of her rage to lash out at him. Instead, the tenseness faded. She seemed suddenly thoughtful and said with unexpected gentleness: 'After that, Steve? After he got out there!'

She swung her arm and pointed at the aviary, where the sunlight glinted beyond the French windows. Hanardy saw birds fluttering among the trees. Their musical cries gave the scene a homey touch, as if it really were a garden. As he watched, the tree leaves stirred; and he knew that hidden fans were blowing an artificial breeze. It was like a summer

379

afternoon, except that just beyond the glasslike wall was the blackness of space.

It was a cosmic night outside, disturbed here and there by an atom of matter – a planet hidden from sight by its own relative smallness and distance from anything else, a sun, a point of light and energy, quickly lost in darkness so vast that presently its light would fade, and become one grain in a misty bright cloud that obscured the blackness for a moment of universe time and occupied an inch of space, or so it seemed. . . .

Hanardy contemplated that startling vista. He was only vaguely aware that his present intensity of interest was quite different from similar thoughts he had had in the past. On his long journeys, such ideas had slipped into and out of his mind. He recalled having had a thought about it just a few months before. He had been looking out of a porthole, and – just for an instant – the mystery of the empty immensity had touched him. And he'd thought: 'What the heck is behind all this? How does a guy like me rate being alive?'

Aloud, Hanardy muttered: 'I'd better get your father free, Miss Pat.' He finished under his breath: 'And then beat it out of here – fast.'

2

He turned, and this time, though she called after him angrily, he stumbled out into the corridor and went down to the depths of the meteorite, where the dynamos hummed and throbbed; and where, presently, he had Professor Ungarn untied.

The older man was quite cheerful. 'Well, Steve, we're not dead yet. I don't know why they didn't jump in on us, but the screens are still holding, I see.'

He was a gaunt man with deep-set eyes and the unhappiest face Hanardy had ever seen. He stood, rubbing the circulation back into his arms. Strength of intellect shone from his face, along with the melancholy. He had defended the meteorite in such a calm, practical way from the attacking Dreeghs that it was suddenly easy to realize that this sad-faced man was actually the hitherto unsuspected observer of the solar system for a vast galactic culture, which included at its top echelon the Great Galactic – who had been William Leigh – and at the bottom, Professor Ungarn and his lovely daughter.

The thoughts about that seeped into Hanardy's fore-conscious. He realized that the scientist was primarily a protector. He and this station were here to prevent contact between Earth and the galaxy. Man and his earth-born civilization were still too low on the scale of development to be admitted to awareness that a gigantic galactic culture existed. Interstellar ships of other low-echelon cultures which *had* been admitted to the galactic union were warned away from the solar system whenever they came too close. Accidentally, the hunted, lawless Dreeghs had wandered into this forbidden sector of space. In their lust for blood and life energy they had avidly concentrated here in the hope of gaining such a quantity of blood, and so great a supply of life energy, that they would be freed for endless years from their terrible search.

It had been quite a trap, which had enabled the Great Galactic to capture so many of them. But now another ship-load of Dreeghs was due; and this time there was no trap. Professor Ungarn was speaking: 'Did you get that part machined before Leigh tied you up?' He broke off: 'What's the matter, Steve?'

'Huh! Nothing.' Hanardy came out of a depth of wonderment: 'I'd better get onto that job. It'll take a half hour, maybe.'

Professor Ungarn nodded and said matter-of-factly: 'I'll feel better when we get that additional screen up. There's quite a gang out there.'

Hanardy parted his lips to say that that particular 'gang'

was no longer a problem, but that another supership, a late arrival, would shortly appear on the scene. He stopped the words, unspoken; and now he was consciously dismayed. 'What's going on?' he wondered. 'Am I nuts?'

Almost blank, he headed down to the machine shop. As he entered, he saw the ropes that had bound him, lying on the floor. He walked over in a haze of interest and stooped to pick up one of the short sections.

It came apart in his fingers, breaking into a fine, powdery stuff, some of which drifted into his nostrils. He sneezed noisily.

The rope, he discovered, was all like that. He could hardly get over it. He kept picking up the pieces, just so that he could feel them crumble. When he had nothing but a scattering of dust, he stood up and started on the lathe job. He thought absently: 'If that next batch of Dreeghs arrives, then maybe I can start believing all this stuff.'

He paused and for the first time thought: 'Now, where did I get that name, Dreegh?'

Instantly, he was trembling so violently that he had to stop work. Because – if he could get the professor to admit that that was what they were – *Dreeghs* – then. . . .

Then what?

'Why, it'd prove everything,' he thought. 'Just that one thing!'

Already, the crumbled rope, and whatever it proved, was fading into the background of his recollection, no longer quite real, needing to be reinforced by some new miracle. As it happened, he asked the question under optimum circumstances. He handed the part to the scientist and managed to ask about the Dreeghs as the older man was turning away. Ungarn began immediately with an obvious urgency to work on the shattered section of the energy screen drive. It was from there, intent on what he was doing, and in an absentminded tone, that he answered Hanardy's question.

'Yes, yes,' he muttered. 'Dreeghs. Vampires, in the worst sense of the word . . . but they look just like us.'

At that point he seemed to realize to whom he was talking. He stopped what he was doing and swung around and stared at Hanardy.

He said at last very slowly, 'Steve, don't repeat everything you hear around this place. The universe is a bigger territory than you might think but people will ridicule if you try to tell them. They will say you're crazy.'

Hanardy did not move. He was thinking: 'He just don't realize. I gotta know. All this stuff happening —'

But the idea of not telling was easy to grasp. At Spaceport, on the moon, Europa, at the bars that he frequented, he was accepted by certain hangers-on as a boon companion. Some of the people were sharp, even educated, but they were cynical, and often witty, and were particularly scathing of serious ideas.

Hanardy visualized himself telling any one of them that there was more to space than the solar system – more life, more intelligence – and he could imagine the ridiculing discussion that would begin.

Though they usually treated him with tolerance – it sure wouldn't do any good to tell them.

Hanardy started for the door. 'I gotta know,' he thought again. 'And right now I'd better get on my ship and beat it before that Dreegh comes along pretending that he's Pat's future husband.'

And he'd better leave on the sly. The professor and the girl wouldn't like him to go away now. But defending this meteorite was their job, not his. They couldn't expect him to deal with the Dreegh who had captured, and murdered, Pat's boy friend.

Hanardy stopped in the doorway, and felt blank. 'Huh!' he said aloud.

He thought: Maybe I should tell them. They won't be able

to deal with the Dreegh if they think he's somebody else.

'Steve!' It was Professor Ungarn.

Hanardy turned. 'Yeah, boss?' he began.

'Finish unloading your cargo.'

'Okay, boss.'

He walked off heavily along the corridor, tired and glad that he had been told to go and relieved that the decision to tell them could not be put into effect immediately. He thought wearily: First thing I'd better do is take a nap.

3

Hanardy walked slowly up the ramp into his own ship, and so to his own cabin. Before lying down for the sleep he needed, he paused to stare at his reflection in the mirror-bright metal wall of the room. He saw a short, muscular man in greasy, gray dungarees, and a dirty yellow shirt. A stubble of beard emphasized a coarseness of features that he had seen before, but somehow ever so clearly, never with such a conviction that he was a low-grade human being. Hanardy groaned and stretched out in the bunk. He thought: I sure got my eyes open all of a sudden to what kind of a lug I am.

He took a quick look back along the track of years, and groaned again. It was a picture of a man who had down-graded himself as a human being, seeking escape in a lonely space job from the need to compete as an individual.

'Nobody will believe a word I say,' he thought. 'All that other junk was only in my noodle – it didn't happen out where you could prove anything. I'd better just keep my mouth shut and stop thinking I understand what's going on.'

He closed his eyes – and looked with a clear inner vision at the universe.

He opened his eyes to realize that he had slept.

He realized something else. The screens were down; a Dreegh in a spaceboat was coming into an airlock at the extreme lower side of the meteorite.

The vampire was primarily intent on information, but he

384

would destroy everyone in the meteorite as soon as he felt it was safe.

Sweating, Hanardy tumbled out of the bunk and hurried out of his ship, and so into the meteorite. He raced along the corridor that led to the other airlock. At the entrance he met the professor and Patricia. They were smiling and excited.

The scientist said, 'Great news, Steve. Pat's fiancé has just arrived. He's here sooner than we expected; but we were getting worried that we hadn't received some communication.'

Hanardy muttered something, feeling immensely foolish. To have been so wrong! To have thought: Dreegh! – when the reality was – Klugg . . . the girl's long-awaited fiancé, Thadled Madro.

But the identification of the new arrival made all his fantasies just that – unreal vaporings, figments of an unsettled mind.

Hanardy watched gloomily as Madro came down the ramp from the lifeboat. The girl's lover was a very tall, slim man in his thirties, with deep-set eyes. He had an intensity about him that was impressive, commanding – and repellent. Instantly repellent.

Hanardy realized ruefully that his reaction was overcritical. Hanardy couldn't decide what had twisted this man. But he was reminded of the degraded people who were his principal buddies at Spaceport, on Europa. Smart, many of them were – almost too smart. But they gave off this same emanation of an overloaded personality.

Hanardy was a little surprised to realize that the girl was not rushing forward to greet the gaunt-bodied visitor. It was Professor Ungarn who approached the man and bowed courteously. Madro bowed in return and then stood stiffly near Hanardy. The scientist glanced at his daughter and then smiled at the newcomer apologetically. He said,

'Thadled Madro, this is my daughter, Patricia – who has suddenly become very shy.'

Madro bowed. Patricia inclined her head. Her father turned to her, and said, 'My dear, I realize that this is an unfortunate way of marrying and giving in marriage – to entrust yourself to a man whom neither of us has ever seen before. But let us remember his courage in coming here at all and resolve to offer him communication and the opportunity to show us what he is.'

Madro bowed to the girl. 'On those terms, I greet you, Patricia.' He straightened. 'About communication – I am baffled by the message I received *en route*. Will you please give me further information?'

Professor Ungarn told him of the Dreegh attack and of its abrupt cessation; he told him of William Leigh, the Great Galactic. He finished: 'We have our report as to what happened from a member of the race of this system – who was somehow infected by the mere presence of this mighty being, and who apparently acquired the ability to see at a distance, and to be aware of some of the thoughts of some people, temporarily at least.'

There was a faint smile on Ungarn's tired face. Hanardy shriveled a little inside, feeling that he was being made fun of. He looked unhappily at the girl. She must have told her father what he had said.

Patricia Ungarn caught his gaze on her and shrugged. 'You said it, Steve,' she stated matter-of-factly. 'Why not tell us everything you felt?'

The newcomer stared somberly and intently at Hanardy; so intently that it was almost as if he also were reading minds. He turned slowly to the girl. 'Can you give me a swift summary?' he asked. 'If there's action to be taken, I'd like to have some basis for it.'

There was a hard note in his voice that chilled Hanardy, who had been thinking for many minutes over and over: *They don't really know him! They don't know him.* . . . He had a mental picture of the real Madro's ship being intercepted, Madro captured and drained of information and then murdered by the vampire method. The rest was skillful makeup, good enough apparently to pass the inspection of the professor and his perceptive daughter. Which meant that, before killing the real Madro, the Dreegh had learned passwords, secret codes and enough back history to be convincing.

Within minutes, this creature could decide that it was safe to take action.

Hanardy had no illusions, no hope. It had taken an unbounded being to defeat these mighty Dreeghs. And now, by a trick, a late arrival had achieved what his fellows *en masse* had not been able to do – he had gotten into the meteorite fortress of the galactic watcher of the solar system; and his whole manner indicated that his fears had nothing to do with either the professor or his daughter, or Hanardy.

He wanted to know what had happened. For a little while he might be forbearing, in the belief that he could learn more as an apparent ally than as a revealed enemy.

'We have to put him off,' Hanardy thought in agony. 'We have to hold back, or maybe give him what he wants.' Somehow, the latter seemed preferable.

He grew aware that the girl was talking. While Hanardy listened, she gave the essential picture of what he had said. It was all there, surprisingly sharp in detail. It even penetrated some of the blur that had settled over his own memory.

When she had finished, Madro frowned and nodded. His slim body seemed unnaturally tense. He said, almost to himself: 'So they were almost all captured —' He paused and, turning, looked at Hanardy. 'You have the feeling there will be one more ship?'

Hanardy nodded, not trusting himself to speak.

'How many Dreeghs are there aboard this one ship?' Madro asked.

This time there was no escaping a verbal reply. 'Nine,' said Hanardy.

He hadn't thought about the exact number before. But he knew the figure was correct. Just for a moment, he *knew* it.

Madro said in an odd tone, 'You get it that clearly? Then you must already know many other things as well.'

His dark eyes gazed directly into Hanardy's. The unspoken meaning that was in them seemed to be: 'Then you already know who I am?'

There was such a hypnotic quality in the other's look that Hanardy had to wage an inner fight against admitting that he knew.

Madro spoke again. 'Were these – this first group of Dreeghs – all killed?'

'Why, I —' Hanardy stopped, amazed. 'Gee, I don't know. I don't know what happened to them. But he intended to kill them; up to a certain moment, he intended to; and then —'

'And then what, Steve?' That was Pat, her voice urging him.

'I don't know. He noticed something.'

'Who noticed something?' asked Pat.

'Leigh. You know – him. But I don't know what he did after that.'

'But where could they be now?' the girl asked, bewildered.

Hanardy remained blank, vaguely guilty, as if somehow he was failing her by not knowing.

He grew aware that Madro was turning away. 'There is apparently more to discover here,' the Dreegh said quietly. 'It is evident that we must re-assess our entire situation; and I might even guess that we Kluggs could through the chance perceptive stimulation of this man achieve so great a knowledge of the universe that, here and now, we might be able to take the next step of development for our kind.'

The comment seemed to indicate that the Dreegh was still

388

undecided. Hanardy followed along behind the others. For a few desperate seconds he thought of jerking out his gun, in the hope that he might be able to fire before the Dreegh could defend himself.

But already doubt was upon him. For this suspicion was just in his head. He had no proof other than the steady stream of pictures in his mind; and that was like a madness having no relation to anything that had been said and done before his eyes. Crazy people might act on such inner pictures, but not stolid, unimaginative Steve Hanardy.

'Gotta keep my feet on the ground!' Hanardy muttered to himself.

Ahead, Professor Ungarn said in a conversational voice: 'I've got to give you credit, Thadled. You have already said something that has shocked Pat and myself. You have used the hateful word "Klugg" just as if it doesn't bother you.'

'It's just a word,' said Madro.

And that was all that was said while they walked. They came to the power room. The girl sank into a chair, while her father and the visitor walked over to the power control board. 'The screens are working beautifully,' said Professor Ungarn with satisfaction. 'I just opened them for the few seconds it took for you to get through them. We've got time to decide what to do, in case this last Dreegh ship attacks us.'

Madro walked over near the girl, and settled into a chair. He addressed Professor Ungarn, 'What you said a moment ago, about the word and the identification of Klugg – you're right. It doesn't bother me.'

The scientist said grimly, 'Aren't you fooling yourself a little? Of all the races that know of the galactic civilization, we're the lowest on the scale. We do the hard work. We're like the day laborers on planets such as Earth. Why, when Pat found out, she nearly went mad with self-negation. Galactic morons!' He shuddered.

Madro laughed in a relaxed way; and Hanardy had to admire the easiness of him. If Madro was a Dreegh, then for all Madro knew this, also, was a trap set by the Great Galactic; and yet he seemed unworried. If, on the other hand, he was actually a Klugg, then somehow he had made inferiority right within himself. 'I could use some of that,' Hanardy thought gloomily. 'If these guys are galactic morons, what does that make me?'

Madro was speaking: 'We're what we are,' he said simply. 'It's not really a matter of too much difference in intelligence. It's an energy difference. There's a way here, somewhere, of utilizing energy in a very superior fashion. But you've got to have the energy, and you've got to get it from somewhere. That's what makes the case of this fellow Leigh interesting. If we could backtrack on what he did here, we might really get at the heart of a lot of things.'

Patricia and her father said nothing. But their eyes glistened, as they waited for the man to continue. Madro turned to Hanardy. 'That question she asked you before' – he indicated the girl – 'when you first untied her. How did *he* leave the solar system after capturing those – Dreeghs?' He hesitated the slightest bit before using the name.

Hanardy said simply, 'He didn't exactly leave. It's more like . . . he *was* somewhere else. And he took them with him.' He fumbled for words. 'You see, things aren't the way they seem. They're —' He stopped, unhappy.

He realized that the two men and the girl were waiting. Hanardy waved his arms aimlessly, indicating things beyond the safeguarding of the meteorite. 'All that – that's not real.'

Madro turned towards his companions. 'It's the concept of a universe of illusion. An old idea; but maybe we should take another look at it.'

Professor Ungarn murmured, 'It would take complex techniques to make it work.'

Hanardy said, straining for meaning, 'You just keep putting it out there. As if you're doing it, even though you're not. That tunes you in.'

'Put what out, Steve?' It was the girl, her voice as strained as his.

'The world. The universe . . . the whole deal.'

'Oh!'

Hanardy went on, 'And then, for a moment, you don't put anything there. That's when you do something I don't understand.'

'What's that?' The girl's voice, almost emotionless, led him forward.

'You stop everything,' said Hanardy wonderingly. 'You let the nothingness rush in. And then – you become the real you . . . for as long as you have energy.'

He stared at the three people, through them, unseeing. As from a distance, Madro's voice came to him:

'You see – it's a matter of energy,' the man said calmly. 'Hanardy?'

He came back into the room, mentally as well as physically. 'Yeah?'

'Where did he get his energy?' Madro asked.

'Uh,' said Hanardy, 'he got most of it out where it was stored – a kind of dark room.'

It was a new thought; a picture came with it of how the energy had been put there by somebody else, not by Leigh. Before Hanardy could speak another word, Madro was over there beside him.

'Show us!' he said, and his voice was like a fire, burning a path of action, demanding counter-action.

Hanardy led the way, his heavy body trembling. He had the feeling that he had made an admission that spelled victory for the Dreegh. But there was no turning back. If this creature was a Dreegh, then resistance was useless. He knew that intuitively.

'If I could only be sure,' Hanardy thought miserably.

And the stupid thing was that he *was* sure. As sure, it seemed to him, as he could ever be. But he wasn't sure enough even to make the attempt to save his own life. As things stood, he'd have to go through with this farce until the Dreegh – satisfied that all was well – destroyed them all in his own good time.

4

It was twenty minutes later.

. . . After they had found the little black room to be merely a drab closet where the professor had always kept certain tools, but otherwise empty.

'Where was it stored?' Madro demanded of Hanardy. 'I mean the energy that Leigh got.'

Hanardy pointed unhappily at the metal wall inside the closet.

'Are you saying the energy was *in* the wall?'

The question once more disturbed Hanardy's sense of the reality of his own thoughts, and so he simply stood there, shaken, as Pat and Professor Ungarn pressed forward and with a portable instrument tested the wall.

Madro did not join them, nor did he again look into the little room. Hanardy felt an inner tremor as the Dreegh, ignoring what the father and daughter were doing, turned and strode toward him.

'Steve,' he said, 'I want to talk to you.'

He glanced back, raised his voice, 'I'm going to take Hanardy for a little private questioning.'

'All right!' That was Pat. But neither she nor her father turned. Madro had not waited. His fingers gripped Hanardy's arm firmly at the elbow. Shrinking, Hanardy realized the other's intent.

A test!

To determine how vulnerable he was.

To the death – if he were that weak.

Even as Hanardy had these awarenesses, Madro drew him away from the storeroom and around a corner. Hanardy kept looking back, not daring to call for help but yet hoping that the professor and his daughter would be motivated to follow.

His final view of them showed them still inside the closet, and the professor was saying, 'A series of tests on this wall should —'

Hanardy wondered what they would think when they found him gone – and dead.

Madro drew Hanardy along the side corridor and into a room. He closed the door, and they were alone. Hanardy still not resisting.

Madro stood there for a few moments, tall, lean, smiling.

'Let's settle this once and for all,' he said softly. 'Myself – against whatever ability you were endowed with.'

And because Hanardy had begun to have fantasies, had nurtured a tiny hope that maybe it was true, that maybe something great *had* rubbed off on him – as Professor Ungarn had implied – for a few seconds, Hanardy actually waited for that something inside him to handle this situation.

That was all the time he had – seconds. The speed of Madro's attack, and the total violent intent of it, instantly defeated that waiting reaction.

He was lifted effortlessly, grabbed by one foot, held like a rag doll, and incredibly was about to have his head dashed against the near wall – when, with a primitive survival spasm of effort, Hanardy kicked with his other foot, kicked hard against the wrist of the hand by which Madro held him.

For that moment, for that one attack, it was resistance enough. The Dreegh let him go. Hanardy fell – the slow-motion fall of less than Earth gravity. Far too slow for the speed of Madro's second attack.

In his awkward, muscle-bound way, only one of Hanardy's dragging legs actually struck the floor. The next moment he was caught again by fingers that were like granite biting into his clothes and body – Madro obviously neither heeding nor caring which.

And there was no longer any doubt in Hanardy's mind. He had no special ability by which he might defeat the Dreegh's deadly intent.

He had no inner resources. No visions. He was helpless. His hard muscles were like putty in the steely grip of a man whose strength overwhelmingly transcended his own.

Hanardy ceased his writhings and yelled desperately, 'For Pete's sake, why all this murder when there's only five women Dreeghs and four men left? Why don't you Dreeghs change, try once more to become normal?'

As swiftly as it had started, the violence ended.

Madro let him go, stepped back and stared at him. 'A message!' he said. 'So that's your role.'

Hanardy did not immediately realize that the threat was ended. He had fallen to the floor. From that begging position he continued his appeal. 'You don't have to kill me! I'll keep my mouth shut. Who'd believe me, anyway?'

'What's normal?' The Dreegh's voice was cold and demanding. The radiation from him – uncleanness – was stronger.

'Me,' said Hanardy.

'You!' Incredulous tone.

'Yeah, me.' Hanardy spoke urgently. 'What ails me is that I'm a low-lifer, somehow. But I'm a normal lug. Things balance out in me – that's the key. I take a drink, but not because I have to. It doesn't affect me particularly. When I was in my teens once I tried taking drugs. Hell, I just felt it didn't fit in my body. I just threw it off. That's normal. You can't do that with what *you've* got.'

'What's normal?' Madro was cold, steady, remote.

'You're sick,' said Hanardy. 'All that blood and life energy. It's abnormal. Not really necessary. You can be cured.'

Having spoken the strange words, Hanardy realized their strangeness. He blinked.

'I didn't know I was going to say that,' he mumbled.

The Dreegh's expression was changing as he listened. Suddenly he nodded and said aloud, 'I actually believe we've been given a communication from the Great Galactic. A twelfth-hour, last-chance offer.'

'What will you do with me?' Hanardy mumbled.

'The question,' came the steely reply, 'is what is the best way to neutralize you? I choose this way!'

A metallic something glittered in the Dreegh's hand. From its muzzle a shimmering line of light reached toward Hanardy's head.

The spaceman flinched, tried to duck, had the cringing thought that this was death and stood there expecting at the very least a terrible shock.

He felt nothing. The light hit his face; and it was as if a pencil beam from a bright flashlight had briefly glared into his eyes. Then the light went, and there he stood blinking a little, but unhurt so far as he could determine.

He was still standing there when the Dreegh said, 'What you and I are going to do now is that you're going to come with me and show me all the places on this meteorite where there are armaments or small arms of any kind.'

Hanardy walked ahead, kept glancing back; and there, each time he looked, was the long body with its grim face.

The resemblance to Thadled Madro was visibly fading, as if the other had actually twisted his features into a duplication of the young male Klugg's face, not using makeup at all, and now he was relaxing.

They came to where the Ungarns waited. Father and daughter said nothing at all. To Hanardy they seemed subdued; the girl was strangely pale. He thought: 'They *do* know!'

The overt revelation came as the four of them arrived in the main living quarters. Professor Ungarn sighed, turned and – ignoring Hanardy – said, 'Well, Mr Dreegh, my daughter and I are wondering why the delay in our execution?'

'Hanardy!' was the reply.

Having uttered the name, as if Hanardy himself were not present, the Dreegh stood for a long moment, eyes narrowed, lips slightly parted, even white teeth clamped together. The result was a kind of a snarling smile.

'He seems to be under your control. Is he?' That was Pat Ungarn, in a small voice. The moment she had spoken, and thus attracted the Dreegh's attention, she shrank, actually retreated a few steps, as he looked at her.

Sween-Madro's tense body relaxed. But his smile was as grim as ever. And still he ignored Hanardy's presence.

'I gave Steve a special type of energy charge that will nullify for the time being what was done to him.'

Professor Ungarn laughed curtly. 'Do you really believe that you can defeat this – this being – William Leigh . . . defeat him with what you have done to Steve? After all, he's your real opponent, not Hanardy. This is a shadow battle. One of the fighters has left a puppet to strike his blows for him.'

Sween-Madro said in an even tone, 'It's not as dangerous as it seems. Puppets are notoriously poor fighters.'

The professor argued, 'Any individual of the race known to lesser races as Great Galactics – which was obviously not their real name – must be presumed to have taken all such possibilities into account. What can you gain by delay?'

Sween-Madro hesitated, then: 'Steve mentioned a possible cure for our condition.' His voice held an edge in it.

There was a sudden silence. It settled over the room and seemed to permeate the four people in it.

The soundless time was broken by a curt laugh from Sween-Madro. He said, 'I sensed that for a few seconds I seemed —'

'Human,' said Pat Ungarn. 'As if you had feelings and hopes and desires like us.'

'Don't count on it.' The Dreegh's voice was harsh.

Professor Ungarn said slowly, 'I suspect that you analyzed Steve has a memory of mental contact with a supreme, perhaps even an ultimate, intelligence. Now, these earth people when awake are in that peculiar, perennially confused state that makes them unacceptable for galactic citizenship. So that the very best way to defend yourself from Steve's memory is to keep him awake. I therefore deduce that the energy charge you fired at him was designed to maintain in continuous stimulation the waking center in the brain stem.

'But that is only a temporary defense. In four or five days, exhaustion in Hanardy would reach an extreme state, and something in the body would have to give. What will you have then that you don't have now?'

The Dreegh seemed surprisingly willing to answer, as if by uttering his explanations aloud he could listen to them himself, and so judge them.

He said, 'My colleagues will have arrived by then.'

'So then you're all in the trap,' said Professor Ungarn. 'I think your safest bet would be to kill Pat and me right now. As for Steve —'

Hanardy had been listening to the interchange with a growing conviction that this melancholy old man was arguing them all into being immediately executed.

'Hey!' he interrupted urgently. 'What are you trying to do?'

The scientist waved at him impatiently. 'Shut up, Steve. Surely you realize that this Dreegh will kill without mercy. I'm trying to find out why he's holding off. It doesn't fit with what I consider to be good sense.'

He broke off, 'Don't worry about him killing you. He doesn't dare. You're safe.'

Hanardy felt extremely unsafe. Nevertheless, he had a long history of accepting orders from this man; so he remained dutifully silent.

The Dreegh, who had listened to the brief interchange

thoughtfully, said in an even tone that when his companions arrived, he, Hanardy and Pat Ungarn would go to Europa. He believed Pat was needed on such a journey. So no one would be killed until it was over.

'I'm remembering,' Sween-Madro continued, 'what Steve said about the Great Galactic noticing something. I deduce that what he noticed had to do with Steve himself. So we'll go to Spaceport and study Steve's past behavior there. Right now, let's disarm the entire place for my peace of mind.'

Clearly, it would not be for anyone else's.

From room to room, and along each corridor, silently the three prisoners accompanied their powerful conqueror.

And presently every weapon in the meteorite was neutralized or disposed of. Even energy sources that might be converted were sealed off. Thus, the meteorite screens were actually de-energized and the machinery to operate them, wrecked.

The Dreegh next cut off escape possibilities by dismantling several tiny space boats. The last place they went, first Hanardy, then the professor, then Pat, and finally Sween-Madro, was Hanardy's space freighter. There also, all the weapons were eliminated, and the Dreegh had Hanardy dismantle the control board. From the parts that were presently lying over the floor, the gaunt man, with unerring understanding, selected key items. With these in hand, he paused in the doorway. His baleful gaze caught Hanardy's shifting eyes. 'Steve!' he said. 'You'll stay right here.'

'You mean, inside my ship?'

'Yes. If you leave here for any reason, I'll kill you. Do you understand?'

Hanardy glanced helplessly toward Professor Ungarn and then back at the Dreegh. He said, 'There's some work the professor wanted me to do.'

'Professor Ungarn,' – it was the vampire's harsh voice

cutting across Hanardy's uncertain protest – 'tell him how unimportant such work is.'

Hanardy was briefly aware of the old man's wan smile. The scientist said wearily, 'Pat and I will be killed as soon as we have served our purpose. What he will eventually do with you, we don't know.'

'So you'll stay right here. You two come with me,' Sween-Madro ordered the professor and his daughter.

They went as silently as they had come. The airlock door clanged. Hanardy could hear the interlocking steel bolts wheeze into position. After that, no sound came.

The potentially most intelligent man in the solar system was alone – and wide awake.

5

Sitting, or lying down, waiting posed no problems for Hanardy. His years alone in space had prepared him for the ordeal that now began. There was a difference.

As he presently discovered when he lay down on his narrow cot, he couldn't sleep.

Twenty-four earth hours ticked by.

Not a thinking man, Steve Hanardy; nor a reader. The four books on board were repair manuals. He had thumbed through them a hundred times, but now he got them out and examined them again. Every page was, as he had expected, dully familiar. After a slow hour he used up their possibilities.

Another day, and still he was wide-eyed and unsleeping, but there was a developing restlessness in him, and exhaustion.

As a spaceman, Hanardy had received indoctrination in the dangers of sleeplessness. He knew of the mind's tendency to dream while awake, the hallucinatory experiences, the normal effects of the unending strain of wakefulness.

Nothing like that happened.

He did not know that the sleep center in his brain was

timelessly depressed and the wake center timelessly stimulated. The former could not turn on, the latter could not turn off. So between them there could be none of the usual interplay with its twilight states.

But he could become more exhausted.

Though he was lying down almost continuously now, he became continually more exhausted.

On the fourth 'morning' he had the thought for the first time: this is going to drive me crazy!

Such a fear had never before in his whole life passed through his mind. By late afternoon of that day, Hanardy was scared and dizzy and hopeless, in a severe dwindling spiral of decreasing sanity. What he would have done had he remained alone was not at that time brought to a test.

For late on that fourth 'day' Pat Ungarn came through the airlock, found him cowering in his bunk and said, 'Steve, come with me. It's time we took action.'

Hanardy stumbled to his feet. He was actually heading after her when he remembered Sween-Madro's orders to him, and he stopped.

'What's the matter?' she demanded.

He mumbled simply, 'He told me not to leave my ship. He'll kill me if I do.'

The girl was instantly impatient. 'Steve, stop this nonsense.' Her sharp words were like blows striking his mind. 'You haven't any more to lose than we have. So come along!'

And she started back through the airlock. Hanardy stood, stunned and shaking. In a single sentence, spoken in her preemptory fashion, she challenged his manhood by implication, recognized that the dumb love he felt for her made him her slave and so re-established her absolute ascendency.

Silently, tensely, he shuffled across the metal floor of the airlock and moments later was in the forbidden meteorite.

400

Feeling doomed.

The girl led the way to what was, in effect, the engine room of the meteorite.

As Steve trailed reluctantly behind her, Professor Ungarn rose up from a chair and came forward, smiling his infinitely tired smile.

His greeting was, 'Pat wants to tell you about intelligence. Do you know what your I.Q. is?'

The question barely reached the outer ramparts of Hanardy's attention. Following the girl along one corridor after another, a fearful vision had been in his mind, of Sween-Madro suddenly rounding the next corner and striking him dead. That vision remained, but along with it was a growing wonder: *Where* was the Dreegh?

The professor snapped, 'Steve do you hear me?'

Forced to look at him, Hanardy was able to remember proudly that he belonged in the 55th percentile of the human race, intelligence-wise, and that his I.Q. had been tested at 104.

'The tester told me that I was above average,' Hanardy said in a tone of pleasure. Then, apologetic again, he added, 'Of course, beside you guys I'm nothing.'

The old man said, 'On the Klugg I.Q. scale you would probably rate higher than 104. We take into account more factors. Your mechanical ability and spatial relations skill would not be tested correctly by any human I.Q. test that I have examined.'

He continued, 'Now, Steve, I'm trying to explain this all to you in a great hurry, because some time in the next week you're going to be, in flashes, the most intelligent man in the entire solar system, and there's nothing anybody can do about it except help you use it. I want to prepare you.'

Hanardy, who had anxiously stationed himself so that he could keep one eye on the open door – and who kept expecting the mighty Dreegh to walk in on the little conspiratorial group of lesser beings – shook his head hopelessly.

401

'You don't know what's already happened. I can be killed. Easy. I've got no defenses.'

He glumly described his encounter with the Dreegh and told how helpless he had been. 'There I was on my knees, begging, until I just happened to say something that made him stop. Boy, *he* sure didn't think I was unkillable.'

Pat came forward, stood in front of him, and grabbed his shoulders with both hands.

'Steve,' she said in an urgent voice, 'above a certain point of I.Q. mind actually is *over* matter. A being above that intelligence level cannot be killed. Not by bullets, nor by any circumstance involving matter. Now listen: in you is a memory of such an intelligence level. In manhandling you, the Dreegh was trying to see what limited stress would do. He found out. He got the message from the Great Galactic out of you.

'Steve, after that he didn't *dare* put a bullet into you, or fire a death-level energy beam. Because that would force this memory to the surface!'

In her intense purposefulness she tried to move him with her hands. But that only made Hanardy aware of what a girlish body she had. So little body, so much imperious woman – it startled him for she could barely budge him, let alone shake him.

She said breathlessly, 'Don't you see, Steve? You're going to be king! Try to act accordingly.'

'Look —' Hanardy began, stolidly.

Rage flashed into her face. Her voice leaped past his interjection. 'And if you don't stop all this resistance, in the final issue *I'll* put a bullet into your brain myself, and then you'll see.'

Hanardy gazed into her blue eyes, so abruptly furious. He had a sinking conviction that she would do exactly what she threatened. In alarm, he said, 'For Pete's sake, what do you want me to do?'

'Listen to what dad has to say!' she commanded. 'And stop looking the other way. You need a high-speed education, and we haven't got much time.'

That last seemed like a total understatement to Hanardy. His feeling was that he had no time at all.

Awareness saved him, then. There was the room with its machinery, and the old man and his daughter; and there was he with his mind jumping with the new fear of her threat. Hanardy had a flitting picture of the three of them lost forever inside this remote meteorite that was just one tiny part of Jupiter's colossal family of small, speeding particles of matter – a meaningless universe that visibly had no morality or justice, because it included without a qualm creatures like the Dreeghs.

As his skittering thought reached that dark depth, it suddenly occurred to Hanardy that Pat couldn't shoot him. She didn't have a gun. He opened his mouth to tell her of her helplessness. Then closed it again.

Because an opportunity might open up for her to obtain a weapon. So the threat remained, receded in time . . . but not to be dismissed. Nonetheless, he grew calmer. He still felt compelled, and jittery. But he stayed there and listened, then, to a tiny summary of the story of human intelligence and the attempts that had been made to measure it.

It seemed human intelligence tests were based on a curve where the average was 100. Each test Professor Ungarn had seen revealed an uncertainty about what constituted an intelligence factor, and what did not. Was the ability to tell left from right important to intelligence? One test included it. Should an individual be able to solve brain twisters? Many testers considered this trait of great importance. And almost all psychologists insisted on a subtle understanding of the meaning of words and many of them. Skill at arithmetic was a universal requirement. Quick observation of a variety of geometric shapes and forms was included. Even a general knowledge of world conditions and history was a requirement in a few tests.

'Now, we Kluggs,' continued the professor in his melancholy voice, 'have gone a step beyond that.'

The words droned on through Hanardy's mind. Kluggs were theory-operating people . . . theories based on primary and not secondary abilities. Another race, 'higher' than the Kluggs – called the Lennels – operated on Certainty . . . a high harmonic of Authority.

'Certainty, with the Lennels,' said the old man, 'is of course a system and not an open channel. But even so it makes them as powerful as the Dreeghs.'

On an I.Q. curve that would include humans, Kluggs, Lennels and Dreeghs, the respective averages would be 100, 220, 380, and 450. The Dreeghs had an open channel on control of physical movement.

'Even a Great Galactic can only move as fast as – he cannot move faster than – a Dreegh,' Professor Ungarn commented and explained. 'Such open channels are pathways in the individual to a much greater ability than his standard I.Q. permits.'

Musical, mathematical, artistic, or any special physical, mental or emotional ability was an open channel that operated outside the normal human, Klugg, or even the Dreegh curve. By definition, a Great Galactic was a person whose I.Q. curve included only open channels.

It had been reported that the open channel curve began at about 80. And, though no one among the lesser races had ever seen anything higher than 3,000 – the limits of the space phenomenon – it was believed that the Great Galactic I.Q. curve ascended by types to about 10,000.

'It is impossible,' said the Professor's melancholy voice, 'to imagine what kind of an open channel that would be. An example of an 800 open channel is Pat. She can deceive. She can get away with a sleight of hand, a feint, a diversion —'

404

The old man stopped suddenly. His gaze flicked past Hanardy's right shoulder and fastened on something behind him that Hanardy couldn't see.

6

The spaceman froze with the sudden terrified conviction that the worst had happened, and that the Dreegh Sween-Madro was behind him.

But it couldn't be, he realized. Professor Ungarn was looking at the control board of the meteorite. There was no door there.

Hanardy allowed himself to turn around. He saw that on the big instrument panel a viewplate had lighted, showing a scene of space.

It was a familiar part of the starry heavens looking out toward interstellar space, away from the sun. Near the center of the scene a light was blinking.

Even as Hanardy watched, the viewplate picture shifted slightly, centering exactly on the blinking light.

Behind Hanardy, there was a gasp from the girl, 'Dad,' she whispered, 'is it — ?'

Professor Ungarn had walked toward the viewplate, past Hanardy and so into the latter's range of vision. The old man nodded with an air of utter weariness.

'Yes, I'm afraid it is, my dear. The other eight Dreeghs have arrived.'

He glanced hopelessly at Hanardy. 'My daughter had some kind of idea of using you against Sween-Madro before they got here.'

Hanardy said blankly, 'Using *me*?'

The meaning of that brought him with a jar out of his own body exhaustion.

The old man was shrugging. 'Whatever the merit of her plan, of course, now it's too late.'

He finished dully, 'Now we'll learn our fate.'

The tableau of dejection held for seconds only. A sound,

a high-pitched human voice, broke through the silence and the dark emotion that filled the room.

'How far away are they?' It was the girl's voice, from behind Hanardy, strained but recognizable. 'Exactly how long till they get here?'

Hanardy's mind stirred from its thrall as Professor Ungarn said dully, 'Less than two hours would be my guess. Notice —'

He thereupon started a technical comment to her about the speed with which the viewplate had centered on the ship, implying – he said – the enormous velocity of its approach.

His explanation was never completed. In the middle of it, the girl uttered a screech and then, to Hanardy's amazement, she raced past him and flung herself, arms flailing, at the old man.

She kept striking at his face then, yelling the most blood-curdling curses in a furious soprano voice. A long moment went by before Hanardy was able to make out what she was saying:

' – You stupid old man! What do you mean, only two hours? Two hours is all we need, *damn* you!'

At that point Hanardy emerged from his surprise. Awkwardly, he jumped over her, grabbed her, pulled her away. 'For Pete's sake!' he cried.

The girl tried to turn on him, her struggling body writhing in his grip. But he held her, uttering apologies the while. Finally, she realized that his strength was too much for her. She ceased her efforts, and with an attempt at control said grimly, 'Steve, this crazy old fool who is my father has twice now accepted defeat – when it wasn't necessary!'

She broke off, addressed the old man. Her voice went up a whole octave as she said, 'Show Steve what you showed me only a few minutes before I went to get him.'

Professor Ungarn was white and haggard. 'I'm sorry, my

406

dear,' he mumbled. He nodded to Hanardy. 'I'm sure you can let her go now.'

Hanardy released the girl. She stood straightening her clothes, but her eyes still flashed. 'Show him, damn it,' she snapped, 'and make it quick.'

Professor Ungarn took Hanardy's arm and drew him toward the control board, speaking in apologetic tones. 'I failed my daughter. But the truth is I'm over three hundred years old. That's just about it for a Klugg; so I keep forgetting how younger people might feel.'

Pat – he went on – was a product of a late-life marriage. Her mother had flatly refused to go along on his assignment as a galactic watcher. In bringing the girl with him, he had hoped to shield her from the early shock of discovering that she was a member of a servant race. But isolation had not, in fact, saved her feelings. And now, their very remoteness from the safeguarding military strength of associated lower-level races had brought a horrifying threat of death from which he had decided there was no escape.

'So it didn't even occur to me to tell her —'

'Show him,' the girl's voice came shrilly from the rear, 'what you didn't bother to tell me.'

Professor Ungarn made a few control adjustments, and there appeared on the viewplate first a picture of a room and then of a bed in one corner with an almost naked man lying on it.

The bed came into full focus, filled the viewplate. Hanardy drew in his breath with a sharp hiss of disbelief. It was the Dreegh.

The man who lay there, seemingly unconscious, bore almost no resemblance to the tall, vital being who had come aboard in the guise of Pat's fiancé. The body on the bed was unnaturally thin; the rib cage showed. His face, where it had been full-cheeked, was sunken and hollow.

'They need other people's blood and life energy to survive,

and they need it almost continuously,' the old man whispered. 'That's what I wanted to show you, Steve.' Her tone grew scathing, as she continued, 'My father didn't let me see that until a few minutes ago. Imagine! Here we are under sentence of death, and on the day, almost on the hour that the other Dreeghs are due to arrive, he finally reveals it – something he had watched developing for days.'

The old man shut off the scene on the viewplate and sighed.

'I'm afraid it never occurred to me that a Klugg could challenge a Dreegh. Anyway, I imagine Sween-Madro originally arrived here expecting to use us as a source of blood and life force. And then when you showed all that Great Galactic programming, he changed his mind and decided to wait until the coming of his colleagues. So there he is – at our mercy, Pat thinks.'

Hanardy had spent his years of association with this couple deferring to them. So he waited now, patiently, for the scientist to tell him what to do about the opportunity.

The old man said, with a sigh, 'Pat thinks if we make a bold attack at this stage, we can kill him.'

Hanardy was instantly skeptical, but he had never been able to influence this father and daughter in any way, and he was about to follow the old, withdrawing pattern, when he remembered again that there were no weapons around to make any kind of attack whatsoever.

He pointed out that fact and was still talking when he felt something cold touch his hand.

Startled, he glanced down and back – and saw that the girl was pushing a metal bar about one and a half feet long, at his palm. Involuntarily, still not thinking, he closed his fingers over it. As soon as he had it firmly in one chunky hand, Hanardy recognized by its feel that it was a special aluminium alloy, hard, light, and tough.

The girl spoke. 'And just in case that dumb look on your face means what I think it does,' she said, 'here are your orders: take that bar, go where the Dreegh is and beat him to death with it.'

Hanardy turned slowly, not quite sure that it was he who was being addressed. 'Me?' he said. And then, after a long pause, 'Hey!'

'And you'd better get started,' said the girl, 'there isn't much time.'

'Hey!' repeated Hanardy, blankly.

7

Slowly, the room swung back into a kind of balance. And Hanardy grew aware that the girl was speaking again:

'I'll go in through the door facing the bed,' she stated. 'If he can awaken at all in his condition, I want to ask him some questions. I must know about the nature of super-intelligence.'

For a brain in as dulled a state as Hanardy's, the words were confusing. He had been striving to adjust to the idea that he was the one who was supposed to go in to the Dreegh, and simultaneously he was bracing himself against what she wanted him to do.

With so many thoughts already in his mind, it was hard to get the picture that this slip of a girl intended to confront the Dreegh by herself.

Pat was speaking again, in an admonishing tone. 'You stand just inside the other door, Steve. Now listen carefully. Do your best not to attract his attention, which I hope will be on me. The information I want is for your benefit. But when I yell, "Come!" don't delay. You come and you kill, understand?'

Hanardy had had a thought of his own. A sudden stark realization. The realization was that in this deadly dangerous situation there was ultimately a solution.

He could cast off in his own spacecraft!

But that meant he would have to obtain the key equipment Sween-Madro had taken from his ship. Obtain it, repair the control board, get away!

To obtain it he'd have to go to where it was – into the Dreegh's bedroom. At least apparently, he would have to do exactly what Pat wanted.

Fear dimmed before that obvious purpose, yielded to the feeling that there was no other way.

Thinking thus, Hanardy abruptly uttered agreement. 'Yep,' he said, 'I understand.'

The girl had started toward the door. At the tone of his voice, she paused, turned back and gazed at him suspiciously. 'Now, don't you go having any plans of your own!' She spoke accusingly.

Hanardy was instantly guilty, instantly confused. 'For Pete's sake,' he said, 'I don't like what you want to do – going in there and waking this guy. I don't see any good in my listening to a lecture on intelligence. I'm not smart enough to understand it! So, my vote is if we're going in let's just kill him right off.'

The girl had turned away. She did not glance back as she walked out of the room. Hanardy grimaced at Professor Ungarn. Moments later he was through the door, following her, weary, hopeless, mentally shut down, but resigned.

Pat heard him stumbling along behind her. Without looking around she said, 'You're a weapon, Steve. I have to figure out how to fire that weapon and escape. Basically, that's all we need to do! Get away from the Dreeghs and hide. Understand?'

He was a man stumbling along metal and rock corridors in a remote part of the solar system, his normal stolidness made worse now by an immense weariness. So he heard the words she uttered; even understood their surface meaning.

It was enough awareness for him to be able to mumble, 'Yeah – yeah!'

Otherwise – she went on when he had acknowledged – he he might go off like a firecracker, discharging whatever energy *homo-galactic* had endowed him with in a series of meaningless explosions aimed at nothing and accomplishing nothing.

So the question was: What kind of weapon was he?

'As I see it,' she finished, 'that information we can only hope to gain from the Dreegh. That's why we have to talk to him.'

'Yeah,' mumbled Hanardy, hoarsely. 'Yeah.'

They came all too quickly to their destination. At the girl's nod Hanardy broke into an uneven lope and ran around to the far corridor. He fumbled the door open and stepped inside.

At this point Pat had already been through her door for fifteen seconds. Hanardy entered upon a strange scene, indeed.

On the bed, the almost naked body was stirring. The eyes opened and stared at the girl, and she said breathlessly, 'That! What you just now did – becoming aware of me. How do you do that?'

From where he stood, Hanardy could not see the Dreegh's head. He was aware only that the Dreegh did not answer.

'What,' asked Pat Ungarn, 'is the nature of the intelligence of a Great Galactic?'

The Dreegh spoke. 'Pat,' he said, 'you have no future, so why are you making this inquiry?'

'I have a few days.'

'True,' said Sween-Madro.

He seemed unaware that there was a second person in the room. *So he can't read minds!* Hanardy exulted. For the first time he had hope.

'I have a feeling,' Pat was continuing, 'that you're at least slightly vulnerable in your present condition. So answer my question! Or —'

She left the threat and the sentence unfinished.

Again the body on the bed shifted position. Then:

'All right, my dear, if it's information you want, I'll give you more than you bargained for.'

'What do you mean?'

'There are no Great Galactics,' said the Dreegh. 'No such beings exist, as a race. To ask about their intelligence is – not meaningless, but complex.'

'That's ridiculous!' Pat's tone was scathing. 'We saw him!'

She half-glanced at Hanardy for confirmation, and Hanardy found himself nodding his head in full agreement with her words. Boy, *he* sure knew there was a Great Galactic.

On the bed, Sween-Madro sat up.

'The Great Galactic is a sport! Just a member of some lesser race who was released by a chance stimulus so that he temporarily became a super-being. The method?' The Dreegh smiled coldly. 'Every once in a while, accidentally, enough energy accumulates to make such a stimulus possible. The lucky individual, in his super-state, realized the whole situation. When the energy had been transformed by his own body and used up as far as he himself was concerned, he stored the transformed life-energy where it could eventually be used by someone else. The next person would be able to utilize the energy in its converted form. Having gone through the energy, each recipient in turn sank back to some lower state.

'Thus William Leigh, earth reporter, had for a few brief hours been the only Great Galactic in this area of space. By now his super-ability is gone forever. And there is no one to replace him.

'And that, of course,' said the Dreegh, 'is the problem with Hanardy. To use his memory of intelligence in its full possibility, he'll need life energy in enormous quantities. Where will he get it? He won't! If we're careful, and investigate his background cautiously, we should be able to prevent Steve getting to any source, known or unknown.'

Hanardy had listened to the account with a developing

empty feeling from the pit of his stomach. He saw that the color had drained from the girl's face.

'I don't believe it,' she faltered. 'That's just a —'

She got no further, because in that split instant the Dreegh was beside her. The sheer speed of his movement was amazing. Hanardy, watching, had no clear memory of the vampire actually getting off the bed.

But now, belatedly, he realized what the Dreegh's movements on the bed must have been – maneuverings, rebalancings. The creature-man had been surprised – had been caught in a prone, helpless position, but used the talk to brace himself for attack.

Hanardy was miserably aware that Pat Ungarn was equally taken by surprise. Sween-Madro's fingers snatched at her shoulder. With effortless strength, he spun her around to face him. His lank body towered above her, as he spoke.

'Hanardy has a memory of something, Pat. That's all. *And that is all there is.* That's all that's left of the Great Galactics.'

Pat gasped, 'If it's nothing, why are you scared?'

'It's not quite nothing,' Sween-Madro replied patiently. 'There is a – potential. One chance in a million. I don't want him to have any chance to use it, though of course we'll presently have to take a chance with him and put him into a state of sleep.'

He released her and stepped back. 'No, no, my dear, there's no possible chance of you making use of some special ability in Hanardy – *because I know he's over there by the door.* And he can't move fast enough to get over here and hit me with that metal bar.'

The tense Hanardy sagged. And Pat Ungarn seemed frozen, glaring at the creature. She came back to life, abruptly. 'I know why you don't dare shoot Steve. So why don't you shoot me?' Her tone was up in pitch, challenging.

413

'Hey!' said Hanardy. 'Careful!'

'Don't worry, Steve,' she answered gaily without turning around. 'It's not because I have any I.Q. potentialities. But he won't touch me either. He knows you like me. You might have a bad thought about him at a key moment, later. Isn't that right, Mr Dreegh? I've got your little dilemma figured out, haven't I, even though I've only got a Klugg brain.'

Her words seemed suicidal to Hanardy. But Sween-Madro just stood gazing at her, swaying a little, saying nothing – a naked scarecrow of a man from the waist up, and below, wearing knee-length dungarees over bone-thin legs.

Yet there was no belief in Hanardy that the Dreegh was vulnerable. He remembered the other's high speed movements – that seemingly instantaneous transition from one location in space to another . . . from the bed to Pat, at invisible speed. Fantastic!

Once more Pat's voice broke the silence, mockingly: 'What's this? An I.Q. of 400 or 500 baffled? Doesn't know what to do? Remember, no matter what action you take, he can't stay awake much longer. It's only a matter of time before something has to give.'

At that point, another sharp anxiety struck through Hanardy. He thought: She's wasting time. Every minute those other Dreeghs are getting closer!

The thought was so urgent in his mind, he spoke it aloud, 'For Pete's sake, Miss Pat, those other Dreeghs'll be here any second —'

'*Shut up, you fool!*'

Instantly shrill, hysterical, terrified – that was her totally unexpected reaction.

She said something else in that same high-pitched tone, but Hanardy did not hear it clearly. For in that moment between his own words and hers, the Dreegh turned. And his arm moved. That was all that was visible. Where did it move to? The super-speed of the movement blurred that. It

414

could only, logically, have been toward the pocket of his dungarees, but nothing like that was visible.

A weapon glittered; a beam of light touched Hanardy's face.

As blackness swept over him, he realized what else it was the girl had said: 'Steve, he'll put you to sleep while that thought about the Dreegh's coming quickly is in your mind. . . .'

8

How swiftly can transition between wakefulness and sleep take place?

As long as it requires for the wakefulness center to shut off and the sleep center to turn on.

So there is no apparent conscious time lag. If you live a dull, human existence, it seems brief enough.

To Hanardy, who was normally duller than most, it seemed no time at all.

He started forward, his lips parted to speak – and he was already asleep . . . so far as he – the self – was aware. He did have a vague feeling of starting to fall.

Consciously, nothing more occurred.

Below the conscious, there was a measurable lapse of time.

During that time, the particles inside the atoms of his body did millions of millions of separate actions. And molecules by the quadrillion maneuvered in the twilight zone of matter. Because of the thought that had been in Hanardy's mind, at some level of his brain he noticed exact spots of space, saw and identified the other-ness of the Dreeghs in the approaching Dreegh ship, estimated their other-whereness, computed the mathematics of change. It was simple in the virtual emptiness of space, difficult where matter was dense. But never impossible.

As he did so, the Dreegh ship with its eight Dreeghs changed location from one spot to another exact spot in space, bridging the gap through a lattice-work of related spots.

In the bedroom in the meteorite, the visible event was that Hanardy fell. A twisting fall, it was, whereby he sprawled on his side, the arm with the metal bar in it partly under him.

As Hanardy collapsed to the floor, the Dreegh walked past Pat toward the open door behind it. Reaching it, he clutched at it, seemingly for support.

Pat stared at him. After what had happened she didn't quite dare to believe that his apparent weakness was as great as she saw it to be.

Yet after a little, she ventured, 'May I ask my father a question?'

There was no answer. The Dreegh stood at the door, and he seemed to be clinging to it.

Excitement leaped through the girl.

Suddenly she dared to accept the reality of the exhaustion that was here. The Dreegh's one mighty effort had depleted him, it seemed.

She whirled and raced over to Hanardy, looking for the metal bar. She saw at once that he was lying on top of it and tried to roll him over. She couldn't. He seemed to be solidly imbedded in the floor in that awkward position.

But there was no time to waste! Breathing hard, she reached under him for the metal weapon, found it, tugged at it.

It wouldn't budge.

Pull at it, twist it, exert all her strength – it was no use. Hanardy had a vice-like grip on the bar, and his body weight reinforced that grip. Nothing she could do could move it, or him.

Pat believed the position, the immovability, was no accident. Dismayed, she thought the Dreegh caused him to fall like that.

She felt momentarily awed. What an amazing prediction ability Sween-Madro had had – to have realized the nature

416

of the danger against him and taken an exact defense against it.

It was a maneuver designed to defeat, exactly and precisely, a small Klugg woman, whose ability at duplication could not lighten the weight of a body like Hanardy's enough to matter and whose ability to solve problems did not include the ability to unravel a muscularly knotted hand grip.

But – she was on her feet, infinitely determined – it would do him no good!

The Dreegh also had a weapon. His only hope must be that she wouldn't dare come near him.

Instants later, she was daring. Her trembling fingers fumbled over his dungarees, seeking openings.

They found nothing.

But he *had* a weapon, she told herself, bewildered. He fired it at Steve. I saw him!

Again, more frantically, she searched all the possibilities of the one garment he wore – in vain.

She remembered, finally, in her desperation, that her father must have been watching this room. He might have seen where it was.

'Dad!' she called anxiously.

'Yes, my dear?' The reply from the intercom came at once, reassuringly calm.

Watching the Dreegh warily, she asked, 'Do you have any advice on how to kill him?'

The old man, sitting in the control room of the meteorite, sighed. From his viewpoint, he could on one viewplate see the girl, Hanardy's unconscious body and Sween-Madro; on another he observed gloomily that the Dreegh ship had arrived and had attached to an airlock. As he watched that second viewplate, three men and five women came out of the ship and into a corridor of the meteorite. It was obvious that killing Sween-Madro was no longer of value.

The girl's voice cut across his awareness. 'He must have used the super-speed again without my noticing and hidden his weapon. Did you see what he did with it?'

What Professor Ungarn was seeing was that the newly arrived Dreeghs, though in no hurry, were heading directly toward Madro and Pat.

Watching them, the professor thought, Pat was right. Sween-Madro had been vulnerable. He could have been killed. But it was too late.

Sick with self-recrimination he abandoned the control room and hurried to join his daughter.

By the time he arrived, Sween-Madro was back in the bed, and Hanardy had been lifted onto a powered dolly which had been wheeled alongside a machine that had evidently been brought from the Dreegh ship.

The machine was a simple device with a pair of bulbous, transparent cups and a suction system. A needle was inserted into a blood vessel on Hanardy's right arm. Swiftly, a turgid bluish-red liquid rose in one of the bulbous cups; about a quart, Professor Ungarn estimated to his daughter in a whisper.

One by one, wordlessly, the Dreeghs went to the machine. Another needle was used. And into each a tiny drain of blood siphoned from the red stuff in the bulbous cup. It seemed as if about half of it was taken.

Still without anyone speaking, the needle was inserted into Sween-Madro's arm; and the rest of the blood from the cup flowed into him.

Pat stared at the dreadful beings with avid curiosity. All her life she had heard of, and been warned against, these creatures; and here they were from all those distances of years and miles. Four men and five women.

Three of the five women were brunette, one was a blonde; the fifth was a redhead.

The women were, every one, tall and willowy. The men

418

were uniformly six feet four or five and gaunt of build. Was height a part of the Dreegh illness? Pat wondered, seeing them together like this. Did Dreegh bones grow as a result of their disease? She could only wonder.

The figure on the bed moved. Sween-Madro opened his eyes and sat up.

He seemed shaky and unsure. Again, there was silent action. The Dreegh men did not move, but the women one by one went over and lightly kissed Sween-Madro on the lips.

At each touch of lips there was a faint bluish light, a flash of brightness, like a spark. Invariably, the blue spark leaped from the woman to the man.

And with each flash he grew more alive. His body became visibly larger. His eyes grew bright.

Pat, who had been watching with total fascination, suddenly felt two pairs of hands grab her. She had time to let out a shriek as two Dreegh men carried her over to Sween and held her above him, her face over his.

At the final moment, she ceased her futile struggle and froze.

She was aware of Sween's sardonic eyes gazing up at her. Then, with a deliberate movement he raised his head and brushed her lips with his.

She expected to die.

Deep inside the back of her head, a fire started. The heat of it seemed instantly unbearable; instantly there was a flash of blue flame from her lips to his.

Then she was back on the floor, dizzy, but – as she realized presently – recovering. And still alive.

Sween-Madro swung his feet over the edge of the bed and said, 'The existence of such brother-and-sister energy flows, Pat – which you have now experienced – and the Dreegh ability to use them make it likely that we could become the most powerful beings in the galaxy on a continuing basis. If we can defeat Hanardy. We only took about ten percent from you. We don't want you damaged – yet.'

He stood up, walked over and looked down at the unconscious spaceman. Presently he beckoned Pat and Professor Ungarn; father and daughter came at once.

The Dreegh said, 'I'm still not well. Can you detect any change in him?' He did not wait for a reply, but said in relief, 'I guess nothing happened. He looks as low-grade a human as you could ever not want to meet or deal with in any way, and that's the way he was before – don't you agree?'

Pat said quickly, 'I don't understand. What did you expect?'

'Hopefully, nothing,' was the reply. 'But that remark about how near our ship was was the first un-programmed use of his ability. A spatial relationship action like that comes in the Great Galactic intelligence curve at about I.Q. 1200.'

'But what did you fear?' Pat persisted.

'That it would feed back through his nervous system!'

'What would that do?'

The Dreegh merely stared at her, sardonically. It was Professor Ungarn's voice that finally broke the silence. 'My dear, the Dreeghs are actually acting as if their only enemy is a programmed Hanardy.'

'Then you believe their analysis of the nature of the Great Galactics?'

'They believe it; so I believe it.'

'Then there's no hope?'

The old man pointed at Hanardy. 'There's Steve.'

'But he's just a bum. That's why we selected him to be our drayhorse, remember?' She spoke accusingly. 'Because he was the dumbest, most honest jerk in the solar system – remember?'

The old man nodded, suddenly looking gloomy. Pat became aware that the Dreeghs were watching them, as if they were listening.

It was one of the dark-haired women who spoke. 'My name is Rilke,' she said. She went on, in a low, husky voice, 'What you've just described – a man as unimportant as this one – is one of the reasons why we want to go to Europa. We must find out what *did* the Great Galactic see in this strange little man. We should know because for our blood storage tanks and energy pool we need the blood and life force of a million people from this otherwise undefended planetary system. And we dare not kill a single one of those million until the riddle of Hanardy is resolved.'

9

Take a sentient being —

Everyone aboard the Dreegh super-ship that flew to the moon Europa in thirty hours (instead of many weeks) fitted that description: the Dreeghs, Pat, Professor Ungarn, and the sleeping Hanardy.

They had brought along Hanardy's freighter to be their landing craft. They came down without incident into Hanardy's permanent spaceship berth in Spaceport, the large moon's principal city.

Consider any sentient person —

That includes a man asleep . . . like Hanardy.

There he lies, helpless. In that fourth sleep stage that Hanardy was in – the deep delta-wave stage – push at him, hit him, roll him over. It is enormously difficult to awaken him. Yet it is in this state that a person can act out a sleepwalker's strange goal.

Force this sentient individual to interact with a grossly vast universe —

'We're taking no chances,' said the Dreegh brunette woman, Rilke. 'We're going to bring him into motion on the somnambulistic level.'

It was Sween who directed a bright light at Hanardy's face; after mere seconds, he shut it off.

There was a measurable passage of time. Then the body on the bed stirred.

A second woman – the blonde – without glancing up from the instrument she was monitoring, made a gesture and said hurriedly, 'The somnambulistic purpose is in the delta-wave band C-10-13B.'

It was a private nomenclature that meant nothing to Pat. But the words caused an unexpected flutter of excitement among the Dreeghs.

Sween-Madro turned to Pat. 'Have you any idea why Hanardy should want to visit with, and have a feeling of affection for, thirteen people in Spaceport?'

Pat shrugged. 'He associates with certain space bums around town,' she said contemptuously. 'Typical hangers-on of the kind you find out in space. I wouldn't waste a minute on them.'

Sween said coldly, 'We take no chances, Pat. The ideal solution would be to kill all thirteen. But if we do, Hanardy might have punitive dreams about us as he awakens – which awakening will happen very soon now, one way or another. So' – the long gaunt face cracked into a grimace of a smile – 'we'll render them useless to him.'

'Ssssh!' said the blonde woman. She motioned toward the figure on the bed.

The somnambulistic Hanardy had opened his eyes.

Pat was aware, then, of the Dreeghs watching alertly. Involuntarily, briefly, she held her breath and waited.

Hanardy did not glance at her or at the Dreeghs, showed no awareness of anyone else being in the room.

Without a word, he got out of bed and removed his pajamas. Then he went into his bathroom and shaved and combed his hair. He came out again into the bedroom and began to dress, putting on his dirty pants, a shirt, and a pair of boots.

As Hanardy walked out of the room, Rilke shoved at Pat.

'Remain near the sleepwalker,' she commanded.

Pat was aware that Rilke and Sween-Madro stayed close behind her. The others had slipped somewhere out of sight.

The somnambulistic Hanardy opened the airlock and headed down the gangplank.

Sween-Madro gestured with his head for Pat to follow.

The girl had hesitated at the top of the spidery 'plank'. And now she stood for a moment gazing out at the city of Spaceport.

The airlock of Hanardy's freighter was located about fifty feet above the heavy lower scaffolding that held the vessel. There was a space of about five feet between the opening and the upper scaffolding which actually constituted a part of the dock.

Almost straight ahead of her Pat could see the first building of the city. It was hard for her to realize that the entire populace of the port, with all their available equipment, had no chance against the Dreeghs. There was no protection here for her, or Hanardy, or anyone.

Awe came. The decisive factor was the intelligence of the Dreeghs.

She thought: and what's in Steve's *memory* of intelligence is all that stands between these vampires and their victims.

Minutes later she found herself walking beside Hanardy. She stole a glance at his blank face, so stolid and unintellectual. He seemed like a small hope, indeed.

The Dreeghs and she followed Hanardy along a street, into a hotel, up an elevator and along a corridor to a door numbered 517. Hanardy pressed a little button, and after a little the door opened. A middle-aged woman shuffled into view. She was dumpy and bleary-eyed, but her face brightened into a welcoming smirk as she saw Hanardy.

'Hi, there, Han!' she yelled.

Having spoken, she must have realized that the Dreeghs and Pat were with the spaceman. If she had any defensive thought, it was too late. Sween made her helpless with his mechanical light-flash hypnotism, about which he commented casually after they were inside and the door shut, 'Nothing more complex is needed for human beings, or —' he shrugged – 'Kluggs. Sorry, Pat,' he apologized to the girl, 'but the fact is that, like the people of this system, you also have a vague idea that hypnotism and other non-conscious phenomena were invented by hypnotists and similar unscrupulous people.'

He added ruefully, 'You'll never surprise a Lennel, or a Medder, or a Hulak with any control method short of — He broke off. 'Never mind!'

He turned to the woman. Presently, under his guidance she was speaking enforced truths about her real relationship with Hanardy.

From the time they had met, Hanardy had given her money.

'What does he really get for it?' asked Rilke.

'Nothing.'

Since their method evoked only truth, Rilke frowned at Sween, 'It couldn't be altruism. Not on his low level?'

It was visibly an unexpected development. Pat said scathingly, 'If altruism is an I.Q. factor, you Dreeghs probably come in below idiot.'

The man did not reply. The next instant his preternaturally long body was bending over the bloated female whom they had so briefly interrogated. There was a flash of blue as his lips touched hers. Half a dozen times he repeated that caricature of a kiss. Each time, the woman grew visibly smaller, like a sick person fading away on a hospital bed.

Finally, a bright light was flashed into the tired eyes, excising all memory of her degradation. But when they departed, the shriveled being on the bed was still alive.

The next person that the somnambulistic Hanardy led them to was a man. And this time it was Rilke who took the glancing kiss, and it was into her nervous system that the blue fire was drawn.

They drained all thirteen of Hanardy's friends in the same way; and then they decided to kill Hanardy.

Grinning, Sween explained. 'If we blow him up with you, the woman for whom he feels a dumb devotion, standing beside him in his home port – the only home he knows – he'll be busy protecting those he loves. And then we, who will be out in space while this is going on, will probably survive the few instants that it will take for him to awaken.'

As she heard those words, Pat felt a hardening of her own resolve, a conviction that she had nothing to lose.

They had started up the metal gangplank that led to the airlock of Hanardy's ship. Hanardy walked blankly in front, behind him was the girl, then Rilke, and, bringing up the rear, Sween. And they reached the final few feet, Pat braced herself and spoke aloud.

'It seems wrong, —' she said.

And leaped forward. She put her hands against Hanardy and shoved him over the side of the plank.

As she expected, the Dreeghs were quick. Hanardy was still teetering over the fifty-foot drop from the narrow walk when both the man and woman were beside him. As one person, they reached over the low handrail, reached out, reached down. That swiftly they had him.

In pushing at Hanardy, Pat found herself automatically propelled by the effort of her thrust away from Hanardy and over the other edge of the plank.

As she fell, she completed in her mind the sentence she had begun: 'It seems wrong . . . not to put that dumb love to the uttermost test!'

10

Spaceport, on Europa, like other similar communities in the solar system, was not at all like an ordinary little town of four thousand human beings. If anything, it resembled an old-style naval refueling station in the South Pacific, with its military establishment and garrison. Except that the 'garrison' of Spaceport consisted of technical experts who worked in complex mechanical systems for the repair and servicing of spaceships. In addition, Spaceport was a mining post, where small craft brought their meteorite ore, gigantic plants separated the precious from the debris, and the resultant refined materials were trans-shipped to Earth.

The similarity to a South Pacific port was borne out in one other respect. Exactly as each little island post of Earth's Pacific Ocean gradually accumulated a saturation of human flotsam and jetsam, so on Spaceport there had gathered a strange tribe of space bums. The tribe consisted of men and women in almost equal numbers, the size of the group being variable. Currently, it consisted of thirteen persons. They were not exactly honest people, but they were not criminals. That was impossible. In space, a person convicted of one of the basic crimes was automatically sent back to Earth and not allowed out again. However, there was a great tolerance among enforcement officials as to what constituted a crime. Not drunkenness, certainly, and not dope addiction, for either men or women. Any degree of normal sex, paid for or not, was never the subject of investigation.

There was a reason for this latitude. The majority of the persons involved – men and women – were technically trained. They were bums because they couldn't hold a steady job, but during rush periods, a personnel officer of the pressured company could often be found down in the bars on Front Street looking for a particular individual, or group. The bums thus located might then earn good money for a week or two, or perhaps even three.

It was exactly such a personnel officer looking for exactly such lost souls who discovered all thirteen of the people he wanted – four women and nine men – were sick in their hotel rooms.

Naturally, he called the port authorities. After an

426

examination, the M.D. who was brought in stated that all thirteen showed extreme weakness. They seemed to be, as he so succinctly put it, 'only marginally alive'.

The report evoked an alarm reaction from the Port Authority. The Director had visions of some kind of epidemic sweeping up from these dregs of people and decimating his little kingdom.

He was still considering a course of action when reports from private doctors indicated that the illness, whatever it was, had affected a large number of affluent citizens of Spaceport in addition to the bums.

The total in the final count came to a hundred and ninety-three persons sick with the same loss of energy and near-death apathy.

11

At some mind level, Hanardy became aware that Patricia Ungarn was falling to her death.

To save her, he had to get energy from somewhere.

He knew immediately where the energy would have to come from.

For a cosmic moment, as his somnambulism was disrupted and replaced by the dreaming state that precedes awakening, he was held by rigidities of his personality.

There was a split instant, then, as some aware part of him gazed in amazement and horror at a lifetime of being a sloppy Joe.

That one glance of kaleidoscopic insight was all that was necessary.

The barriers went down.

Time ceased. For him, all particle flows ended.

In that forever state, Hanardy was aware of himself as being at a location.

Around him were 193 other locations. He observed at once that thirteen of the locations were extremely wavery. He immediately excluded the thirteen from his purpose.

To the remaining 180 locations, he made a postulate. He postulated that the 180 would be glad to make immediate payment.

Each of the 180 thereupon willingly gave to Hanardy seven-tenths of all the available life-energy in their 180 locations.

As that energy flowed to Hanardy, time resumed for him.

The living universe that was Steve Hanardy expanded out to what appeared to be a great primeval dark. In that dark were blacker blobs, nine of them – the Dreeghs. At the very heart of the black excrescences ran a fine, wormlike thread of silvery brightness: the Dreegh disease, shining, twisting, ugly.

As Hanardy noticed that utterly criminal distortion, he became aware of a red streak in the sinister silver.

He thought, in immense astonishment, 'Why, that's my blood!'

He realized, then, with profound interest that this was the blood the Dreeghs had taken from him when they first arrived at the Ungarn meteorite.

They had given Sween most of it. But the others had each eagerly taken a little of the fresh stuff for themselves.

Hanardy realized that that was what the Great Galactic had noticed about him. He was a catalyst! In his presence by one means or another people got well . . . in many ways.

In a few days longer, his blood in them would enable the Dreeghs to cure their disease.

The Dreeghs would discover the cure belatedly – too late to change their forcing methods.

For Hanardy, the scene altered.

The nine black blobs were no longer shaped by their disease, as he saw them next. He found himself respecting the nine as members of the only race that had achieved immortality.

The cure of them was important.

428

Again, for Hanardy, there was a change. He was aware of long lines of energy that were straight and white flowing at him from some greater darkness beyond. In the near distance was a single point of light. As his attention focused there, all the numerous lines, except from that light-point, vanished.

It occurred to Hanardy that that was the Dreegh ship and that, in relation to earth, it would eventually be in a specific direction. The thin, thin, white line was like a pointer from the ship to him. Hanardy glanced along that line. And because he was open – oh, so open! – he did the touching. Then he touched other places and did a balancing thing between them and the Dreegh ship.

He oriented himself in space.

Oriented *it!*

As he completed that touching, he realized that the Dreegh ship was now slightly over six thousand light-years away.

That was far enough, he decided.

Having made that decision, he allowed particle flow to resume for the Dreeghs. And so —

As time began again, the Dreeghs found themselves in their own spaceship. There they were, all nine of them. They gazed uneasily at each other and then made a study of their surroundings. They saw unfamiliar star configurations. Their unhappiness grew. It was not a pleasant thing to be lost in space, as they knew from previous experience.

After a while, when nothing further happened, it became apparent that – though they would probably never again be able to find the Earth's solar system – they were safe . . .

Pat's first consciousness of change was that she was no longer falling. But no longer on Europa. As she caught her balance, she saw that she was in a familiar room.

She shook her head to clear away the fuzziness from her eyes. And then she realized it was a room in the Ungarn meteorite, her home. She heard a faint sound and swung about – and paused, balancing, on one heel, as she saw her father.

There was an expression of relief on his face. 'You had me worried,' he said. 'I've been here for more than an hour. My dear, all is well! Our screens are back to working; everything is the way it was . . . before. We're safe.'

'B-but,' said the girl, 'where's Steve?'

. . . It was earlier. Hanardy had the impression that he was remembering a forgotten experience on the Ungarn meteorite – a time before the arrival of Sween-Madro and the second group of Dreeghs.

The Great Galactic of that earlier time, he who had been William Leigh, bent over Hanardy where he lay on the floor.

He said with a friendly, serious smile, 'You and that girl make quite a combination. You with so much owed to you, and she with that high ability for foolhardiness. We're going to have another look at such energy debts. Maybe that way we'll find our salvation.'

He broke off. 'Steve, there are billions of open channels in the solar system. Awareness of the genius in them is the next step up for intelligence. Because you've had some feedback, if you take that to heart you might even get the girl.'

Leigh's words ended abruptly. For at that instant he touched the spaceman's shoulder.

The memory faded —

12

It was several weeks later.

On the desk of the Port Authority lay the report on the illness which had suddenly affected 193 persons. Among other data, the report stated:

It develops that these people were all individuals who during the past fifteen years have taken advantage of a certain low I.Q. person named Steve Hanardy. As almost everyone in Spaceport is aware, Hanardy – who shows many evidences of mental retardation – has year after year been by his own simple-minded connivance swindled out of his entire income from the space freighter, ECTON-66 (a type classification) – which he owns and operates.

In this manner so much money has been filched from Hanardy that, first one person, then another, then many, set themselves up in business at their victim's expense. And as soon as they were secure, each person in turn discarded the benefactor. For years now, while one human leech after another climbed from poverty to affluence, Hanardy himself has remained at the lowest level.

The afflicted are slowly recovering, and most are in a surprisingly cheerful frame of mind. One man even said to me that he had a dream that he was paying a debt by becoming ill; and in the dream he was greatly relieved.

There's some story around that Hanardy has married the daughter of Professor Ungarn. But to accept that would be like believing that everything that has happened has been a mere background to a love story.

I prefer to discount that rumor and prefer to say only that it is not known exactly where Hanardy is at present.

THE SCIENCE FICTION BOOKS OF
A. E. VAN VOGT

THE books are listed in chronological order of publication. The publisher of the first world edition is given, and where this was an American edition this is indicated by (US). Following this, all British editions are listed.

Short stories are indicated by (collection), Omnibus Editions have a list of contents and these are cross-indexed by the use of In: references. All reissues of a book under a different title are listed with the original title.

Books published in hardcover are indicated by (hd) while all others are paperbacks. The date for each edition is also given. An asterisk (*) indicates that the edition was in print when this list was compiled in 1974.

BIBLIOGRAPHY

SLAN
    Arkham House (US hd), 1946; Weidenfeld & Nicolson (hd), 1953; Panther, 1960*.
    In: *Triad*, 1959, and *van Vogt Omnibus 2*, 1971.

THE WEAPON MAKERS
    Hadley Publishing (US hd), 1946; Weidenfeld & Nicolson (hd), 1954; Digit, 1961; New English Library, 1970*.
    Title change: *One Against Eternity*.
    Ace (US), 1955.

THE BOOK OF PTATH
    Fantasy Press (US hd), 1947; Panther, 1969*.
    In: *An A. E. van Vogt Omnibus*, 1967.
    Title change: *Two Hundred Million A.D.*
    Paperback Library (US), 1964.

✓ THE WORLD OF NULL-A

Simon & Schuster (US hd), 1948; Dobson (hd), 1970*;
Sphere, 1971*.

In: *Triad*, 1959.

OUT OF THE UNKNOWN (*with E. M. Hull*) (collection)

Fantasy Publishing (US hd), 1948; New English Library,
1970.

Title change: *The Sea Thing and other Stories*.

Sidgwick & Jackson, 1970*.

MASTERS OF TIME AND THE CHANGELING (collection)

Fantasy Press (US hd), 1950.

Contains: *Masters of Time* (EARTH'S LAST FORTRESS) and
The Changeling.

✓ THE HOUSE THAT STOOD STILL

Greenberg (US hd), 1950; Weidenfeld & Nicolson (hd),
1953; Digit, 1960.

Title change: *The Mating Cry*.   THE UNDERCOVER ALIENS.
Beacon (US), 1960.   PANTHER 1976

✓ THE VOYAGE OF THE SPACE BEAGLE

Simon & Schuster (US hd), 1950; Grayson (hd), 1951;
Science Fiction Book Club (hd), 1954; Panther, 1959*.

In: *Triad*, 1959.

Title change: *Mission Interplanetary*.

Signet (US), 1952.

✓ THE WEAPON SHOPS OF ISHER

Greenberg (US hd), 1951; Weidenfeld & Nicolson (hd),
1952; Nova Publications, 1955; New English Library,
1969*.

✓ DESTINATION: UNIVERSE (collection)

Pellegrini (US hd), 1952; Eyre & Spottiswoode (hd),
1953; Panther, 1960*.

✓ AWAY AND BEYOND (collection)

Pellegrini (US hd), 1952; Panther, 1963*.

✓ THE MIXED MEN

Gnome Press (US hd), 1952.

Title change: *Mission to the Stars*.

Digit, 1960.   SPHERE 1976

THE UNIVERSE MAKER
   Ace, 1953; Sidgwick & Jackson (hd), 1974*.
PLANETS FOR SALE (*with E. M. Hull*) (collection)
   Frederick Fell (US hd), 1954.
   In: *An A. E. van Vogt Omnibus*, 1967.
THE PAWNS OF NULL-A
   Ace (US), 1956; Digit, 1960; Sphere, 1972.
   Title change: *The Players of Null-A*.
   Berkley (US), 1966; Dobson (hd), 1970*.
EMPIRE OF THE ATOM
   Shasta Publishers (US hd), 1957.
THE MIND CAGE
   Simon & Schuster (US hd), 1957; Panther, 1960.
   In: *van Vogt Omnibus 2*, 1971.
THE WAR AGAINST THE RULL
   Simon & Schuster (US hd), 1959; Panther, 1961*.
SIEGE OF THE UNSEEN
   Ace (US), 1959.
   Title change: *The Three Eyes of Evil*.
   In: *The Three Eyes of Evil*, 1973.
TRIAD (collection)
   Simon & Schuster (US hd), 1959.
   Contains: *The World of Null-A*, *Voyage of the Space
      Beagle* and *Slan*.
EARTH'S LAST FORTRESS
   Ace (US), 1960.
   In: *The Three Eyes of Evil*, 1973.
   Title change: *Masters of Time*.
   In: *Masters of Time and The Changeling*, 1950.
THE WIZARD OF LINN
   Ace (US), 1962.
THE BEAST
   (expanded version of *The Changeling*)
   Doubleday (US hd), 1963.
   In: *An A. E. van Vogt Omnibus*, 1967.
   Title change: *Moonbeast*.
   Panther, 1969*.

THE TWISTED MEN
    Ace (US), 1963.
MONSTERS (collection edited by Forrest J. Ackerman)
    Paperback Library (US), 1964; Corgi, 1970.
ROGUE SHIP
    Doubleday (US hd), 1965; Dobson (hd), 1968*. *PANTHER*
THE WINGED MAN (*with E. M. Hull*)
    Doubleday (US hd), 1966; Sidgwick & Jackson (hd),
    1967; Sphere, 1970.
    In: *van Vogt Omnibus 2*, 1971.
THE CHANGELING
    Macfadden (US), 1967.
    In: *Masters of Time and The Changeling*, 1950.
    Expanded as *The Beast*.
AN A. E. VAN VOGT OMNIBUS (collection)
    Sidgwick & Jackson, 1967*.
    Contains: *The Book of Ptath, Planets for Sale* (with E. M.
    Hull) and *The Beast*.
THE FAR-OUT WORLDS OF A. E. VAN VOGT (collection)
    Ace (US), 1968; Sidgwick & Jackson (hd), 1973*; New
    English Library, 1974*.
THE SILKIE
    Ace (US), 1969; New English Library, 1973*.
CHILDREN OF TOMORROW
    Ace (US), 1970; Sidgwick & Jackson (hd), 1972; New
    English Library, 1973*.
QUEST FOR THE FUTURE
    Ace (US), 1970; Sidgwick & Jackson (hd), 1971*; New
    English Library, 1973*.
THE PROXY INTELLIGENCE AND OTHER MIND BENDERS
    (collection)
    Paperback Library (US), 1971.
M33 IN ANDROMEDA (collection)
    Paperback Library (US), 1971.
MORE THAN SUPERHUMAN
    Dell (US), 1971. *NEL*

A Selection of Science Fiction from Sphere

Some Science Fiction Classics from Sphere

HOTHOUSE (SF Classic No 1)   Brian Aldiss 30p
Winner of the Hugo Award for the best
Science Fiction novel of the year

THE WORLD OF NULL-A
(SF Classic No 2)   A. E. van Vogt 30p
'One of those once-in-a-decade Classics'
– John W. Campbell

CITY (SF Classic No 3)   Clifford Simak 30p
Winner of the International Fantasy Award

THE SYNDIC (SF Classic No 4)   Cyril Kornbluth 30p
This book has been compared by Edmund
Crispin to Orwell's 1984 and is recognized
as Kornbluth's most brilliant and prophetic
novel

THE EINSTEIN INTERSECTION
(SF Classic No 10)   Samuel Delany 30p
Nebula Award Winner

RITE OF PASSAGE (SF Classic No 11) Alexei Panshin 35p
Nebula Award Winner

All Sphere Books are available at your bookshop or
newsagent, or can be ordered from the following address:

Sphere Books, Cash Sales Department,
P.O. Box 11, Falmouth, Cornwall.

Please send cheque or postal order (no currency), and allow
7p per copy to cover the cost of postage and packing
in U.K. or overseas.